Y0-AQH-069

The Pressure of Darkness

The Pressure of Darkness

THE PRESSURE OF DARKNESS

A THRILLER

HARRY SHANNON

FIVE STAR

An imprint of Thomson Gale, a part of The Thomson Corporation

Detroit • New York • San Francisco • New Haven, Conn. • Waterville, Maine • London

Set in 11 pt. Plantin.

LIBRARY OF CONGRESS CATALOGING-IN-PUBLICATION DATA

Shannon, Harry.
The pressure of darkness : a thriller / by Harry Shannon. — 1st ed.
p. cm.
ISBN 1-59414-470-2 (alk. paper)
1. Authors—Crimes against—Fiction. I. Title.
PS3619.H355P74 2006
813'.6—dc22 2006014943

U.S. Hardcover:
ISBN 13: 978-1-59414-470-7
ISBN 10: 1-59414-470-2

First Edition. First Printing: October 2006.
Published in 2006 in conjunction with Tekno Books and Ed Gorman.

Printed in the United States of America on permanent paper
10 9 8 7 6 5 4 3 2 1

This novel is dedicated to three amazing women—the late Devon Doherty, her sister Jaidon, and their mother Jen.

Namaste.

Prologue

Near Mogadishu, Somalia
October 1993

At first there is silence on the terraced rock face, broken only by the vaguely erotic sigh of evening waves stroking the beach. Then comes a man-made explosion of titanic proportions as the modified UH 60L goes pedal to the metal, the darkened Black Hawk helicopter rattling, whining, and thumping as it lifts off and turns away, flying blind. The well-trained pilot in alien-looking black goggles travels night-vision low, dangerously close to the sandy, rock-freckled ground, hoping to avoid enemy radar. Inside a greenish, shadowy cabin rests the human cargo, four elite "D" boys and one shadowy CIA observer.

The quartet of young soldiers, their faces soot-blackened and sweaty, are stretched out near backpacks which, like their uniforms, have been carefully stripped of all military insignia. Silenced weapons have been cleaned, knives sharpened, explosives wrapped carefully, drop ropes diligently re-wound, medical kits checked and re-checked. So now they chew gum and pretend to snooze with the studied insouciance of bloodied males the world over. They have come up together, from Fort Bragg and its Range 19 to Covert Ops in Somalia, and they are at ease in each other's company.

The observer, a youthful "spook" named Cary Ryan, has almost effeminate features but the lithe, compact toughness of a gymnast. He wears a drab uniform, also devoid of any markings, and lives up to his job description by rarely speaking. The men wait. All around them tiny lights flicker, casting purple-pink fingers of shadows up the riveted metal walls. The tallest soldier, a freckled-faced athlete from Nevada, picks imaginary food from his teeth. "Say, Top?"

"Yeah."

The red-haired boy cocks his head. "Where the fuck is this dump we're roping into again?"

"I told you, it's some tribal armpit maybe a few clicks past Mo, over near Ethiopia," Top says dryly. "Why, you got a problem with that?"

Burke shrugs. Around him the other soldiers are starting to tune in. They sense that he's on to something. "Yeah. We're going the wrong way."

"That so?"

"We're moving north, across the bay. Hell, this turns out to be a long enough flight we'll be in fucking Djibouti."

Top lowers and shakes his head. Looks up: "Outstanding, genius. That's because the target is in Djibouti."

Their young medic, inevitably nicknamed Doc, is a wiry black man. "So we're going into yet another fucking backwards country, without official permission. You're shitting me, right?"

"Nope."

"Damn, that is harsh. I was hoping you made us lose our ID in case of a paternity suit or something."

"Like you could get laid."

Nervous laughter all around. Their leader stands up, lurches to one side and grabs onto a leather strap to keep his balance. He looks down at them fondly, shakes his head in mock disappointment. "Bunch of clowns . . ."

"So what's the real mission, Top?" The fourth man is Scotty Bowden. He is stocky, muscular, and always seems to have a two-day stubble on his weathered face. "And what the fuck is in Djibouti?"

"A warlord who needs to learn some manners. I guess Clinton can't get that lying sack of shit Hassan Gouled to do anything, so it's our party."

Burke snorts. "So much for the fucking French, huh?"

"Yeah. They won't touch this guy either, although the frogs do know we're coming. They said they'd look the other way, but other than that, we're on our own."

"Mighty white of them," jokes Doc. No one reacts.

"And if you are killed or captured," Scotty intones, "the secretary will disavow all knowledge of your actions." He hums the theme from *Mission Impossible.* That manages to draw a few chuckles.

"Here's the name of the game," Top says firmly. "Get killed if you have to and we'll bring you home."

Cary Ryan offers his first words. He speaks in a cool, clear voice. "But now hear this . . . nobody gets caught."

An immediate silence follows; all eyes turn away to wander the nearly empty cabin. Death is acceptable, but capture, and the inevitable videotaped confession that would surely follow brutal torture, is strictly forbidden. In short, shoot yourself if you have to; indeed, shoot your friend, but *do not leave anyone behind alive.* Everyone goes home . . . or else.

Scotty cuts a huge fart and breaks the tension. Burke waves a bush hat in the air and pretends to gag, Cary Ryan holds his nose. Doc Washington sits quietly, dreaming of a future he may not see. Top watches with a believable, yet entirely manufactured grin plastered on his face. He is the oldest warrior, thirty-six and pushing thirty-seven; to him the others, in their late twenties, are a solemn responsibility.

"If you ladies are through polluting the rarified air of our home away from home, I'll give you a sitrep and our exact mission."

All business, now, the group gathers in a tight circle. Top reflexively turns his back to the open ramp, flicks on a small flashlight and jams it between his teeth. He drops some photographs onto the floor, illuminates them. "Look these over and memorize the face and vitals. The target is a prick named Yousef Dahoumed. He's a religious nut, a terrorist who is asshole buddies with another rag head called Osama Bin Laden. In fact, they are supposed to be distant cousins. As you girls know, Bin Laden has a real hard-on for the U.S., and may be backing Adid."

Burke mutters something unintelligible. Top eyeballs him until he speaks. "What kind of religious nut, or doesn't that matter?"

"It matters, but not a lot."

Burke gestures expansively, palms out. "You know I like to read about religions, Top. It's a thing with me, okay? So tell us."

"He's a nut job, plain and simple. From what I heard he's set up his own weird mix of Islamic Fundamentalism and Animism, which I've been told is seeing God everywhere, or something like that. You'd know better than me."

"That's close enough. Damn, that sure would have to be one strange brew to work."

"It's strange, all right. We're talking worshipping Allah via animal sacrifice, rolling your ass around in blood, all kinds of weird shit. Which plays right into running a terrorist organization, I might add. He whips those ignorant fuckers into a real frenzy and sends them into Somalia after the white oppressors. Meaning us."

Doc calls, "What you mean *us,* white boy?"

"So what the fuck is he doing over in Djibouti, then?" Scotty Bowden is just making conversation. He won't come alive until the fighting starts.

"Intel says he has a training compound there. The French don't want to piss off that asshole Gouled, and he don't want to irritate his Islamic A-rab majority, so they have all been letting Yousef Dahoumed do whatever he wants to us, long as he stays out in the boonies and doesn't fuck with them."

"Not that it matters," Doc offers, "but anybody tell you why we give enough of a shit about this guy to risk an op like this?"

"RPG's."

The group goes silent. That voice belongs to Cary Ryan. The acronym he used is for "rocket-propelled grenades." "As you know, they've been turning up all over Mogadishu, and one of these days some of the good guys are going to get killed. Intel says Dahoumed is collecting the grenade rifles and shipping them to Adid."

Burke seems satisfied. "So we fuck with him instead."

"Exactly," Top replies. "Now check out the photograph. Memorize it, because you will only have a few minutes to locate the target."

Doc looks, whistles. "Mamma, he ugly. That there is one bad-skinned, limp-dicked, towel-head fuckin' sorry-assed mother-fucker."

More laughter. Burke blows him a fish-mouthed kiss. "I love it when you talk dirty."

"The other photographs are of the terrorist compound. Satellite photos show it nearly empty at the moment, with most of the cadre near the border with Somalia, but there are bound to be some top-notch ragtops there to guard Dahoumed. So keep your shit wired tight at all times, ladies. I don't want anybody hurt."

"How big around is this place?"

"Figures are on the back. Be advised that the compound itself is a couple of football fields long, with a shit load of obstacle courses and some empty buildings used as a firing range, but we're only going in at the southern point, where Dahoumed's quarters are located."

"What about the bird?" Jack Burke.

"He stays airborne the whole time," Top answers. "We haul ass and rope down a little over a mile away. The bird will circle to the west to distract the guards."

"Time in the dirt?"

"Fifteen minutes," Top leans down and uses his foot to indicate a rock face featured in one of the photographs. "We scramble up that face and jog up the back way, across that flat plain."

Burke whistles. "Top, if some asshole turns on a floodlight or something, we're sitting ducks."

"If we rope down fast enough, it will seem like we never stopped."

"Yeah, if the bird does its job."

"It will. You just shut up and do as you're told."

Doc moans in mock terror. "If'n you say so, Boss."

"Now hear me carefully on this, in case you ever have to testify as to your orders." Top comically rolls his eyes and holds up crossed fingers. "We are to enter the compound unseen, using stealth, and then make 'every reasonable effort' to take this man alive. We can, however, fire to defend ourselves if attacked. Are we all clear on that point?"

"Clear."

Burke looks up. "What was that, sir?"

"Huh?"

He locks and loads his modified M-249. "Why, I do believe we just got attacked. Top, did somebody fire upon my sorry ass?"

"You may want to wait until our boots hit the dirt," Top says dryly. "But, yeah. Consider yourselves attacked. Once we enter that compound, we will all notice small arms fire coming from the village. We will then be forced to defend ourselves."

"And, sadly, Mr. Dahoumed will not survive the extraction effort," says Cary Ryan, the spook. "This despite all of your best efforts to capture him alive. Clear?"

"Clear."

Top checks his watch. "Like I said, memorize that layout and the face of our man. Then make sure everything that rattles or clanks is taped down. When we run, I want this chalk as quiet as a nun farting in church." He yawns theatrically, then releases the hanging strap and drops to his knees on the metal flooring. "Look, we've only got another hour or so before the shit hits the fan. Smoke 'em if you got 'em. I'm going to get some more snoring done."

Top rolls over onto his left side. He closes his eyes. He is showing his men that he is cool, relaxed. In fact his stomach is shaking, his palms are wet. Top has a bad feeling on this one. He does not trust Intel, he does not like working with such a small team. Something doesn't feel right.

To his surprise, he falls asleep anyway.

Thirty minutes, twenty, ten . . .

The men on their feet, lined up perfectly. Doc, Top, Burke, and Bowden all slam their clenched fists together and call out, "Brothers!"

"Brothers!" Cary Ryan flashes a wry grin. He slaps them each on the back as they go by. The observer sends them off with a throaty "Go! Go!"

The Black Hawk is hovering, the pilot holding the bird as steady as possible; the massive rotor blades start whipping the sand below into dense clouds. Scotty is out onto the rope and snaking down rapidly; he's twirling in the prop wash, then down on the ground. He trots north to the edge of the dry clearing and goes flat, weapon at the ready, night-vision goggles turning the desert an ominous green. Doc follows him, most ricky tic, his light frame taking him straight down the rope to the sand in one smooth motion. He trots south, flattens with a weapon at the ready. Then comes Burke, whose upper body strength carries him down the rope effortlessly. He drops and hits and heads east. Top follows and takes the west. The bird moves on, as ordered, and the clearing becomes quiet.

The insertion has taken less than fifteen seconds. Top raises a hand and two fingers. He points to the low cliff. In the same order, the men cross the clearing one by one and scale the rock face. Top takes the rear and delays for a bit. He wants to be certain that no one has observed the landing from a hiding place. Then he whips up the cliff and jogs silently into the night.

The small team of men crosses the one-mile area in a few minutes. As the obstacle course comes into view, they slow and fan out, leaving several yards between men. Their passage is so smooth that a low, whining wind covers it completely. Top is pleased. He locates the building believed to be the terrorist headquarters. He waves for Doc, who is wide-eyed from adrenaline, to trot into the lead position. Burke follows Doc. Top motions to Scotty to "leapfrog" and they begin to trade positions as they move closer. Doc drops to one knee and Burke passes him, searching the area. Burke drops and Scotty passes him.

Moments later, they are within a few yards of the darkened building and Top is now on point. He pauses to catch his breath and checks his watch. Four minutes to get in, kill the target, and get out safely. Then a hurried jog back to the waiting bird and a flight home to Mo.

More hand signals. The men fan out silently, raise their weapons. Top takes a long, deep breath and races up the steps. He tries the door handle and yanks once, then again and it springs open. In the greenish glare of the night-vision goggles he sees something that freezes his blood: an altar. Animal parts are all over the place, feathers and chunks of decaying meat mounted on the walls. There is some kind of wooden icon sitting on a prayer rug. He shakes his head and spots six men in their bunks. They are no longer asleep, but now sitting up and scrambling for their weapons. Top fires, feels Burke right behind him also firing and *ratatatatata* one by one the dirtbags splatter blood and sag back down again. Now there's human blood mixed with the hoodoo garbage strewn all over the room.

Top snaps his fingers, whirls around and runs to an open window to see if anyone else heard the muffled shots. Obeying the silent instruction, Burke moves from bunk to bunk, face to face. He shakes his head. No Yousef Dahoumed, not yet. Burke moves back to the door and peers out. Scotty crosses behind him, takes his saw-toothed hunting knife and bends over someone who is still breathing. He slices the man's carotid artery and steps back. A dark fountain pulses out onto the flooring. Scotty flashes a grin and leans forward again. Burke winces as his friend slices off an ear, holds it up as a trophy and whispers, "That makes ten!"

"You're a sick fuck, you know that?"

"Oh, yeah."

Top indicates everything is clear. They back out of the filthy room and close the wooden slatted door behind them. They turn and the new formation puts Doc on point. He jogs to the second, slightly larger building, ducks under a darkened window patched with cardboard. Doc moves up the steps; blows his wind out like a tired horse and tries the door. It is locked.

Doc Washington steps up onto the porch and takes aim at the lock and suddenly someone inside fires *WHAM* and Doc takes a round in the side of the stomach. The Kevlar vest stops it but the impact punches his waist and he spins all the way around. *WHAM* again as another round hits him in the lower back and this one goes through. The young medic rolls down the steps, in shock. He is in agony, but has yet to make a sound.

Emergency floodlights come on. The team has been caught wearing NV gear. They blink rapidly, now vulnerable and virtually blind for around ten seconds. They all rip off the goggles, leaving them to dangle from chin straps, and seek cover wherever they can find it. The entire compound explodes into gunfire. Top tries to make sense of the situation. He finally identifies two gunmen. The one who fired through the door is using what sounds like a Kalishnikov. The other man, at the window, seems terrifyingly efficient with an Uzi. The team is now pinned down, and they are already running out of time.

Doc, sitting flat at the foot of the steps with his legs extended, clutches himself and begins to wheeze/whisper in a high, eerie voice "oh fuck I'm shot" and "I can't feel my legs" over and over again. Burke starts toward him but Top waves NO and orders Red to slip around to flank the man at the window. Scotty starts firing at the door and then rolling, firing again, giving the impression of being more than one man. Top ignores the voice in his head that keeps screaming to abort and tries to make the guy in the window nervous.

"Doc, how is it?"

Doc repeats that he can't feel his legs but his belly *hurts.*

Burke jogs around the back of the dirty building, where the sounds suddenly seem farther away. The lights are not on. Burke passes a white kitchen door, locked from the inside. He sneaks a peek through the broken window, head up and then down again. There are two men in the building and they are sitting in the living room, in the dark, firing out into the light.

Burke slips the night-vision goggles back over his eyes and moves rapidly up the steps to the back door. It is also locked. He moves to one side, carefully fires at the lock. He waits until the man inside whirls and reflexively puts two through the door, just like he did when he nailed Doc. Burke wants to catch the ragtop trying to reload.

"Aw, shit!" someone screaming, out in the yard. One of the terrorists has scored a second hit. Angry, Burke kicks in the door and goes for the one at the window first, a thin Arab in a long white sleeping shirt. Burke walks a line of fire along the floor and stitches the bastard from nuts to nose. The guy at the door has nearly reloaded when Burke turns the gun his way and hesitates. It is their target, Dahoumed. He surprises Burke by dropping the gun and ammunition and fleeing. The leader escapes through the kitchen door and out into the back.

Cursing, Burke follows recklessly, an invisible clock ticking away in his mind. Time is running out. He sees Dahoumed dart back into the guard's quarters, probably hoping to find some protection. From inside, Burke hears an insane giggle start up. The sound makes the hair on his arms rise. He charges into the room.

A figure sits on the now stinking pile of bloody human and animal corpses, holding some long feathers and a primitive wooden icon from the altar. He is rocking and laughing and hugging himself like a child seeing a circus for the very first time. Some of the human and animal skulls beneath him seem to be grinning, their wide, piano-key teeth stained and yellow. Severed limbs pulse while hands and fingers clench at thin air and point, mockingly, at the young soldier in the doorway. This is senseless, appalling, a charnel house; nothing but mindless butchery.

Jack "Red" Burke feels real fear in that moment, a terror more atavistic and overwhelming than any he has known before. This is bloodlust gone berserk. Dahoumed seems like a force of nature, evil personified. The room reeks of gore and the stench of entrails and raw meat. This camp has become the last stop at the edge of the world, where madness begins. The fugitive has smeared himself with the blood of the sacrificed, both animals and his own dead followers. He stops laughing and stands up. In person, Yousef Dahoumed is a squat, fat, unattractive man in a ragged, wife-beater tee shirt and stained boxer shorts. He drops his empty rifle and surrenders. Burke steps closer and peers right into his face. He needs to be certain.

The maniac smiles warmly at him, says, "You take me to America?"

Burke smiles back, articulates carefully, "No, I send you to hell."

The man's smile fades, fear dilates his pupils. Burke opens up on Dahoumed, firing right into that chubby stomach. The burst flings the man against the wall and sunflowers his guts down over his bare feet. Now he fits right in with the rest of the décor.

"Clear inside!" Red Burke calls. "Target eliminated."

After a few seconds, he hears Scotty respond with a note of panic in his voice. "Clear outside! They got Top, too, man. I can hear more bad guys on the way. We'd best get the fuck out of here."

Burke rattles down the steps, legs rubbery from adrenaline. Out of the corner of his eye he sees Scotty giving Doc an injection, but most of his attention is focused on Top, who now lies on his back in the dirt with his knees up and spread, like a woman giving bloody birth. Somehow he's been shot in the lower groin, despite the body armor. Burke approaches, noting the smell of excrement; already reaching to the medical kit at his belt but even before he kneels he knows it is too late. Top begins gagging and clutching at his throat, where he has also taken a round. His larynx has been shattered and he can barely breathe. Burke considers an emergency tracheotomy, but Top is grievously wounded and in pain and he doesn't trust himself to pull it off.

"Go," Top grunts hoarsely, "just go."

"Don't you fucking die." Burke begins to weep. He is instantly ashamed of his weakness, but the sight before him is ignoble, ugly and unredeemable, so devoid of dignity that it breaks his heart. He looks at his weapon. "Top, should I . . . ?"

Top's chest begins to heave. He strangles and something in his neck tears wide open. One long, thin gout of blood shoots straight up and arcs away to splatter like urine in the dirt. Top gurgles. His eyes go flat and empty and it is over.

Burke forces himself to move. He pats Top down, triple-checks that there are no dog tags and all pockets are empty. He opens a waxed package of C4, pulls the pins from two grenades, and carefully places the explosives beside Top's body. He closes his friend's eyes, rolls him over onto the booby trap.

"Let's boogie." Bowden, calling with a razor edge to his voice, and now Burke hears the distant sound of men shouting in Arabic and vehicles heading their way. He looks up. Scotty has Doc over his shoulders and is already a good thirty yards off, heading for the extraction point. Burke tries to think of something to say but comes up empty. He pats Top on the head and jogs low to the ground, weaving back and forth for safety. Then the men run for all they are worth as the noise grows behind them. They shut down their minds and just make time.

But when they arrive at the drop zone again, the chopper is gone.

Burke checks his watch. They are just over three minutes late. The observer has apparently bolted. Burke understands why. He knows that the spooks will have given Cary Ryan and the bird strict orders not to wait. They are on their own.

Red Burke sinks to his knees, shaking and panting, trying not to panic. Nearby, Scotty is also fighting for air. "That fucking Ryan split, man!" Doc is in agony and now stoned out of his mind. "The cracker motherfucker left us here to die."

"Yeah." Burke shakes his head, sadly. "I really didn't think he'd do that."

"Well, he did," Scotty calls. "So what do we do?"

"Give me a minute."

"We don't have one, and if you have any brilliant ideas how to stay alive, now's the time to let us in on them."

Burke's mind whirls in circles. He considers deliberately overdosing Doc and booby-trapping his corpse as well, but doubts he could bring himself to go through with that. Abandoning him is also out of the question. But a suicidal firefight against the fanatics seems just as pointless. Jesus, what now?

And then Scotty grabs his arm. "Listen!"

They hear vehicles moving closer, men shouting in a foreign tongue. Burke puts the enemy maybe half a mile away and closing. He comes to a decision. "We stand and fight. Let's dig in." He frees his entrenching tool, but then hears something else—a low thumping sound.

The Black Hawk! Ryan has ordered the bird to come back for them. Burke grins and Scotty grins and they hoist Doc up between them and stumble into the prop wash as the bird returns for one last pass. And again breaking the rules, the pilot fully touches down to extract the wounded man. In the doorway, Cary Ryan is stressed and pale but seems determined. He drags the men up off the ramp and into the craft, even manages to handle Doc somewhat gracefully. Meanwhile, pinpoints of light sparkle on the far dunes as enemy fighters begin to fire upon the helicopter with a sound like hail hitting a tin roof.

"Let's move!" Ryan calls to the pilot, "Now, before somebody fires an RPG." They hustle higher. The chopper roars up and takes evasive action and the sporadic gunfire is soon far below them. They are quickly out of range. The bird turns rapidly, soars away.

"Cary," Burke shouts over the clatter, "thanks."

The spook nods, mouths *brothers.*

And as the beautiful Black Hawk takes them home, Jack "Red" Burke sits near the open doorway and looks back down toward the distant compound. He sees tiny headlights and floodlights everywhere, the sparks that show men firing into the air from rage and frustration. He thinks about Top, for the first time examines the relentless ugliness of death and senses the constant pressure of eternal darkness. He tries to clear his mind, but cannot seem to erase the nightmare image of that blood-drenched terrorist laughing and rocking on the pile of bodies like some demon from the netherworld, a dark priest performing pagan rites Burke should never have witnessed. He hears rapid gunfire in mental echo and his buddy Doc shrieking in pain, sees Top lying still, guts strewn about on the ground and open throat pulsing blood, dear brothers, maimed and dead.

Come and get some, you bastards . . .

Burke grunts with primitive satisfaction when he sees the small, faraway twin explosions that turn Top's body and anyone near it into red mist and hamburger meat. He turns his face away from death, toward the rest of his life from now on.

One

Los Angeles, California
Present Day
Sunday

"You look tired."

The patient lay prone and still on the crisp sheets, hands folded. Her visitor was a large and muscular man in his late thirties, modestly dressed in torn blue jeans, running shoes without socks, and a plain gray NFL pullover with a Raider's logo. He dragged a folding chair along the floor, indifferent to the annoying shriek of the dented metal as it scraped the linoleum, and planted himself close to the open window. He leaned back and looked at some afternoon clouds. After a moment he turned and spoke softly, so that no one else would hear.

"I've been working too hard."

Her dark, sleepy eyes accused him. Mildly embarrassed, he looked away. "I know, but we really do need the money."

Moments passed. He took a deep breath and looked down into the crowded courtyard. The sky was a darkening blue. It had been sunny and warm all afternoon, a beautiful and remarkably smog-free Los Angeles day. The temperature was still in the low eighties. Pretty women in tight clothing seemed to be everywhere.

"I'm whipped. I'm not getting enough exercise." The man rubbed his eyes. "I brought a book with me, though. I thought maybe you'd like me to read to you." He pulled a thin paperback from his back pocket, *The Red Pony* by Steinbeck. The big man was a clumsy reader, but earnest intensity kept him going. He paused occasionally to take a sip of water from a plastic bottle. The pages turned noisily and time plodded by. Someone called someone on the intercom and the man finally became distracted enough to quit. He set down the book, yawned. "I was a lousy cop, but I wouldn't make much of an actor either, would I?"

"No."

The man smiled in a minor key. He stared out the window again. The sunset was a smear of pale orange and red on the western hills. Shadows elongated to embrace the fiery ball. Down below a beautiful young woman in a white top and shorts, perhaps a student at nearby USC, called out to a friend and waved hello. Pigeons cooed and burbled near the small Greek fountain in the courtyard. The man silently wondered, not for the first time, why God seemed to make gorgeous women younger every year. Eventually he looked up, the fading light accentuating the graying copper in his hair. He studied the braided contrail of a passing aircraft, its engines all but inaudible.

"I started praying again." He spoke so softly he felt compelled to repeat himself. "I've been praying. I think I may go back to that Zen center in the Valley. There was a Roshi there who made a lot of sense."

"Why?"

"You know why. Because I think it helps me with my anger."

"You need to work on acceptance."

"Yes."

The man leaned forward in the chair, dropped his head into cupped palms. He closed his eyes and breathed slowly, deeply. He repeated the focused breath, again and again. Darkness crawled effortlessly down the side of the building until it triggered exterior lighting. The yard stilled and the hospital room grew silent. After a few long moments the man fell asleep; head in hands, hands on knees.

"You have to leave now."

He was on his feet in one fluid motion, fingers spread, reddened eyes searching the room. A stern nurse stood in the doorway, clear plastic clipboard raised high, like a gladiator's shield. She was a toasty-brown Hispanic woman of indeterminate age. Glasses enlarged her dark, wary eyes. Her face was fixed. It was kind, but firm.

"Sorry, but visiting hours were over an hour ago, Mr. Burke. You'll have to say good-bye."

Burke felt irritated in a dull way. He wanted to argue but couldn't quite summon the energy. He nodded to the nurse, hoping she would be satisfied. She remained there, clipboard clutched in one hand and fat fountain pen in the other, determined to check him off as evicted from the premises. Burke walked to the bed, bent at the waist like a mime and kissed the sleeping woman on the forehead.

"Good night sweetie," he whispered. "I'll try to stop by tomorrow."

The nurse looked away quickly, as if surprised by deep emotion. She ushered him out and closed the door once he'd gone.

Burke walked down a long, hollow corridor where footsteps boomed. The walls were a pale green in this section. They soaked up all light and shade, reflected nothing back. The effect was subtly disturbing; everything emptiness and echo, as if he were the last living thing. He shook away a familiar feeling of despair and picked up the pace, mind already beginning to focus on work.

Outside, he paused in the driveway as if to smell the night air and looked around. The lot was nearly deserted, except for a few automobiles in the private-parking area and what appeared to be a yawning, empty ambulance. His eyes efficiently searched corners and doorways, seeking the orange glow of a cigarette or the shape of a loitering stranger, anything that might seem out of place. The sprinklers hissed on and began to twirl mist in sensual circles, moistening the fresh, green grass. Burke yawned and turned to face the glass doors, stretched and rolled his broad shoulders. The movement allowed him to look behind. He had not been followed.

Satisfied, he turned back again. In one sharp burst he sprinted through the sprinklers, almost playfully; ran across the damp grass and into the adjoining lot. Burke looked around one last time and then slid into a used, nondescript white Toyota. He drove away, into the Sunday-night traffic, which was minimal, except for the frustrated Hollywood Bowl customers waiting in long, twin lines on Highland.

The 101 Freeway was an awesome tongue of spider-webbed concrete that stretched from one end of the city to the other. It extended from the gleaming gold of downtown, where tall buildings menaced the huddled poverty of Skid Row, out through the multicultural San Fernando Valley, then roared past the gaudy, overpriced homes of Calabasas all the way out into Agoura and the edge of Ventura County. And Burke, though not from Los Angeles, had settled here. He now knew every inch of the territory as well as he did the deserts of Nevada.

He exited at Lankershim Boulevard and turned north, toward the towering, black structures of the legendary Universal Studios. The concert there, a country music spectacle, had already begun. As Burke drove by the entrance he suddenly swerved to the left, ignored the chorus of annoyed honks, and pulled an illegal U-turn. He started back the other way, one sharp eye on the furious people he'd left behind. Then he turned right, along the sloping ramp that would take him over to Ventura Boulevard and away from the studio and theme park. He watched his rearview mirror carefully until satisfied.

Burke traveled up Vineland, passed the used car businesses and sagging apartment buildings that packed the area, stopped again at the conjunction of Lankershim, Vineland, Riverside, and Camarillo Streets. This intersection, a maze of confusing right, left, and straight-ahead lanes, was a death trap for the unwary and the frequent site of fatal accidents. He turned onto Riverside Drive. Fredo, the Italian restaurant he wanted, was a few blocks back, toward Tujunga. Burke parked on a side street, walked quickly through a darkened alley, and entered through the back door.

The restaurant was decorated in Italian Cliché. Burke saw red-and-white-checkered tablecloths, small vases with drooping dried flowers, condiments and geriatric bottles of olive oil containing sprigs of herb and pepper. A balding, rotund man waited in a booth near the back. He had a notebook in his pocket and a pencil behind one ear and was tapping furiously on a worn laptop. He looked up with a dyspeptic grimace.

"About fucking time, Red."

Burke slid into the booth and forced a smile. "Me? I'm doing fine, Tony. Thanks for asking."

"Oh, fuck you," Tony Monteleone growled. "I've been waiting half an hour."

"Give me more notice next time."

Burke caught the eye of the bored, anorexic waitress. He pointed to an empty glass and mimed drinking. Without changing expression the blonde snagged a pitcher full of ice and a suspicious, clear fluid that may or may not have been tap water. She stalked closer like some praying mantis, poured a glass. He spotted the needle tracks near her elbow; caught a glimpse of death in her flat, disinterested eyes. She floated away like a spider to the corner, seeking food.

"You hungry?"

"No, Tony. Besides, I wouldn't eat here if you paid me."

"Neither would anyone else with a brain." Monteleone shrugged, smirked. "That's why I use it as an office."

Burke almost took a sip of the gray, brackish water, thought better of it. He moved the glass away and called to the bored girl. "Honey, bring me a can of something cold instead, okay?" She returned with a cola. Burke popped the can, took a sip, enjoyed the faint snarl of sugared carbonation. "What do you need?"

Tony leaned back in the red plastic booth. It squeaked soprano, like a rodent. "You know Dinky Martin?"

"The fat guy that uses gym rats as bodyguards? Sure."

"He is into me for ten large on the Cardinals game."

"He took fucking Arizona?"

"No accounting for taste."

"What's the vig?"

"I told him ten percent a day he don't get it to me on time. That was day before yesterday. So that makes twelve large, now."

"I can do the math."

"I should hope so." Tony Monteleone leaned forward again. "And by the way, this is only a piece of what the germ owes me." He struggled to appear concerned, but to Burke only managed to seem constipated. "I get the feeling he's ready to rabbit. Some people do nasty things when they get that scared, know what I mean?"

Burke nodded. "I'll be careful. Where is he?"

"Last I heard, he had packed up his place in Tarzana and was hanging around over at the Horny Rhino."

"Why?"

"My source says he keeps slipping hundreds to that fake-tit collagen princess calls herself Roxanne. He's trying to get her to leave town with him."

"Like you said, there's no accounting for taste." Burke finished his soft drink, slid out of the booth and back on his feet. "I'd better move it, then. Dinky still drive that turd-brown Beemer?"

"The same."

"Who's he got with him?"

"That Arena League football player guy, Kelvin Somebody."

Burke shook his head. "Great. That big bastard is like a Coke machine with a head on it."

"Tell me about it. Take a gun this time."

"Maybe I will. One large?"

Tony rolls his eyes. "You're killing me here! A fucking *thousand?*"

"I come back with twelve grand, it's worth it."

"Okay, okay."

Burke patted Tony on the shoulder. He moved down the hallway and back out into the lot. With some action on the horizon, his pulse began to race. His nostrils flared and his eyesight sharpened. The night seemed more alive than just moments ago. He checked everywhere, carefully opened his trunk. It had a false bottom; half of a fake spare tire and some plush carpeting covered a recessed area packed with weapons. There were short bats, handcuffs, a sawed-off pump shotgun, varied handguns, extra 9mm clips and speed loaders. After a moment of reflection he selected a .38 Special and tucked it into the back of his belt. The gun had no serial number and the handle was wrapped in black electrical tape.

Two

Tarzana, improbably named after Tarzan of the Apes, squatted a few miles west, yet another straight shot down the Ventura Freeway. The Horny Rhino was a so-called "gentlemen's club" where drug-addicted young women could make enormous amounts of cash for shaking booty and offering the occasional hand job, even on a Sunday night. It had valet parking, so Burke circled around the block. He slid to the curb in a residential area and walked briskly to a cement wall at the end of the street. Burke paused, listening to the echo of pounding rap music, but heard no voices. He pulled himself up and over and dropped into the alley behind the club, eased along the brick wall and ducked down behind some overflowing trash cans. The stench of rotting food was damp, foul, smothering.

"The fuck we waiting for?"

A dark, low voice came from right around the corner, at the mouth of the next alley. Burke felt his heart speed-bump his ribcage. He swallowed dryly and edged back a few inches, squeezing into a pile of plastic garbage sacks. He debated pulling the gun but didn't want to risk movement.

"We just guard the back." A different voice with a high nasal twang, read like someone from the Deep South.

"Shit, I'm bored," Mr. Low Voice said. "Let's smoke a J, then."

"No way, man," Twang replied. "You go on inside and do that, you want to. If Willie catches me stoned again it's my ass."

"Suit yourself."

Suddenly the music got louder then softer again as the door closed. Twang sighed and stepped out into view in the alley. He was a male model–type—long brown hair in a ponytail, black designer shirt tight against the sculpted pectorals, expensive cowboy boots. Twang strutted over to the wall, leaned on it. Burke heard the tinny rasp of a zipper and the warm hiss of urine striking the ground. The splatter was just loud enough to cover light footsteps. When Twang turned he was clobbered with a knuckled blow to the throat. His system went into shock. He couldn't breathe. He grunted in panic as Burke artfully steadied him then delivered a second blow to the diaphragm. Twang dropped to his knees, puked and passed out.

Inside the club, the music was deafening. No one saw Burke enter because all eyes were fixed on an Oriental girl. She was writhing about the lacquered black stage while using her vagina to smoke a cigar. The guards outside were likely on the lookout for squad cars or maybe some undercover vice cops out to bust what was obviously a private party.

Burke mussed up his hair, went to the bar and stood next to a red-nosed businessman who was hooting and hollering encouragement. He reached past the overflowing ashtray, stole the man's half-empty glass, slipped into the crowd of drunks. Burke plastered on a harmless, cartoon grin and started looking for Dinky Martin. The air was thick as dirty cotton and made his eyes water. Fortunately, the search didn't take long.

An enormous black man anchored the far table near the men's room. His massive, tattooed arms were crossed over a barrel chest. The scowling colossus was Kelvin, the Arena Bowl player. Burke thought, *He may as well be wearing a sign GUARDING A CHICKENSHIT.* Dinky Martin was wearing a Hawaiian shirt, torpid belly ballooning out over pale blue slacks. He lay sprawled in the booth, a g-stringed beauty under his arm, watching the stage. There were two empty pitchers of beer on the table, along with a bowl of peanuts and some overpriced, watery champagne for the call girl. Burke figured anyone ingesting that much beer would need to pee every twenty minutes. He stumbled along the wall with his face averted and stepped into the foul crapper.

A transvestite in a pink dress was standing at the urinal. The pretty guy shook it, tucked it back into red panties, and lowered his frilly skirt. He turned to the mirror, patted his brunette wig and winked.

"Nature called."

Burke moved aside, face empty. The cheerful cross-dresser left. Burke checked and found all three stalls empty. He stepped into the last and stood on the toilet. He could just see the front door. He locked the stall and leaned back against the wall with his eyes closed, focused on a rippling mountain stream and the sound of cool breeze whispering through pines.

The music was pounding relentlessly enough to vibrate the plaster, so waiting was torture. A couple of tattooed kids festooned with body piercing crashed into the room. They were dressed in baggy fatigues and jean jackets with peace symbols. They peed, finished a foul-smelling roach, and left. Burke remained quiet. After another false alarm—two businessmen from the bar—Dinky entered to use the urinal. Burke heard him tell Kelvin to wait outside.

As Dinky Martin grunted out the last few drops, something cold touched the back of his neck. He whined porcine high and shrill and began to tremble. Dinky reeked of cheap cologne and cigar smoke. Burke whispered in his ear. "Twelve large, Dinky. You know who, you know why."

"I don't have it," Dinky wheezed. "I mean I *do,* but not here for Chrissakes."

Burke grabbed Martin by the back of his greasy hair and

slammed that bulbous nose into the tiled wall. Dinky squealed pathetically and Burke almost lost his resolve.

"My nose!"

"I broke it," Burke said softly. He pushed the head forward into the tile again, but somewhat gently. He rubbed the mess around, so a pinkish smear would be there for Dinky to see. "You know what? You may like it better this way."

"Don't hurt me anymore."

"The money?"

"Okay, okay!"

BOOM the door exploded inward. Burke released Dinky, who dropped down and retched into the urinal. The bodyguard Kelvin drove Burke into the paneled wall of the first stall and Burke heard a sharp *crack* and wondered if it was wood or his ribs. He couldn't reach the .38 in his waistband, so he went for Kelvin's balls, but the bastard was wearing a cup goddamn it, and his fingers slipped off and up the tailored trousers. Kelvin hit him hard once, twice on the top of the head with a ham-sized clenched fist.

"Kill the fucker!" Dinky screamed. He sounded sincere.

"You got it, boss," Kelvin replied. His fist slammed down again and Burke felt his knees weaken. He deliberately let himself sag. He opened his hands and slid them, palms out, up the man's shirt, as if seeking purchase. Kelvin tried to hold him up to hit him again. Burke grabbed his collar and yanked down as he stood up tall. He drove his skull up and into the bigger man's jaw with a sickening crunch. Kelvin swayed, eyes rolling up like windows in a slot machine. Burke whacked the hinge of his jaw and Kelvin dropped like a sack full of barley. Burke stumbled to the bathroom door and locked it. When he turned around, he was feeling greatly annoyed.

Dinky was shaking his head, flattened nose spraying crimson droplets. His eyes were bulging. He went digging into pockets and underwear and socks, pulled out rolls of bills and flung them down onto the piss and blood-stained bathroom floor. "Take it! Take it all!"

Burke felt his head and his fingers came away bloody. He was not overly concerned, since even minor scalp wounds bled profusely. He opened his mouth and checked for a loose tooth.

"There!" Dinky shrieked. "That's all I've got."

Sobbing, Dinky backed away through clumps of paper towels. Burke knelt in the piss and blood to gather a few rolls of hundred dollar bills, distaste for the entire enterprise written on his weathered face. Someone pounded on the bathroom door. Burke moved faster. He carefully counted out exactly twelve thousand dollars and put it in his pocket.

"I said take it all, just leave me alone!"

"You can keep what you don't owe," Burke said calmly. "Just don't be stupid next time."

A thunderous crash distracted him. Men were throwing themselves against the restroom door. Burke moved to the back stall, stepped up onto the toilet seat and grabbed the concrete ledge. He levered the large window open, kicked out the lower pane of glass and slithered through. He dropped down onto a pile of garbage sacks, rolled through some mud, and jogged down the alley.

"Hey, that's him!"

Twang, back on his feet and filled with righteous indignation, was standing by the back exit, talking to a Hispanic guy in boxer shorts and a XXX tee shirt. Burke measured the two of them as they started toward him, clearly set on rearranging his features.

"This is not my night." Burke reached behind his back, down to his belt. He sighed wearily and flashed the snub-nosed .38.

Both men froze and then began to back away, palms up. "It's all good, my man," the Hispanic said with a wide, forced smile.

"Shit, I don't know you, never saw you."

"Easy, dude," Twang added. "No problem here."

Burke tucked the gun away, made the wall on the second try and dropped back onto the residential street. He resisted the urge to run. He strolled to his car, got in, and drove away into the night.

THREE

Monday

She smiles down at him, her beautiful face framed by raven hair and lightly rimmed from behind by a glowing arc of candlelight. Her flesh is warm and soft to the touch. Burke is at peace and content. He wants to say that, wants her to know, but he cannot speak . . . her fingers uncurl, lengthen and splay, then gently stroke his thigh. Burke feels himself thicken. He tries to kiss her, but she shakes her head and pushes him back down. She is focused and intent on pleasing him. In a voice that sighs and rolls like ocean waves she whispers: "Just let go. Let go." But her features somehow writhe and change into something else, a creature that is distorted, dark and strange to him . . . "Let go . . . let go . . ."

Jack Burke cried out. His eyes jerked open. His heart thudded a low timpani roll. He felt small, weak, and terrified. He looked around his sparsely furnished bedroom, eyes seeking purchase.

Outside, the morning was still. Sparrows were pecking at stray seeds on the windowsill.

The clock radio clicked on, played a splashing wave followed by some "cool LA jazz." Burke calmed himself and sat up with a low grunt. The firm mattress barely moved. He shook the dream away, tried to deaden his frayed emotions. He noted a small, sharp pain deep in his chest. He rubbed aching flesh and checked his ribs but found no serious damage. He popped his back. Burke rolled out of bed naked, right down onto the hardwood floor. He did a long, slow series of yoga stretches, followed by a hundred push-ups, a hundred sit-ups, and several sets of hammer curls with thirty-pound weights.

As Burke grunted and sweated through his workout, the innocuous music was briefly interrupted by a newscast. A bored baritone recounted the current status of the 405 and 101 Freeways. The President was denying something to do with his checkered business history. Then: "In a dark coda to an even darker life, best-selling, multi-millionaire horror author Peter Stryker, a controversial public figure, has been found dead, an apparent suicide via what is described as 'self-mutilation.' The coroner has scheduled an autopsy."

Burke thought: *Self-mutilation? That's one way to make a statement.*

Burke slipped into worn Las Vegas PD running shorts and some mud-blackened tennis shoes without socks. He got a bottle of water from the fridge and jogged out the back door, around the side of the small house and down the sidewalk, heading north. He soon felt loose enough, and after a few moments began to run. He made three green lights effortlessly and turned east on Sherman Way. At the next block he caught a red light and had to run briskly in place, pumping his arms.

Some bleary-eyed, hungover, sorry-assed teenagers coming home from an all-night party pulled into the intersection and eyeballed him. Burke imagined what they saw: a tall, aging athlete; good buns with most of a six-pack and a full head of reddish hair, jumping up and down in his underwear at six-thirty in the morning, pouring cold water over himself. Burke stared them down. When the light went green again they roared away farting a trail of brownish smog, the driver peeling rubber in a lame show of macho. Amused, Burke finished the five miles and returned home. He stripped and swam several laps in a small, worn pool that was in need of new tiles. He dried himself, went back inside. After a moment, he turned the radio off. He needed silence.

Burke made breakfast: strong black coffee, dark wheat toast, no butter, and a three–egg white, spinach and mushroom omelet with hot sauce. He washed the dishes, pan and plates, the moment he was finished with them. The routine was the same every morning, structure his only comfort. When the food was finished and the dishes clean, Burke diligently searched the house and emptied the trash buckets into a black garbage sack. He tossed it into the can by the side door. He had already done the laundry for the week, so he vacuumed again. *Do something, anything. Keep moving.*

Burke glanced out the window and watched his neighbors hustle their children off to school. Wives kissed husbands goodbye. People waved and honked and drove away. It seemed like everyone else had somewhere to go, and someone to come back to. Burke's face tightened. He sat alone at the kitchen table, brooding.

When the telephone rang, he jumped and spilled coffee. The phone rang a second time. Burke swallowed, took deep breaths. He answered on the third ring, sounding calm and in control.

"Mr. Burke, this is Detective Bowden's assistant, Alice. Could you hold for him, please? Thank you so much."

Burke contained a flip response and sat back in the kitchen chair. The wood grumbled and creaked. After a few bars of 1970s music recorded for elevators, Burke heard another voice.

"Red, this is Scotty. How they hanging, man?"

Burke smiled. "You have your secretary get me on the fucking phone? What are you now, some big-assed Hollywood producer?"

Bowden snickered. "I knew that would piss you off, brother."

"It did."

"Seriously, Red. How you feeling these days? Is it any better?"

Burke was a half second too late in responding. "I think it is. A little." His voice betrayed the falsehood by sinking deeper into his chest and taking on a faint rasp.

Scotty kept his own tone light. "Good. Okay, so you're still looking for some extra work?"

"Always," Burke said. "The medical bills are kicking my ass, man."

"Then come on over. I got a gimme putt."

"Now?"

"Now. I'll fill you in, slip you a printout of the file, and give you the contact information. You can get started this afternoon."

Burke was already searching for a clean pair of underwear, some fresh jeans, and a tee shirt. He tucked the telephone under his chin. "What's this one about?"

"That dead guy on the news."

Four

The North Hollywood station sat on a rolling green carpet of grass right off Colfax, a main drag close to the Hollywood Freeway. It was an odd, concrete hodgepodge of artsy buildings, apparently designed to link circular and modern to the square and out-of-date. The architect had not succeeded. Jack Burke parked about half a block away. He sat quietly for a few moments, fingering the hundred-dollar bill in his pocket. He did not enjoy being around men and women who were still on the job. It made him uncomfortable. Scotty Bowden knew this, but often insisted on meeting here, perhaps hoping to persuade Burke to apply with LAPD rather than work both sides of the street.

A black-and-white cruised by. The driver, a seasoned homicide dick named Charlie Carney, honked and waved. Burke waved back. Feeling exposed, he slid out of the vehicle and walked down the block, up the steps, and into the freshly painted station.

"Mills."

"Red." The balding, beefy desk sergeant barely looked up. He tossed Burke a guest badge and went back to digesting the racing form. Burke strolled on down the hall, turned right and then left and into the back lobby. He paused by the long plate-glass window to watch his old friend arguing silently with the speakerphone perched on a huge, cluttered desk piled high with file folders and stapled papers. Of the four of them, Bowden had probably aged best. Unlike Burke, he already had a slight paunch, but that was an occupational hazard, and although there were now a few flecks of gray in his thick, black moustache, he was still handsome. Bowden played a lot of handball, and it showed. His face was still ladies'-man perfect, with a faint trident of lines around the dark eyes. Scotty looked up, spotted Burke, motioned.

By the time Burke entered the cluttered office, Scotty had already terminated the conversation. Bowden wore a fraying white shirt with the sleeves rolled up, tight beige slacks, and a brown, food-splattered tie all askew. A 9mm Glock rested comfortably on one hip. When they shook hands, Burke subtly palmed the hundred-dollar bill. Bowden casually slipped it into his own shirt pocket. He dropped back into his desk chair, arms behind his head.

"What are you into these days, Scotty?"

Bowden shrugged. "We got a bunch of homeless guys doing a vanishing act downtown." His voice had the slight rasp of a heavy smoker. "Probably nothing to it but some scrotums sneaking out of town with a dealer's crack stash, or maybe a couple of bottles of wine. You know how it goes."

"Who bothered to report them missing?"

"It was some nun who works the area. They're probably just sleeping it off in some other alley ten blocks away. No big deal."

"The job."

"You miss Vegas PD, don't you?"

"Sometimes."

"But not enough to join up here?"

"No way."

"You're looking pretty good, Red." It was the kind of compliment a vain man makes when he wants reciprocity.

"You could probably still take me, Scotty."

"Oh, I doubt that." It was clear he did not. He smiled, slid a manila file, perhaps one-inch thick, across the desk. It came to rest at Burke's fingertips.

"Meet Mr. Peter Stryker," Bowden said. "Best-selling author of the novels *Passageway, Magician, Black Dreams,* as well as *Deadly Appetites,* and the recent hit *A Taste for Flesh.*"

"The big horror writer."

"Yeah, the same. Although I'm told he preferred being known as an award-winning author of 'dark fantasy,' whatever the fuck that is. Wrote a bunch of shitty campfire stories, you ask me."

"He died last night?"

"And then some. Here's what I got from the Sheriff's office." The LA County Sheriff's office was responsible for the area known as Universal City. "Stryker appears to have checked into a suite at the Universal Sheraton at around seven last night, under another name. We don't know what he was doing in the Valley, or why he used a different name, but we assume it was to avoid being hassled."

Burke stole a pencil from the desk and looked down. "Name?"

"Huh?"

"The name he used when he checked into the Sheraton."

Scotty looked at his own notes. "Dan Ira Palski."

"Mean anything to you guys?"

"Only that it sounds bogus. Anyway, suite on the south side is empty. Some old, very old fart named Clinton Farnsworth and his blue-haired wife are on the north side, in 1124. I know his name from somewhere. I think he's a local businessman who shows up in the papers now and then. We haven't been able to reach the Farnsworths yet to get their statements, but I figure they're both so old they're half deaf and blind anyway."

"Anyone else to talk to?"

"One room service guy went by there and said he didn't hear anything from Stryker's room except classical music and maybe someone humming along, but he wasn't real sure."

"Not much help."

"No, but all the contact info is in the file. Anyway, the maid comes in the next day, around lunchtime. She knocks, opens the door, and makes the bed. She heads into the bathroom, nearly barfs all over our crime scene, and runs screaming out the door. The first guys on the scene find Stryker naked in the bathtub with his guts hanging half out. Guy did himself Japanese-style."

"How did he do it?"

"Medical tools, man. Scalpels and other shit like that. Turns out he was a med school dropout in his twenties. Who knew? He also did a real showbiz number on himself before checking out. Not to be believed."

"Like what?"

"It's all in the file," Scotty replied, a bit too briskly. He wanted to wrap things up. "Let me put it this way, my kind of shit from back in the Mo, man. Not too well-adjusted, okay?"

"He cut himself up first?"

"You could say that, yeah."

"Any last words?"

"A note in lipstick on the bathroom mirror, said 'I can't take this.' "

"Lipstick?"

Scotty laughed. "Yeah, a woman's lipstick. Look, you'll learn that rumor has it the guy was a real freakazoid. He was also into cross-dressing or something. When we searched his house we found a closet with a lot of women's clothing, black wigs, and makeup."

Burke looked up. "Same kind and shade?"

"Good catch, Burke," Scotty said with a quick grin. "Yeah, looks like the very same lipstick. The lab will tell us for sure, but the preliminary says it is."

Burke discreetly thumbed through the case file, but kept it

flat in his lap. He was not supposed to have it. He was not properly licensed in California as a private investigator.

"You need to be a bit discreet, of course," Scotty said. He looked out at the hallway to be sure no one was watching. "But take a second. Check this one out. You won't believe it."

Burke opened the file, shuffled documents. He whistled. There were some ugly photographs of the body in the tub and various blood splatters in the bathroom, along with measurements and details pertaining to the various wounds and the knives and scalpels used, also a preliminary lab report. Burke slipped the file under his shirt. "Strange, but it seems pretty open and shut."

"All ready to wrap up in a heartbeat." Scotty leaned forward, hunched his big arms. "Quick and easy."

"Let's hope so."

Scotty fiddled with his leather watchband. "Trust me on this. Just scan it and file a report, my man. The guy was screwed up. He took drugs and he did himself, and in the nastiest way he could think of. Problem is, the daughter doesn't want to buy that it was a suicide."

"I see."

"And this daughter, who is a stone fox by the way, is also about to inherit one shit load of money."

Burke smiled. "So you told her there was a way to clear up any unanswered questions and that although you couldn't officially recommend anyone, speaking strictly off the record, I might be able to help her out?"

"Yeah, and you can name your price on this one," Bowden said. "You want to string this thing out, it's probably worth fifteen or twenty grand. The foxy daughter's name is Nicole Moberly, but she's dumped her second husband and she's in the middle of changing it back. So call her Nicole Stryker, okay?"

"All right."

Scotty leaned forward with a slip of paper. "Here's the number and address. She's waiting for you to stop by this morning. She claims to be all tore up about this, so go easy on her at first."

Burke got to his feet. "Scotty, I can really use the money. Thanks." He extended his hand.

"No sweat." Bowden cleared his throat. He looked down and away. "Now, if this one does turn out to be a good earner . . . Well, I picked some dog horses this week. I could maybe use an extra little taste this time, you know?"

"That's cool," Burke responded. "I'll take care of you, Scotty. Brothers?"

"Brothers." They slapped palms. Bowden seemed visibly relieved. He brightened. "Stay in touch, Red. Okay?"

"Will do." Burke turned in the doorway. "By the way, Stryker must have had a killer life insurance policy, right?"

"Why you cynical bastard!" Scotty nodded, his eyes sparkled. "A new one, and just inside of the two-year suicide exclusion, too. So your little client could maybe have gotten millions more."

"But the company won't pay out if this is officially called a suicide inside of the two years."

"Bingo."

Bowden picked up the one picture he kept on his desk. It was a small headshot of his estranged daughter, Patty. Bowden's tough features visibly softened. He often seemed to drown himself in her blue eyes.

"Is she doing well?"

"From what I hear, she's great." A wry smile. "You have a nice day, Red."

Five

Like a femme fatale, Beverly Glen Boulevard briefly fondled the trousers of the eternally smoggy valley but then backed away, teasingly, into the lush and numbingly overpriced foothills. At the top of the rise sat famed Mulholland Drive, where a forked left turn and a quick right shot down fancy Benedict Canyon, into the 310 area code and some *serious* money. It was a short trip.

Although decidedly middle-class, Burke had lived around riches, both in Las Vegas and now California. He was familiar enough with those who'd lost track of what they own and still weren't satisfied. The ubiquitous "upper crass" denizens of LA were generally narcissistic people who had somehow scored big in the indigenous entertainment industry or profited from its constant stream of cash.

Nicole Stryker's luxurious house was on a shady, overgrown corner near Peach Lane and Tower Grove Drive. The outside was painted a pale blue with a lacy white ribbon of trim. The entrance and upper rooms had been placed at street level, with the lower floor, presumably the bedrooms, standing on stilts grounded in the hillside. Burke parked in the shade and stepped out of the car. The lawn was impeccably manicured and a silver Lexus sedan crouched like a tiger in the spotless driveway. Burke approached the large oak front door, his eyes searching for a doorbell or knocker.

But then the door opened and time slowed like syrup on a cold morning.

The woman was under thirty, with hair so blonde it looked white in the morning sunshine. Her body was lithe, eyes a vivid blue. She stared up at Burke with the studied superiority of the eternally privileged. After a long moment, she smiled feral approval. Her voice was surprisingly throaty.

"Are you Jack Burke?"

He blinked. "Yes, ma'am."

"It's about time."

She turned and strolled away, hips swaying in worn, but tight white slacks with "Juicy" printed on the back. She moved down some circular steps and vanished into the cool, dark living room. As Burke followed her, the door closed soundlessly on its own. The plush carpeting was white, and without blemish. He walked into the room and found her at the bar, briskly preparing a wine cooler. New age music oozed from invisible speakers. She did not offer him a drink.

"Sit down."

"Yes, ma'am."

"Stop fucking calling me ma'am."

Burke perched on the edge of an armchair. Grief did funny things to people, but whatever the cause of her distress, this girl was already an irritation. Now that the initial, sexually charged effect had begun to wear off, Burke could see the plastic perfection of her breasts and a too-carefully sculpted 90210 nose job.

"I get eight hundred a day, plus expenses," he said softly. He had impulsively inflated his normal fee by more than twenty percent.

Nicole Stryker paused. She arched one carefully plucked eyebrow. "I didn't hire you yet."

"No, you didn't," Burke answered, pleasantly. "But if you're going to be giving me a ration of shit, we may as well start the clock now."

Nicole surprised him. She set down her drink and exploded into loud, good-natured laughter. "Okay, good. That line got you hired."

Burke did not smile back. "Not so fast. First, tell me what you want me to do."

Nicole walked over to the tinted, floor-to-ceiling window and looked out into the canyon. The sun was high enough to have chased cool shadows behind the brush and back under the overpriced homes. One scrawny deer emerged from the hardy foliage to drink from a hidden sprinkler. Nicole sipped her drink. She appeared to choose her words with care. "I want you to look into my father's death. If it was a suicide then fine, but if it was murder I want to know."

"Okay."

"And if it was murder I also want you to tell me who it was, why . . . and *how* they did it."

"That could be a tall order."

Nicole Stryker turned to face him. Her eyes narrowed. *The bitch is back.* "That detective promised me that you were the best man for this. I need to believe he was telling me the truth."

"That probably depends on what you mean by best."

"If I need something . . . unusual done, can I count on you?"

Burke's face remained blank. "I don't kill people for money, Miss Stryker."

"Nicole." She leaned back against the window and took another swallow of the wine cooler. "But you have killed people before, am I correct?"

Fucking Scotty, how much had he told her?

"I'm told you were a police officer until a couple of years ago, Mr. Burke."

"Yes. I was."

"Where?"

"In Las Vegas."

"What happened?"

"I left. Sounds like you already know why."

"To make more money."

"That's right."

He volunteered nothing more. Nicole grinned approvingly. "And before that you were in the service. You saw combat in Somalia."

Close enough. "Among other places."

Nicole sipped. "I think I saw that movie, in fact. You boys got your asses kicked."

Burke did not respond, but the room seemed to chill by several degrees.

"Will you answer some more direct questions, Mr. Burke?"

He sighed and eased back to a standing position. "You know something? I don't think I like you, Nicole."

She frowned. "I beg your pardon?"

"There is a man who can help you, his name is Lynwood. He's in the Encino telephone book under Private Detective Services. Call him." Burke turned, started back up the stairs.

Nicole Stryker cleared her throat. "Nine hundred a day, plus expenses."

Burke kept moving. He was reaching for the front door when she called out: "One thousand a day, plus expenses."

Burke's needs betrayed him. He stopped, envisioning medical bills and a long line of impatient creditors. He swallowed bitterness and his shoulders slumped forward. "On one condition," he said. After a long moment he turned. "Nicole."

"Go on."

"You don't ask questions. I do that. You just shut up and let me do my job."

They glared like alley cats, neither one looked away. Nicole considered, finished her drink and then, conceding defeat, found something fascinating way out in the canyon. "How do we get started?"

Burke, silent as a predator, returned to the living room and his former position. "Tell me about your father."

She saw his hands were empty. "Aren't you going to take notes?"

"I don't need to. Did your father have any enemies?"

"He had several, to be honest." She took a piece of paper from her pocket. She folded it again and again into a tiny square, flipped it at Burke.

He caught it one-handed, annoyed by her little games. "And this is?"

"It's a list of people who hated my father enough to have killed him or ordered his death. These are people who are also, to some extent, wealthy and intelligent enough to have pulled off a murder this . . . sophisticated. You can examine that at your leisure, Mr. Burke, just not on my time."

He tucked the paper into the pocket of his jeans, rugged face bland. "Go on, then."

Nicole sat down on the carpet and crossed her legs, Indian-style. She pulled her hair back, and the pose reminded Burke of something lifted from a Hindu painting. "I assume you know enough about my father's career to know that he was a very wealthy man."

"Yes."

"He also suffered from what appeared to be some confusion about his gender orientation."

"I see."

"No, you don't," she whispered. Her voice cracked with emotion. "But you will in a minute. Please sit down."

Burke slipped off his running shoes and sat on the couch, also cross-legged. He ordered his mind to absorb all relevant information, whether spoken or merely observed.

"Just let me talk for a while, Mr. Burke. Then if you have any questions you can ask them."

"Go ahead."

"My mother was an heiress, the granddaughter of one of the Martingale twins. As you may know, the family made a fortune in canned goods. I am my father's only child. I say my father's because my very wealthy mother died in childbirth and my father raised me. I do not remember Father dating in the customary sense of that word. He employed the occasional mistress for sexual release, but he seldom brought one home or introduced me. As for me, I had a series of nannies, plump and pleasant European women who indulged my every whim."

Nicole Stryker was delivering a monologue of sorts, and as her voice droned on, the sun beyond the tinted windows seemed to drop directly behind her pretty head, creating an odd halo effect, with tendrils of grayish light. As he sank into a trance state, she embodied the goddess and Burke felt the presence of what Carl Jung called "the numinous."

"My father was a remote man, but lest you think passionless just read one of his novels. His soul was burdened by a dark and only marginally contained lust, Mr. Burke. But it was not for mere hedonistic physical sensations. My father craved power over others. And my mother's wealth gave him access to that power. That is why he loved to learn."

"Didn't he attend medical school at some point in his life?"

"In his twenties, on scholarship. He was way ahead of the class. He hated it, or so I was told. He dropped out from sheer boredom."

"And the writing?"

"His writing began as a lark, or so he claimed. He'd always liked anagrams, word games, crossword puzzles, things like that. And he loved to read. Then he happened upon a collection of stories by an alcoholic journalist named Ambrose Bierce, who was an employee of William Randolph Hearst in the eighteen hundreds. Bierce enjoyed writing and publishing very disturbing fiction. My father was inspired by a rather bleak and cheerfully sadistic story called 'An Occurrence at Owl Creek Bridge.' He adored the surprise ending and immediately set about writing a derivative story of his own. With his typical lack of humility he sent it out to a magazine. It was, of course, rejected.

"Mr. Burke, one simply did not say no to my father. He flew into a rage. I remember, I was perhaps nine at that time—he actually threatened to buy the magazine just to humiliate and fire the editor. Father immersed himself in horror fiction at that point. He began with the masters, Poe, H. P. Lovecraft, Stoker, Mary Shelley, and Saki. He moved to the modern best-selling authors, such as King, Straub, Koontz, Anne Rice, and Robert McCammon.

"He educated himself for more than a year. Then he sat down at his computer and tried again. He produced a somewhat derivative novel about an abandoned tenement in a New York City slum that was actually the gate to another, and quite evil, dimension. The book, *Passageway,* won a Bram Stoker Award from the Horror Writers' Association. It then sold to a paperback house and went on to be a bestseller and a film of the same name. The money and accolades poured in. I recall how my father reveled in it all. Of course, now he had even less time for me than before."

"And the author Peter Stryker was born."

"Yes."

Burke absorbed her words greedily, with every fiber of his consciousness. It was easy to do; Nicole was beautiful in the steadily dimming light, sitting like a *fakir,* her face obscured by shadow. His eyes were half closed and heavy. It took him a moment to realize she had stopped speaking. He shook himself awake. "May I ask a few things now?"

"Of course."

"What was your father's real name?"

"Peter Philbin. He was an English teacher when he met my mother. As I heard the story, her car broke down in the rain near a small town in New England. Her driver walked off into the storm in search of assistance. My father happened upon the limousine and offered to assist her. She was intrigued by the fact that he was a medical student at the time. She later invited him to a party at the mansion. They went outside for a drink and a chat. I'm told she was initially just trying to be polite, but then they fell in love."

"How did her family feel about this?"

Nicole Striker chuckled in a low and throaty voice. Burke felt the short hairs on his neck flutter. "My mother's family despised Peter Philbin, Mr. Burke, especially once they heard that he had dropped out of medical school. They hated him even more after my mother's untimely death. My father inherited a fortune, but never their goodwill. In fact, they never spoke to him again."

"Didn't they want to know their grandchild?"

Nicole hesitated. "Not according to my father. If they tried to send birthday cards or telephone, I never heard about it. In fact, they are dead to me."

Burke breathed slowly, allowed his mind to run over what she had already revealed to him, and looked for any unspoken threads. Finally he said: "So now he has money and fame to go along with what you described as a lust for power. How did all that affect him?"

"He continued to write," Nicole replied. "And each book became more successful than the last. Did you know that all but one was made into a movie, and that all of those films topped two hundred million dollars in domestic box office?"

"No, I don't read much horror fiction."

Nicole seemed to read his mind. "Perhaps you have seen a few too many horror facts?"

"Perhaps."

"Well, my father made sure everyone else knew about statistics like that. He would drop those figures at every opportunity. Fame made him even vainer, Mr. Burke, even more insufferably self-centered. Each novel became darker than the last, too. More visceral, more explicit and disturbing. As you noted, he had a medical background and he took great pride in shocking people."

"That seems appropriate for his chosen profession."

"Of course. But in order to stretch the boundaries he also had to research extensively. He read a great deal about witchcraft, human sacrifice, torture, the Holocaust, the Spanish Inquisition. The list goes on and on. To be honest, I remain convinced that such material eventually warped his mind."

"What makes you say that?"

"Father began to lock himself in his study for hours on end, and sometimes I would hear him screaming and crying. He would vanish for days or weeks, always without warning. He was gone most of my high school years, but suddenly ceased flying a few years ago. He became completely phobic about air travel after September 11th and never rode on another plane. He turned to comparative religion and devoured Eastern thought. Nonetheless, his fear of the finality of death became overwhelming."

Burke focused more energy and gathered a deeper sense of the man they were discussing. He did not like the resultant feeling. "You are describing someone very capable of killing himself."

"I know. But hear me out."

Burke shrugged. *It's your money.* Nicole Stryker shifted into a standing position, so effortlessly his pulse raced. She moved away from the tinted window, buttocks rolling smoothly, back to the bar to refresh her drink. Burke was both amused and unduly baffled by this young woman. He shook his head slightly. "Go on."

The tinkling of ice in a glass. "As I said, my father was terrified of death. The more he read about it, and those who explore and worship it, the more frightened he became. If his many fans had realized how pathetic a figure he was in real life, they would have abandoned him in droves. In the last few years his fame was a curse. He could not go out in public without being asked for his autograph. He learned to disguise himself."

Burke smiled. "You're not suggesting that's why he . . ."

"Yes, that's why he began to wear women's clothing. To go out in drag. According to my father, it was the only way he could escape the house without being troubled."

Cross-dressing for privacy? It read as total nonsense. Burke could not tell if she believed her own rationalization, so he said nothing.

"And by the way," Nicole continued, "even discussing the themes he wrote about began to give him anxiety attacks. A supreme karmic joke, wouldn't you say?"

"It sounds that way," Burke replied. "May I have a glass of water, Nicole?"

The fact that he had used her first name increased the static dangling in the air. Burke rose and strolled over to the bar. He moved to the other end and reached out with his right hand. Nicole Stryker poured club soda into a crystal goblet, added ice, and slid it down the bar so their fingers would not touch. It was clear that she felt something, too.

"Was he on medication for these attacks?" Burke was thinking of drugs like Ativan and their sedating effect, also how dangerous they were when combined with alcohol.

Nicole Stryker shook her head. "Not in the way you're thinking," she says. "He saw a psycho-pharmacologist named Markoff at UCLA and was prescribed an antidepressant."

"Do you recall which one?"

"No."

Burke searched his memory bank. "An SSRI, like Lexapro?"

"I've forgotten. That sounds right. Whatever it was, it didn't make him further depressed. In fact quite the opposite. He became more agitated."

"Did your father do recreational drugs of any kind?"

"Not that I know of, but it wouldn't surprise me. My father . . . experimented with life, Mr. Burke."

"That prescription you mentioned? I would like to know what it was." Burke drank the club soda. The fizz tickled his upper lip.

"If it isn't in the police report I will find out."

Nicole reached into her pocket and slid a set of keys across the bar. Burke let them sit on the polished wood. He arched an eyebrow. "The keys to his house and home office," Nicole said. "The police were far more concerned about the crime scene and said they'd get there tomorrow. I doubt you will have any trouble going through his things tonight."

"Okay."

"Search all you want." Nicole Stryker seemed weary. "Remember that this was a man who loved scary stories and secret passageways, so be vigilant. You may find books, women's clothing, religious artifacts, and all manner of strangeness, Mr. Burke. Do not be distracted from your primary purpose. I want to know what really happened up in that hotel suite. And why."

Six

The premium coffee shop was furnished in forest green colors with silver metal bars and extended from the outer wall of a large chain bookstore like some stark, metastasized growth. Jack Burke was seated at a corner table with a long, yellow notepad, a sharpened pencil, and a stack of paperback books written by Peter Stryker. Burke was a speed-reader, and some college girls at a nearby table watched in awe as his eyes and practiced fingers raced through the pages.

"You take lessons to do that?"

"Huh?" He shook his head. There were two of them. One was a lanky blonde in cut-off jeans and a red halter top, the other a plump and slightly busty brunette in a blue pants suit. They were likely students at nearby Cal State Northridge or one of the other colleges. Burke wondered, not for the first time, why pretty girls always seemed to have another, less attractive, female along for company. Perhaps so they could have an audience as they exercised their power. The blonde was trying to flirt.

"The reading thing?" She coaxed him with body language, leaning forward so her breasts were accentuated.

Burke allowed her a thin smile. "I was in the service for a while. I always read a lot, but they had a course in speed-reading and I took it twice."

The blonde widened her eyes, batted those lashes. "Oh, I do love uniforms." Scarlet O'Hara came to mind. Her friend seemed embarrassed.

"That so?"

"I'm serious." She extended her hand like a princess. "My name is Tiffany."

But of course it is, Burke thought. *And this is "mysterious older man day."* He took her hand. "Kevin O'Brien." He gave the name of a long-dead cousin.

The girl moved in for the kill. She edged her chair closer. Her friend sought shelter in a makeup mirror and doodled in the foam of a latte. To her credit, she appeared mortified. Meanwhile, the blonde purred. "And what did you do in the service, Kevin?"

Burke's eyes were slate, face leaden. "Oh, I killed people, Tiff," he said. "Sometimes civilians. Quite a few, in fact."

Her smile froze and soon wavered. She eased away from him, mouth working furiously, like an anal retentive housewife who just found a roach in her broth. Her friend snorted and leapt to her feet. A man at a nearby table struggled not to laugh. Burke looked down and resumed reading. He did not give the girl another thought.

Burke found *Passageway* a pile of crap. It was easy material to speed through. He could see the so-called scary moments coming a mile away. Stryker's first novel was flat and derivative, although the author did have a decent flair for language. Burke finished the book in a few minutes, put a few reminder notes and page numbers on the pad, and started on the next book. It was marginally better, but junk nonetheless. The author tried to write about Native American rituals but got many of his facts wrong. The characters were almost laughably cardboard, the ending cinematic in the worst sense of the word. As Burke read, the real world faded away.

He was on his third coffee when he started the next to last novel. It had more depth of characterization and a lighter writing style, and something had begun to resonate deeply within the structure. It was existential angst, something with which Burke was quite familiar. The author had a macabre preoccupation with concepts like the existence of random chance, and the fact that life may have no intrinsic meaning. Even speeding through these pages, Burke found them disconcerting. Not only did the lead character confront an utter pointlessness to his life and the failure of feeble attempts to be moral and courageous, but evil forces won out at the conclusion. The book was well done, and profoundly disturbing.

As Jack Burke put the book down, he was suddenly cloaked in a gray, weighted melancholy. Peter Stryker may have started out a hack, but he ended his life as a novelist of considerable talent.

Burke had one book to go, the latest and last novel. He turned the book over in his hands. The title was *A Taste for Flesh.* He studied the needlessly inflammatory copy on the back, which described TERROR UNLEASHED and a DEPRAVITY BEYOND DESCRIPTION. The print size and color seemed reasonably restrained, but the jacket hyperbole reminded him of a B movie poster from the 1950s. Despite that, Burke knew that this book was likely to be far better than it appeared.

"Sir?"

The coffee shop was crowded. Burke set the book on the table. A pimple-faced kid in an apron festooned with dancing coffee beans was doing his best to be assertive. "Sir, you've been sitting here for a long time, and there are others waiting for a table."

After a brief flash of irritation, Burke sighed and got to his feet. To his dismay, the kid was spooked by his size and backpedaled rapidly, bumping into a pair of customers still standing in line. Embarrassed, Burke took the final novel but left the others on the table. He walked away.

"Sir, you forgot your books?" The kid was so frightened he made a statement of fact a question, the sentence rising in pitch at the end.

"Thanks. You can keep them."

Burke strolled down the crowded Ventura Boulevard, mildly surprised to find the day coming to a close. He found a parking ticket on his vehicle. He tore it up and tossed it away. The car would change owners several times before the city had registered the existence of the citation, might even be out of the state. Tony Monteleone would take care of it.

Burke drove down Ventura to Hazeltine and turned north. He left his car in the lot of the Trader Joe's store and jogged over to the park around the corner. Hispanic children were laughing and throwing water balloons at a nearby birthday party. Their lips were red or purple from cheap snow cones. Other children hung from the bars of the jungle gym. The sun would soon be setting, but Burke figured he had just enough time. He scribbled notes on the yellow pad, brief thoughts on the tone of the previous work, more to have something to do than from necessity.

He sat beneath the canopy of a sickly elm and opened Stryker's magnum opus. The main character in *A Taste for Flesh* was a middle-aged loner whose life was fading fast. He was being passed over for promotions. His wife had left him for another, much younger man. The beaten-down protagonist elected to take a long vacation in Europe. He wandered east, into the former Soviet satellites. Although he loved the art and culture, the protagonist found the economic and social circumstances depressing. Soon he was drinking too much and seriously contemplating suicide. Burke was pleasantly surprised. The novel had proven to be far more literate than pulp, at least to this point. Indeed, it was well conceived and deftly written. Burke had momentarily forgotten the author's reputation and found himself absorbed by both the telling and the tale.

And that's when Stryker went for the throat, quite literally: the protagonist was bitten by a wolf. His story turned on a dime and became a lurid tale of the mythical and the lycanthropic, the hero as a troubled werewolf. Yet Burke still found the novel compelling, for while the man descended into madness, he also began to re-discover his archetypal masculine power. The man becomes the wolf as the wolf becomes the man. To be sure, both did murder in a plethora of crimson ways. The violence was blunt, to the point, and decidedly messy, but as Burke himself knew all too well, so was violence in real life. It was the subtext that was most gripping; a hint of Nietzsche, lightly seasoned with Joseph Campbell.

He read on. Much weight was given to the ramifications of anthropophagy, the devouring of human flesh, and its varied implications. The protagonist, as the novel progressed, slowly moved from an attitude of revulsion to one of spiritual reverence. This odd concoction was then half baked in recycled Stephen King imagery, but worked nonetheless. At the end of the novel, the protagonist had become something of a god to the peasants in the countryside and a hero to himself again. His inevitable physical death, therefore, was of very little consequence because his spirit lived on.

The acknowledgments made reference to a Dr. Theodore Merriman. Burke decided on the spot to pay the man a visit.

He lowered the book and rubbed his weary eyes. The park was flooding with long, cool shadows and most of the picnicking families had gone home. He watched three males of indeterminate age as they tossed a football in a long, triangulated pattern. Their voices, shrill with enthusiasm and ribald humor, stroked his weary brain. He envied them their laughter.

Later, Burke stopped at a nearly empty restaurant for a plain chicken breast and a salad. He sat alone at a table near the front window, listening to Vivaldi with half an ear, weary eyes on the rush-hour traffic, a sea of headlights, taillights, street-lamps all reflecting and refracting light. Meanwhile a gentle mist of rain, unseasonable but welcome, stroked moist ribbons of color down the clear glass. Burke paid for the meal in cash. He needed no receipt. Over a double espresso, he examined his notes one last time, then left and drove home.

The rain stopped. As Burke pulled into his driveway and got out of the car, he noted the damp, erotic odor of satiated plants. A motion detector flipped on the porch light. He let himself in, double-locked the door behind him and set the alarm for the night. He went into the Spartan bedroom and stripped to his shorts, then took his laundry to the garage. He started the washing machine, grabbed a glass of soda water from the kitchen, and moved into his office.

This was a room possessed, overflowing with books of all shapes and sizes. In contrast to the rest of the pristine house, Burke's office was an ever-evolving chaos where yellow Post-its with scribbled notes lay randomly and crookedly tacked to cork bulletin boards or taped to the lips of crowded shelves. A row of blue plastic tubs contained obese files, facts garnered from random readings, reference papers unlikely to be read again. Burke fired up his computer. He scanned the papers Nicole Stryker had given him, the list of potential enemies and suspects, and e-mailed them to his office with a note: *Gina, check these folks out for alibis.* If anyone could make sense of such a complicated assignment, it would be his partner.

WEREWOLVES. The name in the search engine brought over two million hits. Some of the first hundred were useful, including one that assembled data from medieval times. Another contained an entire translation of *The Book of Werewolves* by Sabine Baring-Gold, first published in 1865. There were Web sites clearly created by mental cases, people claiming to know or actually be werewolves, people just looking to have sex with some. Burke was an old hand at research. He tried the word LYCANTHROPY. He printed out whatever seemed useful, grabbed another soda, and studied the printer as it grunted away. Next, LOUP-GAROU. Half a million hits. A few more selections at random.

When he had nearly two hundred pages of reference material, Burke returned to the living room. He parked on the plain brown couch, flicked on the bronze lamp, began to read. He scanned the pages, fingertips moving rapidly, and absorbed as much information as possible. Burke had no idea what he was looking for. He was merely following what he presumed to be a trail similar to the one blazed by the author of that last novel. He wanted to see what Peter Stryker had seen, go where he had been, in the hopes that path would eventually lead him to the truth.

Finally, Burke turned out the light and sat alone in the darkness. He had learned nothing of import. For a few uneasy moments, he pondered his time in combat: the taste of fear, sight of fresh blood, the split, pulsing flesh of the wounded. He tried to fathom a genuine craving for the taste of raw, human meat, but couldn't manage it. And yet the conceit of the novel had seemed fully plausible to him, unusually compelling. Was Peter Stryker simply an author of true talent, or did his final obsession have something to do with his ugly, agonizing death?

After a time Burke assumed the cross-legged, lotus position. He started to breathe slowly and deeply. He observed the vague sound of traffic outside, released it. Burke observed first his body, then stray thoughts, fall away. He entered a fugue state. Burke knew that the area of his brain that regulated the position of the physical self to other objects was slowly fading into gray, as if controlled by a dimmer switch. The powerful sense of "oneness" was soon palpable. Burke savored it, even as it began to recede and the external world returned. He rose refreshed, tossed the stack of papers into his messy office, and got dressed for the night.

Seven

Jack Burke drove the misty streets with no radio playing, windows up and mind closed. His body knew the route. He sat in his car in the nearly deserted parking lot and prayed for several long minutes, then entered the plain, antiseptic building. Visiting always made him think about death, and death made him feel too achingly alone for words. Burke signed in and walked alone down the corridor; hesitant footsteps booming, quick breath harsh and thin as sandpaper. He slid into the room, moved the chair to the window. He rubbed his eyes and sat back.

"Hello."

Burke closed his eyes and after a long, weighted moment offered a disconnected, whispered response. "I love you."

"I love you, too."

A rubbery, elongated section of silence followed. "I got a new job," Burke said, finally. "It pays very well."

"Oh?"

"It's digging into a probable suicide. A horror author. Guy butchered himself, or at least it looks that way. I spent most of the day reading his trashy novels. The last one wasn't bad, actually."

"You?"

"Yeah, I love to read. What can I say? Figured I might as well see what he was up to near the end, right? Besides, I have to do something to stay on the payroll. Like I said, the money is good."

The wet hiss of sprinklers outside: way down below, a man with a resonant voice was sprayed and bellowed in dismay.

Burke hunched forward. "Scotty got me the job. He still looks pretty good, you know? Of all of us, he's the one who learned how to play the game. He's even better than Cary Ryan, and that is saying something."

"Oh?"

"Yeah. Scotty kisses just enough ass. He can bob and weave and slide around like a champ. You remember how many times he came through for me? Still slips me jobs now and then when he really shouldn't." Burke knew he had told her all of this many times before, but was suddenly groping for words. "I pay him a taste for the contacts, but I think he's a loyal guy. That's a rare quality these days."

He rose, stretched. Cracked his neck and peered out the window. "They really should try and change this view once in a while, just for the rest of us. It's getting old. Maybe plant some new flowers or something."

Too much time passed again. His broad chest clenched like a fist, tired eyes began to sting. "I miss you." The words ached, came flowing out on a faint rush of sadness to hover momentarily and then dissipate.

"I know."

Burke cried softly, for the sweet voice was now suddenly as faint as the sprinklers down below, almost as intangible. "I miss touching you."

She had already gone back to sleep. He knelt by the bed, rested his fingertips on her ivory arm like a man sitting down at an expensive piano. Burke closed his eyes and fell backward, inward, seeking a place where pure consciousness existed, but no longer a lonely, isolated self.

Eight

Tuesday

It was a hazy morning. The filthy parking lot known as the 405 Freeway was packed with multicolored metal dominoes that belched smoke and barely contained their outraged drivers. Burke listened to a cassette copy of an old jazz record, his fingers doing snare drum rolls on the steering wheel. John Coltrane's phrasing captured lines of rage and pain and manipulated them into smoky bursts of sexual heat. Coltrane was both stimulating and relaxing, like the company of a beautiful woman.

Upon arrival, the asphalt was already packed and busy people in expensive suits were milling around the foot of the steps. Though still young, Burke had that rugged, slightly florid face worn by Irish cops the world over. Everyone thought they knew him. His years with the Vegas PD had given him an aura of legitimacy the average street cop was loath to challenge. He breezed past the first guard at Van Nuys City Hall and strolled down the hallway toward the CAS, or Coroner's Ancillary Station. He pinned on a plastic badge lifted during the previous visit. Doc Washington was not in his office. Burke checked his watch and walked toward the back of the building.

The explosion in DNA research and new technologies created a need for a discrete substation. Some bodies were brought there and refrigerated, but most of the heavy lifting was now done in cyberspace by men using high-tech computers. Men like Lincoln "Doc" Washington. Burke heard clacking sounds and ribald taunting from the end of the hall. He smiled.

"You kidding me, right? You think you got game? Think you can take my black ass? Well, come on, then! Come and get some! Yeah, that's right, get some!"

Burke peeked into the commissary. Doc and a new PA were seated at an empty table playing high-speed chess. Each player had five seconds to make a move and slam the clock so that it started again. The physician's assistant, a slender blond man in greens whose badge read Frank Abt, was already perspiring profusely. Doc whooped, slapped the clock, and rolled his wheelchair back two feet. He had a bicycle horn mounted on the chassis. He honked it. "Yo, cracker! That's checkmate, motherfucker!"

The kid called Abt whacked the table in disgust, flashed a rueful grin. "Another round, Linc? Let me get even again?"

Doc spied Burke. "My man!" His face lit up. "No rematch at this very moment in time, yo. I have a man I have to see about a hearse. Maybe tomorrow?"

Abt sighed. "Deal."

Burke was already moving away. He stepped into Doc's laboratory, found a chair. Moments later Doc rolled into the lab, which was a wide room filled with stainless steel, computer screens, and file cabinets. He paused to give Burke a high five. "Brothers. What's up, man?"

"I'm fine, Doc. Doing good, just working too much." Burke's worn face and sunken brown eyes told the truth. "You know how it is."

Doc nodded. "Maybe I do." He turned to the computer keyboard, fingers a blur. "And you want to hear about this Stryker thing, right?"

"Right." The room tilted, rolled. Burke leaned back and closed his weary eyes. "Just give it to me in your own words, okay?"

Doc started the printer, which rattled and wheezed then spat out several pages. "I'll give you a copy of the full ME report, which you never even fucking talked to me about, right?"

"Of course."

Doc scrolled down the screen. "Okay, here is the gist of it. Looks like the dude checked into the hotel around dinnertime under some other name. He orders up a room service salad and two pots of coffee. Then he used his own ass as the main course. This shot here," gestured at the computer screen, "ain't a piece of shrimp. It shows an amputated little finger sitting on the bathroom counter on a neatly folded square of paper towel. Now get this, exactly—and I do mean exactly—twelve inches away, the little finger of the other hand."

Burke, eyes still closed: "He did that to himself? Not once, but twice?"

"Washcloth in the bathroom has bite marks and saliva, lab says both his."

"Give me that report, too."

"Will do." Doc hit the printer again. "Can't be sure about the sequence, but the next event is technically known as enucleation. See this photo? No, ain't no oyster, Jack. That's his right eyeball. Now get this, he has an entire surgical bag with him and doesn't use it. Popped the sucker out with a teaspoon."

"And you have that spoon?"

"A true gross-out, my man. No fingerprints, because he was wearing surgical gloves on both hands, but yeah, we have it. Damn, this had to have hurt like a mother, even with all the drugs."

Burke sat up, intrigued. He rubbed his neck. "What drugs did he have in his system, Doc?"

"First the cancer painkiller, Oxycontin, and lots of it—which I can personally testify is some good shit. In fact, he had enough in him to make the average guy nod off, but I use it myself for chronic pain and believe me, a man can get used to anything given enough time. But we also found a syringe and some bottles in with the guy's surgical kit. Check this out. He had some really top-notch, high-grade, synthetic cocaine in him, too."

"Synthetic coke?"

Doc rolled closer to the keyboard and manipulated a few keys. He turned with a wry smile. "They use that shit for surgeries sometimes, Jack. When the person stays awake, that is. Let's you ride it out without worrying too much, even when you're awake for the procedure."

"He was in medical school for a while. Would have known about stuff like that."

"Yeah, but this type of junk distorts depth perception, your sense of time, even makes you laugh a lot. It's hard to imagine anybody having all this in his system and still doing relatively delicate surgery on his own damned body."

"Unless, like you said, he was pretty used to large amounts of dope."

"Well, there you go," Doc said. "Prove that and we figure the dude just shot himself up. Case closed. So he checks in, has a light supper, pumps himself full of painkillers and stimulants. Over the next few hours he slices off several patches of his own skin and then cauterizes the wounds with a small blowtorch. He cuts off his little fingers and the tip of his nose. He then sets a mirror up at the end of the tub, gets in and lightly turns the faucets, opens up his own belly and watches as his guts fall out. This is not the dude you want dating your daughter."

Burke grinned. "He was a nut job for sure. But let's be thorough anyway, okay? I need to know if anything, anything at all, looks out of place to you. Check it out."

Doc sorted through the files. "Mr. Stryker wasn't dead more than six to eight hours, not quite long enough for serious rigor to set in, so he was a little stiff, but not too bad. Everything in the suite was clean and organized, which I'm told is in keeping with this dude's anal and obsessive personality."

"Seems like."

"Okay," Doc continued. "Like I said, six to eight, so we have some distinct lividity in the lower body, even though he bled out. Kind of a purple patch on his ass, and more on the soles of his feet hanging out the tub. That fits with the time frame, too."

"Okay." Burke was actually feeling a bit queasy, picturing what happened.

"Get this," Doc said, grinning, "along with this lividity thing. The guy probably stops somewhere and buys some decals to stick to the tub so he won't slip in the mess and the blood, I guess. Little yellow duck decals. So now he's got the imprint of one on each ass cheek, like a tattoo. Nice touch, huh?"

"Go on. I don't like hearing this shit as much as you do." He ticked a fingernail on the metal desk. The sound boomed.

"He skinned himself exactly thirteen times," Doc continued. "He took strips about two inches wide and six to seven inches long each time. He sliced the pattern in a fatty area, well clear of arteries, and flayed his own body. We found a pile of alcohol swabs and some strips of bandage."

Burke shook his head. "How could he tolerate that kind of pain?"

"Drugs would help, but believe me, he felt it."

"Why." It is a statement, not a question.

Doc arched an eyebrow. "Pain seems to have been the point, man. Very self-punishing behavior. He doped himself up enough that he wouldn't pass out and be discovered before he could finish the job, but not enough so that he didn't feel every hellish second of the agony. Tissue samples indicate about twenty to thirty minutes went by between sessions of skinning and peeling."

"Jesus."

"Jesus had nothing to do with this one, Burke." Gears whirred as Doc turned the wheelchair. He pointed to a particularly grisly crime-scene photo on the monitor. It showed an angry, reddish patch of flesh that had been blackened by flame. "He dabbed the open wounds with alcohol just a few minutes after inflicting them, see? Damn, that would hurt. Beats me why, since if he was planning on dying he didn't need to worry much about infection, but he did it. And then he fucking burned the wound with the small torch. After that he'd start again on some other part of his body."

Burke stood. He massaged his stomach unconsciously. "How did he stay silent? The classical music?"

"I guess," Doc replied. "That and the chewed dishrag he had in his mouth. Somewhere toward the end he fixed it to his face with some surgical tape."

Burke paced, thinking aloud. "After maybe five or six hours he cuts off the little finger of one hand. Where did he do that?"

"Like most of it, in the bathroom."

"He just sets the finger on the damned sink, cauterizes the amputation, and does the other. Then one of his eyes."

"Appears that way."

"So the finale is, he puts the mirror in place, steps into the tub, and does the Samurai Sayonara?"

Doc shrugged again. "Stoned out of his mind by then, not to mention grossed out and sick from the pain."

Burke closes his eyes. Ugly pictures danced. "Okay, give me how he would have done that part. Reconstruct it for me."

"He did it the clinical way, I'd guess. Began the incision at mid-center, just about the pubic hair, dead on where it had to be. He cut in and then out to the right and upward in a curve. Remember, the large and small intestines are packed in there like a mile of chitlins in a small pail, so once the abdominal cavity was opened they wouldn't have rushed out, not if the guy was sitting in a reclining position."

Burke opened his eyes. "But they *were* out?"

Doc nodded. "Part way. He probably tugged on them a bit."

"I think I'm going to throw up now."

"Pussy." Doc hits PRINT one last time. "Seriously, if I hadn't been doing this shit for so many years I'd come with you. Although I got to say the little ducky prints on his butt cheeks kind of take the heaviness out of it for me, you know?"

"Yeah. Sure."

"Tell you something, this guy knew his drugs."

Burke tilted his head like a man listening to a tune played far, far away. "How's that?"

"Because he used just enough to keep him in the loop, all the time. Like he didn't want to miss a single thing, you know?"

"Any other angles?"

"Okay," Doc said, warming to it. "Another way you could look at it is that somehow somebody gets in there with him. They tie him up."

"No ligature marks on his wrists or ankles."

"Maybe he is wrapped with towels. Or they drug him with something else, something that leaves the bloodstream in a hurry? Not out of the question. I'll keep looking."

"Then they torture this poor bastard for hours over something they think he knows, Doc. Maybe he even tells them near the beginning, but they don't believe him. So they go on until he finally dies. They set it up so it looks like he did himself and sneak back out again."

"No 'they,' Burke. I guess maybe one guy could have, though."

"Or a woman."

"Okay, point taken. But all the damned DNA is his. At least the preliminary tests say that. Blood drops, saliva, tissue samples. Of course, good luck finding useful fiber or print evidence in a hotel suite that's been rented to a gazillion people."

Burke grimaced, looked down. "I'll talk to Gina. Might be worth seeing if there is anything on the voice mail."

"You really think somebody did him?"

"Who knows? But something weird is going on here."

"No kidding."

"Do you buy all this, Doc? That he committed suicide?"

The smaller man rolled his wheelchair to the right. He stretched his upper body. Doc still lifted weights and took pride in his upper torso. "I've seen stranger shit, Burke. On the surface it looks like this guy hated his life and wanted to punish himself for something nasty he did along the way. Besides . . ." He looked away and his voice trailed off.

"Besides what?" Burke raised his head. "What were you about to say there?"

"Think about it," Doc said, "it's like that old locked room thing on *Murder, She Wrote,* or something. If nobody else went in or out of that room, and we can't find a trace of evidence says anybody was there before he checked in, how the fuck would somebody be able to get in there, do him over such a long period, and walk out again without a drop of blood on their clothes?"

"Yeah."

Doc was still thinking it over. "Not to mention 'why.' "

"Oh, that part is easy," Burke said. "The guy was a prick. I have a feeling he's got a list of enemies longer than my dick."

"No sweat, then, brother. You will be home for supper." Doc rolled the chair by hand and scooped the stack of papers and images from the printer tray. He turned and handed them to Burke. "And you never got these from me, right?"

"As usual." Burke slips Doc a hundred-dollar bill. "And thanks."

★ ★ ★ ★ ★

Burke turned, mind already elsewhere. Lincoln watched him go. Doc was always impressed by how soundlessly his old friend could move. Once Burke had left a room there was a brief moment of hollowness, like a pocket of vacuumed air; perhaps the *snick* of the door's tumblers closing, but little else. Burke could be quiet as death.

Doc rolled to the door and locked it. He was beginning to tremble, and did not want to be seen with a Jones on. He flicked a switch and rolled to the bank of telephones. He activated the voice mail and turned his back to the window. A few seconds later he palmed a small vial filled with white tablets; these were time-release Oxycontin. The medication was originally created to treat the pain of terminal cancer patients and soon, after a rash of explosive and widespread drug addictions, became illegal. Doc swallowed a tablet and closed his eyes, waited for the pounding headache to recede. Agony always led to pleasure.

Somewhere along the way, Doc had lost the essential truth of his pain. Now it was real and unreal, at once phantom and unrelenting. When the medication began to wear off and the "rebound" started—the opposite of the initial painkilling effect was always muscular aches and nausea—he took even more to soften that blow. Addiction was an old friend. He also had an electronically powered drug dispenser, of his own design, built into the wheelchair. It could supply him with intravenous Oxycontin on demand.

Doc Washington was no fool. He knew he had a large and very hostile monkey on his back. He just didn't mind. Doc didn't have it in him any longer to give a damn. He leaned his head to the side, enjoyed the rush, and nodded off for a few moments. Less than thirty minutes later, still flushed with opiates, he turned off the voice mail and returned to work, whistling a pop song from the 80s.

Nine

The drab, gray little office building was located in a funky strip mall near the corner of Laurel Canyon and Victory in North Hollywood, adjacent to a barrio Sears. Burke liked it because it was cheap and unassuming. He pulled his car around behind the long line of patrons waiting for the movie theaters and parked near other ordinary-looking cars, under a row of sagging, thirsty elms. Burke jogged lightly through the foot traffic leaving the latest screening. He paused in the doorway, scanned the lot. He had not been followed.

Up the creaky wooden stairs two floors (Gina called the elevator slower than the 2000 Florida recount) to a peeling, off-white door that had been painted one too many times. The sign read BB Investigations. Burke tried the knob, found it locked. He used his key and went inside. The spacious, utility-carpeted, one-room office featured computer equipment, two large desks, and several cork bulletin boards covered with seemingly random photographs and scribbled notations. But these notes were organized, and the penmanship was neat.

"What's up, Gina?"

The stocky, dark-haired woman behind the far desk was compact, muscular and formidable. Her facial expression generally read pleasant, but reserved. Gina Belli wore dark slacks, a simple white blouse, and a Smith & Wesson .38 on her belt. She kept her hair in the short, curt style favored by women the world over who are uncomfortable being perceived as feminine.

Her fingers were pounding hell out of a computer keyboard.

Gina had known Burke long enough to feel like both a stern mother hen and an indulgent sister. Years before, when she'd worked as a Vegas cop and Burke was a fellow officer, he'd performed a substantial service. A former lover, a rough woman given to battery, was stalking Gina and her new flame. She would not back down and her threats were becoming overt actions—sliced tires, keyed cars and broken windows. Burke had a quiet talk with the woman, who rapidly moved away to Chicago. Gina had been a member of the Jack Burke fan club ever since. Her relationship soured, and when he moved to Los Angeles Gina followed as an employee. Her already estimable computer talents had now been augmented by clandestine assistance from both the mob and Major Cary Ryan's top-secret outfit. She was as proficient and dangerous as any determined hacker could be. She also worshipped Burke, would have worked for free, and often did.

"Cowboy." From her the word is a compliment, an insult and a cheerfully affectionate greeting. "I ran the list for you, got the locations and general information on their whereabouts. It looks like a choir of angels from here."

Then Nicole Stryker had been telling the truth, at least about one thing. Her father had made a lot of enemies. Burke and Gina had gone through the entire list and there were still, at minimum, sixteen logical names. Gina seemed to have enjoyed reviewing magazine articles and newspaper clippings about the life and career of Peter Stryker's friends and foes. Soon, between them, they had made careful note of each business rival, aggrieved in-law, or former partner. The list was narrowing.

They sat at their respective desks with long, yellow notepads, plowing forward, writing down and crossing off names. Anyone who could be verified as having been out of town that night was temporarily eliminated. Of course, someone could have been hired to do Stryker, but the brutality of the death struck Burke as too immediate and too personal to be the work of a dispassionate button man.

"Most of his business adversaries were in public, out of town or in jail," Gina said. "We have a couple of folks left, when it's all said and done, but neither one seems likely. A Dr. Theodore Merriman, psychologist, criminologist and author."

"I already have him down to talk to because Stryker thanked him in a book."

"Yeah, Jack, but the old fart is seventy-two or something. Anyway, he and Stryker went to court over some stuff Merriman claimed Stryker stole from him and inserted into a novel without monetary compensation. Stryker settled out of court, probably paid up, but no one is talking."

"I'll interview him anyway," Burke said. The very idea seemed boring.

"We also got a guy named Dr. Mohandas Hasari Pal, lectures at both USC and Cal State Northridge. He writes extensively as well, mostly those boring academic books that sell for eighty bucks to the suckers that take his classes."

Burke stiffened in his chair. He felt his face redden as his composure slipped. He looked away so that Gina wouldn't notice, coughed noisily. "That name was Pal, P-A-L?"

"Yeah, why?"

"I had him for a couple of classes in Comparative Religion," Burke said, casually. He felt a twinge of guilt for keeping something from his partner.

"Good, then you can have him, too."

"Okay. What happened between this Professor Pal and Stryker?" He got up, walked over to the filthy window and looked outside. A homeless black man with wild, filthy dreadlocks was rolling a shopping cart packed with junk across the pavement. Burke barely noticed. He was trying to erase the image of two beautiful brown eyes in an exotic face and the way a very beautiful young woman had once whispered his name during orgasm. *Indira.*

"Not a damned thing, Burke."

"Excuse me?"

"Nothing we know of," Gina said. "They happen to be acquainted. Pal might have given him some research notes along the way. He is thanked in a couple of the novels."

"Not much to go on, is it?"

"Nope."

Burke returned to his desk. "We need to come up with something soon or we won't make a dime off this turkey."

"Here's how I see it," Gina said. She cleared her throat and swung her legs up onto the desk. "Unfortunately for us, Peter Stryker probably did kill himself. In fact, that seems damned near a lock, considering all the existing forensic evidence. Either that, or someone who knew him and happened to be invisible and wearing a body-sized condom slipped into that suite and murdered his ass without leaving a trace."

Burke yawned. "Body-sized condom? Now that's a disgusting image."

"Hmm."

"Maybe somebody killed him, Gina. But it would have had to be someone who knew him well . . . and thoroughly despised him."

"Agreed," Gina replied. "Because if this was murder, it was as personal as a blow job, but *way* more nasty."

Burke's face split into a grin. "Blow jobs aren't so bad, Gina. Your prejudice is showing."

"Fine," Gina deadpanned. "You give one."

Burke thought for a long moment. "You think we should just hang this up?"

Gina shrugged. "I know we need the money, but it sure looks

like a waste of time, at least at this point."

"I should go over and check out the house before we call it quits, though," Burke said. He moved toward the door. "The daughter gave me a key."

"Maybe you should." Gina looked down at the computer keyboard, resumed typing. "At least it'll buy us another full day on the family payroll. Meanwhile, I'll keep digging for more dirt on our two pathetic, boring, geriatric, already drooling on the porch murder suspects. You going there now?"

"A bit later. I have some errands to run."

Gina raised a sardonic eyebrow. "Yeah, that so? You be sure and tell Vito Corleone I said hello."

TEN

Burke trotted down the stairs. He got in his car, circled the parking lot and turned onto Laurel Canyon. He eased into the left-turn lane at Sherman Way and drove west, directly into the smoggy afternoon sunshine, his mind still fixed on Indira Pal. After a few blocks of used furniture stores and dilapidated apartment complexes the street hit a large concrete underpass. Planes could be seen landing and taking off just overhead. Burke entered the drab industrial area adjacent to the Van Nuys airport. He knew the way.

Burke left his car near a pale green wood and aluminum structure and looked for a battered station wagon with familiar plates. He walked over to it, turned, shaded his eyes and glanced up at the darkening sky. After a long moment Burke spotted the small Cessna, swooping a bit too abruptly before sputtering back toward the runway. He hopped up onto the hood of the wagon, crossed his legs, and scooted into a meditation position. *What's done is done. She's gone, let it be.* Burke sat quietly, dark eyes half closed, and waited for the pilot to land. *It would be smart to find a way to drop this one,* he thought. *I might just bite off more than I can chew.*

The blue and white aircraft wove about for just under twenty minutes. Burke watched without moving his body. Finally, the little Cessna vectored in for a landing, with a thin ribbon of white smoke trailing behind. Burke allowed the snarling mutter of its engine to penetrate and draw him back to reality. The aircraft rolled to a stop fifty feet away. Still, Burke did not move. The pilot, a sad-sack of a man both balding and chubby, peered out through a pair of mirrored sunglasses which only served to make him look pretentious. A hesitation followed. Burke could read the man's discomfort from across the hot tarmac. Finally the pilot turned off the engine. Except for the incessant rumble of other aircraft on the horizon, that part of the airport fell blessedly silent.

The chubby man dropped down out of the Cessna. He waved to two airport grease monkeys, kids with bad skin who wandered out to tie off the wing and tail of the rental. The overweight man wore a turquoise Miami Dolphins windbreaker zipped up to the neck, black slacks and shiny black shoes. He stared at Burke, who remained on the station wagon, and shrugged with resignation. Burke slid gracefully to the ground and beckoned with one finger. The pilot approached, rapidly lowering the zipper of the windbreaker, as if he hoped the white collar on his black shirt might offer some legitimately divine protection.

"Jack, my son," the priest said, a bit too politely. "How are you feeling these days?"

Burke shook his head. Father Bennedetto was at once an old friend and a genuine pain in the ass. "Benny, I can't believe you."

"I know, Red." Benny spoke urgently, rapidly. "I'm really sorry. Something came up at the center, is all. I had to get the air-conditioning fixed, and then one of those damned toilets broke. Excuse me, Lord."

Burke grimaced. "Father, do you expect my employers to give a damn?"

"I am a sinner," Benny said. His chins quivered dramatically. "I only hope that I may be forgiven, for my intentions are generally good." He swallowed and leaned back against the vehicle. His color had changed.

Burke raised an eyebrow. "Again?"

"It happens almost every time."

Burke's face twitched as he fought back a chuckle. "Then why the hell do you keep doing this, Benny? If you don't like to fly, stop flying."

Father Bennedetto belched loudly. He was perspiring heavily and seemed woozy. "One hopes to eventually overcome the fear, you see." Suddenly he gagged, turned away. Yellow vomit splattered the gravel. *Eggs for breakfast?*

Burke shook his head. He walked south, toward the drably painted airport coffee shop. Over his shoulder: "When you're finished, we need to figure how you're covering the vig. So come join me for lunch."

Behind him, the retching grew louder.

Outside the next building, Burke dropped fifty cents into the vending machine for the *Daily News*, the San Fernando Valley's local paper. He slipped it under his arm and walked inside. The coffee shop had red plastic booths that squeaked. It also featured a busty waitress named Terri with teased blonde hair. Terri generally wore a short skirt and a see-through blouse, but at her age should have known better. Burke ordered a plain hamburger patty with no bun, fruit instead of fries, and a Diet Coke. He ignored Terri's flaccid attempts to flirt, flipped to the editorial section of the paper and then scanned the classifieds for something interesting.

"Is that how they contact you?"

Burke looked up, startled. He instinctively covered the paper with both hands. "What?"

Father Benny sat down heavily, grabbed Burke's ice water and downed it in three gulps. "Sorry, Jack. I've noticed that you always buy the same paper when you come here and always open it to the classifieds. Since I know you don't date, I thought maybe that's how they . . ."

Terri hovered to refill the glass. With the priest present, she was less blatantly seductive. "Can I get you something, Father?"

Benny nodded vigorously. "A club soda, dear. No, make that two."

Burke waited until the waitress was out of earshot. He glared at Benny, and the priest flinched. "There is no 'they,' Benny, especially not where someone else might hear us. Do you understand?"

"I just remembered that you're still on call for the government. That fellow Cary Ryan hires you sometimes—he's such a nice kid for a lapsed Catholic—and I thought maybe . . ." The look Burke gave him was withering. Benny fell silent. "Sorry."

He seemed so small, so puppy dog pathetic. Burke couldn't stay angry. "I'm confessing here, okay? So this stays between us. It's a simple system that uses different numbered letters in different messages each week. I don't see my code name, I don't call in."

"You haven't had to for a while, have you?"

"I haven't wanted to."

The plain hamburger patty arrived. Father Benny glanced at the food, cringed a bit and looked out the window. He followed an antique Piper Cub as it came in for a landing, engine grumbling like a nest of hornets trapped in an oil drum.

Burke ate efficiently, chewed methodically. He seldom took pleasure in eating. Father Benny rested his fingers on the plastic table, waiting. Finally Burke looked up. "You're two weeks late on the interest, Benny. You know what that means, right?"

Benny wiped his brow. A writhing twitch appeared under his right eye. "You got to hurt me a little, Jack. I understand."

Burke finished his patty and a few bites of the tomato. He sipped at his drink to let the small, chubby man worry for a bit. "I'll cover it. Again."

Benny frowned. "I don't want you to, Jack. Really."

"I'll cover it for another week, but that's it. You have got to come through with the two hundred next time, or I'll have to start telling the man."

Benny stuck out his chins. "I insist, Jack. If you need to break a couple of fingers or something, I'll say I caught them in the cockpit door."

Burke smiled, involuntarily. "Benny, you have no idea what you're talking about, do you? Trust me, that's the kind of pain you don't ever forget. It's not like the movies. So don't be an asshole." Benny eyed him disapprovingly and Burke finally grunted: "Excuse me, Lord."

Benny laughed then went solemn. "Do you have to do bad things to people very often?"

Burke sighed. "Most folks are smart enough to pay on time. Some of the rest, a threat or some property damage gets it done. Once in a while it gets rough. So far, I haven't had to hurt a civilian." Benny did not understand the reference. Burke continued. "That is someone who isn't a player, or a con, or muscle for somebody. If it gets rough, it's usually because the other guy is dirty anyway, so I don't mind all that much."

"And the money is good?"

"The money is very good."

Benny lowered his voice, at once gently familial and professionally concerned. "How is she doing these days?"

A ragged growling noise dialed up from just outside. The next plane distracted Benny and he watched it come in, wings wagging too much, brakes squealing like an amateur wrestled the stick. When he looked back he realized Burke had gone somewhere agonizing, that his question likely prompted the journey. "I'm sorry . . ."

"She's . . . the same," Burke said, finally. He faced down at the tablecloth. His voice was thick and held the faint, cloying whine of a wounded animal. "She's . . . sick. I visit whenever I can and we talk, but . . . I don't know how much longer I can go on."

Father Benny was rarely at a loss for words, but this time remained silent for a stretched moment. His mild eyes reddened. "I'm praying for you both."

Burke became angry at someone or something, but the dark look was quickly replaced by one of resignation. "I know you are, Benny. Thanks."

Benny examined the cracked plastic seat then got busy twirling a straw in his club soda. Grateful, Burke used the dead space to compose himself. Finally he finished his meal and moved the newspaper to one side.

"Benny?"

"Jack?"

"Can I ask you something?"

"Sure."

"Why the hell do you do it?"

Benny was clearly flustered. "Well, I know I'm no gambler, but the center needs money for everything from a new television set to a washing machine for the boys. I never get enough money for the parish . . ."

Burke cut him off with a wave of his hand. "Not that. I mean the flying. It's expensive, time consuming, kind of dangerous. Not to mention it flat-out scares the crap out of you."

Benny slumped. The question was legitimate. He wanted to supply a meaningful response. Jack Burke was a man he'd known for years, someone who had done him many favors. After a long pause, he squinted into the fading afternoon sunlight. "Jack, do you have faith?"

"Probably not," Burke replied, heavily. "It depends on what you mean by that. If you mean spiritual faith, the answer is sometimes yes and sometimes no."

"Exactly."

"Exactly what, Benny?"

Father Bennedetto spread his hands wide in an unmistakably Italian expression of enthusiasm. "So I began to ask myself, what if anything could strengthen my faith. Sustain it through what clerics call the 'long, dark night of the soul,' for example, the pressure of darkness. And I hit upon flying as a way to accomplish that."

"How so?"

"Because it scares me!" Benny chuckled and rolled his eyes, as if to say how obvious could a thing be? "And every time I took a flying lesson, logged some hours, the very moment I signed the papers to apply for my pilot's license, I was testing my faith and making it stronger." He leaned forward, elbows striking the table. Silverware clanged and slid sideways. "Have I told you how much I despise that rental helicopter outside, for example? That bucket of bolts, that twirling death trap?"

Burke was enjoying the performance. "But you qualified to fly it last month, right? Did you hurl during or after?"

"After, of course. And more than once."

"Then why?"

Benny scratched his chin thoughtfully. "A shrink named Victor Frankle once hypothesized that man needed three things to endure the vagaries of existence. They were meaning, purpose and value. I would add one additional thing to that recipe, and the word would be commitment."

"Not faith?"

"That's just another way of saying faith. And if I am committed to facing down my fears, if I remain resolute in my attempts to defy the darkness, it follows that then I should be most likely to feel fully alive, more alive than the others."

"While vomiting into the grass a few yards from your rented aircraft?"

"Precisely."

They shared a deep round of laughter that demonstrated both a keen empathy and the acceptance of differences. "Jack, I'll get you the money at the first of the week. Thanks for covering me again."

"Benny, you need to quit. You're not cut out for it."

"Hey, who thought the Rams could make a comeback like that this late in the season? I mean, damn! Excuse me, Lord."

Burke folded the newspaper into odd shapes, his mind wandering. He did not see the expression of concern carved into Father Benny's face that was both profound and pure. "Jack, you look so tired."

"I feel tired."

"Maybe you need a vacation."

"The medical expenses, remember?"

"Perhaps a week or so, if only to catch up on your sleep."

Jack Burke stared out at the sunset. The dark indentations beneath his reddened eyes seemed like the artful smudge marks worn by a younger man in a faraway war. He grunted, slid out of the red plastic booth. "I sleep, Father. Just not when I want to."

He reached down, grabbed one of the priest's fingers and bent it back slightly. Father Benny jumped. Burke released the digit, patted the hand.

"And Father?"

Wide-eyed. "Yes?"

"Stop gambling."

Eleven

"Where do they have him?"

"He is in the basement beneath the stables, as you requested, Buey."

"Have you softened him up?"

"Old Ortega has gone on at great length about what is to be done to him this morning, *Jefe*. I believe he is very motivated to share what he knows."

"One hopes. Help me with my boots, Ernesto."

"Certainly, Buey."

"Ouch, be careful! You have pinched my toes."

"Forgive me."

"Help me up."

"Yes."

"Let us go. It is a fine morning, no? That pair of starlings have once again nested just above the front door, near the warmth of the light."

"Again?"

"I think they like our humble home, Ernesto. I look forward to hearing the sounds the babies make when they beg to be fed."

"You have a softness of the heart which I find appealing, Buey."

"And you, my friend, are a romantic."

"Do you wish to ride today?"

"Yes, once we are done with the traitor below, I should like to ride. It is a wonderful way to clear the mind. Have them saddle the black."

"Consider it done."

"Perhaps you should come with me today. We could pack some wine and cheese and have our own special picnic."

"I would be honored, *Jefe.*"

"Here we are. Where is the damned light switch?"

"Allow me, Buey. Would you like me to assist you down the stairs?"

"Yes, my knee is a bit sore this morning. So, Ortega. And how is our handsome young thief this morning? I see you have already gagged him. Did you perhaps start without us?"

"I was just telling the traitor some of the things you have ordered done to others of his kind and what he might expect today. He began to babble in a most unseemly manner, so I thought perhaps it would be best to quiet him down a bit before your arrival."

"How thoughtful! Ernesto, do you not agree that this was very thoughtful?"

"I do. Uh . . . perhaps I should go prepare the lunch and the horses?"

"Why, Ernesto. If I did not know better I would assume you to be squeamish, eh, Ortega? *Ha!* That was my little joke."

"Buey, must I stay? You know these . . . events disturb me."

"And you feel faint at the sight of blood."

"*Jefe,* look at the young man kick and try to beg for mercy. And look, the very thought of the punishments to come has caused him to wet his pants."

"Perhaps you are two of a kind, Ernesto?"

"Buey! Please! I would never betray you!"

"Do not be silly, I know that, my darling one. I meant that our brave young thief has no stomach for the very thought of torture. He was courageous enough to steal cocaine from me, but is apparently not strong enough to sit in a chair and picture what is to come."

"I see."

"Yes, the mind is very powerful. Imagination can be a dangerous thing, do you not agree? The gringo Mark Twain once wrote, 'I am an old man who has survived many catastrophes, most of which never happened.' He had such a wonderful wit, Mr. Twain."

"I must read him someday."

"Yes, you must."

"*Jefe . . . ?*"

"Yes, Ortega, what is it?"

"Would you like me to begin now, perhaps with the fingernails?"

"Why look at the boy, Ortega. He is still trying to speak to me. Should we allow that, or wait until he has been . . . prepared a bit?"

"I await your order, *Jefe.*"

"Ernesto?"

"I have no heart for this, Buey. You know that. I would let him speak. Perhaps there will be no need for the rest."

"Ortega, let me closer. I want to whisper to our young man. That's good, thank you. Now hear me, Rudy. I will only say this once. You will be tortured, do you understand? Talking will not save you from your punishment. But if you tell me everything, that is who helped you and where my drugs are and what you did with the money, I will have Ortega move rapidly to bring your life to a close, perhaps within hours. If you do not speak, I am prepared for this to take days, even weeks. Do we understand each other?"

"Should I remove the gag, Buey?"

"Yes, Ortega. Let him speak."

"PLEASE, BUEY, do not do this thing! I swear it was not

my idea and I will tell you everything I know. Just allow me my life, *por favor!*"

"Now, now. Calm yourself. Show *machismo* for a change. Who put you up to stealing from me?"

"Garcia, it was Garcia."

"I see, and how much did he pay you?"

"Twenty thousand U.S. dollars, Buey. My sister is sick and I needed the money and I know I should have asked for a loan but I was afraid and he made it sound so easy that I . . ."

"Hush, or I will have the gag replaced."

"Please, I will be still, I am so frightened . . ."

"The stink of your piss tells me so. Where are my drugs?"

"Garcia took them, Buey."

"Then where is my money?"

"I sent half to my family, sir. I was not lying about that. My sister needs a new kidney and they live in Guadalajara. They have no money, I was only trying to . . ."

"Boy, calm yourself. And the other half?"

"In the wall behind my bed, in the back of the bunkhouse. I was going to give it back to you, I swear it. It was only meant to be a loan, *please,* Buey . . ."

"One final question, we are almost through. I need to know if you told anyone about my new American business partners."

"Those people who come and go? No, I swear it."

"No one at all, not even that goat you fuck?"

"I swear it."

"Also, have you spoken of the project our chemists are involved with, assuming you even know?"

"What project?"

"You wouldn't lie to me, would you? I get very upset when people lie to me."

"No, Buey! I am telling the truth."

"Have you ever heard of an American operative known as Jack Burke?"

"No. Buey, please do not do this to me!"

"Gag him, Ortega. He is beginning to get on my nerves."

"PLEASE!"

"That is better. Now he can only grunt or scream. Don't you think this is better, Ernesto?"

"I should go prepare lunch and the horses."

"You will stay for a bit."

"Yes, Buey."

"You must learn to harden yourself, Ernesto. This man is a common thief, and worse still he betrayed my trust. This has broken my heart, and I demand retribution. Ortega?"

"Yes, Buey."

"Begin. No, wait. I have something else to say. Let me closer. Do you hear me, boy? One last thing, before I go. I know where your family lives, and I will get the other half of my money soon."

"Mmmph!"

"Oh, and your *puta* of a sister has already been raped and strangled. Rest assured that *my* money is on the way back to *my* pocket."

"Buey?"

"Why do you interrupt me, Ernesto?"

"I cannot stay, I feel sick. Can you not end this quickly?"

"Boy, Ernesto seems to like you, and you have told me at least part of the truth, yes?"

"Mmmph."

"Well, unfortunately for you, I am not in a good mood. I hereby retract my initial offer. Ortega?"

"Yes."

"You may take as much time as you wish with this one."

"*Gracias,* Buey."

"Show patience. You must pace yourself, yes?"

"Oh, Buey . . ."

"Ernesto, do not weep. You may leave and prepare our lunch."

"Thank you, sir. Thank you."

"I will be along in due time, yes? Now, Ortega. Let us begin."

"Fingernails?"

"No, not this time, I think. We should warm him up first with the blowtorch."

TWELVE

It has been said that there are many different ways to get to Bel Air, but the easiest is to make a lot of money. Jack Burke drove down White Oak Boulevard, with its rows of weathered, pastel houses, forced his way onto the Ventura Freeway for a few exits. He stayed in the right lanes, where cracked concrete jiggled and thumped beneath the tires, and eased over to the San Diego Freeway, moving south. The sky was a bruised purple with streaks of orange from LA's belligerent pollution.

Burke's mind was wandering, and he almost missed the exit for Sunset Boulevard. A hunched-over elderly man in a finned white Caddy was smoking defiantly and squinting into the taillights of the next vehicle. Burke honked, but the old man refused to yield. Gauging the distance perfectly, Burke floored it and shrieked into a space between cars that opened and closed in a nanosecond. The old man flipped him the finger. The ramp was backed up; Los Angeles traffic was gnarly virtually any time of the day, but in rush hour it was hideous.

Burke hung a left on Sunset and followed it to the overgrown, half-shielded entrance to an exclusive, gated community. He left the main street, followed the winding drive and finally rolled up to a freshly painted guard shack. The rent-a-cop was a buff, blue-eyed kid with steroid pimples. He leaned out of the window and eyed Burke with a practiced gaze intended to intimidate.

"My name is Burke. Nicole Stryker left my name."

The kid made a show of searching his clipboard. He seemed

disappointed when he discovered the name was listed. He nodded grudgingly, reached toward the car with one large hand. "Need to see a photo ID, sir."

Burke debated and then handed over his legitimate license, rather than one of the forgeries he has tucked away in the glove compartment. The extras were there to provide him with different first names—also with his last name spelled as Birk, Berk, or Burk. His eye color was different in some photographs, the same in others; a number of the licenses claimed he wore glasses or was subject to seizures when not on medication.

"Have you been here before, Mr. Burke?"

"No."

The kid leaned on the car. His breath reeked of garlic. "You take a right on Bellefontaine, go maybe two hundred yards until you get to Bogart Drive. Turn left on Bogart all the way to the top of the hill, maybe half a mile. You'll see a fork in the road. Take the left fork onto Warner Drive, and the house is the first one on the right side, you can't miss the gate."

"Thanks." Burke started the car. The kid was looking at him as if about to say something. Burke didn't want the police or anyone else interrupting. "In case you're wondering, I know he's dead. Nicole asked me to come up and get a few things. She's too upset right now."

The kid nodded, a bit dimly. "I can understand that. And how long do you plan on being up there, Mr. Burke?"

"Maybe a half hour." Burke actually didn't have a clue. "No more than an hour. It wouldn't take that long, except I'm going to have to locate stuff from her directions because I've never been here."

The kid still seemed too suspicious. "You work for the family?"

"I'm a friend of Nicole's," Burke said, with emphasis on the word friend. He changed gears and manufactured a lewd wink.

That did it. The kid relaxed, fully convinced. He stepped back. "Go on ahead, sir," he said brightly. "Be sure to check out again when you leave."

The main drag was oddly dark for an upper-class neighborhood, but as Burke turned the car onto Garfield Lane the lighting improved. The next properties could all rightfully be termed "estates," for they were massive. He saw tall rows of trees weaving in and out of giant metal fences with mounted cameras and motion alarms. A Mercedes-Benz sedan passed him going the other way. The driver was a flawless blonde with yet another one of those surgically pinched noses. She smiled, Bel Air–style: *Hi! Are you somebody important, who can do something for me or my career?* The smile flickered out like a pissed-on campfire when she realized Burke was nobody special.

Warner Drive was all one property and the tall fencing stretched for an easy two blocks. Burke was impressed. He arrived at the tall, gothic-looking gates and paused to take it all in. This was a perfect home for a horror author. Far back into the gloomy trees he could just make out a sprawling, two-story property with high gables. The gate looked formidable; the entire, seemingly endless ribbon of impeccable driveway was dark. Burke parked and fished through his pockets for the keys Nicole Stryker had tossed him. There was one large key on the ring, but also one smaller—perhaps for a desk drawer or the lock leading into a library or study. Burke swore under his breath.

Two things sprang to mind: First, *why would Stryker leave such an already isolated setting to commit suicide in a hotel suite?* Second, *why the hell didn't Nicole tell me how to get in the front gate, if she knew it would be closed?*

Burke got out of the car, reached back under the front seat. He pulled out a large, police-style flashlight. He took measure of the fence, sighed. He knelt in the grass, checked that the snub S&W .38 was snug in the holster at his ankle. He removed a small travel-sized bottle of baby powder, sprinkled it on his hands and slipped on a pair of thin surgical gloves, just to be on the safe side. He looked in both directions; nothing. He searched the tree line for cameras directed toward the street; nothing.

He walked closer. There was no key opening on, or even near, the large front gate. Burke dialed Nicole on the cell phone, got a machine. He hung up, not wanting to leave a recording that might later serve as evidence.

Thirty seconds later he was at the top of the metal fence, shining the powerful flashlight beam down onto the lush grounds. He checked again for cameras and quickly found a few placed discreetly atop poles and among the trees. He recognized "sweepers" that were designed to move constantly and search the grounds below. These didn't seem to be activated. He considered, then slithered down some ivy and dropped loose-kneed onto the slightly damp grass. Burke figured he was here legally anyway. The guard could testify to his name having been on the list.

Meanwhile, the closed gate could mean any number of things, but only one that was truly interesting. If Nicole Stryker had left it open for him, then someone else either had recently been on the premises to close it—or that someone else was still here.

Burke stayed at the base of the pines for a few moments, just listening, then crouched low and worked his way closer to the mansion. The grounds had an unnatural stillness to them; the plants were rigid enough to appear artificial and the grass, though cool and somewhat damp, felt like the Astroturf flooring of a domed stadium. From somewhere to the south Burke heard the gruff rumbling of an airliner approaching LAX. His tennis shoes whispered through the foliage. His instincts flared. He was soon moving at a good, solid clip. He angled for the side of the massive porch and duck-walked beneath the picture window.

At the edge of the doorway he reached for his ankle and unclipped the .38. It felt improbably light—and a bit unimpressive—once in his grasp.

Burke blinked sweat from his eyes. He reached up with one gloved hand and carefully tried the doorknob. The door was unlocked and it swung open. Burke slithered into the foyer, the .38 low and pointed toward the tiled flooring. He was surprised how well he could see. He peered down into the huge living room. The house was riddled with night-lights; they were plugged into dozens of receptacles near doorways and closets.

For some reason, Peter Stryker had been abnormally afraid of the dark.

Burke was on the premises legally, with keys that belonged to the family, and he was licensed to carry a firearm. None of those facts were of any particular value to him at the moment. They would not make him bulletproof. In fact, he wished he'd brought the Kevlar vest he left hanging in a closet at home. He eased through the foyer, barely noticing that the ornate, doubtlessly expensive tiles were identical to those that adorned Nicole Stryker's residence.

The living room had thick, plush carpeting. Burke moved through it rapidly and soundlessly. He did not know what he was looking for, but if Stryker's death was something other than suicide, the presence of an intruder would likely be connected. He had taken the young woman's money. Since he was here, he felt obligated to follow through.

A floorboard squeaked on the upper landing. Burke flattened against a wall near the bottom of the spiral staircase, between two massive wooden bookshelves. For the first time, he noticed several small indicators of a careful, possibly recent search of the property. Some books had been replaced upside down and a few papers slipped under end tables or protruded from desk drawers. He listened intently. He could hear faint music coming from upstairs; something classical, although he did not recognize the piece.

Then footsteps, confident and brisk, crossed the floor above him and paused at the top of the stairs. *I saw a man who wasn't there,* he thought. How did that old poem go?

Burke braced the .38 in his hands. He would wait for the intruder to deal the cards. He couldn't retreat to the front door, which was still standing open, without being seen. Neither could he approach the staircase. His best hope was that the man on the landing would decide he'd left the front door open himself and make a run for it, or perhaps would know another way out of the home and not choose to take any undue risk. By staying still, Burke might have the upper hand. All he had to do was be patient and wait. Or so he hoped.

The intruder also waited.

Burke tried to get a sense of the man or woman upstairs. The floorboards had squeaked, rather than complained, as they likely would with someone Burke's size. The person was probably not exceptionally large. The lock on the front door was not damaged in any obvious way, and was the likely point of entry because it was open, so the burglar was either a professional or someone with a key. And this was also someone who could stand in utter tranquility for several minutes after having been interrupted in the middle of ransacking a dead man's home.

More time passed with no movement, no sound. Sweat rolled down Burke's face and tickled his lips. He licked it away. His Delta training had prepared him for long and boring periods of motionless anxiety, waiting for a target to appear. He was confident he could wait his opponent out, regardless of how long it took.

Time slowed, almost stuttered to a halt. Burke could hear the ticking of a clock in another room.

Movement? Yes. The figure was backing away from the staircase now, probably not convinced there was someone else in the house, but unwilling to walk downstairs to be sure. Burke knew he could either call for the police or try to corner the intruder somewhere on the upper floor. But he did not know the layout of the house, and the undamaged lock suggested his opponent may have had an opportunity to familiarize himself with floor plans, or perhaps had even been on the premises before. That gave the intruder a decided advantage.

It annoyed Burke to have to wait. He knew it made sense to call the police and report someone in the house. He even gave the idea careful consideration. But having the person arrested would eliminate a juicy opportunity for some intense, brutal questioning. The footsteps backed away from the upstairs foyer and into a hall or bedroom, somewhere where there was carpeting. Burke did not know if the stairs themselves would make noise. He doubted it. In the dim light of the many tiny bulbs peppered around the house Burke could make out that the stairs had also been carpeted. That meant only the boards at the top of the stairs presented a serious risk that could give away his position. He stepped forward and looked up.

A grotesque, leering face was peering down at him from the upstairs railing.

He raised his gun to fire but stopped just in time. The face was a carved, wooden gargoyle at the top of a wooden rail post. Burke swallowed and stepped to one side. He flattened against the long bookcase and moved to the foot of the carpeted stairs. Still no additional movement from above, so Burke took a breath, released it, and sprinted lightly up the stairs with the .38 raised. His eyes searched the shadows at the top of the stairs. He moved carefully, but each whisper of carpeting was like the shriek of a bone saw to his stressed ears. At the top of the staircase he crouched again. The sounds had come from the left. He had heard nothing from the hallway to the right. That did not prove that no one else was in the house, just that if there was, he or she hadn't been dumb enough to make a noise.

Burke saw no option but to continue with the assumption that he faced only one person. He crawled along the floor, tried not to pressure any particular point with the blunt point of an elbow or a knee. He was hoping to get into the hall without alerting the intruder to his presence. He was less than a yard from the hallway when a board groaned beneath him.

There came a rustle of clothing as someone moved amazingly fast. Burke was on his feet and following, but the man had unscrewed several of the night-lights during his last passage through the hall. Now Burke was at a disadvantage, eyes were not used to the darkness. His gut clenched, waiting for the boom of a gunshot or the blade of a knife. He stopped several yards down the mansion's enormous hallway, listened intently for movement and caught only a vaguely familiar sound, something akin to fingernails scratching at thick fabric.

Burke moved closer. His pulse was thudding. His mouth had gone dry and was coated with the dirty-penny taste of adrenaline. Everything was pitch-black now; huddled clumps of furniture brought back memories of blood-soaked corpses piled in the moonlight after a mission gone wrong. He came to the room at the end of the hall, the source of the faint rustling sound, and whirled into the doorway, weapon raised.

Burke was surprised to see reasonably well. He was in a large master bedroom. On the far side of the canopied, California King bed stood an open window flooded with moonlight. The talons of tree branches were scratching and tapping on one large pane of glass.

Wary of a trap, Burke slid along the wall. He cleared the walk-in closet and bathroom before approaching the window. He eased his head out, withdrew it quickly, waiting for a shot. After a few seconds he peered out again. The tree was as tall as the two-story home, and the branches thick enough to support a large man. Burke was certain when he noticed the carpet of pastel leaves at the foot of the tree. There were four human footprints there, like perfectly spaced exclamation points. As he watched a strong gust of wind erased the evidence.

Damn . . .

He stepped back from the large window, closed and latched it with a gloved hand. Despite the cool of the evening he was perspiring heavily. He closed the curtains, turned on his flashlight, and started to explore the premises.

Whoever searched the house was careful, neat, and had some reason to believe one or more of the many bookshelves contained what he was looking for. In fact, almost nothing else had been touched. As for the shelves, it was clear each one had been carefully examined. Although attempts had been made to put things back, traces of the search remained. As Burke had seen downstairs, some random books were either upside down or not returned to their proper places. Peter Stryker was a very obsessive and anal-retentive man. It is apparent that most of the books had been arranged alphabetically. Now some were clearly out of order.

But what the hell was the intruder looking for? It seemed unlikely that the object or information was found, unless it had happened exactly when Burke arrived, for there were still two bookshelves in the master bedroom that appeared undisturbed. Burke proceeded on the assumption that the goal had not been achieved. He moved to the bookshelf furthest away. He started at the bottom, removing books and fanning the pages; looking into the empty spaces for anything that seemed like a panel or the opening to a safe. He didn't know what he was seeking, but someone wanted something from the house badly enough to have come here illegally.

He was nearly through the second row from the bottom when

he finally started to pay attention to the titles. These were all the classics on mass murderers, *The Eye of Evil, Depraved, Deranged,* and *Deviant* by Harold Schechter and *The Man-Eating Myth* by Arens. There were several true-crime books by authors such as Ann Rule and former FBI agent John Douglas. Stryker also had numerous books about forensics and forensic psychiatry, such as *Bad Men Do What Good Men Dream.* All things considered, probably a normal collection for a horror novelist. Nothing about the bookcase itself struck Burke as unusual. He ran his hands along the sides and behind the edges but found no buttons or switches.

The last bookcase was stuffed with books, many of which Burke immediately recognized. Peter Stryker also had a rather comprehensive library on comparative religion. Here sat the works of Huston Smith and Joseph Campbell, books on the Kabbalah, Christian mysticism, *Zen and the Birds of Appetite* and other works by Thomas Merton, Daisaku Ikeda on Japanese Nichiren Shoshu meditation, and even some tracts on Zen Buddhism by D. T. Sukuki. All in the bookshelf closest to Stryker's bed.

Burke was dryly amused by the concept of a horror author who somehow managed to scare himself into religiosity.

He examined these bookcases as well, but spotted nothing unusual either in or on them. He moved to the large walk-in closet and slid the mirrored door fully open with the tips of gloved fingers. The flashlight revealed a long row of expensive, tailored suits. Each suit was either gray or pale blue and all of the shirts were white. There were dozens of pairs of polished black dress shoes placed neatly on the floor of the closet. It seemed as if Stryker never wore the same outfit twice. Burke closed the door.

What could the intruder have been seeking? Perhaps just a slip of paper he had reason to believe was in one of the books, or maybe a suicide note that revealed something a bit too scandalous?

Shit! What if the man he was chasing had simply slipped around to the front of the house and came back inside from below, perhaps to make one last furtive search of the books?

Burke stepped quietly down the hall to the balcony again, looked down.

The front door was now partly closed. The difference was subtle, but it had been moved.

The tiny hairs on the back of his head fluttered and came to attention. Holding the flashlight as far from his body as possible, Burke let the beam sweep the living room below. Nothing seemed out of place. He trotted down the stairs, .38 pointed at the carpet, and scoured the gloom again. Nothing, no one. *Okay, this is all getting way too weird.*

Burke looked at the books again, even more carefully this time.

The middle shelf was all medical texts, many quite obscure; everything from *Gray's Anatomy* to books on bird flu and other strains of influenza virus, also infections and their varied responses to antibiotic intervention. The fourth row of those texts sat about waist high for a man of average size. It was impeccably arranged, alphabetically organized, not a book was out of place.

And they were not that way before.

Burke grunted softly, moved closer. He examined the sides of the shelves. He ran his gloved hands along them. He found a small switch, on the left side of the shelf, behind the row in question. He pressed it, heard a faint whirring sound. The shelf slid back into the body of the wall; meanwhile, another shelf rose to supplant the first.

Burke used the flashlight. There were papers on this new shelf, most carefully assembled into packets and bound by large, colored paper clips. Some of these had clearly been shuffled around and then replaced. Burke removed a small metal flash camera from his pants pocket, arranged the various pages on the floor and photographed them all.

Some seemed to contain equations of some kind. Burke remembered very little of chemistry or math, but knew Doc could likely decipher them. He took more pictures. Other pages seemed hurriedly scrawled and contained symbols so arcane they might have come from some ancient civilization. Within minutes all the papers had been put back together in the same order, clipped in the same matched way, and replaced on the hidden shelf. He touched the button again and the bookcase returned to normal.

Burke slipped out the front door into the cool night air, jogged across the lawn. He crawled back over the wall and into his car. He stripped off the surgical gloves, stuffed them into a fast-food sack, and drove away. Moments later that sack was buried in a trash bin behind a restaurant off Doheny. Although Burke had done his job efficiently, without having used the key that had been given him or leaving the slightest trace that he had been there, he was not at all happy.

He was at least one step behind.

Thirteen

La Pergola was a small Italian restaurant on Ventura Boulevard in the middle-class neighborhood of Sherman Oaks. Its chief selling point to the health-food conscious denizens of the Valley was that the owner grew his own vegetables on a nearby vacant lot. It was also known for its exceptional homemade pasta dishes. Burke came in through the back of the small restaurant and ordered espresso. He waited until the obsequious waiter had wandered off into the kitchen and opened his cell phone.

"It's me. I had company."

"What?" Gina sounded sleepy. Burke could hear the stilted dialogue and sappy string music of some old black-and-white film playing in the background. Without a relationship to obsess about, Gina was becoming addicted to the Romance Channel. "Damn. Broken-nosed kind or the government kind?"

"I don't know, but he was good."

"The plot sickens."

"He was after something hidden in the house." Burke would not say more over a cell phone. "Gina, I think he might have found it, too. I'm going to speed things up."

She pondered and then caught up. "Okay, do you want me to meet you?"

He dropped sugar and cream into the espresso and downed it in one gulp. "Nope, you get some sleep. I'll handle this part solo."

"You won't be welcome there."

"I'll be careful."

Gina woke up. Her voice rose as she remembered something. "Burke? Major Ryan has been trying to reach you. He was using some dumb-ass Southern accent again, but I know it was him. Why does he bother with that spook shit?"

"I don't know, Gina. I think he enjoys it."

"Call me in the morning."

He broke the connection, folded the telephone and put it back into his pants pocket. He lifted the beaded glass, drank some of the chilled water, left a few dollars on the table and exited through the back door.

Although Burke was always careful to be sure he was not being followed, he now took precautions that bordered on paranoid. He drove up Colfax toward the lower-class part of the Valley, one eye on the rearview mirror, and then took a sharp right onto Burbank Boulevard. Anyone tailing him would be forced to duplicate a very dangerous move. As soon as he was around the corner he pulled into the driveway of a small business, cut the engine and flicked off the headlights. He unfastened his seat belt, turned and studied the street intently. Nothing.

Satisfied, Burke continued on until he arrived at Lankershim Boulevard in North Hollywood. He turned south toward the towers of Universal Studios. The entrance to the theme park, restaurants, and five-star hotel was a long and deeply sloped driveway that ended in a brightly lit circle before the Sheraton Hotel. Burke parked in the self-park area. He did not want anyone to remember his face. He got out of the car and checked out the parking garage. A young teenaged girl was standing near a Bronco, necking with her boyfriend. Burke turned his back to the couple and pretended to screw around with something on the front seat. He made some noise while doing that. Taking the hint, the kids drove away.

Once no one else was on his floor Burke went around to the

back, opened the trunk of the car and removed a small suitcase. The inside lid contained a makeup mirror. He worked smoothly, efficiently, an actor preparing for an old, familiar play. He changed his shirt and windbreaker for newer clothes, located a gaudy knockoff watch, slipped it on his wrist. He closed the suitcase, chose a brand-new briefcase, and slammed the trunk.

A few moments later Burke emerged as a tall, vaguely familiar-looking man with a goatee and entered the lobby of the Sheraton Hotel. He was youngish and obviously athletic and wore the standard LA uniform of a Hollywood producer: an expensive, black James Perse tee shirt and coat, old tennis shoes, and faded jeans. He also sported what appeared to be a platinum Rolex watch to shout that he was actually worth a bundle and could dress expensively if he weren't so humble. The producer, who carried a pristine briefcase, strode through the lobby as if very familiar with the surroundings. Therefore, none of the support staff thought to offer him assistance.

He marched to the house phone, dialed a room number. After a long pause he barked something into the mouthpiece. He kept looking at his watch, clearly impatient and irritated at being kept waiting. A porter walking by heard him muttering something about having "brought the fucking contracts for counter-execution." This, however, was such mundane verbiage for Hollywood that it was immediately forgotten.

The man slammed the phone down, sailed briskly to the bank of elevators, stepped into the first one going up from the lobby and disappeared.

On the 11th floor, Burke stepped out with the same sense of purpose and surveyed the hall. He had already called 1124, the suite rented by an elderly couple named Farnsworth on the night of the murder, and no one had answered. He had insulted a dead phone. The next step in his plan would be the trickiest. He stopped at the corner of the hallway and carefully peered around the edge.

As expected, a bored uniformed deputy was seated in front of the door to 1123, where Peter Stryker's body had been found. He was reading a newspaper, sipping coffee, had a room service tray near his feet. A yellow, plastic card hung angled from the doorknob. Burke knew it would state CRIME SCENE, SEALED BY LACSD. The uniformed cop was there to keep the morbidly curious from disturbing things before the Coroner's office had finished its work.

Burke did not know the officer. He removed a small object from his briefcase, a high-tech metal wand designed to rapidly read and open magnetic locks. Stepping away from the corner, he listened intently at one of the doors. Hearing nothing, he inserted the slender tongue of the silver wand and armed it. After a few seconds there came a slight hum and then a clear, metallic *click*. The device had narrowed the various combinations likely for this floor down to a few hundred, and it could process the rest of those within seconds. Head down, Burke turned the corner and walked briskly toward the deputy, who straightened up and lowered the newspaper. Burke passed him without looking and stopped at the empty suite next door. His back to the patrolman, he coughed and fiddled with his pockets as if looking for the plastic room key. He inserted the tongue in the lock and three seconds later it popped open. Burke hurried inside, closed the door behind him.

The cop went back to his paper.

A quick check with his flashlight indicated that the room was unoccupied. It had already been cleaned and prepared for the next guest and at this time of night, it was unlikely to be rented out again any time soon. Burke opened the door again briefly, without showing his face, and placed a DO NOT DISTURB sign on the knob. He made a loud show of locking it; just a busy businessman going to bed unhappy about something.

Burke would not sit on the bed, touch anything, or risk leaving any sign of his presence. He moved to the door that led into the room formerly occupied by Peter Stryker. Standing carefully over the briefcase, he applied baby powder to his hands and put on surgical gloves. After a moment of reflection, Burke reversed his steps and placed the briefcase on the floor in the bathroom, knowing that the cleaning staff would be most thorough there. They'd use bleach and cleansers immediately upon entering in the morning.

He returned to the dark suite and eyed the ceiling panels. He knew it was theoretically possible to climb up into the ducting and over into the crime scene, but he had something bolder in mind. 1124, where the elderly Mr. Farnsworth and his wife stayed, had been described by Detective Scotty Bowden as *adjoining* the murder suite.

Burke knelt before the lock. It was keyed the old-fashioned way, and the staff doubtless opened or closed it according to specific instructions given by the front desk. He bent low and ran a gloved finger along the bottom of the door and the carpet. There was a reasonable amount of space. Satisfied, he inserted a small locksmith tool and proceeded to pick the lock without scratching or damaging it. After several frustrating moments he reversed the minute teeth on the tool and tried again. Suddenly the lock clicked into place. Burke shoved with a gloved finger and the door hissed open, gliding along the nappy surface of the carpet.

Before going any further Burke soaked up the feel of the place. He danced the crisp beam of the flashlight around the crime scene. While remaining standing in the adjoining suite, he could now imagine how a killer might have stepped into the room undetected. Perhaps if his feet, as well as his hands, were carefully gloved? And if he were a smaller person, light on his feet?

Burke moved into the room.

The crime scene was still tagged and taped. The glare of his flashlight rapidly banned a few ominous, crouching demons lurking in the shadows. Burke efficiently took photographs with a small, high-speed, specially altered infrared camera.

The work rapidly revealed the surreal, horrific spoor left behind by the grotesque death of Peter Stryker: the couch, a plush white piece probably once valued in the thousands of dollars, now had two perfectly placed burgundy circles, one at each end. Stryker's dried blood was splattered up the wall near the reading lamp as if he'd severed a digit there and then momentarily lost bodily control before successfully, no doubt agonizingly, managing to cauterize the wound.

But is that what really happened?

Burke knew that what he wanted was likely in the bathroom. He was reluctant to enter that delicate a part of the crime scene and risk leaving a trace behind. He eyed the ceiling again, and considered slithering up into the air-conditioning ducts and peering down from above, but rejected the idea. He was now satisfied that if anyone else entered Stryker's suite the night of the murder, he or she did it from the adjoining room.

And probably the one on the opposite side, because this one, the suite he now occupied, was supposedly rented to the Farnsworths. The other had been listed as standing empty.

After a long moment, Burke sighed and slipped off his shoes. He went back into the bathroom and wrapped his feet in ordinary clear plastic kitchen wrap, as he imagined a killer might have done. He returned to the door, flashed the beam around to orient himself, and moved carefully into the crime scene.

There were small blood splatters on and around the ornate coffee table as well; one trash can had been bled into and then kicked over. Burke imagined a man insane enough to systematically cut himself to pieces, all the while prolonging his own agony as much as humanly possible with the help of drugs. Everything he was looking at would seem to fit that bizarre scenario, however unlikely that seemed.

He worked quietly and stayed close to the walls and the edges of furniture, as far away from the marked and tagged areas as he could. He moved through the room on his toes, and approached the darkened bathroom.

Wait!

Someone jiggled the lock. Burke was fully exposed, too far from the adjoining suite to escape. He was close enough to the bathroom to hide there, but had not had an opportunity to scrutinize the interior. If he bolted through that door he felt certain he'd accidentally disturb evidence. He swallowed his anxiety and waited. A weird sense of déjà vu overtook him; twice in one night, he and someone else apparently on the same trail had nearly collided.

But where was the deputy sheriff who was guarding the entrance? Or was he in on it somehow?

Time passed, lugubrious and cloying. The air-conditioning *whooshed* on overhead and Burke felt the chill ripple down his back. Nothing but silence followed the initial racket. The guard must have elected to check the lock, perhaps just as a nervous habit, when he'd gotten up to stretch.

Burke edged closer to the bathroom, nostrils wrinkling at an unpleasant odor that was all too familiar. He was careful to shield the flashlight beam so that it did not spill out into the darkened room, even though the constant light out in the hallway would likely diffuse it. He memorized the placement of tape and markers, the chalk lines around forensic evidence and the massive blood splatters. He noted one bloody palm print on the wooden frame of the doorway, about as high as it would have been for a man of Peter Stryker's size and build. He stepped across the threshold.

The bathroom was appalling. So was the stench. Burke had been around death all of his adult life and still gagged. He held his breath. Great gouts of blood and fecal matter darkened the porcelain tub where Peter Stryker had reportedly opened his abdomen. The little duck decals Doc had joked about were still there, but now they were pink instead of yellow. The mirror had a fan of splatter from what may have been one of the last attempts at self-mutilation. The toilet was also marked because the trash can beside it still held quite a bit of semidried blood. The outline of Stryker's buttocks, filthy and splashed with crimson, was still visible on the seat.

The small vanity mirror Stryker apparently used to view his own disembowelment was still propped up on the golden plumbing fixtures. Burke moved carefully around the grotesquely splattered throw rug and some evidence markers and shined his light on the small mirror. It was perfectly positioned. Burke shuddered at the image it brought to mind.

Burke backed out of the bathroom before drawing another breath.

What connection could papers marked with mathematical formulas have with such horrifically masochistic behavior? Could Stryker have gone mad while dabbling in arcane nonsense like witchcraft or voodoo? Perhaps the horror author finally succumbed to some kind of a psychosis generated from researching his own macabre fiction.

Or could someone unspeakably sadistic have done this to him?

Burke moved away carefully, stepping as closely as possible to where he'd passed before. He took one last look around the crime scene. One could almost picture the nightmarish events as they took place over several hours. It seemed likely that Stryker passed out from time to time; the pain alone would have done that, not to mention the stress and the repeated injections of various drugs. In those moments he'd probably have dropped his hand or foot over or into a trash can, thus producing the smaller pools of blood. The pain had gone on and on for hours.

And finally, the stumbling flight into the pristine bathroom, resulting in the one bloody palm print on the frame of the doorway.

But why hadn't Stryker regurgitated? There was no mention of that in the lab report, and there should have been. There was no trace of vomit by the toilet bowl. That fact seemed odd. Burke couldn't shake the feeling that something was wrong. Yet for the scenario to be self-mutilation, the crime scene was flawlessly presented. Perhaps that was the problem. It seemed a bit too perfect to be real.

At the entrance to the adjoining suite, Burke paused again to absorb subliminally. He closed his eyes and allowed the vibes of the room to wash over him. His mind replayed everything he had just seen, sensed, thought, or heard. And that's when he cursed himself. He eased backward, well clear of the doorway. He crouched down close to the floor. He shined his light, peered carefully at strands of carpet.

Damn it, what's that?

He took two small baggies from his pocket and with tweezers removed samples of carpet fibers and dirt from the adjoining suite. This was something he felt reasonably certain the sheriff's office had failed to do. First, they would have had no particular reason to consider doing it, and second there was no mention of fibers in the lab report.

Burke decided to messenger these samples to Doc, just to be on the safe side.

He whispered the door closed, eased the lock into place, and collected his things; tiptoed into the bathroom, leaned over the sink to remove the surgical gloves. Burke unwrapped his bare feet, replaced his shoes and washed his hands. He very carefully cleaned the sink and wiped it down with toilet paper. When he had replaced everything in the briefcase, including the Saran Wrap and gloves, Burke took the calculated risk of flushing the toilet with his shirt-covered elbow.

He exited the hotel suite with his head down and his voice pitched high, mumbling angrily into his dead cell phone. This time he gave himself a slight Southern accent.

"Give me a fucking break. It's late."

He pretended to listen intently. "I'm tired, Parker," he said. From the corner of his eye, Burke was pleased to see that the deputy guarding the crime seen barely looked up from his newspaper. "I'll meet you for one drink, and that's it."

He walked down the hall as if listening to someone ramble, turned the corner toward the elevators and was gone for good.

Fourteen

Wednesday

"Nobody made me."

"You think."

"I know."

The funky Valley breakfast joint was half full. They fell silent when the waitress, a portly gray-haired woman with "Midge" on her stained name tag served their waffles and poured watery coffee in two chipped ceramic cups. Gina drummed her fingers impatiently, rattling the silverware.

"Who the fuck besides us cares what happened to some whacko like Stryker?" Gina whispered, although the place was noisy. "That's the big question. Do you think it was somebody private, or government?"

"Could be either one." Burke leaned back against the side window of the coffee shop. Gina was righteously pissed and sensed something nasty coming on. For some reason it amused Burke to pretend to be clueless. "Or maybe it's all a coincidence and you're being paranoid."

"Oh, sure."

"It wouldn't be the first time."

Her face turned pink. Gina moved her plate to one side, eased closer to him. She didn't notice as the sleeve of her white blouse sank into a small, stray puddle of syrup. "Something shifty is going down here, cowboy. Don't step on your dick."

Burke softened. "Actually, I'm with you, Gina. And I've

stepped in something, all right. The question is what."

Gina tilted her head. "I can't believe it. You're going ahead with this."

"Look, the fees are good, and we both need the money." Burke had already decided to keep Indira Pal to himself for the time being. "Besides, now I'm getting curious."

"You get any sleep last night?" The motherly concern.

"I caught four hours. I'll be fine." It was a mutually acceptable lie. Burke reached into his briefcase and removed the baggie containing hotel carpet samples. He passed it under the table. "Give this stuff to Doc and ask him to tell me what he finds."

"What are you looking for?"

"Anything and everything he can turn up. I'm hoping to get lucky. And please tell him to hustle."

The coffee shop was beginning to fill with people rushing off to work. That made it difficult to keep track of who might be watching. Burke threw some crumpled bills on the messy table and slid out of the booth. He bent over and pinched Gina's cheek, an affectionate "boyfriend" gesture. "Keep your eyes peeled and if anyone leaves right after me, make a note of who they are and what they look like. Leave the information on my cell. Now smile and say good-bye."

Gina smiled broadly, but her voice was thin and reedy when she spoke. "Shit. You're starting to scare me, Red."

Burke exited the coffee shop, whistling. He shaded his eyes against the morning sunshine. Out in the parking lot, he dawdled like a man delaying the inevitable freeway commute. A pregnant woman followed a moment later. She was black, with straightened hair in short braids. She carried a large, woven handbag. The woman marched to a Honda Accord at the end of the lot and seemed to be looking for her keys. Burke watched from his car then started the engine. He drove out of the lot and around the corner. He paused on a surface street, got out and went around to the trunk as if about to open it.

The black woman drove past without looking.

He followed her. He stayed four cars back, risked a change to the right lane along the way. They passed under the freeway at Victory and she continued east, chain smoking. Burke was patient and stayed quite a ways behind. Several long blocks later she pulled into the parking lot of a Target store, grabbed a shopping cart and bumped along the cement until inside. Burke drove on, still undecided. If he was being tailed he'd just signaled that he was aware of it. If the lady was a civilian, no harm done, because only a pro could have spotted his moves.

Burke doubled back on Victory and returned to his office. He took the stairs two at a time and let himself in. The morning sunshine was painfully bright. He closed the blinds, swung his feet up on the desk and opened the Stryker file for another look. He had been to the crime scene now—smelled it, stepped it off, soaked it up; that fact altered how he experienced the photographs the third time around. They were still stomach-churning.

Looking them over, Burke could almost hear muffled howls of pain, reverberations of the cries Stryker would have emitted through the chewed piece of cloth used as a gag. He could smell the stench of scorched, cauterized flesh and the explosive reek of fecal matter, dried blood, and intestinal fluids that finally poured out into that hideously stained bathtub.

Burke closed his eyes, remembered the suite again, and then arranged the photographs in order.

Fifteen

Burke imagined himself as Peter Stryker. He stumbled from the couch to the bathroom. In his mind he placed the small mirror on the tub fixture. He got into the tub with ruined hands, sat on those silly duck decals, and then with those burned and bleeding fingers somehow managed to open his stomach and watch as his own intestines flowed out. The light faded out and he died, one deluded mind shrieking in incomprehensible agony . . .

Burke opened his eyes again. He shuffled through the file to the text section Doc had printed out. He flipped back through the pages and read them from the top once, then all the way through again, then backwards. He blinked his eyes, lowered the rest of the blinds and sat cross-legged on the floor. He slowed his heartbeat and concentrated on one point of color within his eyelids. He brought it closer, moved it further away, all the while breathing deeply. He relaxed his conscious mind so that his unconscious could better communicate. Something had been nagging at him. He wanted it to surface.

The floor fell away, and that small area of the brain known to separate "self" from "other" dimmed. Jack Burke was soon sitting in empty space and felt he *was* nothing but empty space. His breathing continued unabated, untended; the mind emptied itself and there was only white noise over endless silence. Burke was vaguely aware of footsteps in the hallway outside his office door, moving down the hall, but nothing else. The footsteps faded.

Then Nicole Stryker's voice replayed itself: *"You may find women's clothing, religious artifacts, and all manner of strangeness."*

But Burke had seen only rows of gray or blue Armani suits with white shirts, plain ties, and black dress shoes. And although there had been a number of works on comparative religion and other subjects on the shelves near Stryker's bed, he'd not seen any religious artifacts.

The telephone rang. Burke hopped to his feet and answered.

"You want fast, brother? I'll show you fast."

"Hey, Doc. What's up?"

"This ain't real specific, understand. Just the best I can do on my equipment inside of an hour. I'll have a more detailed analysis later on today or tomorrow morning."

"That is outrageous, Doc. Thanks."

"Luke Parker over at the lab owes me a solid. I told him he sneaks this stuff through, I'll let that favor slide."

"Appreciate it."

He heard a slight whirring sound as Doc positioned the wheelchair. Burke sat down at the desk, located a pen to make a note to leave for Gina. He scribbled "Doc says" and waited.

"We got your garden variety carpet fibers, higher grade than usual like they use in really cool hotels. The carpet has been recently cleaned, got serious traces of shampoo on the top third or so. Standard dirt and crap you would expect if it was a motel or a hotel; nothing looks too out of the ordinary at this stage, anyway. Do I dare ask where this came from?"

"A classy hotel."

"Uh oh."

"Doc, relax. It's from the other side of the doorway adjoining the suite next door."

Doc blew out some breath and chuckled. "I saw my career

flashing before my eyes there for a minute. Okay, anyway, like I said there is nothing all that out of the ordinary, except for one thing."

"What's that?"

"If it's from the door adjoining the suite next door, this is a little weird. I found some traces of baby powder, probably a name brand."

Burke grunted. "Yeah, but that's likely mine. I used some on my hands."

"Ah. And I probably don't want to know why."

"That's right, you don't."

"Okay, chief. You can keep that part to yourself."

"Thanks, Doc. And like I said, I appreciate the rush."

"No sweat. I'm on this case file all day today anyway."

"Why is that?"

"Beats me, Red. The Assistant ME called. He wants this sucker bagged and tagged ASAP and I shouldn't stop for lunch."

Burke was puzzled. "They're closing it up already?"

"Like yesterday. It's a suicide, open and shut."

"That's weird." Burke shook his head. "I don't get it. Does Scotty know about this?"

Doc had already changed focus. He was typing something, practiced fingers clacking along the worn plastic. "Scotty knows. In fact, he called me and said to rush it up so he can close out his report. Later."

"Later."

Burke sat quietly, finally listening to his hunch. It grew and expanded. He turned on a desk lamp and went back through the papers again, speed-reading everything that related to the crime scene. One more look at the gruesome photographs, but this time through a magnifying glass. He searched the prints of the disemboweled body in the bathtub and then he paused, short hairs rising. His dark eyes flickered with excitement. Burke spun in his chair and turned on the desktop. He impatiently rapped his knuckles on the desk as it booted up.

Moments later, Burke sent a short E-mail to Doc's personal address with a bcc to Gina at her home: "One clue may be page 18, paragraph 2, line 2, and photo marked CS37." He speed-dialed Scott Bowden's office, but the machine answered. He considered the situation for a moment, made an independent decision and locked his office door from the inside. The blinds were still drawn.

He opened the storage closet, removed the broom and dustpan and opened a disguised wooden panel.

Several firearms hung inside, all unlicensed and untraceable. There were two SIG 9mm handguns from Switzerland, the P210 (widely regarded as one of the world's finest pistols) and the SIG P220, which was a smaller knockoff; Burke selected the P220. It was somewhat lighter at 750g and carried nine rounds in the butt clip rather than eight. He checked the clip and slid the gun into the back of his belt. He locked up the closet and then the office and left.

His meditation had lasted longer than he'd realized. It was nearing lunchtime. Burke trotted down the wooden stairs, paused at the bottom before stepping out into the crowded parking lot. He searched with his eyes and caught a cigarette butt as it sailed out of a parked Dodge sedan and splattered orange sparks onto the pavement. He shaded his eyes, squinted and saw several butts in a pile near the vehicle. Burke emerged from the dark stairwell and walked briskly toward the parked Dodge, eyes locked on the dark form of the smoker in the driver's seat. His blood was up and the pistol dug urgently into the skin of his back like a living thing.

The door opened and the driver stepped out. It was Scotty Bowden. Burke relaxed when Bowden smiled and waved. Scotty walked toward him and they met near a parked blue BMW convertible with vanity plates. His eyes were bloodshot. He looked tired and smelled like vodka and tomato juice. "What the fuck you doing up there, beating off? I tried your door and it was locked."

Burke shrugged and smiled. "I was meditating. I thought I heard somebody go by but you didn't knock."

"I've been on the job too long to knock quietly," Scotty said. "And I didn't want to scare the shit out of your neighbors by kicking the door in."

"You look like hell."

"Yeah, I was up all night."

Burke winked, gesture forced. "Women or work?"

"We keep losing homeless dudes downtown and now everybody's on my ass about it."

"Any bodies?"

"Not yet, just MP's."

"You still think it's no big thing?"

"Hell, man, homeless means they got nowhere to live. So why the hell would they stay in one place for very long? And some of them are bound to end up dead."

"Yeah, you're probably right."

Bowden yawns. "I generally am."

"And you're humble, too." Burke scanned the parking lot, looked back again. He arched an eyebrow. "So what's up, Scotty? You making house calls these days?"

Bowden scratched at his perennial five o'clock shadow. "Just wanted to check in with you, see how that case I tossed you was going. You about wrapped up?"

Something about the question was forced, weighted with subtext. Burke decided to lie. "Yeah, just about, I'd say."

"Good," Scotty said with relief. "I've got a bunch of shit on my desk to get rid of, including the Stryker thing, and if there's going to be any problems I'd need a big heads-up. You'd tell me if there was, pal, right?"

"Sure."

"Hey, the DA wants to close the sucker down soonest. He even leaned on my boss a bit, and well, I'm kind of on thin ice these days, you know? Nothing really juicy, you understand, but I've got a couple of things in my jacket and I don't need anybody upstairs pissed off at me."

"I understand."

Scotty slapped a palm on his shoulder. Burke went hollow. "I knew you would, old buddy. Knew I could count on you. So when will you be giving that Stryker bitch your report?"

"In a day or two, most likely," Burke answered. "We've got a couple of loose ends to tie up first, but I don't see anything to worry about."

"Good, good." Scotty fished in his jacket pocket, produced some breath spray and anointed his tonsils. "Well, I'd best be getting back to work, then. Uh, you plan to copy me on that report?"

Burke, innocent. "I hadn't planned on it. You want me to?"

"If you don't mind. There's no need for her to know."

"Okay, but why?"

Scotty blinked. "Just to put my mind at ease. You know how it is, you were on the job. We want to be on top of everything."

Burke felt concern for Scotty, but did not want to tip his hand. "I'll keep you in the loop. You can count on me."

"I know."

Burke watched as Bowden walked back to the unmarked Dodge. The too-small clothes, poor haircut, and growing bald spot on the back of the head suddenly made Scotty seem pathetic. Burke waved as Bowden started the car. Scotty gunned the engine like a mock drag racer and drove away without looking back. Burke opened his cell phone.

Thirty minutes later he was in Nicole Stryker's living room.

"What's so important, Mr. Burke, that it couldn't wait for me to finish my tennis lesson?" Nicole was wearing tight, white shorts and a halter top. She smelled of sweat and sunscreen. He found the combination intoxicating.

Burke flopped down on the couch and bent forward. "I'm sorry, Nicole." Then, as gently as possible: "I don't believe your father committed suicide. I think he was murdered."

He watched her face carefully. As the implications of his statement slowly dawned on her, she stumbled slightly to one side before sinking into the armchair. *If she is acting, she's a damned fine performer.* She swallowed and nodded.

"So someone . . ."

"Tortured him to death. Yes."

"But who, and why?"

Burke shook his head. "At this point, I haven't the slightest idea. Our work is just beginning."

Her face hardened. "I see. And how much money do you need to continue the investigation, Mr. Burke?"

She has a genius for pissing me off, Burke thought. But he said, "I'm not trying to con you out of more money here. What we have already agreed upon is fine. I'm telling you now because we may be in for some problems, that's all."

"Problems? Explain."

The bitch was back. Burke elected to tell her part of the truth. "I think your father knew something and had something. I think someone was willing to kill him for it. And as it turns out, I am not the only one who is poking around in his things." He explained about the intruder in her father's mansion, the missing papers. "Nicole, do you have any idea what might have been on those documents?"

She frowned. "My father had many hobbies, Mr. Burke, as I told you. He loved word games. He had been to medical school, he studied witchcraft and religion and even some dead languages."

"I know."

"My guess is that those missing papers could have had something to do with any one or all of those things."

Burke got to his feet. "Let's go. I want you to take me through your father's house."

"Now? But why?"

"Because I need you to tell me, if you can, whether or not those papers were the only things taken."

Sixteen

Nicole Stryker insisted on taking her own car, a brand-new ragtop Mustang. The combined racket of wind, traffic and the rock music blaring from her stereo neatly prevented him from asking many follow-up questions. Perhaps she only wanted more time to process things. What Burke didn't know was whether or not she was hiding something.

The Stryker mansion appeared less ominous in the sunshine. Nicole popped the glove compartment and used a battery-operated opener. The metal gate slid soundlessly out of the way. She gunned the Mustang up the driveway and parked before the front steps. In daylight, the two-story house was a cream color, with a forest green trim that allowed it to blend in nicely with the foliage and trees.

Nicole got out quickly. She slammed the door without looking back. Burke, who couldn't help but follow her buttocks with his eyes, thought those tennis shorts did wonders for her personality. He slid out of the car, closed the door gently. He stood watching for a moment.

Nicole jiggled the key in the lock. She was facing the door, head down and hair obscuring her face, when she spoke. "Are you finished looking at my ass?"

Burke cleared his throat and moved around the front of the ragtop. "Sure. For the time being, anyway."

"Good."

She opened the door and walked briskly through the wide

room, going directly for the stairs. Burke kept his eyes focused on her shoulders and that bouncing blond hair. He was surprised to find himself blushing. Nicole raced up the staircase. He noted an odd tension in her shoulders; she became marionette-stiff as she reached the upper floor and also slowed down. Perhaps her memories of her father had begun to intrude? If not, she clearly had something else of import on her mind. He followed.

Nicole turned into what Burke had taken, the night before, to be a bathroom. She opened the door, which was set a few feet into a darkened alcove, and turned the lights on. Burke closed the distance, expecting her to move further into the room, which was actually a guest bedroom of considerable size. Nicole stopped abruptly, unaccountably, and Burke found himself pressed up against her shapely cheeks. She stiffened and so did he. The sensation in his groin was as sharp and precise as the explosion of static electricity from a doorknob.

"Excuse me."

She waited to move. It was a sliver of time that smoothly signaled her positive response to his interest. Then, without turning around, Nicole Stryker walked to a long closet and yanked it open.

"Shit."

Burke followed her eyes. The closet was long and deep, larger than the one in the master bedroom. There were wigs along a top shelf and some dresses, blouses, and women's business suits hanging from the center rod. A few pairs of shoes littered the floor.

"What?"

Nicole turned to face him, pretty features pinched and white. "There are a bunch of things missing, Mr. Burke."

"What kind of things?"

"A few of the women's clothes and most of the purses.

Someone has definitely been here."

Burke moved closer. "We could have it dusted for fingerprints, but the guy I saw wore gloves. I don't think he'd be that stupid."

"And look down there." Nicole pointed to a long wooden shelf set low to the carpet. "He had some icons and artifacts there, and some incense for when he meditated."

Burke's interest was piqued. "He meditated? You didn't mention that."

"Some kind of crazy Hindu shit," she replied. "Now watch."

She slid the shelf to one side, and a panel in the wall opened. It was large enough to step through. The room beyond lit up automatically as Nicole entered, motioned to Burke. There were more shelves here, and also antique statues, carvings, and religious icons of figures he easily recognized: Buddha, Bodhi Dharma, some solid gold Yin-Yang pieces, Kwan Yin, Ganesh, even Shiva dancing before the wheel of suffering. Burke whistled. He carefully examined one image of Siddhartha, deep in meditation beneath the Bodhi tree. It appeared close to a thousand years old.

"Do you have any idea what this is worth, Nicole?"

She shrugged. "A lot."

"More than a lot. You didn't tell me about this."

"My father had an extensive collection of very expensive antiques. He paid cash for the majority of them. I told you that there would be religious artifacts, but frankly I was not in a hurry to let anyone else know how extensive of a collection it was. I'm sure you can understand why."

"Because some of them were stolen."

Nicole faced the wall. "Let's just say that I don't know precisely how he acquired them, but he paid a lot and he always paid in cash."

Burke followed her gaze. "And some of those rare pieces are missing now?"

"That's right."

Burke replaced the Siddhartha and released a deep breath. "Do you have any idea which ones?"

Her shoulders were sagging. She was sinking fast. "Does it matter?"

"Let me put it this way, Nicole." He spoke gently, soothingly. "There are probably hundreds of thousands of dollars' worth of pieces here. If the motive was purely financial, then why not take them all? If you can remember what's missing, you may put me on the trail of whoever killed your father."

"China. No, maybe India."

"Excuse me?"

"Some of the pieces that are gone were from India. I don't remember which ones, but I know he said most of the ones on those shelves were from some obscure sect in, I think Hindu."

"No idea of the name of the sect or the deity?"

"Not a clue."

"Could you sketch me what they looked like?"

Nicole grew irritable. "I wasn't paying that much attention, Burke, okay? This isn't my thing. It was his."

"What I don't understand," Burke mused, ignoring her anger, "is the missing women's clothing. Why take only some of that? Why any of it, why not everything he had? What were they looking for?"

"I want to go now."

She was hugging herself. Her voice sounded thick and Burke could see rows of goose bumps growing on her bare arms. He held her shoulders. "I'm sorry. Sure, let's get out of here." She sobbed at the touch, a sound fraught with vulnerability, dark from remaindered grief. Nicole Stryker whirled around and glued herself to Burke's chest.

When they left, his shirt was smeared by mascara, damp with tears.

Seventeen

"There is something most seriously fucked up going on here, my brother."

Doc was sitting in his specially modified van, tugging on an unfiltered cigarette. The tip glowed orange in the gathering gloom. Tiny sparks soared through the smoke when he exhaled. "The Assistant ME reamed me a new asshole for copying those files."

Burke scuffed his running shoe along a crack in the asphalt. "I haven't shown that stuff to a soul except Gina, Doc."

"You sure?"

"Definitely. How do you think he found out?"

"Maybe he's got a mole in my office or it's bugged up or something. But I don't think so. That leaves one possibility."

"Your computer?"

"Somebody must have hacked into the main frame and downloaded whatever I had accessed and printed out. Now I ask you, white boy, why the fuck would they care about that?"

"Scotty called me. He said he's getting heat to close the case file. I got the feeling he'd rather I drop the ball on this one."

Doc rolled his eyes, snapped the smoke out onto the pavement. "What's up with the brother, man? This sucks swamp water. Damn, I'd best not lose my job over some dead horror writer."

Burke spat on the ground. "It has to be one hell of a lot bigger than that if people at Parker Center and City Hall want to shut things down."

"Fucking great."

"Sorry if I'm making trouble for you."

"I just thought you should know," Doc said. "You figure maybe this is the spooks again?"

"I can find out soon enough."

"Major Ryan?"

"Yeah, it's time I talked to him again anyway."

"Red, just so you know, I lied my black ass off. I told them I have no idea how the file got pulled, much less copied. I don't know if they believe me or not, but you know what that means."

Burke shrugged. "It won't take them long to run the film from the security cameras in the hall and check the logs and see that I was there. Relax. If I get hassled, I'll say I did it all on my own."

"But that's a felony, man."

"Fuck them. The company will cover me."

"We better hope so." Doc started the van. "Man, I don't know what is going on here, but I think you really screwed the pooch this time."

"You checked those pages I e-mailed you?"

"Yeah, I did. Sweet. So a piece of the dude's bowel is flat fucking *gone.* Now, how did the coroner miss that?"

"It was cut in two places, clean as a whistle, probably by a scalpel. And now it's missing."

Doc shivered, grimaced. "Yeah, and then somebody buried that fact for some reason. Look, it doesn't take a rocket scientist to know this whole mother stinks. The guy has already fucked with himself for hours, he's drugged out of his mind, he's sitting in a bathtub, disemboweled and deep in shock, and he stops to cut a piece of bowel out and then what, flush it down the toilet? Or does he *eat* it or something?"

"Because if he committed suicide, where the hell did it go?"

"Exactly." Doc put the van in gear. "And some other dude can re-check his stomach, 'cause that idea even grosses *me* out."

Burke tapped his forearm with stiffened fingers. "One more thing, Doc."

"Not a chance, man. I'm in deep enough already."

"Hang on a second. The baby powder by the doorway, the stuff in the carpet. What kind of baby powder was it?"

Doc scans his memory bank. "Johnson & Johnson."

"You're sure?"

"It was that chemically loaded, lanolin-type stuff. Mind saying why you're asking?"

Burke removed his fingers. "Because mine was corn starch baby powder. I bought it at a health food store."

"Oh, *shit.*"

"Yeah. That means somebody else used surgical gloves in that room. And whoever it was also slipped into the next room, drugged Peter Stryker, then tortured him to death."

"And someone heavy wants this covered up."

"Looks that way."

Doc started to drive away. "Red, I think you just got even more dangerous to be around than usual, my friend. Are you going to tell Scotty about all this, or is he on the shit list now?"

"I haven't decided."

Doc seemed bothered. "He's old school, our asshole buddy. Our brother. Somehow it don't seem right to hold out on him."

The van rolled forward a few feet, Doc's face began vanishing into the shadows.

"I know," Burke said. "But somebody is leaning on him, so he's out. Just let me decide, okay? You play dumb from here on out."

"Glad to." Doc steered the van away. "Color me flat ignorant." He rolled off into the darkness, hissing tires and the fading low drone of an engine.

At first Burke savored being alone. He stood in the parking lot, lost in the gloom, deep in thought. Suddenly he trembled. He did not know if he was feeling the cold or finally becoming afraid.

He needed to speak to her. He drove to the hospital without awareness. Soon he was again by her side . . .

"I'm in trouble again."

"What?"

"A new case. Looked really easy at first, but now . . ."

"Oh, Red."

"I know. But we do need the money."

"Oh, Red."

She did this sometimes. Repeated things in a feathery whisper before moaning back down into carefully measured breathing. Burke hugged his knees and listened for her voice. The hospital seemed even colder than the grounds. Burke was seated near the window as usual, staring out at stars covered by a wispy gauze strip of clouds. The austere room, with its pale walls and lack of furnishings, seemed distorted, oddly elongated this evening, like something from a horror film about a mental institution.

"I love you."

Her voice was a bone sigh, borne on the wind: "I know."

"Are you ever coming back to me?"

There was no answer. Burke felt his eyes begin to water. He forced a wide smile. He did not wish to upset her. He got to his feet, kissed her on the cheek and tucked her in a bit more carefully.

"Sleep well, Mary."

He replaced the chair precisely where he'd found it and took one final look around the room. He found a small scrap of paper on the floor and tossed it into the trash bin. *Nothing but net.* Straightened the one painting on the wall and wiped some dust from the top of the frame. Burke knew that he was stalling, avoiding the dread he would experience once out of her presence, but could not bring himself to hurry. Finally he waved, although her eyes were closed, and walked out.

In the hallway, his own footsteps booming from freshly painted walls, he allowed himself to sob. The moment of weakness was brief, tightly controlled. Ashamed, Jack Burke wiped his eyes.

A faint *ping* caused him to glance back at the elevators. The doors slid open. An old man, bright-eyed and with a wild shock of white hair, was chatting with a plump Hispanic nurse.

Jesus.

Burke's blood turned to ice. He cringed at the sight of Harry Kelso. He stepped away, and flattened against the wall, then ducked into the refreshment alcove to hide between the giant coffee and soft drink machines. Kelso entered her room. The door *whooshed* shut.

Burke did not leave until he heard the voices fade.

EIGHTEEN

The wind whips sideways and then flows downward between towering twin pillars of concrete and glass. It feels hostile by the time it reaches the street; there is a biting chill in the air. The apparently legless man is of indeterminate age, his race obscured by layers of grime and sweat, hair long and tangled. He is known to the others as Willie Pepper. Willie is hunched in the corner of the sidewalk next to the Bank of America building, seated on a small wooden platform. He is counting out change into one filthy hand. He wears an army jacket with sergeant's stripes, a tee shirt, a blue work shirt and two pairs of wool pants.

A small smile creases Willie's dirty face. He has scored enough cash for another quart of Red Mountain. Willie looks up, squinting into harsh slivers of sunset that are bouncing off the windows of the executive suites on the fifth floor of Kingsley Towers. He scans the sidewalk for any likely score, but the streets are already filling with expensive cars. The businessmen and -women who work nearby have already descended *en masse* into the parking garage and will soon pack the streets like shiny roaches. The night crowd will eventually arrive to attend theater events, but not for a couple more hours.

Willie decides to call it a night. He eases his small, rolling platform—made of roller skates and wood—back into the rapidly expanding shadows at the mouth of the alley. He searches his pockets, finds a damp Camel that is bent in a V, sagging but unbroken. He tears the filter off, fires up a smoke, and leans back against the wall. The razor-edge tobacco rush makes his scalp tingle and takes the edge off the shakes.

He looks around. Satisfied no one is watching him, the tramp unbuckles the straps that keep his lower legs hidden in the platform. Tucked beneath him on a carpeted surface, his calves have long since gone numb from lack of circulation. He eases them straight and massages until the blood flow returns. His quietly healthy feet wear two sets of white socks and a pair of unlaced black basketball shoes. When he raises his eyes, he jumps a bit.

A man is watching him from the end of the alley.

Willie Pepper squints. The man has a stocky build and what appear to be smears of dirt on his exposed lower arms. He is wearing a blue Navy watch cap with eye slits. It is pulled down over his face to keep out the cold. Or perhaps hide his features. *Fuck, did that bastard see me count out my change?* Willie Pepper lives in a world where a man may be killed for less than ten dollars. *Or did he think I was really crippled until just now and maybe he's checking out how to do the scam for himself?*

Willie keeps his head down and fumbles with his platform. He designed it himself. Willie used to work in "the trades" as a carpenter, until his drinking got too bad. The device neatly folds up and weighs next to nothing. Willie even left an empty space for hiding a bedroll, some smokes, money, or a little bit of extra booze. He takes a quick peek up the street. The man is still watching.

Willie slips a long, formerly Phillips screwdriver up his right sleeve. He sharpened the point years ago, and can take out a man's eye if he has to. He looks up, yawning and stretching. The stranger has vanished . . . *but there ain't no other way out of that alley. Did he go into one of the restaurants through the kitchen?*

Willie Pepper shivers in the grip of a memory: the way his alcoholic father had chased him through the darkened house growling like an animal *grrrrrrrr, rrrrrrrruff.* Willie had pretended to enjoy it; acted like it was all a game. But his father—a red-nosed trucker with fists like old baked hams—had long since fried his brains on speed and boilermakers. Willie had seen what happened to his mother and his brother when the old man got pissed, and it wasn't pretty. He didn't want that kind of a whipping laid upside his own head, no fucking way. His momma used to tell him "Willie, there ain't no boogie man," but Willie Pepper knew better. He knew a monster lived in his house and its name was Daddy.

Now why the hell did I just think of that after all this time . . . ?

Whatever, because the strange man is gone, maybe he's a dishwasher at the Eye-talian place or something and came out to grab a smoke—*yeah, but I didn't see any cigarette in his hands*—and Willie has important business to tend to, so he'd best get hopping.

There is an impossibly small, tightly packed convenience store located one long block south near the subway station. Willie Pepper insists on referring to it as the subway station, because that's what it is, no matter what these fancy LA fuck-heads want to try and call it. The store is owned by a Korean guy whose name sounds like something off a take-out menu, but Willie likes him well enough. He stays open a little late and lets the street dwellers pick up last-minute things with the change they've scored that day, like packaged junk food, but mostly they get wine, beer, or cigarettes. Willie hurries on down the street, but he can't shake the stranger, not completely, because his body breaks out in goose bumps and somebody seems to be walking just a step behind him going *grrrrrrrr, rrrrruff.* He lets the screwdriver drop down into his hand completely, doesn't try to hide the blade, figuring if he's being followed, let the bastard see he's packing, spot his shiv and know that Willie Pepper won't be anybody's bitch.

"Watch where you're going, damn it!"

Willie has rammed into some portly schmuck on his way through revolving doors trying to catch him a taxi. "Watch your own self," he grumbles. The guy stinks of expensive cologne and even more expensive cigars. Willie knows cigars, can tell a Nicaraguan from a Honduran just by his nose, and this guy just did a Cuban, probably a pyramid Monte C, the fat fuck. Some people have all the luck. Probably ripped the money off in the stock market and walked away with millions after two years in some country club and left the rest of the country holding the bag.

Wun Hung Low, or whatever his name is, has already started to lower the sliding metal panels and lock up his stand. Willie is about to rip the skinny old guy a new one when he smiles that wide dink smile of his and bows a bit. It's hard to get really pissed at somebody who comes off so nice, especially when most of the world doesn't seem to give a damn anymore. Willie slips the screwdriver back up his sleeve. He counts out his money—dimes, quarters, and smelly, oft-folded dollar bills—until he has the requisite purchase price in the Korean's outstretched palm.

Two minutes later, Willie Pepper has a gallon jug of cheap California Red to carry, along with his folded-up platform. He scuttles along the darkening sidewalk, hunched over to hide the bottle—but also because the night chill has begun to slice through the holes in his stiff, unwashed garments like strands of razor wire. Like anyone who lives on the streets, Willie knows his own body oils can provide some protection against the cold, especially in a relatively warm clime such as the one here in Southern California. Although his olfactory senses remain keen enough to recognize the bite and tone of a specific cigar, he has long since lost the ability to recognize the stench emanating from his own body. Truth be told, it is intense enough that a tracker could follow him by stink alone. And someone does.

Willie pauses to finish his cigarette. The man one block behind melts into the shadows until the tramp resumes walking. Willie turns left, toward the LA Center parking lot, intending to camp for the night in the large garbage area next to Cheesecake Factory. Back there, the amount of food thrown out every night is truly staggering. A man can get a terrific drunk on, stuff himself on the remains of expensive meals, and then pass out, all in relative comfort.

The area is nearly deserted. Across the lot Willie can see headlights turning and hear the horns honking; it's a seemingly endless parade of weary, irate worker ants heading home for the night, only to pack the cracked and sagging freeways and return downtown the next morning. On the other side of the row of restaurants and empty office complexes, the brightly lit night-spots will remain busy until after midnight. As for Willie, he intends to be out cold by then. Or perhaps "out warm" says it better.

He approaches the back of the restaurant. The grate near the kitchen gives off huge amounts of steam. If a man burrows back into the garbage and cardboard boxes, he can remain undetected by the head chef or the kitchen crew, who wander out occasionally to grab a smoke or take a piss. At this moment, no one is looking out through the rear doorway.

Willie Pepper relaxes. He opens the jug and takes a deep swig, then another. He wants a smoke, but can't light up without the risk of self-immolation when he's buried in boxes. Best have one now. He finds a Marlboro, tears the filter off, lights up and puffs.

Click-click!

The fuck was that? Willie whirls around, spraying sparks, excited breath hissing out in a smooth, white wave. Shoes on concrete, hitting something, maybe a soft drink can? Willie needs glasses, can't see for shit at night. He now figures somebody is after his hootch for sure.

He drops the sharpened screwdriver back down into his palm and tries to see if he can spot anything, any *one,* moving back there behind him. The headlights around the corner create tricky geometrics of light; the encroaching shadows appear, rapidly change shape, almost seem to chuckle.

Odd. For the first time, Willie Pepper—a man quite given to bluff and bluster, a pro who is used to living on the streets—feels truly afraid to be alone.

"Don't try and fuck with me," Willie calls, but his voice cracks and seems a tad too shrill to be intimidating, even to his own ears. He listens intently but nothing else happens. *Maybe it was just the wind and a piece of paper, Willie. When did you get to be such a pussy?* Willie backs away, his eyes still roaming the darkness, *grrrrrrrr, rrrrufff,* but he doesn't see anything. He swallows, notices he's breathing too rapidly, takes another drag of his smoke and a deep drink of wine.

Willie decides to turn his back on the ominous, rippling black. He will prove he is not afraid. He does face the other way. But then, like a man leaving a darkened garage, he has that one brief moment of atavistic, horrific dread where he realizes that something evil might be sneaking up behind him. He stumbles forward anyway, red-veined eyes glued to the sidewalk in front of his dirty black sneakers. He struggles to keep his panic hidden and to reach the safety of the back porch light behind the restaurant before the boogie man can get him.

Willie runs into something solid; hard enough to take his breath away. His vision clears. It is not a something, it is a man. The man he saw standing across the street. Before Willie can react, the man smiles, spins him like a top, and kicks at the back of his knees. Willie drops like a sack of apples. The jug of wine goes flying, shatters against the pavement, and leaves a blood-dark, widening stain.

"Don't!"

But Willie Pepper's voice is already someone else's voice and coming from somewhere far away. He wheezes and gasps. A soft/tough something has drifted down around his neck and pulled itself taut. The rope cuts into his windpipe and steals his air. Willie struggles but it is useless to resist. The man behind him expertly places a knee in the center of his back and pulls again, hard enough to strangle but not sharply enough to crush his neck. Willie, kneeling in terror, tries to fight back but cannot quite muster the strength as the world spins noisily away.

Nineteen

Thursday

The Institute for Psychoanalytic Studies was located in an otherwise ordinary office complex on Balboa Avenue in the LA suburb of Encino. Burke parked in the nearly deserted lot, where a sign curtly informed him that tenants of the building did not validate their clients. That struck Burke as funny. The large blackboard in the lobby revealed that the school occupied most of the third floor, a sizeable chunk of very costly real estate.

Burke rode up in the elevator next to a tired-looking young couple in business clothing who were squabbling about money. Meanwhile, their infant, who was fussing in a dark blue stroller, grinned and created a stink powerful enough to peel paint from the walls. The argument seamlessly shifted to whose turn it was to change the diaper.

Burke exited onto plush, beige carpeting and into a zone so quiet the Muzak speakers had probably been disconnected. He located the right suite.

In the lobby, a cheerful young woman with impossibly large blue eyes and glasses peered up owlishly from a garish romance novel. The receptionist was under the impression Burke was a reporter, on leave from the *Daily News* and doing research for a novel. To her, Burke might as well have been a rock star. She asked about and arranged for coffee before ushering him into the inner sanctum of Dr. Theodore Merriman.

Before Burke could thank her, the girl vanished like a chaos-theory butterfly determined to set off a tropical storm in the Bahamas.

"Man eating himself is largely a myth."

Dr. Theodore Merriman, the fellow who made the statement in sonorous tones, was perhaps six feet tall, with a carefully shaved head. He wore neat, wire-rim glasses, an expensive salmon-colored tie, and a Men's Wearhouse knockoff of a thousand-dollar suit.

Burke widened his eyes. "Is that so?"

"Absolutely." Merriman tucked the fingers of one hand into his jacket like a man imitating Abe Lincoln. He cleared his throat, began to pace at the front of the empty classroom. "My assistant said you wanted something of a lecture, here. This is so?"

"Actually, that is exactly what I need." Burke started his miniature tape recorder, placed it on the desk in front of him. He summoned his most obsequious smile. "Just pretend you are in a classroom."

"That's where I'm most comfortable anyway."

"Sir, if anthropophagy is largely a myth, what about the sadistic rituals of the Aztecs, for example? Didn't they cut out the human heart and eat it as a way of absorbing their enemies? I have also read that certain African tribes would . . ."

Merriman cut him off. "Those stories may be apocryphal. At the very least, let us say that we have little evidence to support that cannibalism itself, ranging from those sixteenth-century Aztecs to the cultures of New Guinea, was ever actually a socially accepted custom, rather than a bizarre aberration of some kind."

"Still . . ."

Dr. Merriman waved a finger, mock scolding him. "Now, now. I believe I am teaching this 'class,' and you are the student?"

Burke pretended to be chastened. "Of course. Please go on, Professor."

"If you get a chance, pick up a book by Arens called *The Man-Eating Myth.* It will lay out the case much more effectively than I can in the time allowed here."

Burke had already read Stryker's copy, but wrote down the title. "Will do."

"Now," Merriman intoned ponderously, "you say the antagonist in your little novel would be fascinated with cannibalism?"

"Yes."

"And you got my name from Peter Stryker a few weeks ago?"

"Yes, again. He was very appreciative of your having taken the time to give him input when he was writing *A Taste for Flesh.*"

"I have to tell you that surprises me a bit. If memory serves, we had a small legal skirmish over credit on that project."

"He must have gotten over it."

"Indeed. Terrible thing, his death. And probably a suicide, according to the papers. Does anyone know exactly what led him to it?" Merriman placed one hand on the edge of his desk and looked down with feigned benevolence. He seemed quite the egomaniac.

"I haven't really stayed up on it, Professor. I only interviewed Mr. Stryker briefly, and primarily because of his novel."

"Ah. To avoid any similar conflict, no doubt."

"Naturally." Burke risked a probe. "And to steal from the best."

Merriman roared with laughter. "Oh, but of course, my boy. The good ones always do!"

"Please, continue. I'll listen."

"Very well." Merriman resumed pacing. Now he tucked his hands behind the back, like a man trying to channel George Washington. "We find cannibalism and vampirism present in our language in verbal metaphors, such as to devour someone with your eyes, or a parent threatening to 'eat you up.' The anthropophagy myths also appear in Voodoo and even in Latin America, and as you said, most hold that those Aztecs and African warriors would eat the hearts of their enemies to absorb their strength. Any of that play into your novel?"

"No," Burke answered. "Not really."

Merriman returned to the edge of the desk. He shifted to a thoughtful "Thinker" pose. "Well, then let us leave that and examine other aspects of cannibalism, shall we? Consider the Catholic ritual of transubstantiation, the eating of Christ's body and the drinking of his blood. Viewed from a distance, it is alarmingly primitive, no? So the question is why are these images so persistent in our collective unconscious, irrespective of their literal truth? Why do they endure?"

Burke leaned back in his chair. He was not unaccustomed to being the bright student in the front row. "I suspect because the act of transubstantiation is symbolic of something deeper and more abiding than we think?"

Merriman snapped his fingers, alarmingly loud. "Yes! Very good! Benezech, in 1981, held that cannibalism was related to the sado-oral stage of development, that post-sucking stage, when the child awakens to the need to bite. And yet to bite is forbidden, so this conflict is suppressed and then replayed, even in the bedroom, in adult life, as is sucking. Now, let's take the persistently fascinating legends of vampirism. This is the act of drawing blood from an object while taking erotic pleasure in sucking it. Is that not mother's milk? But milk taken in anger? Is it not also quite sadomasochistic?"

"Insanity, but then a psychosis is a memory of something that already happened."

"Indeed."

"That's a fascinating concept to apply elsewhere, then."

Burke was not pretending anymore, he was intellectually intrigued. "What about the concept of zombies and the living dead? Or the aspects of the animalism in the werewolf legends?"

Merriman nodded. "They stray a trifle too far from the current topic to be relevant, but perhaps we could get into those in depth at another time? I am meeting someone for drinks shortly."

"Excuse me, Professor. Go on."

"No, on second thought," Merriman said, "perhaps I will address that interject, however briefly. Do you recall a young Scottish man named Allan Menzies? It was in all of the papers, October of 2003. He killed his best friend, one Thomas McKendrick, to drink the blood and eat part of his skull in the hopes of becoming immortal. Our Mr. Menzies claimed to have been assisted by a character from an Anne Rice novel and film. You see the vampirist fancies that being one of the living dead would constitute a new, perhaps better and more relaxed existence. She copes with her existential death anxiety by envisioning herself as immortal. When the 'love bite' shall we say, or the sucking of the bad mother's breast, turns violent and becomes a bite that sheds blood, it crosses into this territory. And we have all doubtless felt that temptation upon occasion."

Merriman smiled. He had abnormally large canines and poor teeth, giving him an unfortunate, almost vulpine look. The irony almost triggered a giggle. Burke looked down and scribbled nonsense. As usual, he would remember almost verbatim.

"And for your further reference, vampirism as a mental diagnosis probably does not exist by itself. It generally correlates to schizophrenia, hysteria, perhaps severe psychopathic disorder and even mental retardation. The drinking of blood is, as stated, sadomasochistic and appears in blood rituals, fetishism, ritual revenge, and full psychosis with or without drug intoxication. All have some form of premorbid characterological vulnerability. The fantasies arise from residues of early mother–child experiences during the oral sadistic sucking phase. It is probable that the biting and eating images come from maternal deprivation, which arouses in the infant aggressive fantasies and behavior, thus intense oral sadistic libidinal desires."

Burke was nodding, thinking, absorbing. Merriman paused as if expecting affirmation. "Very interesting," Burke offered, tentatively, "and I see you are working your way back to the original topic."

"Yes, shortly. But to further digress, there was a most interesting article from Reuters a year or two ago involving a German man named Armin M. who advertised for a 'young, well-built eighteen- to thirty-year-old to slaughter.' A young man named Juergen actually applied for the position."

"I recall reading that story."

"I don't remember all of the details, but I assure you they were particularly gruesome. The two men imbibed heavily in both alcohol and various drugs. Then Armin surgically removed Juergen's penis. The two then flambéed the organ in brandy and tasted it. Disappointed in the flavor, they then fried Juergen's penis and subsequently devoured same. And all of this was apparently recorded on video camera."

"Castration anxiety makes that concept pretty hard to deal with," Burke said. And in truth, the thought of watching that video made him woozy. "It's a pretty disgusting idea."

"Ah, but disgust, like beauty, seems to be very much in the eye of the beholder. Juergen and Armin had a mutual agreement, it seems, for Juergen is seen on video as submitting voluntarily to his own murder. Armin then dutifully chopped the body into several pieces, froze them, and began to eat the corpse over a series of weekends."

"That part of the story escaped me." Burke had a sudden flashback: he again returned to the night his friend Top died on the disastrous mission to Djibouti—and the ugly little man he saw seated on those body parts, reveling in the wholesale slaughter. The gore had been less disturbing than the man's macabre laughter. His positive *delight* at the presence of death. When Merriman spoke again, Burke needed a few seconds to catch up.

"I assure you it is all true, Mr. Burke. In fact, the German newspaper *Der Bild* printed the grisly police statement word for word. The horrific event seems to have stemmed from the deep homosexual and cannibalistic fantasies shared by both men. The Freudian implications are, of course, quite obvious."

"Sure, but how would a Jungian account for such a story, as the deep shadow of the feminine?"

"Yes, perhaps as it relates to anthropophagy." Merriman stood. "I believe it was McCully, 1964, who first hypothesized that the mythology associated with vampires, werewolves, and anthropophagy could all arise from the destructive side of the feminine. By way of example, consider Hecate of Greece or the Kali-Ma cults of India."

Burke nodded. "Murder in the name of the Goddess of Death."

"Oh, but Kali-Ma is much more than mere death, Mr. Burke. You should read up on her some time, you really should. Quite fascinating." That odd grin again. The man was in danger of becoming a caricature. "The Hindu pantheon is wonderful stuff, and within it the dark feminine is most marvelous."

"It appears in Tibetan Buddhism as well, correct?"

"Very good, young man. Indeed it does." Merriman glanced at his watch. "I am running out of time. You might also look into the concept that schizophrenics—who often manifest persecutory delusions of incorporation, introjection, devouring, and destruction—are lacking any capacity for symbolic thought. To them the ingestion of blood or flesh may be a way to replenish the self, however malignantly narcissistic the behavior. Perhaps that would help you organize the inner world of your murderer."

"That's a good idea. Thanks."

"But he eats people, yes? Then some final thoughts on anthropophagy. Have you noticed that when one group sets out to destroy a subgroup, it tends to lay those charges at its door? The Romans against the Christians, those same Christians later against the Jews? The fantasy that the hated subgroup practices such appalling rites as cannibalism and blood rituals inflames the spirit of the populace and creates the necessary motivation in the masses. Now, I cannot go into it in depth, but this splitting of self and other again echoes of primitive narcissism and borderline psychotic ego defenses."

"Interesting."

Merriman walked to his coatrack, shrugged his way into an overcoat. Burke, taking his cue, packed up his things. He left the recording running.

"Walk me to my car?" Merriman asked.

"Certainly, Professor. I appreciate the extra time."

"No problem." Merriman turned out the lights. His eager receptionist had already gone home. "Just be sure you mention the school favorably when you write about and discuss your novel, eh?"

"Of course."

The two approached the elevator. "When one considers the Goths, sadomasochists, Satanists, and other groups, it seems they all take this fantasy on voluntarily. But here the perceived evil is somehow equated with strength. My belief is that the inner badness these people feel due to their internalized bad objects makes it effortless for them to identify with what society perceives to be bad things."

"I see."

"Of course, there is also an element of adolescent rebellion present, a great pleasure taken in the shocking of one's elders."

Burke turned the recorder off and smiled. "Does the group, or the cult let's say, replace the introjected unloving parents with new objects?"

"Excellent, Mr. Burke. You must take one of my classes some time. You have studied psychology somewhere, I take it?"

The elevator *pinged* open. The two men entered the lobby. "Here and there," Burke answered. "Mostly in pursuit of my interest in comparative religion."

"To answer your question," Merriman continued, "the group certainly provides the injured member with a form of legitimatization, and the possibility of orally incorporating power and strength, but it comes at a severe price. There will be a constant need to expand the group and draw more members in to add to the legitimacy of the lifestyle, which will often then distance these people from the members they wished to be closest to."

"And the cult must seal out the real world. Paradoxically, in order to survive it must become a closed system, which ultimately kills it."

"Mr. Burke, you must really consider going for your Ph.D."

"You flatter me, Dr. Merriman."

"But should the group survive, even as a somewhat closed system, the members will also doubtless be bound to serve their inevitably sado-narcissistic leader. And as someone once noted, absolute power tends to corrupt absolutely."

"It decays from within."

They crossed the parking lot and arrived at a sleek, blue BMW. Dr. Merriman clasped Burke's hand. "This has been a stimulating conversation, Mr. Burke."

Burke refrained from pointing out that Merriman had essentially entertained himself. He remained deferential. "Thank you for your time, Professor. I will be certain to make note of the school in my acknowledgments."

Twenty

Burke stopped at a dented metal newspaper vending machine, inserted some change, and opened the *Daily News.* He searched the classifieds. Suddenly his shoulders straightened. He read the message, sighed, and dropped the newspaper into a trash can. "Perfect timing, Cary."

He walked slowly back to his own car, preoccupied by a creeping sense of dread. He paused by his vehicle, opened and dialed the cell phone.

"Hey, Gina."

"Burke, goddamn it, where the fuck are you?"

"Fine, thanks, and you?"

"This isn't funny. I have two calls from Major Ryan and four messages from Scotty Bowden. They are both going nuts looking for you. I say I don't know where you are or what you're doing."

"Keep saying that, Gina."

She sighed explosively. "I don't understand."

Burke soothed. "For your ears only, I just spent some time with Professor Merriman. He looks reasonably fit, but too old. He may still be our guy, but if he is, I'd be very surprised. He strikes me as a total egghead who is so full of his own bullshit he'd have no room to carry resentment."

"Did you tell him what you're up to?"

"He thinks I'm writing a book." Burke got into his car, started it up. "He was interesting to listen to, but I don't have the slightest idea if what he said is going to apply to this case."

"Can I ask where the hell you're going now?"

After a pause, Burke told her a version of the truth.

Twenty-One

. . . Time curves in upon itself, weaves into a Mobius strip: *Jack Burke is twenty-nine years old. He has already been recruited by the shadow agency known only as The Company, but has been reluctant to sign up. He is only one year out of active duty and not in a hurry to repeat his combat experiences . . .*

It is the blistering, smoggy heat of a Los Angeles summer.

Burke is attending classes at Northridge when he meets a raven-haired, doe-eyed, sultry exchange student named Indira Ray. Indira is a soft-spoken, stunning beauty from a small town in northern India. She is also married to an older man, a teacher. Burke is smitten. Her dusky skin inflames his senses. They are electric to one another—a modern-day Shiva and Kali . . .

The corner of Laurel Canyon and Ventura Boulevards in Studio City features a gleaming, two-story mall packed with restaurants, specialty stores and the requisite brand name California coffee shop. It also has very discreet, underground parking. Burke entered the lot from Ventura Boulevard. He ignored an open spot and drove down, deep into the concrete darkness. He parked, stepped into the stairwell, and trotted back up to the street level. He waited patiently in the doorway. Soon a large, laughing group of civilians passed by headed for the intersection. Burke eased into the group, head down. He used them as cover when the light changed and crossed the street. Moments later he walked briskly into the giant Book Star and asked for the history section.

Several rows back from the entrance, Burke paused to locate a paperback copy of the award-winning World War Two epic, *The Longest Day,* by Cornelius Ryan. He dropped to one knee and thumbed through it as if seeing it for the first time.

"I think *D-Day* by Stephen Ambrose is better."

Burke looked up. "Wasn't he the one accused of plagiarism?"

"He apologized for that before he died, and besides, it's still the best book on that subject."

The speaker was a cheerful looking, bearded Santa of a man, with sparkling eyes and ruddy cheeks. He was carrying a trade paperback copy of *Patton* by Ladislas Farago. Burke despised all this silly spy stuff, but it always made sense to be suspicious of new players. Besides, the man was certainly not as out of shape as he appeared, and his baggy gray LOYOLA sweatshirt left plenty of room for a weapon. He wore loose sweatpants and filthy tennis shoes with the laces untied.

"You're a history buff, too, I take it?"

"Just mid twentieth century." The man had a rich, deep voice and a vaguely familiar accent, like some news anchor originally from the Midwest. "I like from the late thirties and the rise of the Nazi party through the end of the war in Viet Nam."

"That's odd. Me, too."

"Great minds think alike."

Burke got up, extended his hand. "I'm Kevin Kramer."

"David Garrett," the man replied. They both smiled pleasantly at the smooth lies. "Listen, my wife and I were about to get some fresh coffee. Would you like to join us?"

"Wife?" Burke had read the classified ad carefully. The code in it called for a meeting in this section of the bookstore, but said nothing about a second player. The sloppiness made his stomach flutter with alarm.

"Cora?"

A woman who was thumbing through something at the

magazine rack turned to face them. She seemed aloof and scholarly, was dressed in a plain brown business outfit. Her short hair was brown, flecked with gray. The woman had the slightly owlish look of someone unused to contact lenses, so Burke doubted her eyes were actually green.

"Yes, Dave?"

"This young man is a war buff. Would you mind terribly if he joins us for a cup of coffee?"

The woman sighed a bit and checked her watch, a note-perfect impression of a bored housewife. "We need to get home soon, honey." But she had already replaced the magazine, turned away from the rack, and started their way before completing the sentence. She hugged a sizeable purse close to her blouse, hands skillfully covering the contents. No one who bumped into her, on purpose or by accident, would be allowed to feel the weapon inside.

Moments later the three were seated in the back of one of the Valley's ubiquitous coffee shops, heads close together. The war books were in the middle of the table, opened to black-and-white photographs of twisted tanks and shattered bodies.

Burke made the first move. "They didn't say anything about there being two of you."

The man who called himself Dave shrugged. "So somebody fucked up. What else is new?"

"Relax," the woman whispered. She had a large, fake smile plastered on her face, a mild expression totally at odds with her tone. "We're just passing a message from Major Ryan. He wants to see you."

"Tell him I haven't changed my mind," Burke responded. "I'm out, at least for the time being. I've got enough on my plate."

Dave laughed and leaned back. He patted his belly as if joking about food. Cora stayed close in and her frozen smile wavered. "You're not hearing us, Burke. We're not offering you options. We're relaying a direct order. Ryan wants you to come in for a sit-down."

Burke sat quietly, thinking. *I don't know why Cary gets off on this.* He shifted his chair around so that his back was to the room. He pinned the woman with his eyes and smiled. His vibe was decidedly unfriendly. She tried valiantly to hold his gaze, but faltered and looked away.

"Did they tell you about me?"

She swallowed, nodded slightly. Burke heard a snort from his right. Santa Dave was getting his macho up. "Listen, asshole, they told us but we're not impressed, okay?"

Burke grinned again, but now his eyes were steady, cold as frozen marbles. "You should be," he whispered. "I have a silenced Firestar nine pointed at your girlfriend's pussy right now, and if she goes facedown on the table it will look like a seizure. I'll be out the door screaming for a doctor before anyone can identify me."

Dave leaned closer, hand now sliding under his sweatshirt. "Oh, and you figure I'm just going to sit here and let you do that?"

In a flash, Burke snaked his hand onto the man's sweatpants. He grabbed at the genitals and twisted. A quick glance showed the first shock of agony and then a complete loss of blood to the face. Burke turned the testicles again, just enough to keep Dave paralyzed, in pain, and filled with dread.

"Dave, if I wanted you dead it would already be over." His face was still pleasant and hadn't broken a sweat. Dave's features were streaming perspiration. Cora was pale except for two little pink dots on her cheeks.

The waitress chose that precise moment to call out cheerfully, "You folks having fun over there?"

"Say you're having fun."

Cora waved back. “A ball, thanks.”

Burke released Dave, who moaned with relief. “Now that we have established that I have the biggest dick, let’s get down to business. Why does Ryan need to see me?”

“Need to know basis,” Dave grunted, then added, “asshole.”

Burke ignored the epithet, though he admired the effort. He shook his head. “He knows me, Dave. He knows I’d ask. So he gave you something to say if everything else failed. Cut to the chase and tell me what’s up.”

Cora was not doing a very good job of covering her anxiety. She needed to bring the meeting to a swift conclusion. “He said to tell you this one is live ammo. He said you would know what that meant.”

Live ammo. Burke drank coffee to buy time. “Where?”

Cora swallowed. “All I have to do is page him. He said he will be waiting back at your car, in the underground garage. We made certain you weren’t followed.”

“Gee, thanks.” Burke rose. “Tell him to be there.”

“Yes, sir.”

Burke looked down at Dave, who had regained his composure but was obviously seething. He experienced a small twinge of remorse. “And by the way, stud, I was lying about that silenced Firestar nine. I didn’t even bring it with me. I’m just having a bad day.”

Burke left some cash to cover their coffee. He walked out. He caught the light perfectly and crossed Laurel Canyon with a clump of other pedestrians, feeling frustrated for having such a short fuse—and for thinking that a woman he saw looked a lot like Indira Pal. Ever since her husband’s name had come up, Burke hadn’t been able to stop thinking about her. When he reached the stairwell he chastised himself for all the grandstanding. Dumb move. Dave and Cora had no idea what was actually on his mind, and he might need them to watch his back someday.

Burke entered the underground garage. A slender, middle-aged man with a precise crewcut was leaning against the side of his car, holding a thick accordion folder.

"Why do you always need to pull this silly movie shit, Cary?"

"I didn't write the manual." Major Ryan was impeccably dressed, as usual. He wore Gucci slacks, a jet-black, form-fitting knit shirt and a new pair of loafers. Ryan was tall, nearly Burke's own height, and could be one tough customer, but his delicate features and effeminate movements could make him seem like a woman in drag as a man. "Nice to see you, too, Red."

Burke automatically searched the garage. He approached, one hand sliding casually toward the small of his back. They were alone. Satisfied, he opened the passenger door. Ryan slid in and placed a CLASSIFIED folder in his lap. Burke moved around to the driver's seat and started the engine. Ryan's eyes widened when Burke backed out of the parking space. "I thought we could talk here."

"No," Burke replied. "If you want to play spook, let's stay on the move."

Ryan was silent. He'd worked with Burke often since their black ops days in Somalia, so he knew better than to argue. Burke roared up the circular driveway, handed the attendant some cash, and joined the flow of traffic headed west along Ventura. As he drove he planned his usual series of turns—up Fulton and along Riverside to Colfax and then back down—and a route that would eventually bring him back to the same shopping center.

"What is going on, Cary? I told you I was taking a break."

"It's important, Red." Ryan attempted a soothing tone. He was generally a slick customer, and a born politician. That part of his personality had always annoyed Burke, never more than now. "I can run this down for you fairly quickly. You give me a yes or a no. If you're not up for it, I'd like your input about who we should send."

"That's it?"

"That's it."

Burke arrived at Fulton and turned. "Shoot."

"As you know we have pretty nifty satellite surveillance of Mexico and South America going on at all times." Cary was clearly reciting something he'd said dozens of times before. "The system is basically designed to give us heads up on any cocaine and marijuana crops our erstwhile allies are neglecting to tell us about."

"Cary, I led a small LURP team to kill Buey for you just last year, remember?"

"You missed him by a pubic hair, but you burned an entire field of coca plants without being discovered or suffering a single casualty. That's exactly why I'm back to talk to you about this situation."

"Which is?"

Cary Ryan slid some photographs out of the manila file. He checked to make sure they were in the proper order. He waited patiently for Burke to arrive at a stoplight before handing him one.

Burke studied it. "This is from a Predator drone, right?"

"Yes, at five thousand over a piss-ant town called Los Gatos in northern Mexico. You have a sharp eye." The smarmy stuff again. "We sent the Predator two nights ago, with the permission of the Mexican government, ostensibly on a drug mission."

"This isn't about drugs?"

"We don't know yet, Red. Let me bring you up to speed, and then you can ask all the questions you want." Burke sighed and returned the photograph. "Now, look at these," Ryan continued, with a subtle tension in his tone. "We have Spectra, Gamma,

UV, and SLR. But let's look at the Gamma shot more closely."

"Hang on." Burke pulled to the curb and parked. He grabbed the photograph and examined it. Now he could see something that was not there before: a swirl of color, like the eye of a hurricane on radar. "What is that, some kind of hydrocarbon smear?"

"Nitrogen for the most part, but normal is around seventy-eight percent and this is low eighties."

"Which means?"

"Considering the fact that there are no swamps in the desert near Los Gatos, we think it may be the spoor of buried, denitrifying bacteria, starting to leak aboveground."

Burke felt yet another chill pass over him. *Who just walked on your grave?* Something was rotting, down deep in the earth. "Leaking from what?"

"Our boys agree that the most likely explanation is some kind of killing field, like in Cambodia or Bosnia."

"A mass grave." Burke thumbed through the photographs front to back and back to front. "And now you want to insert a team to check it out."

"I have decided on that option."

Burke returned the photographs and Ryan closed the file. Burke held his gaze. "What is it you're not telling me?"

Ryan's eyes fluttered, and for a moment he seemed like a nervous girl. "I don't know what you mean, Red. Why would I be keeping something back?"

"Because you're not going right to the Mexican government, so somebody is being told hands off. Who's applying pressure, and why?"

"Come on, Red. There's no pressure." Frowning, Ryan shook his head and pointed to the roof of the car. *He's wired.* So their conversation was being taped. The hands-off instructions were coming from above him, high up.

Burke nodded in understanding. “All right, Cary. I’ll take your word for it. Forget I said that. What else is going on in that area? No offense, but what has the spooks giving a shit about this, mass grave or garbage dump?”

“Like I said, Los Gatos is a one-horse town. It means nothing in and of itself, but Juan Garcia Lopez has been spotted in the area.”

“Buey again.”

“Yes. Buey owns a large hacienda at a compound in the foothills, just a few hundred feet away from where that photograph was taken.”

“So?”

“Burke, he brought down a drone last night, probably with a Russian-made SAM.”

“You’re kidding me.”

Ryan ran delicate fingers through buzz cut hair. “I shit you not.”

“That took guts, or he’s dumb as a box of hammers.”

“We had clearance from the Mexican government for a flight over in that general area, so whoever gave that order has *cojones.* He will clearly fuck with Uncle Sam, his own government, whatever.”

“Why?”

“We think he’s building some kind of fortress out there. The over-flights made him nervous.”

“Great. So any team going in there will run right into a posse of spooked druggies with AK-47s and an attitude.”

“We have a plan to distract them. The pay is one hundred thousand for a couple of days’ work, wired straight to your bank in the Netherlands Antilles. Will you do it?”

“No.” Burke started the car and headed back to the garage. “I had my shot at Buey last year. I’ll pass on this one. I’ve got too much on my plate with private clients.”

"I can't change your mind?"

"Not this time."

They rode in silence, down Ventura to the garage entrance. Ryan tapped the dash. "Let me out here. My driver is picking me up." He got out, leaned back into the vehicle. "Should I use Weston, or maybe Lukac?"

Burke was intrigued, despite himself. He pondered. "Lukac has better Spanish. You might need that if he can grab a prisoner. Off the record, I think Weston should be riding a desk. He's a year or two past burned out."

"I'll ask Steve, then. Take it easy, Red."

Ryan started to close the door. Burke leaned across the passenger seat, held it open. "Cary?"

Ryan thought Burke was about to change his mind. He looked both ways, put his head back in the vehicle. "Yeah?"

"Keep me up to speed on this one. I'm into it, although I don't exactly know why. Just not now, okay? Maybe I can help out later."

Somewhat mollified, Ryan agreed. A Lincoln Town Car rolled slowly around the corner, tires squealing on the pavement. Major Ryan's driver unlocked the electric latch. Ryan slammed the door, got into his own vehicle and drove away.

Jack Burke remained behind for a long moment, brooding. He was starting to feel like a piece on someone else's chessboard.

Twenty-Two

Hidden Hills was a ranch-style community near the far suburb of Calabasas, right on the edge of LA County proper. It covered a large, sunburned area and featured white, rail fences and Western-style estates with horse corrals and riding trails. Burke gave his name at the gate and was handed convoluted directions to the property owned by Dr. Hasari Pal.

After two false starts—streets with similar names that led to dead ends—he found a two-story house, relatively modest for the area, perched at the top of a long and curving drive. Beyond the fence, a weary old Palomino studied Burke with something like suspicion, and then shook his long head to dislodge the relentless horde of flies nesting in his mane. Burke parked the car and stepped out into the shaded driveway. He checked his watch for the tenth time and brushed imaginary lint from his clothing. The walkway was flawless brick and curved through the lawn to a heavy wooden front door with a large brass knocker. Upon closer inspection, the knocker proved to be a brilliant carving of Lord Shiva, dancing before the wheel of life. Burke was nervous but determined not to show it. He lifted Shiva's feet and rapped them against the world to announce his arrival.

The clacking sound boomed through what sounded like a largely empty foyer. After a time, small footsteps approached. The door opened with a low moan. The small, fit, elderly man who stood behind it wore a turban and traditional cotton clothing. His short, white beard was neatly trimmed and he wore round reading glasses. He peered up at Burke with a palpable sweetness.

"May I help you, sir?" His accent was charming, probably Calcutta.

"I am here to see Dr. Pal." Burke was suddenly aware of his own accent, a flat, nasal twang that seemed annoyingly bland compared to the lilting, pastel lisp of the Indian. "My name is Jack Burke."

"Ah, yes! Mr. Burke, you are very welcome. The doctor and missus are expecting you. Please." The little man backed away from the door, motioned expansively. "My name is Mr. Nandi. May I offer you some tea?"

"Tea would be nice."

"Consider it done, sir. Dr. Pal asked me to tell you he is very, very sorry but he will be running a few minutes late. He hopes that this will not pose a difficulty."

"No, I have plenty of time."

"Very good."

The small feet pattered away. The living room was immense, yet sparsely furnished. Burke noted several beautiful pieces of art, carefully placed for maximum effect. There were Buddhist items, but the majority of the artifacts came from the Hindu pantheon. He saw numerous Shivas, some of the elephant god of wisdom Ganesh, the monkey god whose name Burke had forgotten, even a few striking representations of the Goddess Kali, the dark aspect of the feminine. Many of these pieces were even more striking and expensive than those in Stryker's small collection. Burke strolled over to admire some framed art and a photograph of a massive Tibetan Buddhist sand painting. He worked his way along the walls. To a man of his interests, the assembly was captivating.

The smell of strong tea entered the room, but when Burke

turned a bit belatedly, the little man called Mr. Nandi had already vanished. He continued to look around. A small tea set was now carefully angled on an end table near the leather couch. Burke approached and spotted a large, leather-bound volume that rested on the mahogany coffee table.

He sat down, added two lumps of sugar to the strong black tea and opened the book, which had been painstakingly produced and seemed handwritten. Someone had very carefully quoted classic Hindu poetry and then translated the lines into contemporary English. There were only a few illustrations and the poetry did not seem to have been arranged in any particular order.

> "Is Kali, my Divine Mother, of a black complexion?
> She appears black because She is viewed from a distance;
> But when intimately known She is no longer so.
> The sky appears blue at a distance, but look at it close by
> And you will find that it has no color.
> The water of the ocean looks blue at a distance,
> But when you go near and take it in your hand,
> You find that it is colorless and clear."
>
> — Ramakrishna Paramhansa (1836–1886)

Burke carried the book, which was heavier than he'd expected, over to one of the representations of Kali. Seen up close, it was a clever wood carving painted over in black, silver, and red. Burke knew the black goddess to be many things to many people. Here, she was seen in her most terrible aspect, as Kali-Ma, the dark mother, a raging black woman with four arms. She had the head of a victim—some say a demon—in one bloody hand, and a sword in the other. Her two free hands were raised as if to demand the worship of her followers. Kali wore a necklace of skulls and a waistcoat made from the hands of corpses. Her enormous red tongue rolled out of her mouth like some terrible serpent; she stood on the prone body of her husband. Burke looked down at the book, turned the page.

Behold my Mother playing with Lord Shiva
Lost in an ecstasy of joy!
Drunken with a draught of celestial wine,
She reels
And yet does not fall . . .
Erect, She stands on Shiva's bosom,
And the earth trembles under Her tread
She and Her Lord are mad with lust and frenzied
Casting aside all fear and shame.

— Ramprasad (1718–1775)

"Do you know the story behind that one?" The voice came from nearby, but Burke managed to disguise his surprise.

He forced a polite smile. "Good to see you again, Dr. Pal."

Mohandas Hasari Pal, Ph.D. was a tall man, quite muscular for a practitioner of both tantra yoga and several Chinese martial arts. He had dark hair and eyes and the slightly bronze skin of a full-blooded native of India. His English was clipped, precise, and virtually free of accent. Pal did not seem to have aged a day since Burke last saw him, although he was certain to be in his fifties. He walked his obsidian eyes over Burke and then inclined his head gracefully.

"Ah, yes. Young Mr. Burke. I remember you quite well, actually."

"Should I be flattered?"

"Not necessarily, I'm afraid. You were often intellectually self-important and obnoxious."

Burke smiled. "I suppose I was."

"Ah, but at least I recall you as the kind of student who actually paid attention. That is a rare thing in a class dealing with comparative religion. You were in that class my wife audited for amusement, no?"

"Yes. And I remember her well." Burke's pulse leapt, but he willed it to slow again. "And is she well these days, Doctor?"

"Quite. Indira will be joining us shortly." Pal floated across the floor, moving closer. Like Mr. Nandi, his feet barely seemed to touch the floor. "And you may call me Mo, Mr. Burke. It is a nickname somewhat disrespectfully derived from Mohandas, but I'm afraid I have become quite used to it during my many years in this, my adopted country."

Burke was treading water. "If I remember correctly, you brought Mrs. Pal here with you when you became a citizen."

"Yes, Indira was raised in a small and rather primitive village called Meeta. Her people could not read. I married her when I was forty and she was but fourteen. I purchased her from her family. This is a practice which I recognize would be deemed scandalous in America. But she was impossibly beautiful and I was madly in love."

"When we were in your class, I think we were both in our twenties."

"Yes," Pal replied, without apparent subtext. "I suppose she is much closer to your age."

"A few years younger, actually."

Stay on guard. Pal missed very little. Burke knew that he'd grown up in the city, in Calcutta's hardscrabble slums, but attended good schools as a young man, likely due to the fire of his intellect and an obvious flair for manipulation. As a Professor, Mo Pal was an intense man both fiercely Americanized and wedded to the violent and mysterious mythology of his youth.

Pal smiled politely, pointed to the poem Burke was reading only seconds ago. His hand came closer and the skin smelled slightly of scented oil. "Legend has it that the demon known as Daruka is endangering the world. So Lord Shiva asks his wife Parvati to eliminate the threat. Parvati acquires the body of

Shiva, drinks of his essence, and becomes a creature known as Kali. And this new goddess is so horrific and ferocious in her likeness that all beings quake in alarm. Kali and her assistants, all of whom feast on human flesh, attack and defeat the demon Daruka."

Burke remembered. "But Kali has awakened her blood lust. She cannot stop the slaughter."

Dr. Pal nodded. "Indeed. Her hunger and rage, once aroused, are so potent that they threaten to destroy this entire plane of existence. She goes on a rampage and murders everyone and everything in her path."

"I've forgotten the ending, but it had something to do with a baby."

"Lord Shiva is unable to stop her with words or commands, and so he ultimately transforms himself into the shape of an infant and hides himself upon the battlefield. He cries out for sustenance and Kali, deceived by Shiva, puts down her weapons to suckle him. And that night Lord Shiva danced *tandava.*"

"The dance of creation."

"Yes. To please the goddess Kali, who became so happy she began to dance it with him. For most of her followers, though, Kali-Ma is the Great Mother. Her demonic aspects are generally hidden, but must never be completely forgotten, lest she become aroused and destroy us all."

"As we males know women can."

Pal blinked. "As we know all too well, yes. Some left-hand tantra followers in the lesser cults dress as women, not for any sexual reason but to remind themselves of the awesome power of the feminine."

Pal took Burke by the sleeve and walked him to another work, a painting clearly hundreds of years old. Here Kali was depicted at rest, less enraged. She was still quite formidable. "But you see there is much more to the story, because Kali offers freedom, Mr. Burke. If we come to her as a child comes to his mother, she teaches us the true nature of reality."

"And the temporal nature of the self, taking us all back to the curse of our ego."

Pal touched the painting lightly with perfectly manicured fingers. "Yes. If man lives his life unwilling to become accepting of pain and death, he automatically dooms himself to further suffering. If his ego tells him he will not die then die he must."

"And so we all must die."

"One does not have to become a transvestite to know that Kali teaches the great doctrine of non-attachment by both the grossest and clearest of means. She uses death to teach us a gentle and profound acceptance of life the only way it may truly be possessed . . . and that is in the given moment."

Burke walked to another statue, made of dark brown clay. "This one is Aztec, right?"

"Yes. She is Tonantzin, 'our mother.' The Aztec version of Kali, you might say. Notice that she wears a skirt of live serpents? Coatlicue literally means 'serpent skirt.' She is once again the feminine principle as both creator and destroyer of men and gods alike."

"Didn't she have a couple of other names? Something about childbirth, maybe Toci for grandmother?"

"Oh, yes, you were a fine student, Mr. Burke." Pal grinned broadly. "But one would suspect perhaps a young male college student would remember her other visage more enthusiastically. She was also called Tlazolteotl." He waited, curious to see if Burke could make the connection on his own. He couldn't.

"Goddess of impurity, Mr. Burke," Pal chuckled at his own joke, "and thus, every hormone-addled young man's dream."

The two men locked eyes, stared for a fraction too long; a strange tension appeared to hang like a mist in the air.

"I've always been drawn more to Buddhism than Hinduism,"

Burke said, breaking an awkward silence. His own deep voice sounded far away. "Zen in particular. But I suspect that we Americans seldom have the patience to study long and complex mythologies."

"Kali-Ma is not a myth, Mr. Burke. Any more than Tonantzin is surreal."

"Enlighten me."

Pal turned. "She is not mythological in the strictest interpretation of that word. She is more psychological. Think of her in Jungian terms and you will follow me. She is a way of viewing the darkest side of the feminine, the Johari Window aspect of women that is neither loving nor nurturing but destructive and wild. Something they are rarely able to see within themselves."

"I understand."

"Yes," Pal exclaimed happily. He patted Burke on the sleeve. "Yes, I believe you do! Now let us sit down." On the couch, sipping tea from the second cup: "If memory serves, you wanted to ask me some questions about my relationship with Peter Stryker."

"You heard the news?"

"Just that he had committed suicide in a rather unpleasant way. It all sounds so very tragic." He did not ask further, merely waited.

"What did you two talk about?"

Pal set the cup down on the table. He yawned and stretched like a sleek panther. His face was remarkably free of lines for a man his age. "Let's see, now. Kali-Ma, certainly, but if memory serves, Mr. Stryker was mostly interested in the Thugee sect."

"The robbers who practiced mass murder."

"Yes. They have been much abused by Hollywood over the years. Karma, no?"

"What did Stryker want to know?"

"How it originated. The truth is, of course, that no one knows for sure. I gave him a copy of *Confessions of a Thug* by Meadows-Taylor. We discussed the Mahomedans and how they plundered India both before and after the Tartars and Mongols arrived. Some believe the Thugee began there, but the Hindu used to hold that the sect had a divine origin and was thus derived from the goddess Bhowanee. In any event, the group ran wild in India until the British attempted to suppress them, and even the Empire made little headway in perhaps the 1830s."

"So perhaps Stryker was researching a book on the Thugee? Did he tell you anything at all about the project?"

"I never asked." Pal wrinkled his nose. "It was another one of those ridiculous potboilers of his, no doubt. I think he might have said it was for a silly novel about a new sect springing up to assassinate politicians in Washington, something like that."

"Did he ask you about anything else?"

"We talked a bit about Kali-Ma because of the Thugee," Pal replied. He seemed to be searching his memory bank. "Oh, and about the Aghora and the left-hand path of Tantra. In case you've forgotten, the Aghora seek enlightenment by reveling in the distasteful, shall we say. They carry the left-hand path to implausible lengths."

"I remember, now. The emphasis is on the acceptance of everything, regardless of how dark or hideous it might at first appear."

"Yes. They might eat excrement or sit on a dead body, for example, as a way of eradicating every conceivable trace of disgust. Or even eat the flesh of the dead. By embracing the awful, one breaks down dualism, you see. And begins to experience the world as it really *is,* a thing of 'terrible beauty' rather than allowing it to continue to be perceived as merely terrible *or* beautiful."

"I recall it sounded pretty extreme."

"Oh, to a Westerner it most assuredly would," Pal replied.

"And yet there are smaller splinter groups deemed even more extreme than the Agouri."

"A group with practices more extreme than eating shit or the flesh of a corpse?"

"Well, let us take the Shahr-e-Khamosh, by way of example. The shamshan it uses and the group it describes are known as 'The City of Silence' because the term means cemetery and also that the spiritual work is to become virtually dead while still alive."

"To die to more than just desire." Burke steepled his fingers. "Or, to pursue the One in that manner as well, in other words?"

"Yes. And to connect with the spirits of the deceased. To a devotee of Shahr-e-Khamosh there are many spirits, Mr. Burke. As all seers, they see the Preta, who have died without proper services, Dakinis, who died in childbirth, the Bhuta who clings to physical life and refuses to let go. And these spirits instruct them about how to live better lives. Thus, as I said, the way of Shahr-e-Khamosh is to die while still alive, or to live while openly communing with the dead. Simply fascinating superstition, no?"

"It's all a bit too far-fetched for my taste." Burke didn't want to think about the little man who haunted his dreams. He spotted a waist-high, lovingly crafted statue to his left. "That's Egyptian, isn't it? Ammut or Ammit?"

"Or Ammenmet. She was an Egyptian demoness."

The figure had a crocodile's head with the torso of a leopard and the buttocks of a Hippo; Burke remembered that all three of those creatures were fierce and terrifying to the Egyptians because all were eaters of men. That awakened his interest again. Burke squinted, read aloud, "*Hat em emsuh; pehu-s em tebt her-ab-set em ma,* is that correct?"

"Close. It is a description of the creature. As you may recall, in *The Book of the Dead* Ammut sits near the scales of Ma'at.

When any dead person's heart weighs incorrectly, is found unworthy, she is there to devour and excrete their immortal souls. She was also known as the 'devourer of Amenta.' "

"The underworld."

"Yes, and also the west bank of the river Nile. To the Egyptians, west was always a direction linked with death. One papyrus contains a speech made to Thoth regarding the soul of the scribe Ani. It says something like 'His word is true, is holy and righteous. He has not committed any sin and has done no evil against us. The devourer Ammut must not be permitted to prevail and eat him' or words to that effect. The exact wording escapes me."

"Fascinating."

"Sadly, I am getting older, Mr. Burke, and my memory is not what it used to be."

"Your memory is remarkable."

"Are you boring Mr. Burke, Mo?"

The voice was sultry, flowed like warm honey; the accent was irresistible. Burke felt the hair rise on his arms and his stomach jangle like a bucket of ice cubes. Pal jumped to his feet. Burke struggled to remain composed. He rose more slowly, and when he could no longer politely delay, turned to look at her.

Indira Pal had also changed little. Her raven hair was swept back and to the right, where it dropped down to coil around her shoulders like a serpent. The luscious hair framed a face as seductive and exotic as her name. Indira had wide brown eyes with arched black brows, plush red lips, and a slender nose. She was dressed elegantly in a beige strapless evening gown that hugged her lithe frame. Carefully placed gold jewelry caught the waning light and glowed with mystic fire.

Jack Burke swallowed and thought that nothing on earth had ever frightened him as much as the presence of this one woman.

"Red, it's good to see you again."

Burke found himself close to her, inhaling her jasmine scent and touching her hand before he was aware his body had crossed the room. His own voice sounded alien to him, both reedy and unstable. "Mrs. Pal, how nice to see you again."

"Yes," she replied, meaninglessly. She slipped her hand away quickly, gracefully; the gesture was specific, the insult intentional. She joined her husband, gave him a kiss on the cheek. "Mo, I think we need to be going."

"Of course. And go we shall. Mr. Burke, perhaps we can meet again another time? Or if you have any further questions for me, you can e-mail them care of the university."

Burke held his ground. "Just one more moment, please. May I ask how well you knew Peter Stryker, Indira? Were the three of you friends?"

Indira tilted her head and her eyes were lava. "I am not sure I ever met the man. Did we meet, Mo? Perhaps at one of those awful office Christmas parties?"

"Perhaps," Pal replied, as if to soothe her growing irritation. "But if you did it was very briefly, dear. No reason you should remember."

Indira shrugged. "I guess that answers your question."

"I guess it does."

"So nice to see you again." Icicles dangled from the words. "You'll excuse us now, please."

Burke stepped back as if slapped. "Yes, I guess I should be on my way."

The man called Mr. Nandi appeared at Burke's side and gently took his left elbow. Burke was getting the bum's rush. He allowed himself to be led to the door by the much smaller man. He called back over his shoulder. "Thank you for your time, Dr. Pal."

"Oh, my pleasure."

Good, Burke thought, his attitude sour. *Because it certainly wasn't mine.*

Twenty-Three

Friday

"This sucks." Detective Scotty Bowden doesn't want to work. He would rather grab some breakfast. He is pissed off and more than a little drunk. Also, Bowden doesn't like skid row, the stench of urine, vomit and that nagging vibe of hopelessness. Bowden is ending an all-nighter and has already packed away two shots of Wild Turkey dropped into mugs of cold, draught beer. He slides down Broadway, parks and exits onto the sidewalk. He pauses at the mouth of the alley to use a little breath spray.

Dawn is peeking over the towering office buildings with a baleful eye. A handful of driven executives are already turning into underground parking garages and rushing out of the doughnut shop, breath and hot coffee steaming in the frigid morning air. The sun will be up soon, but the full moon still hangs in the gray sky like a pocked piece of slate. Most of the bums are already stalking the pavement for handouts. They look like an army of the undead. Since Bowden was drinking when he heard the radio traffic, he is way late to the party.

A cherub-faced, stocky uniform is holding a couple of curious vagrants at bay. Bowden recognizes the kid. His rabbi in the department has been grooming him for Robbery/Homicide.

"What's up, Kasper?"

Patrolman Jon Kasper looks exhausted and a bit green. He speaks with a faint Boston accent. "SID was already here, sir.

They dusted and photographed everything. The ME wagon is getting ready to load him up. I told them to hang on until you got a chance to look things over."

"Thanks. I got tied up with something else. You okay?"

Kasper blushes, pink on pale lime. "Actually, I nearly lost my doughnuts, sir. I thought I'd seen a few things in South Central, but this one is pretty bad."

Bowden is distracted by Sergeant Bob Tanner. "Scotty? About fucking time!" Tanner is a loathsome toad of a man, given to copping free blow jobs from the hookers near Selma and Hollywood in exchange for leniency. He is seldom caught without a cell phone at his ear and a wet cigar butt clenched between yellowing teeth.

Bowden approaches the crime scene. He is surprised by a rapidly festering sense of anxiety. There seems to be something hanging like bug spray in the morning air, something intangible but ominous. He shakes the feeling away. Bowden stamps his feet against the cold and winks. "Morning, Bob. Is some asshole actually making you do a little work for a change?"

Tanner spits a foul stream of brown juice into a nearby pile of trash. "Fuck you and the horse you rode in on, Bowden."

"So what happened here?"

"Some homeless dude got his ticket punched, probably over a bottle of screw-top Thunderbird. What do you care? This ain't your regular turf."

Bowden shrugs. He is not above a little gossip, but he's also not about to trust a motormouth like Tanner. "I've caught a couple of missing-persons cases around here lately, and I just pulled an all-nighter in the area. When I caught a piece of this over the radio, figured I'd come over and have a look." Then, as casually as possible: "So how did the guy check out?"

"The assistant ME says somebody strangled the dude, probably with a piece of rope or something. So far, it looks like no big deal. You get used to that. Shit, these ass-wipes will off each other over a pack of cigarettes or a porn rag. But catch this part. Our boy takes a knife to the vic, right? And I mean does him good. He tugs down his pants and cuts him up like a side of beef."

"Before, or after?"

"ME says probably after, from the splatters and preliminary tissue samples. Which makes it, like, why the fuck bother doing it?"

"Rage."

"More than that." Tanner chews the foul cigar butt, a whimsical smile tugging at his upper lip. He is enjoying this.

Bowden lets him have the moment, waits for the secret to build pressure. If Tanner knows more than he's letting on, he is bound to let it slip eventually. Bowden raises his left eyebrow high enough to indicate a question mark.

"Okay, you didn't get this from me but it looks like the perp carted away a few chunks of his leg." Tanner says this in a low, amused voice. "Now hear this, though. The ME found a couple of good-sized baggies lying in the fucking mud!"

"Like refrigerator baggies?"

"The very same. So this may be some crazy Hannibal the cannibal shit. Nucking futs, huh?"

"Yeah."

"Have a good double shift, Scotty," Tanner says. "I'm out of here."

Bowden pats Tanner on the shoulder and crosses in front of him. His eyes are on the far end of the alley, where the yellow tape has sealed off the area and the corpse lays waiting in a partially zipped black body bag. The ME wagon guys are standing, smoking, careful to catch the ashes in their hands. They are a Mutt and Jeff duo, one tall and acne-ridden and the other short and chubby. Bowden squints, but he does not recognize either man.

"Let me take a look."

Mutt squats down, opens the bag the rest of the way. The man inside is naked, his body surprisingly hairy and quite simian. His face is twisted in a death grimace and his face darkened and mottled. The veins in his eyes are occluded with spider-webbed blood. His neck bears the indentation of something hard, yet flexible, like a bungee cord. Bowden wrinkles his nose at the stench. He looks around the area and notes a small picnic blanket, a candle, some fast-food sacks, and a large, empty wine bottle.

"What kind is it?"

The short ME cocks his head, bewildered.

"The wine," Bowden says patiently. "Can you tell what kind it is?"

"Sutter Home, sir. White zinfandel, I think."

Strange choice for an old man with no money. That means the perp probably sprang for the wine, even offered some kind of low-rent night on the town. Bowden motions with his hand and Mutt unzips the body bag the rest of the way. The stench is palpable, the sight grotesque. The body has been butchered below the waist, chunks of flesh removed, probably by something extraordinarily sharp, possibly medical in nature. Bowden swallows and leans back. This is no ordinary killing. The sight brings back buried memories of combat, and is surprisingly disturbing—especially to a man who used to collect human ears. Bowden nods and Mutt begins to zip the bag up for removal to the coroner's office.

"You know something?"

Bowden knows what is coming. His bad reaction to the carnage was obvious. He plays along anyway. "What?"

"I think I'm hungry," Jeff says, smirking. "How about a nice, juicy rare steak over at the Sizzler?"

Mutt snickers. They both watch Bowden closely, but he just grins. "I think steak tartar would be better, maybe with some fava beans and a nice Chianti."

The meat wagon boys roar their approval. Bowden gets to his feet, dusts off his knees, and starts back up the alley. The air feels heavy with the possibility of rain. A frigid breeze, lightly scented with ozone and mold, twirls down the alley. It moves a small pile of litter with a sound like fingernails scratching the concrete. Three yards away, Bowden pauses, turns. "By the way, who found the body?"

"I did."

The voice comes from the shadows behind him. Bowden whirls, one hand grabbing for the 9mm Glock at his waist. His heart kicks jackrabbit fast and his mouth sours with fear. "Who's there?"

A tall, gaunt black man in filthy clothes emerges from a triangular section of bricked wall. His scalp excretes long, matted dreadlocks and his sallow face sags like heated clay. Only the eyes seem alive. His flesh is covered with burn scars, pink blossoms on black enamel. "You ain't never gonna catch him, you."

"And why is that?"

" 'Cause I tink you all fools," the man says. Bowden struggles with the accent, but then places it as Cajun. The dude is from Louisiana bayou country, or a damned good actor.

The black man points at the corpse down the alley. "This man got a curse on him, else nobody do him this way, butcher him up like a fucking cow."

"What's your name, sir?"

"I done give my name to the fat one with the cigar already. You don't talk to your friends, cop?" Bowden considers a knee to the balls, but the man—as if reading his mind—holds up one hand, palm out. "Peace, mon. My name be Jean-Pierre Ladice, but in the life dey call me JP."

Bowden takes his foot off the gas, forces one plastic Jesus of a smile. "So the man with the cigar got your full statement, name and address?"

JP coughs a sandpaper laugh. "Dis was my address, mon. Not after what I found. I tink maybe the shelter, or I go home again."

"You don't go anywhere without our permission," Bowden scolds. "We might need to talk to you again."

JP offers wide-eyed innocence. "I'm staying right here, me. I'm a good citizen, officer. Cross my black heart." When he laughs again his breath carries gum disease and tooth decay.

Bowden wants to leave. But a hearty breakfast is no longer an option. Maybe another drink. Behind him he hears the meat wagon start its engine. "You see anything, hear anything?"

"Not a ting, boss."

"What was the victim's name, JP?"

"Called hisself Bruno, sir. Never heard another name."

"How well did you know Bruno?"

The tall black man shrugs. He steps back, leans against the wall. Bowden unconsciously imitates him directly across the alley. They allow the ME boys to drive by slowly, tailpipe farting smoke. The driver is listening to some classic rock on the radio. Bowden shivers, tucks his hands into the pockets of his jacket.

"I told dem fools this already," JP says. "Only ting I can say may be good for you is the man I seen wit him."

Bowden feels his heart twist. "What man? Describe him."

"He not a man. He a demon."

"JP, don't fuck with me. Describe him."

"Dis man not small not big, but very strong wit tattoos all over. Wear navy clothes, you know? All blue, cap down over de eyes. That's it, all I saw."

"What kind of tattoos?"

"Never got close. Blue, maybe black. All over his arms."

"And he was with the vic, Bruno?"

"Last night, buy him wine. They laughing, talking. Seen him around before, but never up close."

"Did they ask you to help us by sitting down with an artist, maybe about making a sketch at the station?"

JP shrugs, shakes his head. "That all I know, big mon. Never saw his face, never got close to him. Can't help you more than that wit how he looks."

Bowden sighs. "Be easy for us to find, okay?"

"Okay." The tall man melts back into the eerie shadows. "Bruno, he say one ting, though. While he dying in the dirt, he say 'the end begins.' "

"The end begins?"

"I hear him clear, mon. He say 'the end begins."

Bowden shivers again, thinks *I better not be coming down with something.* Says: "JP?"

"Yeah, boss?"

"If you never saw the man up close, never got next to him, how come you said he was some kind of demon?"

"Tings in my world you don't see in yours, mon," JP said. His voice echoes strangely in the dark, damply bricked corner.

Bowden backs a little closer to the light at the mouth of the alley, where the LA sun is now rising, the day turning toasty warm. JP's voice follows him like a wraith. "Dis man feel evil. You tink I'm crazy, maybe, that's okay. Truth is I didn't want to get no closer to him. He feel like a big spider in clothes, mon. And who else but a demon do something like dat to a fellow man, you? I ask you that."

Bowden continues to back away and does not stop until he feels the heat of sunshine on the back of his neck.

"Policeman?"

Bowden turns. The bum called JP is now invisible in the shadows. Bowden imagines he's the Cheshire cat, nothing but large, white teeth.

"You take good care of dat little girl you got, eh?"

Bowden sputters. "H-h-how did you . . . ? Hey! Come back here!"

But JP has dissolved into the chuckling black.

"Who the fuck are you?"

No answer. In fact, no one is there. Bowden shivers and hugs himself again. When he turns, he sees a few street people watching and whispering among themselves. He wonders if he looks ill. His face is streaming with perspiration and the color has left his cheeks. Bowden has never been a man inclined to give in to fear, but this morning his nerves are shot. Head down, hands in his pockets, he walks back to his car, slams the door. He drives away, mind a whirling dervish, and only when he is on the already crowded freeway does he speed-dial his cell phone.

"It's happened again," he says tersely. And after a long moment, "Yeah, but this time he left something behind."

Twenty-Four

Across town, Burke sat on the floor of his home office, trying to stay busy and literally up to his ears in research papers, cassette tapes, and books taken from Peter Stryker's residence. He had opened volumes on mass murderers, serial killers, and sexual psychopaths of all stripes, shapes, and colors. He slammed a cassette into his portable system and leaned back to listen to the voice of Peter Stryker, horror author extraordinaire.

Some hissing and fumbling, then a man's baritone voice: "Why would Carter hang around town, knowing what he knows? Maybe give him a woman he wants to fuck, or some motivation for revenge against the mayor. Maybe make it both. Check, make sure last couple of novels not too close to that in subplot." The voice was stiff, self-conscious and somehow grating all at the same time. It droned on with reminders, ideas, commentary, self-criticism, changes. Most of what Burke heard was boring, repetitive, and occasionally brazenly self-congratulatory. He had no idea what he was listening for; he was just hoping to find something. The labels on the tapes indicated that they contained notes on the novel Stryker was working on when he died. A click from the tape. "Great idea. See if their brains were ever dissected for abnormalities," Stryker drones. "Specifically those creatures covered by Schechter. Might be interesting to theorize an enzyme irregularity related to serotonin, dopamine, and thus perhaps tie to the murderous rages and grandiose religiosity of the paranoid schizophrenic.

One should carefully scrutinize the compounds in methamphetamine and lysergic acid and PCP particularly as it relates to auditory hallucinations followed by fully homicidal ideation and action. Find a book on 'Son of Sam' for reference."

Burke couldn't recall the subject matter, an unusual event. He stopped the recorder and thumbed through his own notes, many of which had been written on yellow notepaper in a slanted scrawl. He found no mention of religious delusions in any other section, yet this was a specific and highly detailed reference. Stryker's interest in the collection of artifacts predated his work on this particular book, but Burke could not help but wonder if there was a connection. He wrote, *Grandiosity, paranoid rages, religiosity in serial killers?*

He knuckled his eyes and stacked the reference material. He had already written down the specific pages which were marked with Post-it notes, and the passages outlined. Some of the books related to one another. Harold Schechter's works *Deviant, Depraved,* and *Deranged* were each about different serial killers. Ed Gein, who served as the inspiration for the movie *Psycho,* made lampshades and masks from human skin and gutted and butchered several women like deer. Gein was a mild farmer driven mad by his overbearing and demanding mother. He died in a mental institution. H. H. Holmes, America's first serial killer, created a house the press dubbed "the castle of horror" because of its horrific hidden rooms, trapdoors, greased body chutes, and dissecting table and instruments of torture and disposal. He died on the gallows in 1896, and although his neck broke immediately it is said it took him nearly fifteen minutes, kicking and twitching, to fully expire. As Professor Pal would have said, "Karma, no?"

Seeing the reference to a "castle of horror" which contained secret rooms and hidden trapdoors, Burke made another note. It interested him that Stryker's house had some hidden panels and rooms, so he scribbled *Perhaps we should go back and look for more evidence?*

He sped through *Deranged.* An elderly man named Albert Fish kidnapped and butchered perhaps fifteen young children in the 1920s and 1930s. What he did to their flesh bordered on unspeakable. Fish was so sadomasochistic that he'd inserted needles into his own anus; they were finally discovered during a routine x-ray exam. He ate human feces and drank urine. "None of us are saints," Fish explained, rather blandly. "I am not insane, I am just queer." He died in the electric chair at Sing Sing in 1936.

Burke read several of the books, ignoring things that seemed irrelevant to the notes Stryker was working with, notes that seemed to suggest a book on ritual murder and/or serial killing, possibly with religious overtones. The "organized" serial murderer generally killed at random. He was meticulous in both design and execution, very into the use of handcuffs, restraints, and the enjoyment of the terror and humiliation experienced by his victim. Death brought an end to the experience, and he promptly lost interest in his subject. He was a psychopath who left few clues, and watched his pursuit with amusement. By contrast, the "disorganized" type, typified by Gein and Jeffrey Dahmer, was psychotic at the core. His fantasies involved acts performed with the dead body. This is how he exerted his need for domination. The disorganized type would have sex with the body, disfigure or dismember it for no logical reason, and generally knew his victims. Dahmer devoured human flesh.

Burke read and studied all day long. The window was darkening when he finally finished. He vaguely remembered stopping to use the bathroom or make fresh coffee, but other than that the day had been a blur of pages and nightmarish black-and-white photographs. He did some slow stretching, collected some of the mess into one large pile. He remembered that he had turned off the telephone, saw that his answering machine was blinking. His heart pounded a bit. Burke settled himself, touched the machine. He studied the red light as if it could tell his future. He rewound the tape.

Beep. "Red, this is Doc. I have a couple of things I need to go over with you. Get back to me as soon as you can, okay?" *Beep.* "Burke? It's Scotty Bowden, man. Just checking in, figured we could grab a beer. Hey, you ready for a new side job yet? I might have something. Let me know if you have wrapped that silly-ass Stryker thing. Okay. Later."

Beep. "It's me asshole, that little dyke who is supposed to be your trusted partner. Call me." *Beep.* A voice captured by his tape recorder in mid-sentence, "And if you come and see this beautiful resort you will automatically be eligible for a three-day weekend getaway in Palm Desert, just for showing up. Remember, that number is 800—" Burke fast-forwarded. "Mr. Burke? It's Nicole. Stryker. I would like to talk a little, okay? Call me." She sounded a little flirty, and an awful lot drunk. Burke felt a responsive twitch in his loins, but mentally slapped his own wrist. *Not with a client.*

Beep. "Hello?"

Somehow he'd known this call would come, even prayed it would. Burke's legs deserted him and he sat down heavily. He closed his eyes. "I'm sorry if that hurt you," the voice said quietly, tearfully, gently. "You can call me around dark tonight. I should be alone by then. We should meet."

Twenty-Five

An hour later, Jack Burke—showered, clean shaven, and dressed in reasonably clean clothes—was seated at La Pergola. He sampled ice water, hummed tunelessly and fidgeted while staring out at the last of the rush-hour traffic on Ventura. Each pedestrian was her for a split second, statuesque, exotic, and refined, but then morphing into someone disappointingly normal. Then the side door opened. Burke felt a primal quickening, caught the brisk scent of her perfume. She ran her fingers along the nape of his neck, sat down across the table. His throat seized, eyes softened.

"I am so sorry," Indira Pal whispered. She stroked his palm. "I was so hurtful and rude. I prayed you would understand why."

"You told him."

Her dark eyes closed. She released his hand. "I never meant to tell him, I swore I would take the secret to my grave, but somehow he already knew."

"How?" Burke heard his voice continuing the conversation, but watched as if from high up in one corner of the room. He saw the weathered, still somewhat youngish man in the corner of the patio area, seated by a gargantuan clay flowerpot filled with roses—a big man, with short, reddish hair, scarred knuckles, and the broken eyes of a combat soldier. But more importantly he viewed the striking woman seated across, her black eyes moist with tears that shimmered in the candlelight.

Indira was beyond beautiful. Her clothing was not spectacular—she wore a purple pants suit of vaguely oriental origin, efficient black shoes, and minimal jewelry—but her body thrilled. She was trim, muscular, feline as a coiled jaguar. Her beauty seemed timeless, her facial features nearly flawless; Indira Pal was the sort of woman who could start a war—or drive a man to murder.

"Jack?"

He'd been lost somewhere, in another time and place. His face betrayed his confusion, his hands were trembling. "I'm sorry. What were you saying?"

"I was telling you that Mohandas came to me one night, full of wine, and crying like a child. He told me that he had hired someone to follow me, even take pictures of us, and that he knew about you, even from years ago. He actually . . . begged my forgiveness."

"For what?"

"For intruding on my privacy. Somehow that broke my heart."

Burke did not, could not answer. He lowered his eyes to the sugar bowl and studied several packets of sweetener known to cause cancer in laboratory rats. The blond, buff waiter, unquestionably one of LA's ubiquitous would-be actors, brought ice water and recited the daily specials like a man who'd practiced in front of a mirror. They both ordered dinner salads. Indira asked for a glass of white wine. The waiter moved away, but just then an older couple and their grown children move noisily past the table. More precious moments were lost. Finally, Indira continued, sotto voce. "He has forgiven me, or so he says. But there are times he doubts me. A woman knows these things. And so I needed to show him it was over, dead, gone. I wanted him to see that I hold only contempt for you now in my heart."

Burke looked up. "Do you?"

"Of course not," Indira whispered. "Red, what's wrong?" Her pretty face was clearly tormented, clenched with worry.

Burke felt a white-hot bolt of jealousy course through his gut like electrical current. He wanted to hit her, shame her, find a way to make her share his pain and loss. The rage was abrupt, thoughtless, and nearly overwhelmed him. He swallowed water. The rattling of the ice cubes seemed abnormally loud. "I think you know."

"And your wife?"

He shrugged, but his face pinched. His eyes gave him away. "I don't want to talk about that."

"Maybe we should."

"Not now," he snapped.

The intensity startled her. Indira flinched slightly. Her knees rocked the small table just as the waiter brought the glass of white wine. Some of it spilled on the glass surface, but when he began to fuss she waved him away. For a few moments, they both listened to the syrupy, melodramatic Italian pop music coming from the nearby bar.

Burke's chest muscles trembled rapidly, like the feathers of a captured bird. Indira looked frail to him now, like a little girl caught stealing cookies from a bakery. He was ashamed of his anger but could not find a way to explain something he did not yet understand. "Do you ever think about death?"

Her eyes widened. Indira created an uncomfortable smirk, as if he had told a rude joke. "Not a very romantic subject."

"I'm serious." He was, and also listening for her response with an uncharacteristic sense of urgency. "Do you?"

"Yes," Indira replied. Her features went softer, sadder. "Of course I do."

"Because I have been thinking about it a lot for some reason. And about what Victor Hugo called 'the pressure of darkness.' Maybe I'm just getting older, but suddenly I really want to know what the hell all of this is really about."

"What is the meaning of life?" She was leaning forward now, subtle irony in her voice. "Lately, I wonder about that, too."

She listened. He had missed that quality in a woman. "See, that's the issue, isn't it? What meaning we manage to give our own lives. There is that famous line Jean-Paul Sartre wrote, the one that says that 'man is condemned to be free.' Because no matter what else he does, he must always choose his life and either give it meaning, or surrender to ennui. We have these givens of existence to contend with, making sense of it, freedom, isolation, and death anxiety. Those things inform our spirits and affect every single thing we say, think, or do. In fact, the existence of death infuses life with meaning."

"Death is life."

"Something like that. I think it haunts everyone, in one way or another."

"Everyone?"

"Scotty, Doc, and I were on a mission once," Burke said, changing directions. His voice became scratchy. "This was a lifetime ago. I saw a man who had found some kind of meaning in debauchery, torture, and slaughter."

"What happened?"

"I shot him as he sat on a pile of dead people. Somehow that moment terrified me. It stays with me. I even dream about that bastard. Because what's even worse than what he did is that he seemed so . . . happy."

"And you," Indira said, a bit too quickly, "have you found meaning?" His story had clearly unnerved her.

"Meaning? Not yet." Deflated, he sat back and his eyes changed lenses; Burke relived intimate history, summarized it for someone he loved. "I have looked for it in books, in religion, even in being a soldier. I think I looked for it in you."

He startled Indira; someone younger, more skittish and frail, peeked out before closing the curtains. "And I thought I'd found it in us, too. But it does not work that way, does it?"

"No, it doesn't. Because when it is all done we are alone with whatever we have created. Life just is, begins and ends. We are born alone, die alone, and we answer to God, if there is one, alone."

"Red?"

"What?"

"Perhaps you should try your hand at writing romance novels." Her smile was impish. She crossed her eyes, and he responded. Just like old times; she had dragged him back into the light.

Burke laughed a deep, true, rich laugh; the first he could remember in a long, long while. "I really turned you on with that line, huh?"

Fluttering eyes, a smirk. "Oh, yes."

"My fecal alchemy again." He'd once told her he thought he had the ability "to turn anything to shit." One of them had dubbed it fecal alchemy, and the joke had kept them going for weeks. Burke looked at her fondly, gently. The sexual heat was gone and the frustration and loss melted away to be replaced by affection, history, and something like forgiveness—or perhaps the sense one had been forgiven. "Does he treat you well?"

"He does."

"Good." Burke, to his considerable surprise, meant it. "That's good."

Their salads arrived. The waiter hovered, babbled; his well-rehearsed bonhomie seemed especially cloying on the heels of an honest emotional moment. Indira started to giggle. Sensing he'd been dismissed, the actor glided away.

Einstein, explaining relativity, once noted that a few minutes in a dentist chair can seem like two hours, but two hours with a beautiful woman can seem like a few minutes. Burke remembered that anecdote when the check came. He could sense her concern and knew she had to leave, but that fact created subtle unease and caused the encroachment of a hollow sadness. Their words blurred and ran together. Burke walked Indira to the nearly deserted parking lot, where eerie shadows crouched near stuffed trash cans where the kitchen crew loitered to smoke. The rectum of a restaurant is the alley directly behind it.

"Can I see you again?" He knew and feared the answer.

It did not come. Indira Pal hugged him, but when he tried to kiss her, she pushed gently with her fingertips and separated them. "Take care of yourself, Jack."

Something tight and cold as ice sculpture lodged in his throat. Burke had no words, less control over his pulse. She walked to a red BMW sedan and an inconvenient burst of lust focused his attention on her small breasts in the tight suit as she slid into the driver's seat. She waved and he managed to smile back. The car rumbled like distant thunder. Pinned in the headlights, Burke waved, fearing that he looked like a lost little boy. Then it was dark and Indira was gone.

When Burke turned, the kitchen help had vanished. He noticed two half-smoked cigarettes adjacent to the trash cans. They were still burning, but that fact did not fully penetrate until he was near the far end of the parking lot, going onto Dickens Street in search of his car. No sound, no voices; those two Hispanic workers had simply vanished into the interior of the restaurant. *Why?* He looked back just in time and saw someone large and wide bearing down on him. He was momentarily blinded by having stared into the back porch light, but still managed to gauge the size and speed of his opponent. He dropped to one knee and leg whipped the larger man just as he'd finally closed the gap.

Burke had moved a fraction too soon, but still managed to catch the man around the shin. The assailant careened into a parked car, hissed his frustration. When he turned, Burke was almost back on his feet. The man closed the distance and bear-hugged. He lifted Burke high and shook him like a toy. Burke kept his muscles tight, knowing that a breath would compress his chest and allow the man to squeeze his lungs empty. He brought his palms up and slapped at the ears, working to deafen the assailant, who howled but shook the pain away. Burke tried to knee him in the testicles, but the attacker raised his thigh. Burke saw multicolored, pinprick stars. He knew his ribs couldn't last. He suddenly let himself go limp. He forced a harsh, moaning noise, as if unconscious.

"Don't kill him yet."

Burke recognized the voice. It was fat Dinky Martin. So the larger man would be Kelvin, the Arena-bowl bodyguard. Kelvin allowed Burke to collapse to the lawn adjacent the pavement. His hand dropped into something moist. He opened one eye slightly and saw Kelvin's nose has been braced and taped down and that the fat gambler has traded in his trademark Hawaiian shirt for a cheap suit and a loud, wide tie. Dinky leaned closer, clearly feeling very brave because he believed Burke to be out cold. "Let him wake up again. I want the fucker to know who offed him and why."

Kelvin cocked what sounded like a large revolver. "Somebody is bound to come along, boss." Kelvin sounded nearly as stupid as he looked. Burke didn't want to get shot. He made sounds, writhed a little bit, groaned like a man with cracked ribs.

"He's waking up," Dinky chortled. "Hey, motherfucker, guess who this is? Guess who's about to punch your ticket?"

Burke acted dazed. "Who are you?"

Dinky leaned over to tell him, wide tie dangling down. Burke grabbed it, yanked, and kicked Dinky in the balls. The fat man emitted a loud chuffing noise and sagged into blubber. Burke, now up on one knee, strained for leverage. He kept Dinky between his body and an alarmed Kelvin, who was looking for a clean shot. Burke stood, gathered his legs, and rushed Dinky's fat body forward. He rammed it into the bodyguard, forcing Kelvin into the side of a nearby parked car.

"The fuck?"

Burke reached around Dinky and knuckle-punched Kelvin twice in the throat, then broke his nose again. The .357 went off, the noise was more like a dog barking than a gunshot. Dinky started to struggle. Burke punched him in the diaphragm with the palm of his hand. He let Dinky drop to the sidewalk, stepped to the left, got closer to the gun. Angry, he broke three of Kelvin's fingers while taking it away.

The football player screamed as Burke pistol-whipped him. Satisfied, Burke allowed him to fall next to his boss.

"The only reason I don't kill you is that I'd have to ask Monteleone first, since you owe him so much." Burke wiped his prints from the gun and tossed it over a tall fence and into the restaurant's vegetable patch. "Here it is, just so you know. The next time I see your sorry ass, I'll drop you on the spot. No questions asked. Maybe it's time you moved to Vegas."

Dinky was moaning. "Okay, okay."

Burke, still wired up and furious, kicked them each once in the head. Moments later he was in his car driving home, sucking his knuckles and aching to be with Indira Pal.

Back on the sidewalk, in the darkness, Kelvin was the first to recover. He sat up, holding his re-broken nose with broken fingers. His breathing was an obscene gurgle; tears were running down his face. Dinky rolled over with a low groan.

"Boss?"

"What the fuck you want, you fucking loser?"

"Look over there. Who's that?"

Something in Kelvin's voice made short hairs stand up all

over Dinky Martin's substantial body. The bodyguard was pointing a shaky finger in the general direction of the restaurant parking lot. "What? Where?"

Someone moved, no—*oozed* out of the darkness, someone who had witnessed the entire incident. Dinky rapidly ran several options through his mind; perhaps to bribe, threaten, make up a story, but before he could come to a decision, Kelvin's humiliation and pain got the best of him. He barked: "What the fuck you looking at, white bread?"

Dinky blinked. The mysterious man's features did not seem Caucasian, nor did he move like a typical white male. Dinky saw the reflection of a porch lamp stroking pale skin. No, he *was* Caucasian. But those bare arms were stained—almost camouflaged. No, just busily tattooed. And instead of running away because of Kelvin's challenge, or being intimidated by the violence he has just witnessed, this man was moving closer. In fact, he ran like a predator, low to the ground, eyes searching the shadows.

It was suddenly obvious to Dinky that the stranger had not intended to be seen by anyone, in fact *could not allow that to happen*—and therefore would soon eliminate witnesses. "Kelvin, get him!"

But the man was already there and fell upon them. He made a graceful, spinning move with something in his hand and Kelvin grunted, grabbed his throat and sank to his knees. Dinky could see blood gushing from the carotid artery through huge, broken fingers. Then the man shoved the back of Kelvin's skull, almost with affection, the way someone might slap the head of a young boy. Kelvin fell forward onto the grass.

"Don't hurt me!" Dinky heard his own voice from far away, and it was the whining plea of a frightened child.

Kelvin produced a gurgling sound but did not move again. *He's fucking dead.* Dinky was oddly fascinated by that fact, and how briskly Kelvin had been dispatched, even as he heard a long-forgotten rosary running through his mind and observed snot and tears streaming down his face. He just had to ask. "Why?"

The man paused, amused. He stared down at Dinky and his sunken eyes were bright, wise, and in a weird way, rather kind. "Hello." He knelt and patted Dinky on the shoulder. "My name is Gorman."

Dinky sobbed. "Wait. I could use a man like you."

"In some other life, perhaps."

Gorman rapidly slipped a cord around Dinky's throat and fluidly stepped behind. He crossed his tattooed arms and slowly, quite lovingly, strangled Dinky Martin to death.

Twenty-Six

Willie Pepper wakes up with his chapped lips pressed against hairy flesh that smells freshly bathed. The hobo jerks his head up, emits a grunt, and lowers it again. His skull is throbbing and his entire body feels sore. His vision swims back into focus. The arm he smells is his own. Confused, he feels his body and checks his face and chin. Someone has given him a short haircut, bathed and shaved him, even applied aftershave lotion. It smells like that cheap, department store kind with a sailing ship on the bottle.

Willie sneezes, which makes his head ache again. He has some kind of cold or sinus infection coming on. He opens his eyes. He finds himself in a small area that seems like a combination hospital room and holding cell. Everything around him seems to be made of glass, porcelain, or metal.

The cell contains a tiny toilet, a cot, and a small table—fastened to the floor—that holds a plastic beaker of water. Willie sits up gingerly, holding his head. His nasal passages are clogged. And he feels stone-cold sober for the first time in years! But he has no memory of going through DTs. What happened? If this is a city detox clinic, it's the strangest one he's ever seen. The lights are bright; they hurt his eyes. The walls are blank metal, with not a single photograph or painting to provide distraction.

"Hello?"

No one answers. Willie, who now notices that he's wearing

some kind of paper slippers and a hospital gown, swings his feet around and lowers them to the cold flooring. It seems that he's fine, so long as he moves slowly enough. His throat feels parched and dry. He reaches for the water with a trembling hand and gulps. His stomach rolls for a long moment but settles. He feels his face, his head. His hair has indeed been shaved close to the skull and his beard is completely gone. Willie knows this happened recently because he knows how quickly it grows. It feels strange to be so exposed. Willie Pepper is accustomed to hiding his facial expressions, and thus his true feelings, behind a wall of filth and matted hair.

"Hello?" A little more loudly this time. Still no reply.

The throbbing in his skull is gradually changing to an odd feeling of pressure. His teeth hurt. He is parched from thirst. Willie takes another drink of water, gulps with greed and gratitude while his eyes roam what appears to be his new home. Didn't he hear somebody talking about some kind of new government program for the homeless? Maybe he got sick and they picked him up off the street. But no, he wasn't sick, someone had attacked him! The memory comes back like an icy wave. Willie Pepper feels his neck, and the abrasions from the rope, or whatever it was that strangled him, are still fresh. Wherever he is, whatever happened, he hasn't been unconscious for more than a couple of days.

Willie leans against the cold, impersonal wall and struggles to his feet. Again, a slight wave of dizziness assails him. He sees Christmas tree lights on a black velvet background, but the nausea passes quickly. His vision seems to waver like a mirage but when it comes back into focus he can see colors more clearly. He sneezes again, expels a large gout of clear mucous. He wipes it on his arm. The paper gown and slippers are a very pale green, hospital-style, and the metal and ceramic walls and tiles have an odd sheen to them, rather like varnish.

Jesus Christ, is this a morgue?

His heart goes *POW* at the idea, contributes a ghastly vision of his chest pried open and blood smoothly pumped into a drain by an impersonal black hose. He shivers against the cold and is forced to sit down on the cot again.

No, it can't be the city morgue. Dead folks don't get cots to lie on, and besides, there ain't no one else in here.

That door.

Assuming it is a door. What if it opens?

Maybe there are people on the other side, doctors and nurses who don't have a clue that he's awakened. Hot meals and some good dope for the pain, and maybe someone to talk to so he can complain and find out what's going on.

Willie Pepper eases back up to his feet. He narrows his eyes and tries to clarify the vague outline he sees in the far wall. It appears to be in the shape of a door, although the edges have been sealed in what seems to be black rubber. Perhaps if he pushes on it, it may simply open into the next room? He works his way along the wall, leaving clusters of knuckle- and fingerprints on the perfectly polished surface, his feet shuffling and whispering in their paper shoes.

This is definitely a hospital gown. Willie is conscious of the cool air on his bare buttocks. Another sneeze and this fucker *hurts.* His nose seems to be running like a damned faucet. He pushes on the flat surface outlined in black rubber, but it does not move. Willie Pepper shoves harder, tries to slide it to one side but it is rock solid and perfectly sealed.

"Hey!" The effort to speak punishes. His sinus passages are on fire. This cold sucks the big one. Willie hears some static coming from a hidden speaker. He looks around for it but can't see anything. Then a melodious, calming baritone voice speaks to him.

"You are in a hospital, sir. We recommend that you sit down

on the bed, if you do not mind."

The man has an accent of some kind. Willie knows he has heard that accent before, Mexican or Greek or something; he cannot quite place it. Like from the movies maybe. Whoever he is, the dude certainly sounds like he's in charge. Willie considers the request, elects to comply. He works his way across the room again. Once seated on the cot, hands folded in his lap like a good schoolboy, he tries again.

"Excuse me, but where am I?"

A hiss, the voice: "This is a medical facility, sir. We are sorry to inform you that you have been quite ill."

"Somebody tried to kick my ass, is what happened."

"Excuse me?"

"Hey, I said some asshole tried to strangle me. What the hell do you mean I've been sick? For how long?"

The voice laughs, rattling the speaker. Willie begins to search the room again with his eyes, and now he finally notices the small box above the doorway and the four video cameras mounted in the upper corners of the room. "You have been very ill with alcoholism, sir. We have taken the liberty of performing a rapid detoxification procedure."

"Huh?"

"We first administered some Halcyon and then used an intravenous solution of glucose and benzodiazepine to slowly withdraw your body from the alcohol while you slept. Except for your cold, you must be feeling better than you have in years, yes?"

Willie Pepper rolls his shoulders. He doesn't want to admit it, give the son of a bitch the satisfaction, but except for his sinus problem he does feel good. *Very* good. He grunts instead of speaking.

After a long moment the voice continues: "May we have your age, sir?"

"I'm forty-five. No, forty-six." *Jesus, am I that old? Yeah, last November. That means it has been nine years since I talked to my sister Lisa up there in Santa Rosa.* Willie shakes his head, sets off more throbbing. He is amazed at the passage of time. He also feels something unfamiliar but not entirely unpleasant happening in his midsection. Emotions are surfacing. It has been a long time since he has felt anything but rage, fear, or the ravaging lust of his addiction to alcohol.

"And have you had any other serious accidents or illnesses in your life?"

Willie picks at his fingernails absently, mind elsewhere. "Measles when I was a kid, and I broke my leg once."

"Anything else?"

"Not that I remember." But he suddenly does remember being a boy, playing with Lisa in the yard of their home in Pomona, waiting for his father to get home. Amazingly, he can recall the scent of the freshly cut grass and the faint, snoring drone of an airline passing overhead. The back of his neck heats up as if the summer sun was burning down, reddening his skin. Willie Pepper suddenly wants to curl up and cry. He rubs his eyes. Another sneeze.

"Are you still with us, sir?" the impersonal voice asks. He clearly cares little one way or the other.

"Yeah. Fine. I'm fine. How did you people find me?"

The speaker clicks. "We brought you here."

An odd and chilling thought occurs to Willie Pepper: *They haven't even asked me for my name. I don't carry ID, I'm not wearing any bracelet like they give you in the emergency room in Santa Monica or over at Cedars Sinai, so what the fuck is this place? Where did they take me?*

"Doc?" This must be a doctor, right? "You still there, Doc?"

"Yes," the voice replies, "we are still here."

Another sneeze, another wipe on the top of his forearm.

Hundreds of ants crawling his flesh: this time there is some blood in the clear mucous.

"Fuck!"

"What is it, sir?"

"Look, I want to know where I am and what's going on, all right?" Willie gets to his feet, surprised to find that he feels pretty strong now. Most of the wooziness is gone. "What have you people done to me?" His limbs are flushed with blood and fear is giving him strength. *Weird.*

A low chuckle. "You are feeling somewhat better now, sir. Quite suddenly, yes? We can see that."

Willie rubs his belly. "Yeah, but I have a shitty cold, man. And I think I'm gonna be sick to my stomach. Can I have some more water?"

"I doubt you would be able to keep it down at this stage."

The fuck does he mean by that? Willie shivers abruptly, licks his lips. His now chattering teeth really hurt. He stumbles to the mirror while the cameras carefully track his every move. He opens his mouth and shrieks. There are pustules on his gums, black dots that look like blood blisters. Before he can manage to form new words the drinking water comes back up in a rush and splatters the mirror.

"Doc, h-h-help me!"

"Be calm. It will not be long, now."

What won't be long?

Willie Pepper looks at the pustules again. He watches himself in the gooey mirror, helpless to intervene or cry out, as his facial muscles begin to twitch and tremble. The right side of his body goes completely numb for a few seconds. Now that his mouth is open, it seems to lock into place as if he had rabies. He cannot close his jaws or move them to speak. He feels an electric shock run through his entire body and he stiffens, like a mannequin. After a long moment his rigid body leans forward against the mirror, tilted like a fallen statue. He is silent, still. The cameras zoom in for a close-up of his full body.

Hunh!"

The frozen feeling only lasts for a short time. It is followed by something akin to an epileptic seizure. Willie Pepper hits the hard surface of the floor, twitching and moaning and grunting like an animal. He chews in a grinding, devilishly effective manner until he begins to devour his own lips and tongue. A few seconds later he hears a voice, from somewhere far away, say something about *damage to the mid-brain* and *basal writhing.*

Willie shits himself. *Bowels evacuated.*

His spine arches hideously, impossibly, until it bends so far back it seems certain to break. Blood is gushing from his nose and eyes, now (meanwhile, the voice says *epistaxis*) and Willie Pepper knows in some dark and dim corner of his mind that he is going to die. He no longer cares. His eyes have rolled back into his skull and he is rigid and silent and nearly insane from the pain. A deep and racking cough occurs; another gout of blood, this one bursts from his mouth like an alien creature to land on the now-messy floor, a foot or so away. Willie Pepper feels all of the tension leave his body and it feels good, almost orgasm good, to have the fit over with. His eyes glass over and his vision darkens. It comes to him that he is no longer breathing, he tries but *cannot* breathe. The image of his sister in the sunshine returns.

The voice: "We have respiratory failure at 10:19:26."

. . . Willie Pepper gives his little sister Lisa a big hug. It is so good to see her again, and wonderful that she is still a child. Then the most remarkable thing happens, Willie can really feel the hot sun on his skin, warm and gentle, smell that newly cut lawn. He lets himself slide down a hill made of that fresh, green grass and drops away into an endless summer . . .

Twenty-Seven

"Okay, one more time from the top."

Less than an hour after the fight with Dinky Martin, Gina brought a weary Burke an ice bag and commenced playing mother hen. They were seated in the office, blinds lowered and lights high. Gina had proffered five aspirins and made coffee strong enough to lube a lawn mower. Burke held the ice close to the bruised rib on his right side. He cleared his throat, but carefully. "Your turn, run it down."

Gina was wearing a tight tee shirt and jeans with a large belt and cowboy buckle. She was a night person anyway, so she was already focused. "Okay, we have a horror novelist who likes silly word games. He seems to have committed suicide at the Universal Sheraton. Cuts off various body parts, anesthetizes his ass, and then starts up again. He does it all over several hours. The daughter probably wants more money from insurance, wants it to be foul play, so Bowden turns her on to you and me."

"Check."

"You go to toss the guy's house and somebody else has already been there, in fact is still there. There's a load of books on all kinds of spooky stuff, religious artifacts, a couple of hidden panels. He has some kind of symbols on pieces of paper in a hidden place, they get swiped."

"Uh huh."

"Lots of people hate Stryker, the daughter says. You interview

Merriman and Pal in the same day and come up empty both times."

"Yeah."

"And finally Doc does a little digging for you, and among other things says the baby powder from the adjoining suite doesn't match yours. So now we have to figure somebody else *did* go in there to slice-and-dice Stryker."

Burke sat up carefully. "You left something out."

"Dinky Martin?"

"No, I doubt that's related to any of this. I think Dinky just wanted to even the score for the whipping I gave him Sunday night."

"So what are you talking about?"

"I meant the fact that Doc has gotten some serious heat for helping me out. And add to that Scotty Bowden suddenly acting so weird. Jesus, you'd think he was on the other side, or something."

"Other side of *what,* Burke?"

"That's the question, isn't it? Beats the hell out me."

Burke leaned forward, elbows on the desk. He'd been pounded on before, but not at this advanced age. He remembered a line from an old Indiana Jones movie, something about it not being the speed but the mileage that finally got you.

"Okay, Suite 1124."

"Say what?"

"That old couple who rented the suite next to Stryker at the Sheraton," Gina said impatiently. She looked down at her notes, unconsciously pursed her lips. She looked like a small child. "Here it is, Dorothy. Clinton and Dorothy Farnsworth. I looked them up on the Internet, Burke. They pop up on the society pages a lot. Fund-raising for hospital wings, doubles tennis for the prune juice set, that sort of thing."

Burke grunted. "Likely to be squeaky clean, in other words."

"Well, I got to wondering. What would a rich Bel Air couple owns their own mansion be doing renting a not-that-swanky suite at the Sheraton for a night? Construction on their mansion, what?"

He felt a chill jogging on thin, hairy legs. "You know something, that is a damned good question, isn't it? So you checked on their whereabouts the night of Stryker's death, just to be sure."

"Oh, they were in town all right, but they were supposedly attending a private birthday party at Shutters in Santa Monica, and stayed quite late. Whoever checked into that suite, Burke, it wasn't them."

"Did you get a description from the staff? I don't remember there being anything in the police report we could use."

Gina produced a folded piece of paper. "I schmoozed, I wheedled, I begged. Scotty almost shit himself, but then he faxed it over."

Burke grabbed it from her hand. It was a copy of the hotel's registration documents for Mr. and Mrs. Clinton Farnsworth. "The handwriting?"

"It's a reasonably good forgery," Gina said, "but it's fake. I checked." She yawned. "But witness the colossal arrogance, my man. The business address is correct for the real Farnsworth, over on Avenue of the Stars in Century City. But take a look at the home address they gave."

"Did the cops ever follow up on this?"

"Not so far. And trust me, Scotty sounded scared."

"Tell him I'll be dropping by his second office later tonight, okay?"

"Oh, fuck. You're going there, aren't you." It was not a question. They both knew Burke had no choice. The address given as the Farnsworth residence was not in upscale Bel Air. It was in Panorama City. That meant the barrio. Gang country.

TWENTY-EIGHT

Twenty minutes later, Burke was on his way.

Sepulveda showed signs of strain around Burbank Boulevard, near the overpass entrance to the 405 Freeway. That's where the crack whores started to appear, at first half in shadow, like emaciated citizens of a third world country, but eventually strutting openly along on the sidewalk. They wore butt-floss shorts, halter tops, and black high heels, and sported a carpet of goose bumps from the cold night air. Some were still adrift in puberty, some nearing menopause, but their faces looked the same due to makeup thick as dry-wall mud. A few were bold enough to stick their thumbs out as though asking for a ride, not looking for a john, but most merely paced in circles, waiting for work.

Burke continued north, past the rows of neon strip malls packed with middle-class cars and shopping carts. At around Victory, the first signs of gang graffiti appeared, one florid NHBZ, the spray-painted signature of the North Hollywood Boys. Crowds of rootless young men and women dominated the cracked sidewalk by the time Burke neared Saticoy, still heading upstream. The males had their heads shaved close to the scalp and sported sagging blue jeans, wife-beater tee shirts, and padded fluorescent jackets baggy enough to hide automatic weapons. The police working this neighborhood did so with considerable anal tension.

Burke drove on, the address repeating itself in his brain like a mantra. Lawrence Street finally appeared just north of Roscoe.

He turned right into the gloom, down a row of pastel-painted 1940s wood frame homes fronted by stacks of tires and used cars that were works-in-progress. His shoulders tensed a bit. Two of the four weary streetlamps had been broken, or perhaps shot out.

The house was at the end of the street in a cul-de-sac. It looked deserted, nearly uninhabitable. The slatted wood was splintered, peeling, and in places regurgitating large nails already orange with rust. Burke pulled to the curb and parked just two doors away and on the opposite side of the street. He checked the rearview mirror. A group of five adolescent boys had followed his slow progress down the street. Their body language was already agitated and stiff, sporting various hand signs. They were working themselves up, discussing this arrogant *gringo* invading their turf. He hadn't much time before the young sociopaths—and perhaps several of their erstwhile friends—decided to challenge his presence.

Burke armed his 9mm Glock, grabbed his flashlight. He stepped out of the car into the humid night air. The nearest streetlamp was still working, making him clearly visible to the gang. After a moment Burke allowed his gun to hang loose at his side, in plain view. He hoped to read like a private citizen out to settle a score, maybe with some drug dealer. Perhaps that impression would slow the boys down. Of course, another possibility was that the kids came down the block ready for all-out war. If that was the case, things could get ugly in a hurry.

The lawn was thick with weeds and piled high with trash; the ground parched. There were footprints everywhere, going across and in and out of the area, so Burke's own would be impossible to identify. He walked across the cluttered lawn, stepped on cans or crushed fast-food containers wherever possible, and got to the foot of the wooden steps. Nothing moved within the darkened house. Burke glanced back over his shoulder.

Like a trick shot from a horror movie, the clump of angry boys had gotten one hell of a lot closer; they were still doing exactly what they were doing before, but were now less than half a block away. Their hostile muttering became audible.

Burke used the flashlight to nudge the door open and roll back the darkness. He discovered a room filthy and reeking of decay. There were needles, condoms, empty bottles, and all manner of cushions, pillows, and lawn chairs. This was a former crack house, from the look of it, although the dust everywhere suggested it had not been used for some time. He stepped wide over the threshold and into the living room, listening intently. A vague humming sound caught his attention. It was the faint sound of static from a radio that had lost signal, or perhaps from a broken television set.

Another glance over his shoulder. The gang members were now spread out on the sidewalk, arms hanging loose at their sides. Three of them carried baseball bats, one seemed empty-handed, but the last was holding a shiny silver automatic. They moved no closer, almost as if they were afraid.

Of what? Something that lives in this house?

Burke swallowed dryly and moved deeper into the gloom. He swept the dark with his flashlight. More trash, traditional waste products from drug use and prostitution. He moved toward that annoying, low humming sound, eased down the hallway and closer to the back rooms. Soon it was not a humming sound. It was a buzzing.

A stench assailed his nostrils. Burke knew what he'd find. He kicked open the bedroom door, recoiled in disgust. *An ugly little man seated on a pile of reeking corpses, rocking back and forth and laughing and laughing . . .* Burke blinked away history. He saw an elderly man and woman hanging upside down from a wooden beam. Their bodies were covered with an excited, rolling carpet of gorging, black and green bottle flies. They had been gutted, and their darkening entrails were festooned along what seemed to be a piece of thick, plastic drop cloth spread beneath them. Burke had seen death many times, but the disrespectful abuse of these old people made him tremble. He moved the beam of the flashlight. Pieces of their flesh had been carved away. They had been butchered, but the coroner would have to determine what had happened before and after death.

Burke heard a sound behind him. He raised the 9mm and turned.

"Madre de Dios!"

A stocky gangbanger wearing a checkered scarf as a headband was two yards back in the living room. His mouth was hanging open, eyes bullfrog wide. The handgun was hanging useless at his side. His friends were behind him. Burke twirled the light and pinned them in the glare. They were all visibly upset, a bunch of bewildered, shaken kids.

"What the fuck happen here, *ese?*"

Burke lowered the light. "I don't know exactly. Somebody brought these people here, killed them, and left them as a message."

"On *our* streets, man? Holy shit." The three boys holding up the rear looked lost and terrified. But their leader was already summoning machismo. He puffed his chest. "Then we gonna find them and do them back, right?"

Burke backed away from the crime scene. "I don't think the message was meant for you and your homies."

"Then who did it, man?"

"I don't know for certain, but I'm thinking this might have been left for me."

The kid, who has seen far too many rap videos, jerked the .38 in the air, pointed down and at an angle. The gesture was intended to be at once casual and threatening. Burke had the Glock aimed at the kid's forehead before the idea reached his conscious mind. No one blinked. Burke lowered his weapon and the kid followed suit.

"You might want to put that away before someone gets hurt."

The kid's lower lip trembled, but he held his water. "Who the fuck are you, *ese?* What did you bring down on my street?"

"Don't worry, I'll never come back here again," Burke replied coolly. "But I doubt whoever did this chose your turf for any particular reason."

"You better hope so, man."

"Here's what I think you guys should do. First, forget you ever saw me. Get someone to call this in. Let the cops handle it. You'll do your block a solid."

"Shit," one of the kids in the back moaned. "They'll blame it on us, *vato!*"

But the first kid smiled. "I get you, man. Maybe they want to nail us, but we didn't have nothing to do with it, so they can't. But the word gets out that we're bad, either way."

Burke nodded. "People will leave you alone. And I can get back to trying to track down who did this without being interrupted."

Gato examined the offer carefully and finally smiled. "I can get behind that, man. Did you know these people?"

"No, but I think I know who they are." He gave the kid his props. "Hey, do I have your permission to leave?"

A stately consideration, followed by: "Yeah. Get the fuck out of here."

Twenty-Nine

The drive from the barrio down to the cop bar on Magnolia Boulevard in Studio City was a blur. The aftereffects of the crime scene were severe. Burke broke out in a cold sweat. He put The Wave on the radio and tried to slow too-rapid breathing. The sight of old people gutted like deer had distilled the truth of the situation. He was crossing swords with people ruthless as enraged Columbian drug dealers. They already knew about Jack Burke—but he still had no idea who they were, or why they were committing these horrific crimes.

The converted storefront called the "Love Inn" started out as a gay hangout. Frequent visits from vice and undercover LAPD officers gradually transformed it into a cop bar by the early 90s. Now it was one of Scott Bowden's favorite watering holes. The parking lot was unpaved, the outside lighting poor. Burke eased in through the back way, walked past the stench of urine coming from the men's room, entered the dark bar and stood near the antique jukebox. He saw Scotty Bowden, unshaven as always, in a nearby booth. His handsome head was weaving slightly as he stared into a candle flame with reddened eyes. Burke sat down.

"Brothers!" Scotty was pretty sloshed. "Have a drink with me, man."

"I went to the address the hotel register had listed for the Farnsworth's," Burke said. "Do you know what I found up there, Scotty?"

Bowden couldn't meet Burke's eyes. He remained silent. Someone disengaged from a cluster of drunks at the bar and moved their way. Burke thought the woman looked vaguely familiar, so he shrank back into the gloom until she'd passed by.

Bowden responded to the movement. "Thanks for that, man. It will go better for me if I'm not seen talking to you."

Burke's mind was still riveted to the crawling flies and two dead bodies. He put his elbows on the table, kept his face down. "Some gangbangers will call it in any time now. I don't think they had anything to do with it."

"With what?"

Burke leaned a lot closer. "With potential Stryker witnesses Mr. and Mrs. Farnsworth hanging from the rafters, sliced open with some pieces missing. I figure they've been dead at least a day or so."

Bowden looked up, eyes wide. "Witnesses to what, Red? I don't think they were even there at the Sheraton that night."

"I don't think they were, either. But they must have known something about what was going to happen to Stryker, and someone couldn't take the chance they'd talk."

Bowden looked back down, sipped his drink. "I am *so* fucked."

"Scotty, talk to me. What the hell is going on?"

"I don't know, man," Bowden said. "But when it comes to the Stryker thing, I am being told to zip my mouth and wrap it up yesterday."

"By who?"

"It's from high up, man. I can't say. If I open my mouth I'll be so toast even Cary Ryan won't be able to save me."

"Scotty, somebody else was in Stryker's suite that night. Somebody who probably used surgical gloves and covered his tracks well. But then, I suspect you have already figured that out on your own, haven't you?"

After a long pause, Bowden nodded. "It crossed my mind."

"But you still tossed my name to Nicole Stryker, so I guess that was just to control the situation. Then you told me to wrap it up quick, that there was nothing about the case that wasn't righteous."

"I'm sorry man. It's cover-my-ass time. And if she was going to hire somebody, I wanted it to be a friend of mine, you know? Besides, somebody asked for you by name."

"What? *Who* asked for me by name, Scotty?"

"I don't know." Bowden looked up, then back again. His eyes blazed. "Fuck you, Jack. I've been good to you."

"Sure, but you also might have set me up in the process of covering your sorry ass. Did that ever cross your mind?"

"What do you mean?" But Scotty understood. He hadn't thought this one through well enough. More people would die, and Burke might be one of them. Bowden wiped his brow. Burke let him twist in the wind for a while.

Finally Scotty mumbled, "I'm getting some real heat to let it slide, Red."

"Even though you know something stinks."

Scotty eyed the middle distance. "Yeah."

"So help me fight."

"I can't." His expression was wan, haunted, but even in the poor light of the bar, colored with shame. "Because I got IA on my ass, too, Red."

"Shit, Scotty . . ."

"Oh, I'm not actually dirty, more like a little bit smudged. Some meals here and there, a few hundred bucks from a bookie last Christmas. But they've got enough to hang me out to dry if they want to. That would leave me with a bad jacket and no pension. I'd be fucked."

"So the deal is you shut up and drop this, IA closes the file."

"You got it. You are on your own here, pal. Just consider that little fax I sent kind of a gift for old time's sake."

"What happened to you, Scotty?"

Bowden shrugged. He forced a thin, bitter smile. His face reassembled and became a studied mask of indifference. "Life happened."

Burke slid out of the booth. He stepped back, stayed close to the wall and opened the side door. Scotty lit a cigarette. With his hand masking his mouth: "So what are you going to do?"

"In the long run?"

"Yeah."

"I don't know. Right now I'm going to go report to my boss."

"The Stryker girl is crazy, you know that. Why are you going to tell her anything?"

"Her check cleared."

THIRTY

Saturday

"That is just horrible." They were in Nicole Stryker's kitchen, late the next day. She seemed truly upset about the Farnsworth murder. Nicole was wearing a plush, beige bathrobe that covered some kind of lacy black nightgown. The blonde hair was mussed and her dazed, slightly pink eyes said she had already smoked a little Saturday afternoon dope. "They were such nice people."

Burke had told her about the deaths. He'd neglected to mention he'd seen the bodies personally, saw no compelling reason. Nicole looked up at him as if reading his mind. "Just how did you hear about all of this?"

"A contact at the police department."

"And you think this is connected with what happened to my father at the Sheraton? But *why?*"

"One of my people hacked the guest register." Burke worked to avoid staring at her breasts. "As I told you, the suite on one side of your father was empty. The other was registered to Mr. and Mrs. Farnsworth. Only they weren't there that night, they were somewhere else at a party."

"But then why kill them?"

"I don't know yet."

"God." She dropped her head. The already yawning robe opened a bit wider, likely by design.

Burke looked away. He ordered his mind to stay on track. His mind told him to take a hike. "How well did your father know the Farnsworths, Nicole?"

Muffled, dazed: "They met for dinner and drinks now and then. I remember them from parties at the house, before my father withdrew from the world. They always seemed nice enough to me. I can't imagine why someone would . . ."

Nicole did not describe the picture in her mind's eye. When her hand crabbed sideways across the table to grip his, Burke felt hormones race through his body like blue fire. *What the hell is going on?* He had been dormant and numb for too long. Burke knew the ache he felt for Nicole was the polar opposite of his need for Indira—one female inspired love, the other lust—but at this moment in time, lust was the stronger emotion.

"Stay with me," Nicole Stryker whispered, as both of them knew she would. Her head was bowed in submission, that long golden hair flowing down to caress the damp sheen on the pale, white skin of her arms. "I need to be with someone."

Her fingers dropped to stroke his leg. Burke felt his flesh tremble and twitch. He heard a roaring in his ears, his bloodstream was suddenly oceanic, rhythmic, the pulse of the universe. Before he could reason a way out of it, he'd moved his chair and pulled her into his arms like a baby clutching at the breast; their mouths were ravenous, all tongues and teeth and panting, humid breath. The quickening was fluid. Nicole genuflected; moved her head to his swollen lap, feral fingers clutching at the zipper of his jeans.

"Wait."

That was someone else's voice, he thought. Some damned fool across the city, up on a mountain, from some other time and place. "Wait, stop."

The tip of his sex was already between her taunting teeth, the shaft being licked and sucked and fondled. The heat was explosive and relentless and it was almost over right there, before it began, but Burke knew it must *not* begin, mustn't happen at all. With a Herculean effort of will, he pulled her head away and clutched it to his chest. He rocked both of them, while their breath streamed through the kitchen.

Nicole Stryker was irritated, confused. "What are you doing?"

"I can't," he managed, half of him screaming frustration. He adjusted his stiffness in the chair, rose and zipped his pants. Nicole, pretty mouth puckered, young cheeks red with excitement and embarrassment, was humiliated. She jumped from her knees to her feet, uncurling like a startled gazelle, and slapped his face. Hard.

"You are *so* fired."

He tried to keep it light. "I think this might constitute sexual harassment."

She tried to slap him again but he grabbed her wrist, twisted lightly, and forced her back into her chair with a thump. The power shifted immediately and Nicole seemed frightened, so Burke sat down and held on to her arm.

"Look, I couldn't be more flattered," he said, and meant it. "You're a beautiful woman and I'm very attracted to you, as I'm sure you can tell. But I work for you. Now, we need to keep that straight, and get our heads clear."

"Get out." She shoved his chest with her palms. The chair squealed two inches across the kitchen floor. "I said get out. Now."

Burke did. He moved away to allow her to recapture some of her dignity. "Nicole, I don't mean to offend you. The people we are up against play for keeps."

"You don't think I know that?"

"I think we need to stay focused."

She glared at him, those eyes flashing bright shards of rage like slivers of broken glass—Burke half expected her head to spin around and spit a stream of pea soup. "Leave!"

"All right, then," he snarled, surprised at his own vehemence. "Go fuck yourself." Though a dim part of his brain called it childish and dramatic, he slammed the door hard on his way out.

Thirty-One

The young woman tried desperately to nurture primal rage. She hoped it would shield her, inoculate her against the sting of his rejection. She stomped out of her kitchen and into the living room, made a tall Dewar's and soda, downed it in a few gulps.

Who the hell does he think he is?

Nicole paced the room, hugging herself, struggling to remain offended and angry rather than hurt, fighting to keep the oppressive fact of two murdered old people from dominating her thoughts, trying to keep the hideous image of her father's death out of her mind. Down deep, she knew that there was something unnatural about intense sexuality surfacing at a time like this, something even childishly needy, but she didn't care. She wanted to get high, escape, get off, and get *out* of the pain. A good orgasm was just another kind of drug. A wave of dizziness followed. She waited for it to pass, poured a second drink anyway. Nicole examined the roach in the ashtray and tried to light it, but burned her lip. She was out of dope.

Nicole shrugged the robe to the floor and walked through the windowed living room in her sheer nightgown. She watched her figure reflected in the glass, the long, lithe legs, perfectly formed breasts that bobbed so arrogantly. She was desirable enough for any man. Again: *Who the hell does he think he is?* But somewhere deeper, darker in the belly: *Don't think about Daddy, don't think about Daddy . . .*

Nicole Stryker, carefully balancing the drink with both hands, went upstairs to her bedroom. It was large, opulent with a round princess bed, the kind of bedroom a little girl dreams of having. Its pink fabric and plastic immaturity were a bit incongruous, considering the lusty, reckless young female who'd approached Burke moments ago. She used the remote to start her CD player and selected some music appropriate for the mood.

Go fuck myself? Sure, why not.

Nicole located the dimmer switch and lowered the lights. She took another drink and put the glass on the nightstand. She removed the nightgown; closed her eyes, massaged her breasts. She could still feel his thick hardness in her mouth, taste the salt from his skin. Her hips began to move on the bedspread and her right hand snaked lower. Nicole pleasured herself . . . *don't think, don't think* . . . Her fingers rubbed gently, persistently, patiently . . . *don't think, don't think* . . . The climax would be quick, she could tell, she was already wet and ready, her body twisting, her mind focused on a small galaxy of light eons away but moving closer and closer.

What was that?

Nicole froze. *Jesus Christ, I left the front door unlocked.* Her body was now both aroused and panicked, and thus paralyzed. The sound came again, from down the hall, something crisp and quick, like the breaking of a small piece of glass.

Or a window.

She sat up in bed, naked, heart and hands both at her throat. The "panic button" for her alarm was across the room, by the makeup table, where she'd left it just the night before. Now Nicole was a little girl again, with a monster in the closet, and she couldn't bring herself to move. Her terrified mind rationalized: perhaps it was Burke, coming back because he'd changed his mind and wanted to apologize. Sure, and then he'd knocked something over on his way upstairs, and . . .

Squeak!

Nicole was up and running for the panic button, despite her nakedness, bare skin abruptly hived with rolling bumps from preternatural fear. The intruder caught her by the hair and yanked, hard. Her feet continued forward, absurdly determined to reach the goal, but when her torso hit the floor it took her breath away. He held onto her hair and her scalp burst into flame.

The man grabbed her from behind, sat her partway up, took one tender breast in each hairy hand. He squeezed and twisted the sensitive flesh. Nicole grunted an animal sound of surprise at the searing pain.

"Where is it?"

The nipples, this time, pinching hard and twisting; Nicole tried to call out but his left hand abandoned her breast and clamped over her lips, bruising them. "No screaming, just words. Where is it?"

"Where is *what?*"

More pain, a wave of agony beyond belief. "Please, stop!" Nicole was panting with terror. Her already aroused body was quickly tipping over into a mindless state of hysteria.

"Where is it?"

"I don't know what you mean, I don't know what you mean." She repeated herself, over and over again like a woman saying rosary. She could smell the man, and his repulsive stink caused her stomach to clench and her heart to sink into a deep, dark well. The man, or perhaps creature, reeked of shit and matches, sweat and offal; he had become death, destroyer of worlds. As his right hand crept up her trembling flesh, it scorched like a soldering iron, then clamped over her nose. Nicole Stryker began to struggle for air. She bucked and twisted and kicked her legs. The sounds she emitted were pathetic and heartbreaking. They seemed to bring the stranger real, sensual pleasure.

When she wet herself, he chuckled. Nicole could not fight

anymore. She fell off a cliff into darkness . . .

. . . "Tell me where it is."

The voice brought her back. Nicole gasped for air and opened her eyes to see who or what was speaking.

The demon was terrifying. He squatted before her now, like some savage on a gory battlefield. His bare arms were covered with tattoos, ribbons and snakes of them, and his eyes burned, though they were black as slate. His awful breath reached her, and her nose twitched, the hare smelling a predator.

"Where is it?" He twisted her breasts again and she cried out. The man smiled pleasantly, and brought his bland face close to hers.

Nicole Stryker held her breath. She knew she was about to die. *Dear God, he doesn't even care if I see him, he's decided to kill me anyway!*

"You pissed yourself, little girl."

He reached down, arms rippling, and moved a finger around in the puddle of urine on the floor. He tasted it and smiled. And Nicole was now just small, helpless; emotionally crippled and humiliated and could only whimper for mercy. The stranger licked his fingers again. His other hand produced a hunting knife with a long, saw-toothed blade.

"Don't. Please."

But he did and the knife probed her vagina lightly, like the cold, sharp mandible of an insect. Meanwhile, the man leaned forward and kissed her tears away. "Tell me where it is and I promise I'll make this quick."

Nicole understood him perfectly; her mind was as focused and pure as a nuclear implosion. She would suffer the torments of the damned if she did not speak the truth, answer his question immediately and do what he asked. She would die horribly, much as her father had, and it would surely be far better to die at once. There was only one problem. *She did not know what he wanted!*

"I don't know what you mean or where it is. Please, believe me. I don't even know what you're talking about."

The knife probed and tender flesh protested. Nicole closed her eyes. She was panting, needed to vomit, felt herself tottering on the edge of madness. She wanted to fight but was frozen in a block of cold, steaming, ice and could not move for fear of the sharp blade.

But then nothing else happened. The blade was withdrawn.

Nicole opened her eyes. The man had hopped soundlessly as a tarantula and was now crouched a few feet away. He waited, listening and sniffing the air, senses reacting to some pure, atavistic instinct. Nicole's own desire for survival finally kicked in. She was already scuttling away, back on buttocks and heels and palms, when the man lashed out with the blade, so instead of her throat, he sliced empty air. The man jumped to his feet, intending to pursue her—

And Jack Burke flew into the room like a hurricane of feet and hands. Burke had her robe over one arm and used that to block and parry the knife. The fight was so fast and furious it seemed choreographed. It was over so quickly that Nicole would later be unable to describe much of what she'd witnessed. Something—an extended leg, perhaps—eventually slammed Burke back into her bedroom dresser. He lost his footing, slid down with his back to the furniture. He seemed dazed. Nicole wanted to call his name. The foul killer moved in, knife extended. Before the intruder could cut his throat, Burke produced a small, but wicked-looking gun. The killer moved. Nicole heard two quick sounds, a bit like balloons popping. The stranger rolled across the bed and scrambled out the door and was gone.

Burke did not follow, seemed to intuit that he'd never catch up. He got to his feet and jogged down the stairs. She heard him locking the front door, talking to someone on the cell phone as he moved back up her staircase. He entered the room.

"I came back to say I'm sorry."

Nicole was now gasping, shivering, snot running from her nose. She barely noticed when Burke draped the robe around her shoulders to cover her nakedness.

"I called my partner, Gina." He spoke softly. "She is going to come and spend the night. I'll arrange for a bodyguard to stay with you in the morning."

"Who was that?"

"I don't know."

"W-w-why can't *you* stay?"

"I have too much work to do." He kissed her forehead, quite gently. "What did he want, Nicole? Did he say anything to you?"

"Where is it?"

"Where is what?"

Nicole shook her head, hugged him tighter. "That's what he kept on saying to me, over and over while he . . . hurt me. 'Where is it?' Burke, I don't know what the hell he was asking about. Do you?"

"No."

"Should we call the police?"

Burke glanced down and away. He was thinking about Scotty Bowden. After a time, he shook his head. "I don't think we can."

Nicole's eyes focused on an invisible tunnel to China. "Burke, he said he'd go easy on me if I told him, but if I didn't . . ." *Don't think about Daddy.*

"Don't talk. Relax."

"He said if I didn't he'd . . ."

Don't think about Daddy . . . But she could not help thinking about it now, and soon the tears overcame reason. Perhaps because of the stimulus of her fear, all the buried grief, need, and loss exploded. "Oh, my God, my poor Daddy . . ."

Burke accepted her into his arms. Nicole cried in roaring bursts. He held her tightly, gently, a bit like the father she never really knew.

Thirty-Two

Sunday

Scott Bowden again watches his breath stream out into the frigid air in a long, feathered plume. His hands burrow into his armpits. He hugs himself against the cold. His bleary eyes search the cement corners, battered trash cans, and piles of corrupting garbage. It is still the dead of night, when the desperate and the violent own the mean streets, so Bowden is anxious, yet depressed and angry enough to block that feeling and transform it into aggression. He is alert but moving slowly, carefully, with the calculated stiffness of an aging man who knows he is drunk but believes he can still pass for sober.

"Who is she?"

"They call her Bloody Mary."

Somehow it is always harder on Bowden when the stiff is a female. He turns to the young, cherub-faced cop who called him. "And you kept this just between us, right? Nothing went out over the radio?"

Officer Mike Gallo looks shaken as well as cold. He rubs his hands together. "I kept my mouth shut. Scotty, I'm hope I'm not going to get in trouble for this."

"Are you kidding, Mike? You did the right thing. And believe me, the man upstairs will appreciate it when he hears about this."

"You sure this is straight from Parker Center?"

"You have my word, kid."

Mike Gallo nods rapidly, a man eager to vanish. "Can I go now?"

"Yeah, sure. And remember, you never saw this."

"Yes, sir."

Hurried footsteps crunching through the frost, the sound fading away. Bowden kneels a few feet from the corpse, sets his torch down for a closer look. The middle-aged homeless woman formerly known as Bloody Mary is sideways on the ground, bloodied eyes enlarged, face contorted in a twisted grimace. A small clump of purplish vomit lies several inches from her half-open mouth like a puddle of expelled afterbirth. Like most of the homeless, she wears several sets of filthy clothing, but the stench from her evacuated bowels is unmistakable.

Bowden trembles, but this time it is not from the cold. He wonders what the woman was thinking when her time came. Initially, just that she had the flu, or maybe needed to go to the emergency room. Then the creeping awareness that something more serious was at work, deep in her body. The panic would have started with the convulsions, but by then it was already way too late to seek help. Bowden has only seen one other body that looked as tormented as this one. It was a street whore whose pimp had punished her for holding out on him by pouring a can of drain cleaner down her throat. The chemicals had eaten her alive from the inside.

Damn, what happened to her? What have I gotten myself into?

Bowden leans back on his haunches and lights a cigarette. Now the fear has washed his system clean and the warm alcohol buzz has vanished. He sucks the nicotine into his lungs with a greedy gasp. It helps a bit.

He grunts to his feet and looks around the filthy alley. Eventually his eyes settle on a black garbage bag that has split open. He yanks on one lip and pulls the bag free. He spreads it out and lets it float through the cold air and settle down over the body like a plastic blanket. Then Bowden scatters some empty cans and milk cartons over the surface to make things look good.

Jesus.

One bony hand, fingers blue and crooked, is sticking out like a lobster claw. Bowden takes a deep breath and uses his foot to push it back under the makeshift tarp. He stands back to look things over.

Fucking with a crime scene, I'm fucking with a crime scene. The thought plays and rewinds, pops and fries his brain like something searing on a hot griddle. Bowden could lose his career and his pension over this, and couldn't even say why.

All he knows is that someone upstairs wants this done.

Bowden finds a broken broom in a pile of trash. He uses it to sweep the pavement—and remove any footprint evidence—as he slowly backs out of the alley. He surveys the scene to see if he has missed anything, then stays in the shadows and dials his cell phone.

"I found her."

He listens, gives the address. "Better send someone . . . tactful to pick her up. Yeah. I'll wait here for a while." Bowden listens again, interrupts. "Look, I said a while. I'm not going down over this." Bowden closes the phone. He stands alone in the dark, trying to remember what the hell happened to the feeling he used to call integrity.

Bowden joined the force fresh out of the Army. He'd intended to be a good and ethical cop. In the beginning he'd resisted the smallest of bribes and even been known as a tight-ass in the ranks, but somewhere along the way, he'd lost himself. Maybe, he thinks now, it was after that second marriage failed and he was broke and on his ass again. Or when Marjorie sued him for the back child support? No, it was when one of the wise guys hanging around the Sunset Strip dealing upscale coke had offered to let him "wet his beak" a little. Scotty Bowden had opened his mouth to say "no," but nothing came out. Finally he'd nodded to the little bent-nose fucker and bargained away the first piece of his soul. That's when it officially began, and from there on it only got easier. Accept a little bit of a kickback from guys taking small bets on the football games, just for looking the other way. Harmless enough, especially since Bowden had become a betting man himself by then.

Nowadays, Bowden doesn't often ask himself why or when, he just takes the bribe. Oh, he isn't a pimp hustler, doesn't take free blow jobs from the working girls or anything, but he isn't above shaking down a high-rent escort service that works the Hyatt for a little protection money, either. If you're on the wrong side of something you might have to buy your way out. That's the way of the world, right?

Now, your heavy drug dealers, Bowden always busts them hard and clean. He never takes any of the cash or drugs for himself and won't ever look the other way if someone else wants to pilfer meth, coke, or heroin. Not a chance. A guy has to have some standards to sleep at night. But somehow, between his adventures at the track and his drinking and the end of his third marriage, the worst just happened. Someway or another, the great Scotty Bowden finally stumbled a little too far over the line. And now he can't get back.

And a few bad decisions and some big-shot bets have placed him right here in the mouth of an alley full of garbage and guts, covering up a nasty situation, waiting for some kind of amateur meat wagon to come and pick up the corpse of this poor bag lady. He was all tangled up in some kind of a murder case. *But why poison some old broad who likely never hurt anyone? And for Chrissakes, why do it out here in the open, on the damned city streets, in front of God and everybody? What the hell is going on?* The risks are too great and the gain too little. This just doesn't make any logical sense.

Now, pressuring Bowden is one thing—Scotty knows he is burning out, on the edge, just a card-carrying fuckup—but then demanding that he suck in the poor beat cop likely to find the woman? That only widens the potential for trouble. What if Gallo talks to someone outside of the group?

Little Mike Gallo is a good boy, and Bowden knows the kid idealizes him and trusts him, but Gallo is also burdened with something Bowden lost a long time ago. A conscience.

So what if he talks and it's to the wrong person?

Bowden lights another smoke. An errant wind whistles down the rain gutters and ruffles his hair. He makes a mental note to check in with Gallo in a day or two, just to keep him in the choir. *This really sucks.* More wind. Bowden blinks, his eyes tearing from the cold. A second or two later, something near the body at end of the alley . . . *moves.* Bowden's mind starts flickering horrific images from a zillion B movies, one after another: the pile of trash bulges and shimmies and ripples in the wind, then slowly but surely something under it begins to stir. The milk cartons, stained napkins, and pieces of rotting food start to drop away as it sits up; that black plastic bag rolls down and peels like burned and blistered skin to reveal Bloody Mary, her face locked into a grimace that reveals yellowing, bloody teeth and a protruding tongue chewed all the way through . . .

Stop it!

Bowden inhales smoke, burns his fingers on the cigarette. He swears and drops it to the ground in a meteor shower of orange sparks. He stomps it out. He sees his own shadow where he didn't before and whirls around.

Headlights.

Instinctively, Bowden steps further back and hunches his coat up to obscure his face. The vehicle approaches slowly, cautiously, lamps on bright. It's probably the pick-up. Anyone driving through this neighborhood before dawn is bound to be cautious. Bowden shields his eyes and tries to make out the shape of the car. He can't see for shit. Bowden is no longer only worried about the safety of the young patrolman, Mike Gallo. Not for the first time it occurs to Scotty that he, too, may be dispensable.

Bowden kneels. He reaches into his leather ankle holster and pulls out his "throw down," an untraceable .22 with the serial number filed away. He is wearing leather driving gloves, so if he is forced to use the weapon he can leave it behind. The car stops two doors away. The make and model are still obscured, but it sounds old, like some ghetto car. The raggedy engine is still running, chuffing out foul smoke. But is the driver looking for him, or just lost? Should he wait here as instructed, or run for his life?

"Yo. Cop. *Buenas noches.*"

Bowden clutches his weapon with both hands. He takes a deep breath, releases half of it, and steps out into the light with the gun pointed up in the air. He keeps his eyes zeroed on the driver, who seems to have come alone. He moves his head to one side to indicate the alley.

"Down there. She's at the end, under a garbage bag."

"Hokay, then. You go."

Bowden risks a quick glance behind him, sees the street is empty. He starts to back away toward his car. He keeps his tired eyes glued to the front and keeps his gun at the ready. When he moves to his right, he can see the driver. The man behind the wheel is enormous. He gets out of the car. He is dressed in hospital garb of some kind, like an orderly at a mental hospital, or a nurse. He ignores Bowden and goes to the back of the vehicle. Once he opens the rear door, Bowden can see that the car is an old, wood-paneled station wagon. The man wrestles a large wooden trunk to the edge of the vehicle. He opens the heavy lid. He grabs something that looks like a body bag and vanishes into the back of the dark alley.

Bowden wants to throw up. He slides behind the wheel of his own car and drives away. He is surprised to find his entire body soaked with sweat. He stops at the on-ramp to the Hollywood Freeway and attempts to light another cigarette, but his hands are shaking too badly. Bowden takes a photograph of his daughter out of his pocket and studies it. He wonders what this girl, now nearing puberty, would think of her brave daddy, the heroic policeman.

Or perhaps the man she thinks is dead . . . *is* dead.

A horn startles him. Bowden looks up and into the rearview mirror. A drunk in a Chevy is behind him, waiting to get on the freeway. Bowden rolls down the driver side window to flip the prick off. He laughs and gets on the freeway. He keeps the window down and lets the cold fresh air wash over his damp body. It's refreshing, but fails to make him feel clean again.

Thirty-Three

Burke left Gina to stay with a terrified and confused Nicole Stryker, stumbled home, undressed, and was soon asleep. He began dreaming of a long, hot beach with brilliant white sand. In the dream, he was getting a massage, and the hands that touched him were clearly the hands of a young woman. It excited him that he did not know who she was, couldn't see her face. But then the dream changed . . . *Burke walked into a room filled with blood, gore, and body parts. In the center of the room sat a man who had smeared himself with offal and excrement. His eyes were wide, his teeth wetly red, and he was roaring with laughter. Burke searched for his weapon, struggled to raise it, but he could not find the strength . . .*

. . . But then he was back on the beach, being massaged by a woman he couldn't identify. A large bird passed overhead. It made an odd, guttural chirping noise, almost metallic . . .

The telephone.

Burke shook himself awake. He checked the clock. It was not quite five in the morning. The whole world seemed cold, dark, and silent. He fumbled around on the nightstand, found the receiver in the darkness.

"Hello?"

Silence, but for a light, feathered breathing and his own, bass heartbeat; Burke instantly knew who it was, what was happening. "Hello?"

"I need to see you."

Varied emotions hit him, all from different directions; feelings of every temperature and color, most too vivid and powerful for words. "Yes. Where are you?"

"Where do you want me to be?"

And then she knocked on the front door.

Burke ran barefoot to the living room. He paused at the door, damp palms pressed against the varnished wood. The porch light, a quick look for safety; he opened the door and embraced her, clutched at her clothing and kicked the door closed. She dropped the cell phone on the area rug. They kissed long and wet for several moments. Not a word was exchanged.

He dragged her toward the bed, a bit too roughly. His mounting heat had become an agony and it drove him forward, left him almost indifferent to her feelings. He crushed her lips, ripped at zippers and buttons. He forced her to her knees. She took him in her achingly warm, soft mouth. He cried out in torment as much as pleasure. He stopped her a moment later, before it was too late. He took her there on the rug, staring down at her wide-open eyes.

Later he dragged her to the bed, threw her down, licked her dripping sex and entered her from behind. She groaned in a way that spoke of other worlds and shared climaxes. He still held back, until she reached the cliff a second time. When he finally shouted loudly and poured hot lava into her, she was weeping. They curled like spoons and Burke fell into a dark and dreamless sleep.

. . . The dawn, leaking like warm butter through the window blinds: Burke had a sudden flash of instinct and awakened. He opened his eyes. Indira Pal was staring down at him, dark skin still glowing from their frenzied bout. She had an odd expression on her face; those dark eyes seem more sad than happy.

"I love you," Burke whispered. Deep inside, another part of him winced with guilt and objected like some strident prosecutor. *She is married, shut up.*

Indira Pal did not seem pleased. In fact, her sadness deepened visibly. "I should not have come here, Red."

He nodded. "You're probably right, but I'm glad you did."

She lowered her head to his chest, listened to his pounding heart. He stroked her hair, acutely aware that she had something she needed to say, not sure he wanted to listen. He had always been keenly attuned to her and had desperately missed that feeling.

"I have to go back to him."

He did not answer. Could not.

"He needs me."

Let her talk, let her tell it.

"Mo hasn't been well. And that makes my having done this seem even worse than it did the first time."

"Do you want me to feel bad about us? I can't do that." *Not true.* Deep down he did feel bad, for his own reasons as well as those she had just articulated, because selfishly, greedily, he wanted her to stay, to have sex one more time. His flesh needed the sustenance. Burke had been a corpse and she had brought him alive again.

"I have missed you. I have thought of you always, since school. The feelings never went away."

Another flash of guilt, for different reasons: in the spaces in between, Jack Burke had lost himself in someone else, married that someone, and for him these intense feelings had seemed ancient history. He had never forgotten Indira; the memories were precious and rare, but until recently they'd been carefully tucked away in a mental scrapbook, tied with twine, left on a dusty shelf. The past was dead and gone—but now it had returned. For him, things could never be the same now, and he knew it. An affair would not suffice. Their coming together had been irresistible, but he was bound to want more, and soon.

Burke had learned how fickle passion could be, likewise how steady real love could become. Perhaps it was one of the parts of him that had already grown old.

"I'm glad you came here." He repeated himself because he was at a loss for words. His hand, even while stroking her forehead and playing with her long, dark hair, paused for a new thought: "How did you know where I live?"

"I had your address in my book." Had she stiffened a bit? "Perhaps you have sent me a holiday card. No, did you not leave your business card with Mo?"

"That doesn't have my home address."

Indira sighed. "I think of you so often maybe I got it once in the last few years, I don't know. I had it when I looked for it and the computer gave me a map. I waited for Mohandas to fall asleep. He stays up very late sometimes. But then when he went to his room I left to come here."

"You sleep in separate rooms, then?" The thought of their marriage failing so badly instantly made him jubilant, but that response soon provoked a third twinge of guilt. *What, that makes me the golden penis or something?* "It sounds like you have been unhappy for some time."

"Yes."

Moments passed. Indira roused herself to speak again. "But how have you been? Are you . . . working?" That question also was burdened by back story, heavily weighted. Indira had known of his violent adventuring and had always disapproved.

"Not much," Burke lied. "And very little of the wrong kind."

"That is good." Her voice was becoming slurred, her breathing turning lighter and moving faster as she fell asleep.

He considered trying to arouse her again, but let it slide. "Too tired?"

"Hmm. Yes."

Reluctantly, Burke put resurgent lust aside. "Sleep, now. Get some rest." He closed his own eyes and inhaled the scent of her: perfume and perspiration and the heavy musk of sexuality. It had been such a long, long time. He fell asleep. *The dream came again, a man sitting in a pile of gore, laughing* . . . Asleep or awake, Burke couldn't seem to find a way to kill that demon.

When he opened his eyes again, Indira was gone.

Thirty-Four

Burke awoke groggy and depleted from the odd combination of sexual fusion and graphic nightmares, feeling both stimulated and exhausted. He ran his fingertips along the indentation in the white sheets and on the pillow where her head rested; plucked a long, dark hair from the covers. He inhaled the scent of her perfume. A great sadness seized his heart, and he wondered—not for the first time—how a man could so deeply love two women. He did a series of yoga stretches, then stomach exercises and push-ups, used the free weights and gave himself a thorough workout. When he was dizzy and his muscles were trembling, he stopped. Then it was time to repeat the stretches and unwind a little before taking a long, hot shower.

He made a protein shake with fresh fruit and skim milk. He turned on the television in the living room to watch CNN. The blender screeched like a surgeon's bone saw. When he turned it off, he caught the last minute of a story involving "Juan Dominguez, one of South America's biggest drug lords," who had died of some lingering illness at a remote location in Mexico. Unsurprisingly, both American and Mexican officials were not displeased.

What had brought international attention, however, was an outrage involving Maria Consuelo Dominguez, the drug lord's spouse. At the written request of Senor Dominguez, and with the full approval and involvement of his gang, the wife was gagged and bound and thrown onto her husband's funeral pyre.

Although that practice was well known in the East it was virtually unheard of in South America. Human rights activists and feminists the world over were in an uproar.

The telephone rang. Burke answered. “Honey?”

Tony Monteleone. “My office. Half an hour.”

Burke heard the same program in stereo. Tony was also watching CNN. “Tony? Hey, did you catch this story on Dominguez and his wife?”

A grunt. “Some of it.”

“How low can you go?”

The CNN anchor introduced a video piece. Someone had done their research. A short, narrated clip referred to an obscure, now discredited Hindu practice called *Sati,* where a man’s widow was required by law to burn beside the body of her spouse.

“The old ‘if I can’t have her, nobody can,’ huh?”

“How about that,” Monteleone offered, dryly. “Maybe you can take it with you.” In comedy, timing is everything. Tony broke the connection.

The shower felt wonderful on aching muscles. Burke locked up, left, and was surprised to find himself whistling tunelessly as he drove through the city. Even one annoying schmuck who cut him off at the Riverside exit failed to fully arouse his ire. He parked behind Fredo, as usual, and sailed in through the back.

“Have a seat.” Tony Monteleone was in his usual booth, papers everywhere. He looked wrung out and short on sleep, his hair divided into two small hillocks not unlike the horns of a satyr. “Want some coffee?”

Burke was already pouring from the pot.

“What the fuck you so happy about?”

Burke sipped, smiled. “Nothing.”

Monteleone shook his head. “You scare me, Red. You really do. Just when I start believing you got some brains to go with your balls, you go and fuck up."

Burke felt his smile falter. *How the hell does he know about her?* "I didn't plan on it, Tony. It just happened." *Jesus, he's really pissed.*

Monteleone leaned forward. Silverware clanked and tepid coffee pooled in his saucer. His features went pinched. He was having a difficult time keeping his voice level. "What the fuck do you mean, you didn't plan on it? What did you think would go down after the last time?"

When Burke didn't reply, Monteleone became even more irate. "Listen, Red, do you know what I think?"

Burke leaned back in his seat, honestly bewildered. "No, Tony. And I'm not sure I give a damn what you think."

"What?"

"You heard me."

Monteleone's features darkened. His mouth turned down and slanted into a jack-o-lantern scowl. "I owe you favors. You are a man of respect, but don't presume upon our friendship by talking to me this way ever again."

Burke realized, a bit too late, that being with Indira had clouded his thinking—something was very, very wrong here. That there had been an extra car in the back parking lot, a dented Volkswagen bus, yet no one else was inside the restaurant. That the curtain separating the entrance from the main part of the restaurant was always open when the restaurant was this empty—but now it was halfway shut, and below the lower trim Burke could just make out the shape of a large pair of shoes. Someone was watching them argue.

This was a hit.

He slid his hand from the table and allowed it to stray to his weapon. He extended his peripheral vision, soaked up some additional details: The door to the kitchen was open a crack and a thin shadow extended to the edge of the bar. *There are two of them, one straight ahead and one slightly behind me, both probably mob soldiers. What the hell is going on?*

Monteleone slowly extended a trembling finger and pointed to Burke's left arm. "Bring your gun hand out and set it down on the table, nice and slow."

Burke did not comply. "Tony, I would very much like us to start over from the top here, okay?"

Tony Monteleone was red-faced and seething. He picked up a napkin, dipped it in some ice water and dabbed his perspiring forehead. "And just how do you propose we do that?"

For his part, Burke was tense, but cold; his fingers were at the butt of his Glock, and he was determined to get out alive. He hesitated. A new approach occurred to him. He slowly brought his hand back into plain view, set it down on the red-and-white-checkered tablecloth. "Start over. Tell me why you're pissed. I don't get it."

"What?" Monteleone, clearly stunned. "The fuck you mean you don't get it?"

"I'm serious. Look, my hands are empty. You've got two of your studs drawing down on me right now, and a gun of your own under the table. I'm going to trust you, here. We go back a long way. Now, tell me why you're pissed."

Monteleone shook his head. "You're a piece of work, Burke. You think you can just hit anybody you want? Take out a customer of mine who owes me forty large, without even clearing it first?"

"What are you talking about?"

"Dinky Martin, damn it. Don't yank my chain. You left me in the dark and holding my dick, here."

Burke blinked. "Somebody wasted Dinky?"

"And the Arena Bowl Elephant, too. Down in Sherman Oaks somewhere. You trying to tell me it wasn't you who did it?"

"No way. I swear."

"Don't lie to me, damn it." But Burke's shocked face was convincing. Tony slowly relaxed. "Maybe you'd best tell me what transpired."

Burke sighed. "He and the big guy tailed me out of a restaurant and braced me. We danced a little, sure, but I left them both breathing."

"You wouldn't shit me?"

"Tony, I've done some strange things in my time, but I don't kill people for no reason. And if it had been me, it would have been in self-defense. And don't you think I would have called you and put you in the loop?"

Monteleone pondered. After a time, he relaxed. "It didn't sound much like you, Red. You don't like knives and I never heard of you strangling somebody, either."

Burke was worried, deep in thought. "Down in Sherman Oaks, you said. That bothers me, man. Because it must have happened right after I got into it with them. Did he owe big anywhere else?"

Monteleone dabbed his forehead again. "Not half what he owed me! I'm the biggest sucker around. And now I'm out a lot, and that means my bosses are out, too. They are not happy campers."

"Tony, it wasn't me. We were talking about two different things at the start, there."

Monteleone squinted. "Okay, but answer me this, then. What the hell did you mean when you said it wasn't my business?"

"That was about a girl," Burke offered weakly. "And . . . well, she's married."

"Pussy? You were going to croak for *pussy?*" Monteleone snapped his fingers. "Down, boys." A rectangle of pale light appeared on the curtain as the first man stepped through the front door. He smiled amiably at Burke and walked back outside. The one in the kitchen quietly closed the door; his footsteps slapped the damp flooring as he exited through the back.

Burke forced a wry grin. "Why do I feel a sudden and almost overwhelming urge to go to confession?"

Straight-faced and dour, Tony Monteleone responded. "Because you were maybe a pubic hair from being dead."

"Well, no wonder."

Tony squinted. "Okay, then here's how it is. I want to hire you to find out who hit him. Who the fuck wasted a client on my turf without asking. Whoever it is, he took bread out of the mouths of my family. I want him notified that his behavior is unacceptable."

Burke drank some coffee. He was surprised to see that his hand was steady. "I guess that brings us to a second topic."

"Which is?"

"I'm out."

"Say what?"

"I'm out." Burke put the cup down, gently. "You've been good to me from the day I hit town from Vegas, Tony. You've looked the other way when I asked you to. You worked with me so I could pick up a government job or two. Never bitched when I had to turn you down for something, never dragged me too far into anything delicate. I owe you big, friend."

"I'm getting an ulcer, damn it." Tony leaned back and rubbed his belly. "It's the stress. Okay, I heard a 'but' in that speech, right?"

"But I just can't do it anymore. I think I can find other ways to make the cash. Maybe I can figure out a way to lower the medical expenses, I don't know. But this tap dancing on the edge, it needs to stop."

"Tell me it ain't so. You're gonna play it straight?"

"Have to."

Monteleone was amused. "And you think *they* will let you walk away, just like that," another snap of the fingers, "whenever you want? Me, I trust you. I might be okay with something like this, but Wee Willie and Sonny D . . . you know how they are."

"I know. So it might please them to know I'm not in a hurry for the rest of the money that is owed me. You can take your time."

Burke was calm and perfectly composed and the reason gradually dawned on Monteleone. He fought down a smirk. "Don't tell me. You have a little insurance policy of some kind put away."

"What we have here is a 'live and let live' kind of thing," Burke replied. "There will be no problem so long as nothing happens to me, or anyone close to me, that could in any way be considered suspicious."

Monteleone allowed the smile to blossom wide. He actually seemed pleased, even proud. "And needless to say, if anyone were to try something and fail, you'd take that very personally."

"Very. I would feel compelled to speak directly to whoever gave that order."

"Like I said earlier, you got balls."

Burke shrugged. "I know I might be putting you in a very awkward position, Tony. Do you mind passing the message for me, or should I fly to Vegas and do it myself?"

"I don't mind. I want to see their ugly faces. And for what it's worth, if anybody can pull off yanking the Corelli brothers by the dick, it's probably you. The government thing scares them shitless, you know. They remember hearing stories about the Kennedy family."

Burke got out of the booth. "Thanks, Tony. You're a good guy. And I meant what I said. I owe you for all you've done for us."

"You and your wife are good people, Red."

"Just take the compliment."

Monteleone considered. "Aw, fuck. I probably owe you, too."

A sip of coffee, another dab with the napkin. "But answer me something."

"Okay."

"This married broad. You love her? I mean, *really* love her?"

"Yes." Burke surprised himself. "In fact, I think I always have."

"I kind of envy you that shit," Monteleone said. His eyes changed filters, rolled inward. "Me, I never had it. Been married to Louise since we was both kids in Newark. She was a real sweet piece of ass back then, and I liked her well enough. But now . . ."

Burke waited, politely; wondering where this was headed.

"Now, she's mean as a snake." Monteleone sighed. "What I envy is you got a woman who might really want to be nice to you. That can be a very fucking good thing, important in a man's life. A man needs that shit." He extended his hand. They shook, hard. Monteleone held on for a few extra seconds, clumsy machismo preventing him from voicing his true feelings. Burke nodded, getting it. He squeezed back.

"Red? Good luck."

"Thanks, Tony. You, too."

Monteleone, who had been prepared to do murder only moments before, was embarrassed by the vague hint of real sentiment. He returned to his clutter of papers, face down and shoulders stiff. Burke paused at the back door, looked back at a man truly out of his proper century. Monteleone barked, without looking up.

"Don't be a stranger."

THIRTY-FIVE

Monday

Bowden could still remember when smoking in a city or county building was not considered a mortal sin. But somewhere along the way those tree-hugging, animal-rights, health-food freakazoids wormed their way into state politics. By the time they had completed their rampage, smokers had become an endangered species. Other than a brief, all-too-trendy resurgence of cigar smoking in the 1990s, the zeitgeist had condemned the smoker as foul, filthy, and morally repugnant. Bowden was currently outside the garage entrance, smoking one last cigarette before his meeting with the Deputy Mayor of Los Angeles. He had his back to the parked cars and stood, quietly, inhaling desperately into cupped palms. His cell phone rang.

"Yo! Scotty? It's Doc." His old friend sounds tense, hurried. The dark voice has a flinty edge to it. Doc sounds like a man who just got bad results from a biopsy. "You where you can talk?"

"What's up?" Bowden forces enthusiasm. "How are they hanging these days, my man?"

"Scotty, I don't know who else to talk to. I got specific orders form the ME's office to close the file, but I was fucking around killing time and I noticed something."

Bowden drops his smoke, steps on it. His mouth turns down. "You've lost me, Doc," which is a bald-faced lie, "which file are you talking about?"

"27ME1642," Doc replies. "You know, that writer guy, Stryker."

Bowden kicks the wall in frustration. "Doc, where are you?"

"I'm on a land-line, but it's a pay phone outside the office. Don't worry."

Yeah, but I'm on a goddamn cell phone, Bowden thinks. He's getting pissed off, but it's really just fear. "I'm worried, believe me. Drop it here, Doc. Please."

"Scotty, I found something really weird."

"You tell anybody about it?"

"I left a message for Burke, but he hasn't gotten back to me yet."

Bowden grunts, runs sweaty fingers through his thinning hair. "Doc, leave him out of the loop. You hear me?"

"Scotty, there's a piece of the guy's bowel missing."

Bowden is speechless. Then: "Say *what?*"

Doc is excited, a bit fascinated. "I was flipping through the files when I came across something so odd it doesn't fit any scenario I've ever seen before, not suicide or homicide. Dude, remember that he did himself in the bathtub, the old *hari kiri* thing?"

"Yeah. It kind of ruined my lunch to read that."

"Catch this, dude. I found an area of the lower bowel where two surgical cuts had been made, neat and clean and professional, one on each side of what was probably about a ten-inch section."

"So?"

"So there is absolutely no way the guy could have tortured and disemboweled himself, then made two neat surgical cuts in the mess of his own lower GI. Not a fucking chance. He would have been too deep into shock."

Bowden tap dances. "I read he took a lot of drugs, Doc, all different kinds. Hey, you're the Doc, but, with the right mix of painkillers and stimulants, who knows?"

"Scotty, catch this." He pauses, the timing of a little kid about to give the punch line to a dirty joke. "You know that maybe nine- or ten-inch long, stinky hot dog of a bowel piece?"

"Yeah?"

"It's missing."

Bowden closes his eyes as the sidewalk collapses around him and becomes a black hole in space. "Doc, don't tell Burke."

"Why not?"

"Don't tell Red, my friend. Please. We need to talk, okay?"

"But . . ."

"Doc, I can't go into this now, but it is not in Burke's best interest that he hear about this, man. It will dig him in too deep. I'm trying to cover him and he's almost out of the woods."

"What woods are those, man? You're not making any sense, here."

"If you tell Red about this, you are going to drop him into one hell of a shit storm. Just take my word on that. Can I come by later?" He looks at his watch with blurred eyes. "Maybe around closing time, five or six?"

Doc's voice loses steam, gains suspicion. "Yeah. I guess."

"And don't talk to anybody else about this before then, okay?"

"Scotty . . ." A warning mixed with growing mistrust.

Bowden interrupts him. "Think Feds, Doc. Think witness protection, top secret, for-your-eyes-only, need to know–type shit, okay? And then trust me and keep your mouth shut. I'll explain later."

"Yeah. Okay. Sure thing."

Bowden closes the phone, blows air like a man running track. *Well that is just what I fucking needed.*

A bookish brunette in a knit woolen business suit and large glasses strides by with her eyes locked forward. She seems offended. Bowden realizes he's spoken his thoughts. He gives her a weak smile and follows her into the tiled, gilded lobby where footsteps echo and voices generally whisper, but big money shouts. He rides up in a bronze elevator with other city functionaries, all of them jammed together like Vienna sausage.

The buxom receptionist eyes him, bird to worm. Bowden shows his badge, gives his most winning smile and his name. He wanders over to thumb through some out-of-date magazines while the receptionist carries on a hushed conversation with her high-tech headgear. "He'll be with you in a moment."

Bowden grabs *Sports Illustrated* and stares down at an article that attempts to explain the collapse of the St. Louis Rams. He is too preoccupied to read. His descent into hell has been so rapid, so dizzying, that he still finds it difficult to retrace the steps. Now Doc is going to need to know what's up. Bowden doesn't like that. He has already told Jack Burke part of the truth, the part Burke needed to know. He'll have to keep his story straight with Doc. Say just enough.

Because the rest, an embarrassing collection of sordid events involving prostitutes, recreational drugs, and off-duty chores for corrupt city officials like Deputy Mayor Paul Grace, Bowden had elected to keep secret. This is a mess becoming a whirlwind. One thing has to stay under wraps . . . and that's this meeting. Paul Grace is not someone he is proud to know.

Deputy Mayor Grace, a sleek and well-tailored young Harvard law graduate, comes from what was once old LA money. His family built its fortune the new-fashioned LA way, meaning in the entertainment business. His father, Jack Grace, co-founded Cyclops Productions, a company known for cranking out bad films and worse television. By the time young Paul had graduated from Harvard, his cocaine addled, sex-addicted father had run the family business into the ground. So young master Grace made the logical move. He switched from entertainment to local politics—considered by many to be one and the same.

Paul Grace's superior, Mayor James Shelton, does not merely stand on a platform of "family values," he paces around ranting and raving about the same. Mayor Shelton is not the sort who handles unpleasant issues personally. Being a man who dreams of federal office, the Mayor, ever conscious of the need to leave himself "plausible deniability," delegates those to Deputy Mayor Grace.

Scott Bowden, under pressure from IA for his peccadilloes, suddenly found himself summoned for a personal conference with Mr. Grace. Ever the suave attorney, Grace managed to make the terms clear while keeping the precise agreement completely off the record.

Bowden caught on rapidly. He promptly "volunteered" to work special assignments for the Deputy Mayor's office. In exchange for that clandestine service, his IA record would be expunged and the charges filed against him deleted from the system. As Bowden thumbed through a magazine he could not see, he remembered a quotation from somewhere—Mark Twain perhaps?—that the "greatest trick the devil has ever pulled is convincing us that he doesn't exist."

He does. *And his name is Paul Grace.*

The "assignments" began simply enough. Bowden got a call asking him to meet Mr. Grace for a drink. Grace had a bodyguard with him, a former homicide dick named Roy Garner. In the men's room, Garner patted Bowden down, pronounced him clean. Then, with the water running to foul up any electronic bugs, Grace showed Bowden a piece of paper with a name and an address. He made it clear that Bowden's job was to find something, anything, to pin on the guy.

"The guy" was Jack Reilly, a congressman from northern California who was leading a movement to block the flow of illegal immigrants into the state. Bowden didn't know much about politics, but he did know that the Mayor had a lot of money invested in industry from south of the border, and was friendly to businesses that employed workers at below minimum wage. It didn't take a rocket scientist to see that Reilly was starting to cost thc Mayor somc serious bucks. Bowden switched to a day shift and followed Congressman Reilly during his off-duty hours, looking for a chink in the guy's armor. Turned out he didn't drink or party much, didn't gamble, and didn't seem to have any white-collar scams going; if he did, they were very well hidden.

But the guy was a chicken hawk.

When Bowden uncovered Reilly's penchant for young male hookers, Deputy Mayor Grace was thrilled. He slipped Bowden a grand and promised that a bit more of his jacket had been cleaned up. For a little while, Bowden had believed him. *I wanted to believe him.* But now, nearly two years later, Scotty found himself back in the office of the Deputy Mayor, waiting for another assignment, wondering what it would be this time: character assassination, a slight beating, blackmail? Bowden thinks he'll print some new business cards soon. Hey, maybe something like SCROTUMS 'R US would look cool. What made him feel the sleaziest was that he had been handing assignments to Jack Burke for months that in some way originated with the Deputy Mayor without Burke realizing it. Bowden didn't like using his friends, but the idea of being a cop behind bars was even less appetizing.

Miss Boobs speaks: "Deputy Mayor Grace will see you now." She stands, turns on her high heels, and leads the way down the hall. Bowden thinks she walks like she has a corn cob up her ass. Must be those stiletto heels.

The receptionist knocks on a tall, thick door. After a respectful few seconds she opens it and ushers Bowden into a spacious conference room. One long window faces the city of Los Angeles. Grim, smoggy clouds hang like pads of steel wool over the toothy skyline of irregular buildings. Grace is seated alone at the head of a ludicrously long, varnished wooden table, with a coffee service and croissants on a tray before him.

"Hello, Detective."

The Deputy Mayor had his chin cupped thoughtfully in one hand, staring out the window, a poseur channeling a burdened leader. Grace was that kind of elemental narcissist, always performing for a hidden camera.

"Pull up your shirt," Grace says mildly. "Then turn around." Bowden complies. The air-conditioned atmosphere strikes his bare skin like a slap. Grace glances over just long enough to verify that Bowden isn't wired. "Have a seat. This room is swept for bugs on a weekly basis."

Bowden moves closer, but still a few chairs away. He feels strange in the empty, cavernous meeting room. He sits. Grace does not offer him refreshment.

"We have a couple of new problems, Scotty."

Hearing his first name issue from this fur ball puke makes Scotty cringe, but he hides the reaction. "Go on."

"Your friend Burke, for starters, seems quite tenacious. He is not backing off."

"I warned you he was stubborn. I told you that if there were any slipups, I might not be able to control him."

Grace looks up. His eyes are narrowed, pupils contracted into marbles. "If you can't handle him I'll find someone else, someone less squeamish."

"I'll talk to him again."

"You did a good job with the old woman," Grace says quietly. "Our man took her directly to a mortuary and requested cremation."

"That's good."

"Unfortunately, despite your best efforts, it seems a report was filed."

Bowden feels the skin on his neck quiver. "Excuse me?"

"A young officer named—" Grace consults a small notepad. "—Mike Gallo. I think he's one you trusted to call you."

"He made a report?"

"Apparently he had an attack of conscience, or wanted to make sure he was in the clear. So he entered a line or two about spotting a homeless woman 'who may have been ill or dead' into his daily log."

Damn it, Gallo. You moron!

"That's unfortunate. Out of curiosity, how did he explain not calling for an ambulance?"

Grace steeples his fingers, posing again. "I believe he claimed his radio malfunctioned, so he left to find a pay phone. He was also out of change, it seems, and when he returned the woman was gone."

Bowden shrugs. "Okay, so what if he covered his ass in case anything comes up? He can admit he saw her, say he tried to do his duty. It's no big deal."

"Oh, but I'm afraid it is."

"How so?"

"Someone was a busy beaver last night. Someone called around and found the mortuary we had taken her to. Someone put a stop order on the cremation and made a formal request for an autopsy."

I'm fucked. "Who is that someone?"

"Why, a gentleman of color in the coroner's office." Grace's voice had gone soft, and the effect was disturbing. "I believe you know him, too. His name is Lincoln Washington." He raises his eyes, pins Bowden like a bug.

A chill, stark as a wave of high fever, runs through Scotty's upper body and he sits back as if slapped. "Doc."

"What?"

"His nickname is Doc. And he just called me about a

completely different situation. It seems he noticed something odd about the Stryker death, a section of bowel missing. I asked him to sit on it. Told him there was some federal stuff going on, high priority, and that I would explain later."

"Ah. I can understand your reasoning. Sadly, this is not a different situation."

"You mean these two incidents are related?" Bowden hears his own bloodstream hissing, aches for the well-being of his old friends. *Judas and the pieces of silver.*

Grace poses again. This time the stern father, pointing his finger. "I am not at liberty to discuss details. Let's just say that your concept of top secret is not far off the mark. Please understand that my superiors are very unhappy with you at present. Despite assurances, your compatriots, the young patrolman and Mr. Burke and this black fellow, are not proving as functional as you had initially represented. In fact, they are briskly becoming irritants and obstructions."

"Do you thumb through a thesaurus in the morning? Didn't anyone ever tell you nobody actually talks like that?"

Bowden likes the reaction. The younger man's cheeks turn pink. "You're a piece of shit, Bowden. It is not in your best interest to anger me. I think you should remember that."

Ignoring him, Bowden shakes his head. "Doc probably doesn't know."

"Know what?"

"Doc doesn't have any reason to think these two things are related. The Stryker suicide and the old woman. He's doing his job, that's all. He found a couple of loose ends and blew the whistle."

Grace thinks for a moment. "Let me put it to you this way. The people I report to cannot afford to have him put those pieces together. That must never happen. Do I make myself clear?"

"I'll talk to him today."

"I have already taken care of that."

"Don't!" Bowden hears the plea in his voice, cannot help it. "Let me handle him."

Grace stands, motions to the door like Nero at the games. "I would prefer you devote your limited time and attention to Mr. Burke. He looks to be a far more complicated individual." Those eyes again. "Convince him to look elsewhere, Mr. Bowden. Do it quickly."

Bowden gets to his feet. For a moment he considers blowing the dick away and then turning the gun on himself. *I just wish I had the balls . . .*

Bowden is numb during the ride down the elevator, in the lobby, and all the way up to his car. He starts the engine. When he puts his hands on the wheel they are shaking. He looks around the garage, finds it empty. He slides a pint bottle of vodka from under the seat and gulps.

"That rat bastard." The tears come. Bowden ends up sideways on the front seat, shaking and crying. The episode lasts for several minutes. Eventually he sits up, starts his car, and drives out into a crisp daylight that has somehow darkened.

Thirty-Six

Tuesday

"Have you seen this film, Esteban?"

"No, Buey."

"That is Mr. Steve McQueen who should have got the Oscar for the job he did. I love this fucking movie, Esteban. It is called *The Sand Pebbles* because the boat is the San Pablo. You understand?"

"No, Buey."

"You make me laugh, Esteban. That is why I enjoy to drink with you. Come, sit by me on my couch. Later, there will be women."

"Yes, Buey."

"Watch. Watch. This part is good."

"May I have a drink, Buey?"

"What? Oh! Of course, Esteban. Help yourself to some fine whiskey, or perhaps a *cerveza.* The tall one is called Taj Mahal, it is imported from India, some very good shit. There is coke on the table. Do a line, relax."

"Ah, blow does not relax me, Buey. It makes me want to fuck."

"Well, then you can do that, too! I said there will be women, didn't I? Ha!"

"This is a good movie."

"Yes, Mr. McQueen is so upset when he has to shoot his Chinese friend in the head to save him from torture. This breaks your heart, no?"

"Very sad."

"Yes."

"Buey?"

"Esteban, I am watching the movie. *Shhh,* it is nearly over. He will go to the courtyard to save the woman and they will shoot him."

"Who will shoot him?"

"The Chinese, you fool."

"I thought they were his friends, Buey. I am mixed up."

"Some are his friends and some are not."

"Ah. I see."

"Look, they shoot him now. And listen, he says 'what happened, I was almost home,' or something like that. I love this fucking movie."

"This is good shit."

"The best. Now, please. You asked to see me."

"Buey, I am a loyal man and I have served you for many years. Please do not think I would question your judgment."

"But?"

"I am troubled by something."

"And this is what?"

"It is this new man we are doing mucho business with these days. The one who works with our scientists. He worries me, Buey. I do not trust this man or the people he brings here."

"You are concerned for me. I am touched."

"You are not angry?"

"Oh, of course not, Esteban. I admire your courage in coming to speak with me this way."

"This is good."

"Ah. You have not shared these feelings with the others, behind my back, have you?"

"I have said nothing, Buey! I would never do such a thing."

"This is good. Because then I would have to kill you, Esteban. I would not like being forced to do that. Continue to say nothing. You see, this man from America is going to make me very, very rich. He will also give me revenge on a man who tried to shoot me last year, an American operative named Burke. So I value his friendship, you understand?"

"Yes, certainly."

"But know this, my friend. I have not lived this long or grown this fat by trusting people, eh? And certainly not some asshole from America who thinks he is on a first-name basis with God."

"I see."

"Fear not, Esteban. I have a plan of my own in mind. I fully anticipate to confront him, and soon. I expect his treachery and will meet it with a nasty trick or two of my own."

"That makes me feel better, Buey."

"I wish you to feel well."

"And I promise that I will keep your confidence."

"I know you will, my friend. Because you enjoy breathing too much! Ha! Ha! Look, here are tonight's young women. Ladies, come. Join us. Tonight we spend in bed, but we do not sleep."

Thirty-Seven

Deep in LA's San Fernando Valley, a large man walked through an empty Catholic church on Lindley Avenue in Tarzana and knocked on the door to the private offices.

"Jack?"

Father Benny was shocked but delighted. Burke closed the door behind him. They walked down a short hallway to Benny's office.

"Why in heaven's name are you showing up here?"

"Bet you never thought you'd see me in church."

"Exactly." Benny's office was chaos. Pillows, file folders, unwashed dishes everywhere. To his credit, the priest was clearly embarrassed. "Have a seat, my boy. If you can find one, that is."

Burke shoved two ornate pillows aside and sat on the sagging leather couch. He cracked his knuckles and toed the floor, obviously stalling.

Benny prodded, ever so gently. "To what do I owe the pleasure?"

"I need to talk to someone."

"I don't recall you ever saying you were Catholic."

"Lapsed is too mild a word."

Benny leaned back in his office chair, folded his hands across his plump belly. "Well, that's all the better, then. You can lie to me and not worry about it being a damned sin, right? Excuse me, Lord."

Burke did not smile. "I have a question for you. And I came

here because I don't know anyone else I can ask. Maybe you can answer it, maybe not. All I want is the same answer you would give another priest, the spiritual answer."

Cautiously. "Okay."

Burke, voice muffled. "I have done a lot of bad things in my day, Father Benny. Some of them I regret, some I think of as just doing my job. But there are damned few I feel really ashamed about. I don't want to add anything to that pile if I can avoid it."

"Go on."

"Just give me an honest answer to my dilemma, and I will be on my way. That's all I'm asking."

Benny grinned. "Okay, I am officially in priest mode, now. Shoot."

Burke rubbed his hands together. "There's a woman."

"There's always a woman."

"I have loved her for a long time."

"Since before Mary?" Benny's voice was gentle, probing.

"Yes. I knew her a long time ago. Since I was in school with her, and she was an exchange student from India. It started then."

"And . . . ?"

"She's married."

Father Benny's face softened, sagged with sorrow. "I see. And so are you."

"And so am I." Burke looked up, his anguish now fully apparent. "Over to you, Benny."

Father Benny sighed. He walked his fingers along his shirt, fiddled with his collar. "Have you ever read the prayer of St. Francis, Jack?"

"Yeah, a long time ago."

"Where he says 'let me be an instrument of thy peace' and 'let me seek to understand rather than to be understood, to love rather than be loved'?" Benny closed his eyes. "I adore that passage because it resonates so well with the teachings of the Buddha—the admonition against attachments, a dedication to the compassionate release of all worldly things."

"It does, but I'm no saint."

Benny laughed gently. "None of us is a saint, Jack. The best we can hope for is to strive to be better men than we were yesterday. I'm just saying that the answer to life's dilemmas is never to cling to what was never ours in the first place, and that eventually means even life itself."

Burke's eyes widened half in shock. "Do I understand you correctly, here?"

Benny shook his head. "No offense, but I doubt it. I am not taking an ethical position, or trying to give you pat answers. You didn't come to me for that. I'm saying that the ultimate truth is that nothing belongs to us, Jack. Not even our bodies, much less someone else's soul. God owns it all, lock stock and barrel. He calls us home on a damned whim, excuse me, Lord. Because we serve at his discretion. Go on, name me something you actually own."

Burke understood and accepted the tenets of Buddhism. He saw where Benny was going but elected to play along. "My house."

Benny grinned triumphantly. "The bank owns your house."

"What if I've paid it off?"

"Don't pay your property taxes for a while, and you'll quickly find out that the state owns that house."

"What if I pay it off and pre-pay my property taxes indefinitely?"

Benny leaned forward. "The universe always wins, Jack. Sooner or later you die. The house is torn down and becomes dust. Everything goes back to where it came from. We don't own anyone or anything, we just borrow a bit here and there."

"Okay, now back to my problem."

"You don't own either one of these women, Jack. Neither does anyone else. They don't possess you, or your heart—you have chosen to give them something. The pain we feel comes from confusing attachment with love, or affection with ownership."

"They are already gone."

"Yes. You will lose them both in the end, and they you."

"Agreed." Burke grunted, ruefully. "Okay, now you've really made my day."

"The issue confronting you cannot be dealt with through emotion, or outmoded ideas of romance or attachment."

"Then how do I think this through?"

Benny pondered. "You remember why I said I keep flying? Because I think I have to face my fear to know God?"

"Yeah."

"Maybe that's a bit of what you're looking at here as well. You need to be willing to face some of your deepest fears if you're going to come to the right decision. Hell, if there is such a thing as a right decision, excuse me, Lord."

"How do I do that?"

"What *is* your deepest fear, my son?"

Burke shuddered. "My deepest fear is probably what you just described, Benny. The damned impermanence of things, death and the cosmogonic cycle, the loss of my own life and the lives of those I love."

"You must rethink your priorities, Red. Open up your mind. One simply has to change the camera angle, as it were. To pull back and see the bigger picture. What would serve the greater good?"

Burke winked. "What would Jesus do? I thought you were Catholic."

Benny blew a raspberry. "Hell, the majority of the people

who slap that bumper sticker on their car don't have a clue what it really means. We're not talking about any individual religion here, and you of all people should know that. We're talking about a spiritual principle."

Burke leaned back on the couch. "Go on."

"So you must ask yourself this . . . if I felt nothing but compassion for everyone involved here, both myself, the lady in question, and the wronged spouses, what would I do? What would serve the greater good?"

"Ah. That's not easy."

"No." Benny rested his elbows on the desk. "Take your time. Think it over, pray about it. The answer might surprise you. From personal experience, I assure you that it is also seldom as simple as it first appears. And in the end, you are the only one who can decide."

Thirty-Eight

The volleyball coach is an Hispanic woman with dishwater-blonde hair. She is a young thirty, dressed in tight, red shorts and a halter top. She brings the whistle to her lips and stops the calisthenics. The all-girls team collapses to the ground in a heap. Their giggles carry easily on the afternoon breeze.

The man with the bloodshot eyes sits in the plain brown sedan. Those eyes are glued to one pre-teen with a lithe and almost tomboyish figure. He watches her stand ahead of the others. She is the first to start running in place. He smiles.

When the coach turns his way, as if growing suspicious of the parked car, the driver lowers his glasses, starts the vehicle, and drives off.

She looks like me, Scotty Bowden thinks. *She's a jock, and I'll be damned if she doesn't look a lot like me.*

THIRTY-NINE

"234?"

"234 here."

"We have a possible 182 in progress at 18745 Lansdale Street, North Hollywood. Be advised that is south of the intersection and west of Vineland."

"We're on it. ETA four minutes."

Officer Mike Gallo feels the familiar thrill. He grins—bright, white teeth in the darkness—lowers the mike and starts the powerful engine. He pulls the patrol car away from the curb and out of the darkened area of the street. His new partner, as usual, doesn't react. Gallo has only known Frank "Bulldog" Gillespie for a couple of days. Bulldog just transferred in from South Central. Bulldog already has the "thousand-yard stare" of a young man who has seen far too much, and way too often.

"Lock and load." Gallo immediately despises himself for sounding macho. *Over a year on the force and still insecure, like I got something to prove. What a dipshit.* Gallo weaves in and out of the light traffic and cuts down Vineland. Lansdale is a quiet residential street south of Blix; it touches a long fork that extends south from Vineland and then veers west, into the shadows. A few porch lights are on, but the street is otherwise quiet. "What was it again?"

Bulldog grunts, checks the computer console in the patrol car. "18745 Lansdale. Must be in the next block."

"Check us in."

Bulldog grabs the microphone. "234 on the scene."

This section of the block is as still as a painting. The house on the left appears uninhabited, although there is one battered Ford truck parked in the oil-stained driveway. The house on the right, an impossibly small, one-bedroom cottage, is several yards back from the sidewalk. Someone inside is watching television; black-and-white images flicker eerily on the closed, beige blinds.

"Okay." Gallo wishes he knew his new partner better, could trust him more. He takes a deep breath. "Let's do it."

The young cop opens the car door, one hand on his weapon and the other holding his heavy flashlight. He waits for Bulldog to clamber out of the passenger seat. They examine the house. It is a plain, white one-story 1940s house, most likely two bedrooms and one small bath. There is an empty carport on the left side, rather than the standard one-car garage. The faux redwood frame is warping under the weight of tree branches and a pool of stagnant rainwater that has not been properly drained. The rear of the carport is filled with cardboard boxes and tall slats of used plywood. No one, nothing.

It could be a trap.

Gallo veers left, shines his light into the carport and works closer. Bulldog takes the vegetation on the right of the house without being asked. The two men keep their hands on their holstered weapons and move quietly. 18745 is the kind of dilapidated home generic to this part of the Valley, where the long-suffering middle class still struggles to uphold a sense of community pride. The dark street has not quite yet descended into gangland, but it is turning into what some cops euphemistically refer to as "poor white," and chances are the gang graffiti will start popping up within a couple of years.

Gallo pauses. A common feature on this sort of property is a tall bank of runaway ivy. Sure enough, the entire backyard is overrun by thick, green vines. Three doors down, what sounds like a gigantic Doberman roars an alarm. His loud *wuff* agitates other dogs in the neighborhood and within seconds the night is cluttered with barking.

Gallo shines his light through the kitchen window, sees nothing out of the ordinary. He moves to the far side of the carport. This gig has a "pucker factor" of nine, so his heart is soon doing a very slow, very loud rain dance. *Why was it called in? There's nothing going on here.*

Footsteps in the ivy.

Gallo has his 9mm halfway out before his ears properly place the sound; it is Bulldog, crossing the far part of the yard, exploring a pile of trash and old tires near the fence. *Jesus H. Christ. Take it easy.*

Another noise, right in front, and Gallo flinches a little but holds back this time. He is starting to feel a bit like a scared old woman jumping out of her pantyhose. Sure enough, the sound comes again. It is low and to the left, behind some cardboard boxes at the foot of the rapidly metastasizing wall of yellowing ivy. Gallo moves in a bit closer, peeks around the back of a box. A large, striped gray-and-white tomcat with badly chewed ears and abscessed skin has cornered something. A slight rustle in the ivy, another pounce a foot or two away from the original position; jaws strike flesh. The cat turns, a stunned rat dangling bloodily from gaping maw, and flashes Gallo an arrogant, possessive grin before trotting off into the darkness with its prize.

Gallo relaxes his shoulders. He hears footsteps again. Bulldog must be finished patrolling the yard. Mike Gallo turns around with his mouth open to relay what just happened. A firecracker goes off and someone punches him in the groin, just below his Kevlar vest. Confused, he sinks to his knees, mouth still open, pained air hissing out. A sticky, warm wetness flows into his hands. Gallo moans. His vision morphs and he sees Bulldog down at the far end of the ivy, spread-eagled in the moonlight, throat cut and blue uniform covered with blood.

Oh, fuck. Gallo grabs for his gun. The second shot neatly removes the top of his head.

Three houses down, the Doberman falls silent.

Forty

Wednesday

"What the hell?"

Doc Washington rubs his weary eyes and sits back in his wheelchair. He has slight reddish-white circles around his eyes from using the lab's electronic microscope for too long. He types his findings into the computer and waits.

Doc knows himself to be a reasonably skilled pathologist, but the blood sample he is examining has him stumped. What he is looking at doesn't make any logical sense. Oh sure, you would not be surprised to find that a homeless woman called "Bloody Mary" had a form of *Chlamydia trachomatis,* or any other contagious sexually transmitted disease. But this particular form of *rickettsia* is new to Doc. It appears to have attacked the woman's immune system with a prototypically voracious appetite, yet something about its hot vector is abnormal. Almost as if it had been affected by another, quite mysterious form of infection, the *Chlamydia* made stronger by the presence of something else—something far more virulent.

Doc grabs the switch to his electric wheelchair and rolls away and over to a standing table. He pours some ice water, grabs an ice cube, and rubs it over his forehead, regretting that his insatiable curiosity has opened such a can of worms. The ME's office, on behalf of the Deputy Mayor, clearly instructed him to allow the cremation of the old woman known as "Bloody Mary" to proceed posthaste. And Doc had done just that, but only after paying a nurse's aide named Joyce fifty bucks to go down to the mortuary to draw a sanitary sample of her blood. If this woman died of the flu, Doc wanted to know what kind had done her in.

Curiosity killed the cat.

After three hours of examination, the cause is no clearer to him than before. In fact, the presence of what appears to be a severe and abnormally strong influenza infection simply muddies the waters. And was this an H1, H2, or H3? The apparent oddities in the protein coat, or surface characteristics of the virus, left his findings inconclusive.

Flu is actually a class of diseases, a fragile but constantly evolving group that modifies rapidly every year in response to a number of environmental factors. Many of the seasonal "bugs" that strike Americans actually begin somewhere in the world's bird population, with wild fowl as far away as China. Then they migrate through human beings, eventually to burn themselves out and become dormant again in another attempt to modify and gain superiority. These bugs are mankind's oldest and deadliest foe.

What few people outside of the medical establishment realize is how dangerous and potentially lethal the entire community of influenza virus types may one day become. Doc remembers reading about a 1918 flu bug dubbed "Spanish Lady." Fatalities in the United States exceeded the deaths in both world wars and the Viet Nam conflict combined, and all of this took place within a few, hellish months: the stricken ran fevers as high as 107 degrees and suffered brain damage before dying; experienced vomiting, explosive diarrhea, crushing headache pain, leucopenia, nosebleeds, gangrene of the genitalia, partial or complete blindness, and loss of hearing. Spanish Lady slaughtered over thirty million people in four months.

The world hears about a new strain like SARS or bird flu,

and reacts with trepidation. However, the minute the immediate threat has been eradicated, everyone in the press goes back to sleep; however, the medical community does not.

The Center for Disease Control in Atlanta sends out flu-season requests for reports on any fresh or seemingly aberrant strains of virus. Doc had recently seen one posted in the cafeteria at USC Medical Center, where he occasionally assisted the Pathology department with computer-generated disease vector demonstrations and audio-visual presentations.

Doc chews his lower lip, fishes in his pocket and palms a pair of Percodan. He washes the painkillers down with ice water. He is giving some serious thought to contacting the CDC directly and e-mailing them a detailed file on what he has thus far. But he doesn't want to get fired. The Assistant ME, a Nisei named Miyori, is known for his refusal to share credit with subordinates. Doc realizes all too well that he is endangering his career by disobeying orders. Going around Miyori without offering to share credit will be tantamount to writing a letter of resignation.

Doc leans back, closes his eyes and waits for the pills to take effect. As the drugs begin to increase the production of Dopamine in his brain, Doc comes, with great reluctance, to the logical decision. He unlocks his chair, steers it back to the computer keyboard with a slight whir, and sends his annoying boss a carefully worded E-mail. RE: HOMELESS FEMALE. FOUND SOMETHING ODD IN BLOOD SAMPLE. POSSIBLE NEW STRAIN INFLUENZA. NEED TO SPEAK WITH YOU SOONEST, WASHINGTON.

Doc rubs his head, wonders if he's goofed. Hey, what's done is done. He guides his wheelchair back to the electron microscope and resumes his work with renewed energy.

Forty-One

Burke drifted down the hospital corridor like a wraith. As usual, the facility was nearly deserted. As he turned the last corner he heard sloshing and what sounded like faint, high-pitched squealing over toy drums: a scowling young janitor with massive, gym-rat arms was mopping the floor. The kid wore headphones and had a CD player strapped to the waist of his overalls. He did not look up.

Burke paused, placed his fingers gently on the pale green metal door as if expecting to feel a positive change in her condition. His stomach muscles knotted and invisible fingers seized his throat. He entered the room.

Mary Kelso Burke, supine under starched white covers that were rolled down to her absurdly thin waist; her cold, white, blue-veined arms were flat against the wizened body, fingers curved like talons. A vague hissing and clicking was all that kept this room from feeling like a morgue. This machine managed her breathing and kept hope alive. Burke approached, went down on one knee, and gently kissed her right hand.

"Hello, sweetheart."

Hello, he heard it, the sound breeze-faint and carried on the upper tones of this chirping, impersonal machine. Burke kept his eyes squeezed shut, willed his heart to keep on believing. *She answered me. She always does.* But the logical side of him knew better. *She's gone, she's gone.* It fought back, and this time it seemed to be winning.

I miss you, Jack. But then she didn't really say that. Or did she?

"I miss you, too."

"She looks like she has lost more weight."

A man's voice, from right behind him. Burke jumped back from the bed and sprang to his feet in one fluid motion. Before he pulled a weapon, his mind identified the speaker. Somehow it seemed appropriate. It was time for this confrontation to take place; in fact, it was long overdue. Burke turned to face Harry Kelso, father of his comatose wife. The Einstein look-alike, a soft-spoken, blue-collar man, stood leaning on the storage cabinet. He was nearing seventy, weathered visage giving ground, but the wide eyes were bright, alert and intelligent. "You've been avoiding me, Jack."

Burke pulled his chair away from the window. He reversed it and sat facing his father-in-law. "I suppose I have, Harry."

"There's no change."

"That's not true," Burke replied. He wanted his voice to sound convinced, but there was something fragile and foreign crackling there, like the surface of a thin sheet of ice. "She spoke to me the other day, just a word or two, but she spoke to me."

Harry Kelso's eyes moistened. In that moment it was impossible not to love him. "No, Jack. You imagined it, heard what you wanted to hear. I ought to know because I've done that myself."

"It was only a word or two, but I heard her."

"In your mind, not aloud."

Jack Burke lowered head to hands. "Harry, I can't do it."

"We have to. It's time to let her go."

Burke felt hot tears coursing down his cheeks. He loathed himself for such an involuntary expression of weakness. "Why are you in such a hurry?"

Harry Kelso touched his shoulder. "I'm in no hurry, Jack. She has been brain dead for over two years now, nothing has changed. And this is something Mary said she never wanted to have happen. You know that as well as I do. She would hate being like this."

And Kelso was crying, too. He moved away and leaned against the storage cabinet before continuing. "I had her when I was halfway to fifty, remember? Hell, no man wants to bury his own child, but I never figured to live long enough to see grandchildren. The last thing I expected . . ." His voice trailed off, words winding down to entropy.

Neither man wanted to articulate the harsh and hurtful flash of a manufactured memory they both shared: *they are on vacation and Mary is driving down an icy road, coming back from seeing a friend higher in the mountains, alone in the car in that freak snowstorm. She is trying to call home on her cell phone when the truck appears, looming like a dinosaur in the dense fog. Mary is screaming and spinning out on the frozen highway, maybe thinking of how much she loved one or both of them until the lights went out and most of her mind died . . .*

"It's time."

"No." *Because Jack Burke is no longer in the hospital, he is back in the snow, holding her body, rocking it and himself . . .*

Harry Kelso had crossed the room now, come closer to touch him again. Burke opened his eyes. "I should have been there and we both know it, Harry. I took a job I didn't need to take just because I was bored, or I would have been there with her when it happened. Maybe I would have been driving. Maybe I could have . . ."

Harry Kelso grunted. "Jesus, boy. You mean you haven't stopped playing the 'maybe' game yet? Everyone does, but the truth is, what is . . . *is.* And the rest is bullshit."

Burke wiped his eyes. "I have to go, Harry. I have something

I need to take care of, and it could get heavy."

Kelso did not know the details of his son-in-law's work, but he knew that it was clandestine and often dangerous. "You saying good-bye?"

"Maybe. Could be."

Kelso nodded. "Long as you are alive, you have the legal right to decide if Mary stays or goes. Something happens to you, it's my choice."

"I understand."

"Even with that, I pray you come back okay."

"I know, Harry."

"But please think on it some more, kid. She would loathe being like this, brain fried, always in a coma. I can't allow it to go on much longer. Neither can you. Think."

"I know. I do. I will."

Forty-Two

Gina Belli sits quietly in Nicole Stryker's home office. She is using every dirty trick she knows. Using codes provided by Major Ryan, she has hacked into the database of VISA Credit and is searching for any numerical combination that might lead her to the real owner of the specific card used to rent the adjoining suite at the Universal Sheraton. Gina is operating on the assumption that the card, which is a brilliantly constructed fake, was created by combining the real names and numbers from two disparate accounts into one new, almost legal identity.

"Gina?" Nicole Stryker, at once comforted and disturbed by her presence, keeps offering refreshment. "How about some coffee?"

Gina mollifies her. "Sure. Black." She returns to work, but Nicole remains in the doorway like an expectant puppy. "Something on your mind?"

"How long have you worked with Jack Burke?"

"Too long. He's a pain in the ass."

"I heard that."

The two women smile, although clearly for different reasons. Gina softens a bit. "Let it go, girlfriend," she says, finally. "He's been in love with somebody else for a long time, now."

"Who?"

"Does it matter? It's not you, that's all. Let it go."

"I see." Nicole's pretty features grow pinched. She nods rapidly and turns away before the hurt can show. "Black, right?"

"Black." Gina slowly goes back to the computer screen, feeling a sudden, odd sadness deep in her chest. The numbers from one account, the names and identification information from another, and yet the Visa database failed to catch the fraud. Somehow, someway, the creators of this new identity managed to fool a very sophisticated system. Gina wants to know how it was done, and by whom. She works quietly, diligently. She is only vaguely aware of the passage of time . . . and completely unaware of the man who stands in the shadows across the street from Nicole's home, watching her through the open window. He is a muscular man with heavily tattooed arms.

Forty-Three

Scotty Bowden was the Homecoming King, also the dude voted "Most Likely to Succeed." Hell, he was also the college quarterback who would have made the pros if he hadn't blown out a rotator cuff during his senior year at Arizona State. The Cardinals gave him a tryout anyway, but they cut him before the start of the season. That's how he ended up joining the Army. Now he sits in a strip bar drinking beer and wondering how his promising life has dwindled down to this, gone from excellent to tawdry.

This is Darwin's Delight, Bowden's second favorite hangout. It's a bump and grind in an industrial area located out near the Burbank Airport, situated so businessmen traveling through won't have to strain the brain too much in order to find a lap dance between flights or right after their dinner meeting. Stella Starr has just done her thing on the round wooden stage, figuratively and literally, masturbating against the chrome-plated pole that seems to hold up the ceiling. Bowden's ears are still ringing from the DJ's speakers and some generic turkey of a rap song.

The kid calls out: "Give it up for Stella," and feeble applause follows. There are a handful of other losers scattered around the cheesy, Vegas-style bar. Bowden doesn't look them over; they mind their own business. The DJ takes a break and the sweet and sour odor of marijuana wafts across the room. Bowden doesn't react, just smokes a Camel. Once you break one law, the next comes easier. He stares down into his overflowing ashtray like he's trying to read somebody's future in it, perhaps his own.

Right now, like so often lately, he's going up and down his life, peeking into corners with a lit match, seeking out the major turning points. Every man reads his life backwards from time to time: *how did all that come to this?* But Scotty Bowden figures he might soon hold a patent on self-pity. It all started fumbling with bras in the backseat of his car, quick doggie-style humping under the night sky in his old, ragtop Mustang. He seemed bottomless then, could handle liquor like some kind of automaton and never act drunk or make a fool of himself, not really. Damn, he'd get up the next morning with a fresh hard-on and a headache and run five miles. That Scott Bowden was immortal, invulnerable, and even somewhat admirable.

This Scotty Bowden feels old, beat up and increasingly ashamed.

That Scotty aced his physical and mental exams for Special Forces and blew through Hell Week with a barely disguised smirk. He talked back and took a beating without ever giving up his pride. The first Scotty Bowden saw eight combat missions in and around Somalia and collected human ears on a bloody string of leather. He was young, tough and bad.

This middle-aged man is dented, aching and scared shitless of dying.

This is not my story, Scott Bowden thinks miserably. *I'm halfway to dead and living some other fool's life.*

Bowden is waiting for Lacey, the pole dancer. In fact, he has booked her for a "private dance," the local euphemism for a dry-humping, tits-in-the-face lap dance in the back room. After five lukewarm beers, some watered-down scotch, the dance and a blow job, Bowden will be out yet another hundred and fifty bucks he cannot afford. Still, that's how it's going down. Some weeks you just can't win for losing. The DJ in the back of the room stumbles back to his equipment and plays an antique seventies disco hit. Bowden finishes his beer and reads the dirty jokes on the napkin. He finally places the moaning, groaning singer as Donna Summer.

"Fuck me, it stinks in here."

Bowden looks up and to the right. Bud Holm sits down heavily on the next bar stool. Holm is a desk jockey who had been a homicide dick in South Central, back in the day. Bowden barely disguises his annoyance about having his contemplations so rudely interrupted. He ventures a jibe. "They fuck you, it's bound to stink worse."

Holm whistles for the topless waitress, a vacuous bovine who goes by the name of Holly. All the girls here give fake names. Bowden finds that both sad and funny. Some can't even keep their own stage names straight from one week to the next.

"Babe, a beer and a shot!"

Holly takes the order without missing one chew of her bubble gum. She relays it to the surfer-dude bartender, who couldn't look any more bored if he were a gay gynecologist.

"You off duty, Scotty?" Holm has the kind of personality booze doesn't improve. "Me, I was sort of in the neighborhood."

Yeah, right. Instead, he drones: "I pulled a double, so now I've got forty-right free."

"You believe those fucking Packers, man? They laid out Minnesota last week like they was a bunch of Girl Scouts playing soccer."

"Didn't catch the game."

"I wish I hadn't. Lost forty dollars on those goddamned Vikings. Man, they sucked."

"On any given Sunday, my man."

"Eat my shorts." Holm's drink arrives. He drops the shot

glass into the beer in time-honored, cop-style "depth charge" fashion and chugs. A long, slow, foul-smelling belch. "Hey, you hear about what went down last night?"

"What?"

"You know that kid Mike Gallo, right?"

Icy cobwebs creep down Bowden's spine. "Yeah, I know him."

"You didn't hear?" Holm reads his face. "I'm sorry to be the bearer of bad news, pal. The kid got himself blown up catching a house call."

Bowden cannot speak or think. He covers himself by sipping at the now-empty beer mug. "Any idea who did it?"

"Gang pricks, probably."

Bowden examines the ashtray. He feels the beer starting to come back up. "What happened?"

Holm leans closer. "He and this other kid I knew at SC, we called him Bulldog, they go to check out a 182 in some cheese-dick neighborhood. Time it's over, Bulldog has his throat cut. Then poor Gallo gets his brains blown out."

"And they say that's gangbangers?"

"Yeah, I know. It sounds like a pro hit to me, too. But downtown is chalking it up to some North Hollywood Boys who've watched too many episodes of *The Sopranos.* They figure it's the same bunch of taco-loving dick wads did that old couple and skinned them alive the other night. Like they got a real taste for it, and they're out to do them some rich white folks and cops."

"I guess."

"Think so? Me, I figure that's a crock of shit."

"What do you mean?"

"I mean there must be something else going on. Otherwise, why we sitting on everything in the press? That horror guy, the couple, and now two cops all in a few days? And as far as the public is concerned, nobody out there even knows the gory details. If it's just gangs, why is it such a big secret?"

Bowden raises trembling fingers to signal another round for both Holm and himself; he's having what Holm is drinking this time. Scotty wants a boilermaker. He needs something to numb out as rapidly as possible. "So poor Gallo, he was DOA?"

"Oh yeah. He was deader than Custer's nuts at the Little Big Horn. It was a real shame, man. He seemed like a real nice kid."

"Yeah? Fuck him."

"Huh?"

"Fuck him because he should have been more careful, right? Gallo should have done a better job of watching out for his own sorry ass."

Bowden is snarling, trying to justify the death, does not notice the odd expression on Holm's chubby face. Even Holm, who is a bit of a dullard, catches the rage just beneath the studied indifference, just can't make sense of it. Why is Bowden so calloused about the death of a near-rookie he knew personally? Or just as strangely, be so enraged at the kid?

"Gentlemen, give it up for Lacey!"

The music changes to the grinding, galloping pulse of Rod Stewart wailing "Do You Think I'm Sexy." Bowden does his best to tune out Holm, what he represents and the terrifying message he brings, even more so the image of Mike Gallo lying face-up in a pile of garbage bleeding from the ear, probably with one eyeball engorged and shot through with exploded veins, *yeah well fuck him, he didn't listen to me so fuck him.*

Lacey is a peroxide blonde with dark pussy hair, long legs, and impossibly large tits. The boobs are difficult for Bowden to accept. Whenever he buries his face in them he keeps flashing on two bags of silicone. It seems bizarre that when Lacey is an old broad in a rocker, drooling on the porch of some rest home, she'll still have tits to die for. He watches Lacey twirl around the chrome phallus. She licks and humps it and—knowing he has booked a private show for afterwards—flashes him a lewd wink. Bowden winks back, does his best Kiss impression and licks the air. The boilermaker arrives and he downs half in a couple of gulps.

Meanwhile, Holm finishes his first, clicks mugs, and sips the second. Bowden watches Lacey's ass, so perfect in that spangled, thin butt-floss underwear. It occurs to him that Holm has been talking.

"What?" He hears the annoyance in his own voice, is unable to curtail it. Bowden wants to shoot the messenger.

"I said that's pretty cold, man. Saying he should have taken better care of himself. You really mean that?"

Scotty knows he should get up and leave, go dance with Lacey, disappear to take a piss, anything but get it on, but as it turns out, he can't help himself. He grabs Holm by the tie, yanks him closer. He ignores the breath soaked in beer and whiskey. "Just in case you missed the bulletin from God, Holm, you're all alone in this world. You came in that way, you're going to leave that way. So you look out for number one. Those of us that remember that have a better chance of going home alive."

"True shit, man."

He releases Holm, resumes staring at the ashtray. Bowden senses when Holm finishes his drink and gets up to go, but he does not react. A few crumpled bills hit the bar.

"And you have a nice life, asshole."

Bowden feels a flash of insane rage. He gives serious thought to pistol-whipping Holm, sliding his sorry ass facedown on the bar and off into the bottles at the end, then over into the DJ's equipment. Instead, he says, "Yeah, you, too." His shoulders tremble as he imagines smashing Holm's chubby face, feeling the cartilage give, maybe ripping off one of his ears for good measure and adding it to the collection.

But he does nothing.

Not a thing.

No, Scott Bowden sits and drinks and contemplates the ashtray and waits for his pathetic solo dance and a quick, condom-inhibited blow job in the back room. To kill some time, he remembers once upon a time he was a football hero, a first-class soldier, even an honest cop. He broods on the wayward course of his life, the great pity of it, and lets Holm walk away untouched, not a mark on him.

Because that Scotty Bowden is long gone, too.

Forty-Four

The sun was setting in the darkened rocks, out by Chatsworth, smearing the lunar mountains with cotton pastels. Burke was stretching on the back porch, getting ready for a long run around his small neighborhood, when he heard a car enter the driveway. The engine was too well-tuned to be Doc's van, not ragged enough to be Bowden's funky car or Gina's little Metro. It purred in a smooth and clearly expensive way, like maybe a top of the line Beemer. Burke hopped onto the back porch, peeked around the corner, spotted the brand-new silver Lexus. He reached down under the leg of his sweatpants, palmed his spare .22.

Aren't we being a little paranoid?

The doorbell rang. Figuring most hired killers wouldn't drive up before dark and knock, Burke opened the sliding glass door and went into the living room. He tucked the .22 into the back of his pants and pulled the sweatshirt down to cover it. After a few silent steps across the room and a peek through the eyehole in the door, his jaw dropped. He opened the door without thinking.

"May I come in for a moment?"

"Uh, certainly Professor."

Dr. Mohandas Hasari Pal entered the room. Standing behind him on the porch was the unobtrusive butler, Mr. Nandi. Burke, expression pleasant, slid his hand around the sweatshirt to touch the gun. "Mr. Nandi?"

"My servant will wait on the porch, if that is acceptable."

"All right."

Burke closed the door gently, let the gun go as he turned to face Indira's husband. Mo Pal had a manila folder under one arm. He was dressed impeccably, as usual, in a perfectly tailored gray suit and a black silk shirt with no collar. The effect made his shaved head and severe countenance all the more imposing.

"I hope I am not intruding, Mr. Burke. I need a few moments of your time."

Say something, idiot. "Can I offer you a drink?"

"No, thank you." Pal held himself tightly, barely containing nuclear emotion. "I will try to be brief. I suspect you know why I have come here."

Oh, Jesus. Face a blank. "Not really, sir. Is it about my visit the other evening? Have you thought of something else you wanted to tell me about Peter Stryker?"

Pal, clutching the manila folder like a flotation device, strolled deeper into the sparsely furnished living room with the air of Patton on parade. Facing the plateglass door and the backyard, he cleared his throat. "One of the advantages to shaving your head is that no one notices when you begin chemotherapy, Mr. Burke. I have come here to tell you two things. The first thing is that I am dying." His large fingers snare-drummed the folder. "This is a Xerox of my medical file, should you wish to establish the veracity of that statement."

"I-I'm sorry to hear that."

Pal turned with a smile thin as a dime. "Not half as sorry as I am, I assure you. In any event, it is a highly aggressive form of bowel cancer. I have been given a reprieve by the final round of chemo, probably only a few more months. I intend to make good use of that time, Mr. Burke. I intend to spend it with those who mean the most to me." Pal moved closer. His eyes bored black holes. "And that brings me to the second thing."

"Which is?"

"Don't play me for a fool, Mr. Burke. I'm here to ask you to stay away from my wife."

Burke wobbled, dumbstruck. His face turned pale but then flushed. His gut churned with self-loathing and remorse.

"Indira may appear to be a sophisticated woman, but at heart she is still an ignorant savage from a dusty little town in India." Pal abruptly hugged himself, as if cold. He closed his eyes before resuming. "She cannot think properly, and has seen little of the real world. This, I fear, is a failing on my part. You must understand that she is a weak person, Mr. Burke. Do not take advantage of her, I beg you. Or, frankly, of me. Respect our marriage."

Burke tried. "Wait a minute, Mo. I don't know what you're talking about, here. Indira and I are only friends." The protestation sounded jeeringly feeble. He couldn't maintain the façade, caved and looked down.

Pal shoved the folder into his hands. "You can keep this or shred it, that's entirely up to you. I have also told my oncologist that you may call and that if you choose to do so, he is to answer any questions you may have."

Burke glanced briefly at the file. It appeared genuine. He was not reading, just stalling for time, and wondering how much, if anything, Indira had elected to share with her husband. Did he know for certain, or was he merely probing?

Pal paced the room. "I don't know that there is any more I can do, frankly. I came here hoping I would be able to reach you, man to man."

Burke decided, closed the file. "You have."

"I see." Pal watched the shadowed garden. Outside, a shiny black crow picked at a dead insect. "Or perhaps this can all be settled for a sum of money?"

Burke dropped the file on the coffee table, gunshot loud. "Go ahead, insult me. I suppose you're entitled."

"May I assume you did not know I was ill?"

"You may."

Pal hitched up his trousers, perched gingerly on the couch, crossed long legs. The calf and ankle seemed shockingly white, belly tissue of a gutted fish. There were some small, discolored patches on the flesh of the lower muscle, like purple nickels and quarters. "Indira does not wish to dwell on that fact," he whispered, mournfully. "It upsets her. She often acts as if she were in a full state of denial, as if nothing whatsoever had changed in our lives."

Burke moved to the easy chair, parked opposite Pal. He leaned forward and clasped his calloused hands. "But something has."

Pal smiled, ruefully. "Oh, most definitely. You know, the most amazing thing about dying is how . . . physical an experience it is. Those of us who have spent decades in academia researching and reading, studying mythology, folklore, and religion as they pertain to death come to think of it as an abstract, metaphysical thing; more of a construct, or an idea, than a fact."

"And it's not."

"Oh, no. It is most certainly not." Pal's eyes burned tiger bright. "When Kali strikes your bones, it is a most grounding thing. The body fails in the most elemental of functions. The soul feels defeated and degraded. All of the abstract concepts turn to dust and blow away."

Burke squirmed. "Are you sure I can't offer you a drink, Professor?"

"Perhaps a little water, then."

Burke sprang to his feet, relieved to have an assignment. He escaped into the kitchen. "Do you mind talking about this?"

"Not at this point," Pal replied. He was up and roaming the

living room, condemned man pacing the cell. "What's done is done."

Burke poured some ice water at the cooler. His mind, eager to escape the awkward situation, wandered off on a tangent: why was it that Los Angeles had a public water and power company, paid exorbitant fees for service, yet no one who could afford it ever drank from the tap? He carried the glass back to Pal. "Here you go."

Pal gulped with a Legionnaire's greed and spilled one teardrop-shaped watermark on his coat. "As I said, the final thing I came here to discuss is that I want you to leave my wife alone. At least until I am dead and gone. Do you understand clearly, Mr. Burke?"

"Oh, I understand you, sir. But in the end, doesn't Indira have as much to say about that as either one of us?"

"In a perfect world, perhaps she would." Pal pressed his advantage. "I know you had an affair with her many years ago. I realize there may still be strong feelings between you."

"I won't lie to you. There are."

"But now I am begging you. Please stop seeing her."

Burke stiffened from an intense vision: just pulling the .22, whirling around and drilling Pal through the forehead. The violent idea sprang from nowhere and momentarily seemed to have merit. Cary would probably cover him and dispose of the body. Of course then he'd have to do Mr. Nandi, too, but hell, Indira would never have to know what happened. The fantasy was so sharp and crisp Burke came close to acting it out.

"You have nothing to say to me, sir?"

Burke shuddered. "Professor, I will think about what you have told me."

"Thank you."

Pal rose up—the preacher ends the sermon. He adjusted the expensive suit and tie, walked briskly to the front door. The action left Burke behind, subordinate. He remained seated, feeling an odd mixture of guilt, resentment, and fear. Pal opened the front door. The dapper Mr. Nandi leapt at once to attend. Pal hesitated, with the eye lightening of someone who just remembered a long-lost joke. "The cause of suffering is desire, yes?" His tone was sweet, the meta-message corrosive. "If you can find it in you, please try to have the decency to allow an old man to die in peace."

Mohandas Pal left. Nandi gently closed the door. Their exit seems to suck all the air out of the living room.

Forty-Five

Later, Burke would have no idea how long he'd sat alone, impaled by the consequences of his behavior, writhing in exquisite shame. The shadows lengthened over the area rug and somewhere down the hall a timer lamp kicked on. The light reflected on the hardwood flooring, like a yellow flare over a darkening sea. Burke began to mourn, small sobs at first. Finally, he slapped his own face. He had betrayed Mary in her endless, sleepless sleep and disgraced himself by interfering in the Pal's marriage a second, even more damaging time. Burke felt beneath contempt.

Well, what do I do now?

Fifteen, perhaps twenty minutes later than that someone knocked. Burke palmed the .22 and padded to the door, more afraid of a return visit from Professor Pal than a hired gun. He peeked out and saw a man in a brown delivery uniform under the glare of the porch light; he was tall, slight, and blond with a thick moustache. The driver was holding a small, manila folder-sized package.

Burke opened the door, shaking his head. "Bro, what the hell are you doing? I think you need to get some professional help."

"Don't start," Major Cary Ryan muttered, as pushed his way into the room. "Do you ever turn any lights on around here?"

"I was thinking."

"About what? Your recent visitor?" Burke blinked, wondering how much he should say. Ryan went on without a break. "I was down the street in the delivery truck when I saw the little fart on the porch. Then I watched the bald guy leave. Who is he?"

"An old professor of mine," Burke replied. He clicked the table lamp, brightened shadows. Ryan seemed ridiculous in short pants. His fake moustache looked exactly like a fake moustache. "Cary, what are you doing here?"

Cary sat on the couch with the package in his lap, noisily unwrapped. "This couldn't wait for me to run an ad or fuck around with the usual stuff, and I didn't want to say anything over the phone."

Burke turned with spread palms. He couldn't guarantee his own home wasn't bugged.

"No, you can relax," Cary said, offering a slightly apologetic smile. "I had your house swept earlier today."

"Thanks for asking." Burke parked in the easy chair. He was not annoyed. It would be good to have something to distract him from the awful sense of anguish Pal had left behind him like the fluttering tail of a kite.

Cary finished unwrapping the UPS box and removed some files. He spread several photographs on the table like a bad poker hand.

Burke spun one around, right-side up. "You already showed me these the other day. The Gamma shots from the Predator drone, right?"

"Los Gatos, northern Mexico. But look at the date stamp."

Burke squinted. "Last night."

"And now look at these UV prints."

Burke thumbed through the aerial photographs. In some, small crimson clusters dotted the landscape like sloppy flower arrangements. The shots were taken every ninety seconds over a nine-minute period. "Is this what I think it is?"

Cary removed the fake moustache and rubbed his red upper lip. Burke noted his face looked wan from lack of sleep. "We sent in Steve Lukac and a short team. He picked that new kid, Charlie Carney, also Del Howison and Kevin Kramer. We jammed radar, did a fake drug flight and took them in low over the border from Texas. The chopper dropped them a half mile downwind of Los Gatos. The insertion went perfectly."

Burke remained silent. He liked Steve Lukac and served with him for a time. It is suddenly, chillingly obvious what happened. *A fire fight.*

Cary spoke in a monotone that belied his tension. "You know this has never happened to me before, Red. Not in fourteen years of service. I have seldom lost a man, much less an entire team."

Burke blanched. "The whole team?" He looked down at the UV scan again, those scattered little splatters of light. "So this was a running gun battle, those are muzzle flares and explosions."

"Yes."

"The team is presumed dead."

"As near as we can tell, Howison and Kramer bought it right away. Charlie Carney and Steve Lukac got pinned down. They were badly outnumbered, but did their best to make the LZ. They never got there. One of them was killed, the other captured. We don't know which."

Burke felt stunned. "Caught and questioned by a freak drug lord like Buey? You know what they're going to do to him, don't you?"

Cary swallowed. "The last DEA agent he got his hands on ended up flayed from the crotch to the shoulders and then buried alive. We know because they found dirt in his lungs."

"Jesus H. Christ."

Burke and his former boss glared at the pictures. Finally Burke got to his feet and stumbled toward the kitchen. "I need some coffee. You want a cup?"

Cary Ryan stayed behind. His body sagged so deeply into the couch he looked physically diminished. "Sure. Just black for me."

Burke understood why Ryan had come. He wanted time to think it over. Cary stacked the UV photos again, shuffled them just to have something to do. He heard the gurgling of the coffee machine. Burke came back into the living room, sat down.

"What's the rest of it, Cary?"

Ryan removed more photographs from the folder. He slid them over. "These photos are from the day before. That area we suspect may be a mass grave just got larger. At least one other object about the size of a grown man's body was added to the pile."

"You're thinking that the agent that survived, Lukac or maybe Carney, is likely to be next. Let's get real. He's probably already dead. You know that, don't you?"

"Maybe, maybe not."

"And the kind of torture a prick like Lopez uses would break any man down. They know everything about your operation, now. And why you sent a team into Mexico."

Cary shrugged, miserably. "Worse case scenario, Buey knows what Lukac knew. And Steve didn't know where the headquarters would be moved to this month, or what the new codes would be, because we never told him. If it was Carney that lived, he knew even less. I'm not that worried."

"Then why come here?"

Cary Ryan tapped the photographs with a stiffened ring finger. "Because this fucker is toast, brother. I want him punished for what he did to my boys."

"You want me to enter a foreign country illegally and off the record? Sure, what the hell. But drop into a drug lord's compound right after he's already slaughtered a solid, professional team? You're out of your mind."

"I want someone good and you're the best we've got."

"I'm the best you had, Cary. There's a difference. I'm just a contract guy, now. I pick and choose. And this one looks like a suicide run."

Ryan leaned back into the swallowing couch. "I'll double your fee."

"Still not interested." Burke's stomach clenched and his self-esteem took another swan dive.

"You and Steve were friends, Red. I know you well enough to know that this gets to you."

From down the hall, a wall clock ticked inexorably forward. Neither man spoke. Burke sat quietly, weighing his obligations and the varied challenges piling up. He had a wife in a coma, a former lover who was married to a dying man, a mountain of outrageous medical bills, a client who had just been assaulted by a professional for mysterious reasons, and a suicide that rapidly morphed into a murder investigation. These days, everything he touched seemed to rapidly spiral out of control. *Fecal alchemy, man.*

"I need to mull this over," Burke said, finally. He drained the coffee mug. He put it down on the table. End of discussion.

"You'll at least think about it?"

"I will. You had my home swept?" He waited for Cary to catch on and nod. "Okay. If I understand you correctly, officially you want a fresh team to go in there and see what's up and also investigate the long shot that our boy may still be alive."

"Yeah."

"But *un*officially you want my team to go in there, find those miserable cock suckers and level the place when we leave."

Cary Ryan leaned forward to rest his knuckles on the coffee table like a challenged simian. "Off the record?"

"Off the record."

"No cute euphemisms necessary, Red. I want Juan Garcia Lopez taken out, terminated, wasted. I want you to find Buey, and the rest of the lowlifes who killed my boys and blow up their shit."

Burke responded quietly, firmly. "I don't do hits, you know that."

Ryan shrugged. "Come on, Red. If you take this job, you know as well as I do how this is going to go down. It will be scorched earth, baby. Buey and his boys won't let you do it any other way."

"Cary, this isn't like you. What is it you're not telling me?"

"Nothing."

Eye to eye for a long beat. Ryan broke first. "There's a lot of heat. The Mexican government is a little pissed off, and our own guys upstairs are less than thrilled about things getting botched. Even Homeland Security is pissed because we didn't fill them in."

"You're in hot water."

"Let me put it this way, a lot of folks would prefer I let this slide. But I can't do that. I'm not willing to, okay?"

"I understand."

"But?"

Burke rubbed his knuckles. "Cary, I've got a lot on my mind right now."

"Does that mean you're not up to working? If you are going to take this on, I need you at the top of your game. I have my neck right on the chopping block. I need you cool as ice, man. It's too hairy otherwise."

Burke stared into the middle distance, hearing long-ago battles in deep mental echo. "What about Walker, can you use him instead?"

Cary seems to deflate. "If I have to, sure. But I was hoping you'd see this my way. Why don't you think it over and then get back in touch?"

"No, I can give you my answer right now." Burke ceased debating, grimaced. "I don't want to pass on this, I really don't, but I have to. I'm sorry."

Forty-Six

Thursday
The tinny, impersonal voice comes from the computer speakers, but somehow manages to sound smug anyway. "Check."

"Damn!"

Doc Washington slaps his hand down on the keyboard in frustration. He rolls his wheelchair back; stretches his arms, rolls his neck. Needles of pain are starting to tingle all over his shattered body, particularly down his neck and upper spine. Doc looks around the office and is surprised to find it empty. He has been playing chess alone for several hours and is being roundly trounced by the advanced level of the computer program.

Doc closes his eyes, willing himself to be elsewhere and in another time when: . . . *A young stud again, a high school running back from the LA ghetto, feeling his cleats dig into the crisp, scented fall grass when he makes one sweetheart of a cut and smoothly shifts the hard-cornered pigskin to his outside arm; Doc can see the defender bite on the hip fake and slip and fall and he can still hear the echoing crowd . . .*

But he's here, now. Fucked up beyond belief, strung out on dope, and frozen forever in a cripple's go-cart.

Rolling himself to the counter, Doc parks the chair and opens his med box. He has tried to wean himself before, and this is his latest attempt; it is an Oxycontin IV drip coordinated by an electric pump and a timer. It is out of the illegally obtained painkiller. Doc carefully pours another day's dose into the glass container and replaces the tiny mechanism. He moves the IV to a different vein; he rotates it daily. He is still heavily addicted to the powerful drug, but now a normal dose lasts him two full days. He must adjust things carefully. The entire dosage, all at once, would doubtless prove fatal.

"Check," repeats the voice. The computer flickers and rolls to get his attention.

"Fuck you and the horse you rode in on, you stinking pile of junk," Doc mutters. "I taught you everything you know." The computer stares back without blinking.

Doc is sweating lightly, now. His stomach has begun to feel queasy and the aches have begun to spread. He eyes the dosage meter again, rests the tip of his finger on the button but holds back. He tells himself to wait thirty minutes, endure feeling sick for thirty minutes and then he can give himself another dose. He knows it is the only way he will ever get clean and sober.

His hand shakes.

Doc turns the electric wheelchair and rolls it back to the computer. He types in a forfeit and closes the program. He checks his E-mail. It puzzles him that no one has responded to the tissue samples he sent. Out of curiosity, he rolls back through his SENT mail and finds the mail is not listed at all. It has been deleted. *Say what?* A chill runs down his neck, along with rivers of perspiration. Doc types in several commands and traces the communication. No luck. Someone has blocked it somehow, made it impossible for him to send a file to his superiors. The E-mail has not even remained on his computer.

What the hell is going on?

Doc opens his files and checks the folders. As he watches, the one regarding the homeless woman, marked MARY, winks out. *Deleted!* Eliminated by someone who has access to the main-frame computer? The chill comes again. Whoever it is, he is working at precisely the same moment to eliminate Doc's hours of work. But why?

Doc types as fast as he can. He shifts a rough draft Word copy of the file regarding MARY to the first folder that comes to mind, BURKE. He changes pages and checks. The document is present. He rapidly changes the title to UNSUB and hits "save." As he watches the screen, the Burke file called STRYKER winks out. Doc goes online, types an E-mail to Gina at Burke's office, then adds UNSUB as an attachment. He drops it in "mail waiting to be sent" and puts it on a timer. Seconds later UNSUB winks out as well. For a long moment all he is aware of is the clacking of his fingers on the keyboard and the timid patter of his pulse. He stops, reaches for the telephone.

And the clattering continues.

The noise is coming from behind him. Doc gasps. Someone else is with him in the darkened room—someone else who has been busily typing on a different computer.

Oh, shit!

Doc tries to turn the wheelchair, but his hand is shaking and damp and his fingers slip off the small red knob. Meanwhile, footsteps rapidly cross the floor. Someone turns the desk lamp off and the room plunges into shadow. Something round and cool presses against the back of his neck.

"Just stay quiet," a male voice says. Doc begins to hyperventilate; his nostrils catch an odd odor. The stranger stinks of unwashed flesh and decay. "Unless you want the rest of you to get paralyzed, too."

Doc swallows, remains still. His muscles twitch from adrenaline and opiate withdrawal. The stranger is quick as a panther. Small plastic bands rapidly encircle Doc's arms and the battery is removed from his wheelchair. A gag is inserted into his mouth. It's a rag with a golf-sized ball in it. He is helpless.

"Now, I have turned out the lights for a reason," the man says. "If I planned to kill you, why would I bother?"

Doc finds his voice, tries to speak around the gag. "I don't know what you want."

"We'll see."

The gun is withdrawn from his neck. Doc hears a rustle of clothing as the intruder shifts position. That repulsive odor comes again, making Doc gag. The man moves a high-intensity lamp and bends the neck so that it shines directly down on the laminated desktop in a concentrated beam. He places a stack of rolled fabric on the desk, opens it. Several polished, shiny medical tools are revealed: scalpels of various sizes, some scissors, and wicked-looking metal probes.

"Please," Doc mumbles. It sounds like a faint *pleeth* because of the gag. A shudder passes through him as a combination of death anxiety and continuing opiate withdrawal racks his body.

The man is wearing gloves. He will leave no prints. He removes something else and puts it near the medical tools. It is a long barbeque lighter with a wide mouth. Doc's eyes widen comically above the gag. Images from the grotesque Peter Stryker death scene are flooding his mind.

"I need to know what you have done," the man whispers. "And what you know." His voice is low, gentle, and obscenely intimate; he is like a sadistic lover coaxing a woman into trying something humiliating and painful. "If you try to lie this will be a very difficult experience for you, but then I'm sure you realize that."

"What?" Doc asks, thinking: *Jesus Christ I'll tell you anything, what is it, what do you want from me?* "What?"

"Who knows?"

Doc shakes his head, does not understand the question. The man strokes Doc's left hand in that sensual way. He plays with the little finger, bending it back and forth in a teasing fashion.

He pulls it up and then rapidly slices it off.

The drug withdrawal makes the pain unbearable. Doc shakes and writhes, tries to scream. The gag blunts the sound. He struggles to beg for mercy, but only hoarse gargling noises emerge from his strained vocal cords.

"Shhhhh." The man who smells like shit soothes, comforts like an amused parent. Doc looks at his violated hand. Blood fountains, an arc of crimson beneath the high-intensity lamp.

The man flicks the lighter on and cauterizes the mutilated finger.

Doc shrieks; his body jerks and convulses, then finally comes to rest. He hovers on the edge of consciousness, his head pounding and his hand in flared agony. Meanwhile, the man waits patiently, his breathing calm, even, and undisturbed; such complete indifference is almost as horrifying as the sadism.

Again: "Who knows?"

Doc feigns unconsciousness, stalls for time. The man selects another finger. It hits Doc then that he will say anything, do anything, to avoid what is to come. He will give up Red Burke and Gina and make up stories about other people, anything to avoid the horror of being dismembered alive. The man who stinks of excrement is a demon, and he will patiently do what he has come to do without regard for time or truth or the slightest hint of compassion.

Doc imagines the E-mail and the file flying through cyberspace. He wills them to be sent on time, offers up a short prayer. Then begs: "Wait!"

The man ignores him. The torturer slices off his second finger. Doc bellows a sound he would not have believed possible for a human to make. His upper body snaps back and forth like a passenger in a car crash. He begins to babble nonsense.

"Tell me what you have done."

The cauterizing follows. Doc's intact right hand locates the homemade device that monitors his hidden Oxycontin supply. He shrieks in pain again, bangs his head against the top of the wheelchair, but his shaking fingers still somehow manage to deactivate the small timer.

When the flame hits the bleeding socket of the second finger, the world whirls into a tornado of rippling darkness and Doc passes out . . .

Everything is red and black when it returns. The left side of his body is in agony and behind the body odor of the assassin, Doc locates a smell like something left too long on the grill: his own scorched flesh. Someone dabs the sweat away from his forehead. The melancholy voice comes again, by his right ear. "Would you like to tell me something now?"

Doc nods rapidly. The sound of his own coughing sob shames him. His body arches involuntarily. Small, white tendrils of smoke are rising lazily from the scorched flesh of his left hand. Doc's two severed fingers lay side by side like little brown fish, mocking him.

Doc's right hand searches. The man who stinks carefully removes the gag and tucks it under Doc's chin like a child's bib.

"Umph." Doc mumbles, incoherently. His tongue feels like an emery board.

The man dabs Doc's sweat-soaked face again, leans closer to listen carefully. "Yes?"

"Go fuck yourself."

Doc taps the plunger with his right hand. The entire two-day dosage of powerful Oxycontin enters his bloodstream in one immense wave. A warm rush of pleasure hits his brain. Almost simultaneously Doc feels his heart begin to labor, already failing. His lungs forget to breathe and his chest seizes up, but he does not care.

Someone screams something. "No!"

But now Doc Washington is young and tall, he has his legs back and he is standing on top of a gigantic metal elevator as it descends deep into the bowels of the earth. See you soon, my brothers. Some old Marvin Gaye music is playing. Above him is a tiny square of light and an angry man who is thumping his chest and shaking him, someone who'd been terrifying seconds before, but as the loving night overtakes him, Doc can't remember for the life of him why he ever felt so afraid . . .

Forty-Seven

"Excuse me, Buey."

"I asked you not to bother me, Esteban."

"But . . ."

"Can you not see I am busy?"

"This is urgent. We must speak alone."

"Alone?"

"My apologies to this young lady if I have embarrassed her in any way, *Jefe,* but I know you will understand when I tell you the content of the message we have just received."

"Blanca, leave us."

"But what shall I do?"

"After this? Go and brush your teeth! Take a bath or something and leave the men to talk of business."

"Ahem."

"Do not stare at her if you value your *cojones,* Esteban."

"Sir . . ."

"Wait. Okay, now what was so important it required you to stomp into the room like an angry bull?"

"The strange American, Buey. He is coming again."

"And so? You fucking idiot! I already knew he was coming."

"But did you know *why?*"

Forty-Eight

"I know he came to speak with you."

Indira Pal was standing on the sidewalk, beneath the harsh white of the streetlamp, hugging herself against the evening chill. Burke could see goose bumps rippling along the beige flesh of her arms. She wore smart brown pants, an Oriental patterned beige blouse, and had her black hair up in a bun that was tied with golden cord.

"I can't talk to you." Burke turned away, faced a parked car. He watched a stream of milky white light from the streetlamp as it pooled in neat rows down the long, silent residential street. He could smell night-blooming jasmine, the crisp odor of a nearby fireplace, and the faint scent of her warm, perfumed skin. His shoulders ached; they were hunched beneath his denim jacket and it felt like roofing nails had been pounded into his flesh.

Somewhere to the north a dog barked. Burke felt his eyes sting, and his sad pulse sang opera. "You need to leave."

"I'm begging."

"Indira, don't. I can't."

"I love you."

He closed his eyes and stood rigid and trembling, a racehorse in the starting gate. Indira closed the gap, stood behind him and stroked his waist with her delicate hands. Her bracelets jangled. More dogs barked in alarm.

"He said he's dying."

"It is true, Jack. He has months, a year at most."

"You didn't mention that."

"No."

"I think I had the right to know."

Her hands trembled. "I was afraid you would send me away if I told you. I was afraid you would not be there for me. And I needed you to be there for me."

"So what you needed was more important than the truth?"

"Hasn't it always been that way for us?"

"Indira, I feel ashamed."

"And so do I."

He turned and she melted into him, body sculpted to his own. He leaned back against the car and looked down into almond eyes wide, crying and clearly free of guile. He pondered how someone could appear so innocent yet perpetrate an act as unconscionable as infidelity to a dying man. He wondered if he would ever be able to trust her again. Indira pressed her face into his chest. His shirt was damp. "You should have told me."

Her voice, muffled and hoarse. "Yes. I should have told you. But then I would have had to tell you the rest of it."

Burke grabbed her shoulders, forced her away. "The rest of it?"

"He will not go alone, my love."

"Excuse me?"

"I must go with him. He believes that this is his right."

"Indira, what are you talking about?"

"Sati."

"What?" Yet Burke knows the meaning of the word. It is that barbaric Indian custom, now outlawed in virtually all provinces, that holds that when a man dies, his wife is expected to follow him onto the funeral pyre. "Indira, what the hell are you talking about? He can't possibly mean that."

Her voice, still muffled. "Mo paid my family's debts and

bought me from my father when I was still a girl. He dressed me, educated me, and brought me here to America."

"And that means he owns you?"

"Mo has very deep spiritual beliefs. He leads a group of sorts, a collection of old friends and business acquaintances. They believe anything he tells them, they feed his ego. For a long time I believed him, too."

"Not anymore?"

"No. He frightens me, Jack. He brings the group designer drugs and leads them in deep meditation. They are all devout followers of the left-hand path of Tantra, but in the extreme. And they also all believe in *Sati,* even in the idea of sacrificing their own lives to follow their guru into death, if asked."

"This is craziness."

"It is real enough to them. And so I am to follow Mo when he dies, and nothing will persuade him—or his followers—otherwise."

Burke angered. "Why didn't you ask someone for help? Why not go to the law?"

"He owns my life."

"*You* own your life."

"You don't understand."

Burke slipped fingers under her chin, lifted her face, kissed her; soon was drinking her in, savoring even the salt of her tears. "Then tell me more. I want to understand."

Indira broken, body wracked with silent sobs. "I am going to do it. I have to. I must go into the void with him."

He rocked her for a moment. He looked around. At the west end of his block, a large Taurus quietly turned the corner, splashed through a pool of water, run off from overworked lawn sprinklers. The headlights were off, surely a red flag, and then the driver stopped. A miniscule orange glow announced he was lighting a cigar. After a long moment the car began moving again, rolling closer. Burke spun Indira and placed his body between her and the approaching vehicle. He urged her along the sidewalk, up the steps, into his house. The car drove on.

"Sit down. I'll make some tea."

She crumpled onto the couch, then curled up as if feverish and disoriented. Meanwhile, Burke busied himself in the kitchen; teapot, chamomile tea, a spoon of honey. He was in overdrive and a tight band compressed his skull, causing white dots with red trim. He knew the feeling well, had never been able to escape it for long. His heart was black with rage.

Burke leaned against the sink and concentrated as intently as he could on the stream of water coming from the faucet. He took a deep breath, held it for several seconds and released it through his nose, first one nostril and then the other. Then he turned off the water, brought sweetened tea back to the living room. Indira was sitting up. She could not meet his eyes. When he put the saucer down his hands were steady.

Hers were shaking so wildly she had trouble bringing the cup to her lips. Burke gave her time to compose herself. He sat cross-legged on the armchair, across from her, loving her presence.

Indira replaced the cup. She studied it, and her vibrating hands. Her cheeks seemed to burn with small pilot lights of shame. "I should not have told you."

Burke contained his anger, spoke soothingly. "But you did. So you may as well tell me the details."

Indira looked up. She set her jaw and jumped directly to the truth. "He calls the group Shahr-e-Khamosh," she says quietly.

"The City of Silence."

"Yes."

"Like a graveyard."

"More or less. The *smashan.* This is the charnel ground, where bodies are taken to be buried or perhaps burned. That word is taken from *ashmashana,* the ground where rocks are found."

"Left-hand Tantra."

"Mo has become a kind of *Rudra.* A man who makes others cry out to the sky because he brings them death itself. He can do it, Jack. He's become one with *Shiva,* the destroyer of worlds."

Burke did not argue with the implanted delusion. He could see conflicting emotions flickering. Indira had already begun to doubt herself. "But Shiva needs a consort, correct?"

Her lower lip trembled. She had never seemed so young. "He means to honor me, Jack. By being burned I would become a deity as well. Mohandas means to make me his *parvati,* a manifestation of Ma, the Mother Goddess. He thinks we have been in Kali Yuga, the fourth age of man, but that we are at the end of the 432,000-year cycle. We believe that the Old Gods will soon return."

Burke nodded politely. "I have noticed something. When you speak of this, you seem to switch back and forth from 'he' thinks to 'we' believe and back again. So I have a sense you recognize this apocalyptic nonsense for what it actually is, the ravings of a scared man who is terminally ill."

Indira jerked back as if she'd been slapped. "Many of us have joined him in *sadhana,* Jack. He is a master."

"Or a charlatan."

"Please. You said you would listen."

Burke tilted forward. "Okay, I'm sorry. I should not be arguing. Now, my understanding of the left-hand path is that the 'dying' which is to be devoutly pursued is one of ego boundaries and old ideas. Death on the physical plane should not be feared, but it need not be sought out, either. What am I missing?"

Indira continued, and as she recited the tenets she grew more enthusiastic. "We have been living in a corrupt age, Jack, with drugs and sex and violence on a scale unprecedented in human history. *Shahr-e-Khamosh* is the way of the true believer, for we are ushering in the end of the 432,000 years. The Kali Yuga is almost over."

He watched the brainwashed eyes film over. "I see."

"Mo even believes we should reawaken the concept of the Thug, or Thugee, because they served Kali directly in the olden days."

"They drugged and robbed people and then strangled them for human sacrifice."

"Well, I don't think he means to go that far . . ."

"One would hope not." Burke touched her hand, rubbed it gently. He smiled, went for broke. "And next you're going to be telling me you will all die together so that you can hitch a ride on the tail of a passing comet."

"Now you're mocking me."

"I'm trying to wake you up. I know you come from a superstitious background, but this is America in the twenty-first century. He's got you good. Come on, Indira. Do you *really* believe all this shit?"

"No. Yes. Maybe."

"Maybe?"

The shocked look again. Her eyes filled with water. "I don't know what to believe anymore." She grabbed his hands, squeezed tightly. "When I saw you again, my faith began to weaken. Once we'd made love . . ."

"What?"

"I wanted to live."

Burke kissed her. "I lost you once. Here is what *I* believe. I must not allow it to happen again."

"I feel so sorry for him."

"Sorry is not a good reason to agree to be burned alive. Wake up from this very bad dream," Burke whispered, urgently. "This is a cult thing, okay? History is filled with them. They are all built around one megalomaniac who thinks he is on a first-name basis with God and can predict the end of the world. They all end up the same way, too—with a very public humiliation or a bunch of dead followers."

"But our practice . . ."

"Let me tell you," Burke said. "There were psychedelic drugs involved, perhaps in the food. There were mushrooms, most likely, if not some version of LSD. The meditations were guided and he spoke hypnotically. Members of the group are forbidden to discuss its secrets and must cut off all contact with the outside world."

She remained silent. "He has a medical background, yes. There are drugs he says are holy. He makes them in a laboratory somewhere."

"So, I've pegged it all correctly so far."

With a sigh, Indira said, "I think some part of me has always known I should leave, that I do not belong with him. But I was so young. I cannot explain. I don't know how I allowed this to happen."

He tugged her arms. Indira stepped over the coffee table and sat in his lap. Her face nestled in his neck, feathered breathing slid down his chest. For his part, Burke had gone cold with purpose. "How many people are involved in this?"

"I have only met some of them, perhaps thirty or forty. I do not know any of their names."

"Who are they, Indira?"

"Mo says that they come from all walks of life, academics and politicians and scientists, some are even from the military."

"What is he planning?"

"His death, my death. A large funeral pyre somewhere and a celebration of the beginning of the end."

"Other than that. What is he planning?"

"I don't know." She looked deeply into him. "He is a man of

limitless ambition, capable of anything." She steeled herself. "I could go back again now and ask questions, try to find out."

Burke stroked her hair. "You will not be going back. Not now, not ever. Like I said before, I will not lose you again."

They melted together like hot wax and despite the fear—or perhaps because of it—the loving was delicious.

Forty-Nine

"I told you I would fucking handle it."

Deputy Mayor Paul Grace has thin white striations surrounding his lips. His face is pale and drawn. Bowden can smell the stench of fear lurking behind the expensive cologne. "Well, you *didn't* handle it." Grace sits down heavily, the plush office chair rocks. "So they took care of it for us about an hour ago."

Scotty Bowden's stomach drops to the parking garage like a depth charge. His mouth fills with a sour taste. He stares at Grace, whose worried face is now in shadow just beyond the glare of the high-intensity lamp. He knows what he heard, but cannot accept it.

Grace purses his mouth and shrugs like an accountant delivering bad news. "That's just the way it is."

Bowden turns away, lightheaded. Outside, the city lights ripple along the plateglass window. At first he cannot find his voice. "What have you done?"

Grace massages his temples. "It wasn't me. I didn't do anything. I just told them the truth."

"Who are you talking about?"

"The people we work for."

"Who?"

"Don't get any ideas, Bowden. They are not to be trifled with." Grace's voice drops to a mellow, eerie baritone. "I warned you to keep your friends away from this particular situation."

Scotty Bowden stumbles to the window and looks out. He

leans on the glass and it is cool against his palms. When he lifts them away, ghost prints remain but gradually fade. "This isn't right." Bowden watches the world tilt sharply. He feels a twitch beneath his left eye, hears whistling in his ears.

"It is what it is."

"Doc Washington was a good guy."

Grace exploits the opening. "That's too bad. He should have listened to you."

"Level with me. Exactly what happened to him?"

"Officially? It was a suicide, nothing more. He overdosed on painkillers. He's dead, so let it go."

Bowden turns, anguish in his voice, face contorted. "Jesus, Paul. *Why?*"

Grace takes a gold pen from his desk and fiddles with it, screwing it open and closed. "He dug into the Stryker file and passed confidential information about it to your friend Burke."

"We knew that. Burke didn't get much, for Chrissakes."

"It turns out that wasn't all, though."

Bowden turns to face Grace. "What else?"

"He was screwing around with a blood sample from one of the bodies. The old woman, to be precise." Grace puts the pen in the top drawer of his desk. He leaves his hands there.

Bowden is baffled. "Well, so what? That was his job. It doesn't mean he ever put the two cases together."

"I was told I couldn't take that chance."

"You gave the order?"

Bowden reaches for the gun at his belt. Grace takes his hands out of the drawer. He is holding a .38 in his right fist. "Don't."

Bowden drops his hands to his sides. "Fuck you. You expect me to stand still for this?"

Grace clears his throat. The gun does not suit his personality. Bowden is not convinced he will use it. "We now have you on videotape acting as a bag man for your squad, Bowden." The cop lingo sounds forced and artificial, but the content is alarming. "We also have you paying loan sharks, keeping a cocaine stash from a drug bust you did in NoHo last year, and all kinds of material. You're also on video taking payoffs from me in the parking garage. If I go down, you go down. Hard."

Bowden shakes his bowed head, a man trying to recover from a beating. "Maybe I should just shoot you now."

Grace shrugs. "Better shoot yourself. You know what happens to cops on the inside, don't you? Might as well be a death sentence."

"Maybe I don't care anymore."

"Don't be absurd," Grace sneers. "You're not going to die for some little nigger in a wheelchair."

Bowden reaches for the holster. His eyes are pinpricks of concentration and hate; one line of sweat runs down from his pale forehead. He watches Grace carefully and raises his own gun. Grace cocks the .38, but his hand is shaking. "One last thing," he offers, watching carefully. "Your kid will know you died a corrupt cop. Do you want that?"

Bowden approaches. His own grip is steady. Grace cannot fire. He lays down the .38 and raises his hands. His voice becomes thin, reedy with fear. "We're being filmed right now. I'm not armed."

Bowden wedges his 9mm between Paul Grace's teeth. He leans in quite close. "Smile for the camera, asshole."

"Don't."

After a long moment, Bowden wrinkles his nose. "You disgust me." He withdraws the gun. "Even on drugs and in a wheelchair, Doc Washington was ten times the man you will ever be. Now hear this, Grace. I'm out. My debts are paid."

"Bowden, look . . ."

"If you try to weasel one more thing out of me I'm going to come back here and give you two more nostrils."

Grace is squirming. His eyes fill with tears. "They don't let you leave, Bowden, take it from me. You're never done."

Bowden looks down. "I'll ask you one last time. Who are you talking about?"

"They run things," Grace is babbling. "They have money and power and a plan. That's all I can tell you. You can shoot me, but I say more than that and my family dies. Yeah, my family is on the line, too. I shit you not. These people are ruthless. Nobody goes free, Bowden. You keep playing ball or they'll come after your kid."

Bowden kicks the desk. It slams into Grace, pinning him against the wall. He aims a second time. "That's twice you mentioned my kid. I think maybe you need killing."

Grace, sobbing, writhing, raises his hands in a pathetic, all-too-common attempt to ward off the bullet with flesh. "I said it's not me, damn it! It's them! Look, this is all on videotape now. You can go ahead. Kill me if you want. Then they'll come after you and your family."

Bowden wavers. "They'll find me if they want me?"

"Gerber, the fat prick from downtown that plays the horses all the time? They own him. Your friend Talbot, the desk jockey who just put in for retirement? Him, too."

"Fuck them both."

"One of them would come to give you your new orders maybe twenty-four hours after I'm found. It would be like nothing ever happened."

Somehow, Bowden believes him. But who the hell would have that kind of power and reach? Not even the mob. Meanwhile, Paul Grace is a wailing, snotty mess. "They just keep turning the screws, man. Once you're in, you can't get out, that's all there is to it."

Scott Bowden lowers the gun. "You know something? I don't even think you're worth shooting."

Bowden slams the office door on the way out. His chest muscles constrict with grief. He needs a drink, ten drinks. He stuffs his hands into jacket pockets and stomps down the hall to the elevators, mind whirling and gorge rising. *Doc, poor Doc.*

Back in the office, Deputy Mayor Paul Grace gets to his feet, face crimson with shame. He looks up at the camera buried in the ceiling. The camera even the city bosses do not know about.

This humiliating experience will be watched by superiors and his sad performance evaluated. Worse still, the details will be shared with others. He will be openly mocked, then demoted. Finally, no longer considered useful . . .

Grace screams to summon courage and before he can change his mind, jams the .38 in his mouth, jerks the trigger. The low blast is somewhat muffled by his skull. The back of his head explodes into mist and creates red, white, and gray modern art on the pristine wall behind the desk.

Fifty

The messenger's truck is little more than a glorified golf cart. It pulls to the curb and parks directly in front of Nicole Stryker's stylish home. The driver, a muscular man with tattooed forearms, busies himself scribbling notes on a clear plastic clipboard. He glances up at the house as if to verify the correct address. He drops earphones over his ears, begins bopping to the music, grabs an envelope from his sack and starts up the dark sidewalk.

But it is very late for a delivery.

"Gina!" The voice sounds strident, on edge. Gina finishes typing the URL she's been trying to break. Nicole Stryker is a nervous pain in the ass. Gina sits back with a groan and rubs her tired eyes. "I'm right here."

"I think it's him."

A starburst of adrenaline courses through Gina's system. She reaches into her leather Alessi holster, palms her little aluminum-framed Astra A-75. The Spanish pistol holds seven .40 shells with decent stopping power. Gina shoves her rolling chair backwards, away from the computer desk. "I'm coming."

They meet in the hallway, near the broad foyer. Nicole Stryker is holding herself against an icy, imaginary wind. "Gina, he has tattoos."

Gina flattens against the wall. The little gun is gripped tightly in both hands and pointed muzzle-down at the floor. She slips the manual safety catch at the left rear of the aluminum frame and waits. The doorbell rings. Nicole Stryker emits a squeal and steps back into the office at the end of the hallway.

"Yes?"

A muffled voice from the porch: "Letter for a Ms. Stryker."

Gina raises the gun. "Oh, gosh. Leave it on the porch, okay? I just got into my pajamas."

"I need somebody to sign for this, ma'am."

Gina makes herself sound chipper. "Oh, can't you do me a favor on this one, pal? I'm a mess right now. Just scribble something on it. Hey, they'll never know the difference."

Heartbeats accentuate the long pause that follows.

"Yeah. Sure. I guess that's okay."

"Thanks."

"You have a nice night."

A minute passes. From the back office, Nicole calls out. "He's going back to the truck."

"Does he have anything in his hands, Nicole?"

"Just the clipboard. I don't think it's him," Nicole says, finally. "He looks too young."

"Keep watching."

"He's driving away. Gina, what is this? What does it mean?"

Gina lowers the Astra, swallows her fear. "Beats the crap out of me." She slides the safety back into place. Nicole comes back down the hall, her feet scuffling like a small girl's and her arms still tightly wrapped around her upper body. "Don't open the door, Gina. It might be a bomb or something."

Gina eyes her. "What did you see him carry up to the porch?"

"The clipboard."

"And he took that with him."

"Yes."

Gina sighs and tucks the Astra A-75 back into the leather holster. "Let's take a look at what's out there, then."

"But isn't there such a thing as a letter bomb?"

Gina already has the door yawning wide. She looks carefully out into the shadows of the yard, then down on the door mat. There is a small white envelope with Nicole's name and address on it. Gina picks it up carefully, looks at the return address.

"Hot damn."

Gina closes the front door and locks it behind her, turns off the porch light. She examines the envelope, sniffs the seams, and holds it up. It contains only a piece of paper. There is a small date written under the return address. "Looks like he arranged for this to be delivered tonight. Maybe in case something happened."

Nicole's eyes fill. "You open it."

Gina does. The single sheet of paper contains a long series of symbols and equations. They have been reduced to an almost infinitesimal size and printed out. There is a scrawl at the bottom. "Is this his handwriting?"

"Yes."

The sentence reads: *SEND GOV AT BEGINNING OF THE END.* Nicole is crying softly at the sight of that familiar, powerful handwriting—at once horrified, touched, and confused. Gina brushes by her and trots down the hall. She sits down before the computer. Her fingers dance over the keys and she feeds the page into the scanner. She dials her cell phone.

"Burke?"

"Yes?" He answers softly, for he is lying on his bed naked, one arm around Indira. Burke gently extricates himself and pads into the bathroom. He closes the door. "What's up?"

"I just e-mailed you something you need to see."

Burke feels his pulse quicken. He slips into his jeans. "What is it?"

"Peter Stryker sent his daughter a page full of some kind of equations, looks like math or chemistry stuff. The note on the bottom says she should give it to the government at the beginning of the end, whatever that means. Okay, this is getting to be some really strange shit."

"No kidding. And I'd be willing to bet I've seen this paper before. You scanned it?"

"Yeah. You should have it on your computer by now. Hey, you want me to ask Doc to take a look at this, too?"

"No. He's catching enough heat already." Burke thinks for a moment. "We need to get it analyzed as quickly as possible. I'm going to send a copy to the JB." JB is their slang for the E-mail account Burke uses for government work. The acronym is a cynical reference to James Bond. Any E-mail that goes there is automatically encoded and forwarded to Cary. Burke figures government scientists should make short work of the formula, whatever it is. "Hang on, Gina."

Burke slips into a tee shirt, sneaks back through the bedroom and into his office. His computer is already booted up and sitting online. He downloads the one-page file. "Yeah, this looks like the same thing I saw at Stryker's house the night someone broke in. Whatever this formula is, somebody probably killed him over it."

"And he sent it to his daughter through a messenger service, in case something happened to him."

"That's why the bastard kept asking Nicole where 'it' was, too. He tortured Stryker into admitting he'd sent it to her."

"Jesus. What now?"

"We'll find out soon enough." Burke prints out one copy of the page. He then encodes and forwards the E-mail containing the file to his secret account with five stars typed in the message line. This is a signal to Cary that the matter is urgent. "Everything okay there?"

"It is so far," Gina replies. "Watch your ass, Burke."

"You, too. I'll get back to you later on."

They break the connection. Burke studies the printed copy. What could a horror author like Stryker have possibly been up to that would get him killed, much less over a set of numbers and images?

"Red?"

Burke whirls, leaps to his feet. Indira stands in the doorway in her bra and panties. She recoils from the look on his face. "I'm sorry. I wondered why you were up."

He calms himself, wraps his body around hers. "I need to leave for a little while," he whispers. "I have to make a few arrangements. Then you and I are going to go run far, far away."

"Jack, I can't just go. I have all of my memories at the house, the pictures of my family, the jewelry and other heirlooms. If I leave them behind, Mo will destroy them once he sees I'm not coming back. That would break my heart."

"You can't go back there. Not ever."

"Well, you can't leave me here alone."

"I have to, just for a bit."

"Please don't go." Indira reaches down, touches the piece of paper containing the printed formula. "Where did you get that?"

Burke covers rapidly. "It's nothing, something I'm working on with Gina."

"It looks familiar."

A chill passes over, perhaps the shadow of a demon. "It does?"

She nods, her eyes still filled with sleep. "Some of it, anyway. I saw something like that on his desk once."

"Your husband?"

"Yes. It was with some other medical papers of some kind. He got upset with me and scolded me for prying."

Mohandas Pal? What the hell?

"Indira, listen to me. I need to get some money together." He looks deep into her almond eyes. "I want you to promise me you'll stay here for a while, and that you won't answer the door."

Burke opens a desk drawer. He removes a small but functional Heckler & Koch .22 caliber pistol. "Do you know how to use this?"

"I suppose."

"You have to be fairly close for it to do much good, but if you have any room I want you to run like hell instead. You understand?"

"You're scaring me."

"I need to." Burke checks the time, hugs her. "There's a lot going on, Indira, and I don't understand any of it yet. I have to assume we're both in danger. It would be foolish to think otherwise. I don't like leaving you, but I won't be gone long, I promise. So just trust me on this and wait right here, okay?"

Fifty-One

"I need the rest of my money, or as much of it as you can get together."

"Is that all?"

"And I need it in cash."

Tony Monteleone grinned like a threatened possum. "Burke, anyone ever tell you what a pain in the ass you can be?"

"You, just the other night." Burke closed the distance and slid into the booth. The plastic squealed. "I'm serious, Tony. Something has come up. I know I said I could wait, but I'm in a bind."

"And I owe you."

"I didn't say that."

"No, but it's true." Monteleone stirred espresso with a tiny, stained spoon. "Maybe you ought to tell me about this." He added two cubes of sugar. "I'm not too busy just now." He drank with an audible slurping, in the Sicilian tradition. "Who you running from?"

"I wish I knew."

"You need some help?" They both know what that means.

Burke shrugged. "I might at some point, but not yet. I'm serious about not knowing exactly who or what I'm up against."

"You want a drink?"

"No, Tony." Burke touched his hand, a personal gesture highly uncharacteristic of their relationship. "Look, somebody with clout has it in for me. There's a girl involved, someone I really care about. I want to get her away from here."

Tony Monteleone scowled. "Anybody with ears knows you work both sides of the street. But you do it without pissing people off, and you're a man of respect. This somebody is fucking with the wrong people when they fuck with you."

Burke shook his head. "The support is appreciated, Tony. But these people don't play by anybody's rules. Whoever they are, they seem to think they're above the rest of us. That's why I need to get her away. I need some time to think."

"And you need some cash."

Burke waited. Tony snapped his fingers. A stocky, muscular man moved noisily through the curtains and into the room. He acknowledged Burke, who didn't recall having seen him before. "Sal," Monteleone barked. "Get this man thirty large against the fifty and change we owe him. Make half of it in small bills. No funny money, the real deal."

"Thanks, Tony." Burke leaned back onto squealing plastic. Thirty thousand would get them far enough away, at least for now. In his mind, he was planning the route: a drive to Vegas and a plane to Denver, then from Denver to New York City and over the border into Canada. Nobody had that kind of power in two different countries. He hoped.

The money arrived quickly, already neatly packed in bundles, perhaps for some other nefarious purpose. It was a surprisingly small package, wrapped in brown butcher paper. The man called Sal dropped it on the table and moved away, face blank as a slab of granite.

Monteleone chuckled. "Hey, do you want fries with that?"

Burke tucked the package under his left arm, got out of the booth. "Now I owe you one."

"Damn right." Monteleone stood. "So stay alive, you hear?"

Burke nodded, looked behind him. He backed away out of habit, wary eyes fixed on the man called Sal. For some reason

Tony Monteleone found that funny. "Look at this hard-ass, he don't even trust his best friends."

Burke cased the gloomy parking lot. The stash of money seemed like a flashing red light that could attract unwanted attention.

He opened the trunk of his car, removed the cash bundles and packed them into the wheel well, around the undersized spare tire; ripped the brown paper and buried the money as best he could. He covered everything up with tools, a grimy beach blanket, and an earthquake kit, slammed the trunk and got into the vehicle. He started the car and drove away, with one wary eye on the rearview mirror, but he was not followed.

As Burke approached the freeway, his cell phone vibrated. Gina sounded upset.

"Burke, I tried to call Doc."

"Why? I told you he was catching heat."

"I figured I'd say hello, maybe ask him to stop by my place for a drink. Then if he did, just as a friend, he could maybe look over what came in the mail without any hassle."

"And he said no."

"Burke," Gina's voice cracked. "Doc is dead."

Burke felt punched out of air. "What?"

"When I called I got that friend of his, the guy he plays chess with, a kid named Frank Abt? He said the meat wagon had just picked Doc up. The homicide dicks were on the scene, but Abt heard the cause of death was an overdose."

Burke was racing up the freeway on-ramp now, heart slamming like a wooden gate in a wind storm. "No other details?"

"No. This guy, he was figuring Doc did himself by accident. Doc liked his drugs. I guess it might be that simple, huh?"

"Not if the homicide boys were there. Something stinks."

"Yeah."

"Damn it to hell. Gina, I need to know the whereabouts of

Professor Mohandas Hasari Pal. Right fucking now. Get on it. I'll keep this line open."

"Sure, but what's he got to do with this?"

"Do it, Gina."

"Okay, okay."

Burke dropped the cell phone and floored the gas pedal.

Fifty-Two

Red won't be gone long, he promised . . .

Indira Pal, still in panties and a bra but wearing one of Burke's oversized robes, is half watching some ridiculous old black-and-white Mexican horror film on the giant screen television. She is curled up on the couch with a tall, white-wine cooler, lost in thought. When the station cuts to a histrionic car commercial, Indira sets down the glass. She gets to her feet, somewhat unsteadily, and walks to the bathroom. She drops the robe, sits down on the toilet to pee. She thumbs through a magazine.

Something rustles in the bushes outside the bathroom window.

Indira huddles forward, instinctively clasping her knees with her forearms. The gun is back on the couch. She does not flush the toilet. Tense, she waits for another sound. Nothing comes. After a time she cleans herself, then grabs the robe and walks on her toes, moving back into the now cavernous and desperately lonely living room. She slips into the robe, tucks the small Heckler & Koch .22 into her pocket and curls up again. After a moment she sees her cell phone on the coffee table, drops it into the other pocket.

"Hello?"

The voice is scratchy, weak, and yet its very presence startles Indira. Her nervous system reacts badly, tears spring to her eyes. She jumps to her feet and stands between the couch and the coffee table.

Knocking. Again: "Hello? I know you're in there. Answer me!"

There is something surreal about the experience; standing half naked in someone else's home, cringing at the presence of a stranger at the door. Something about the voice is feeble, nonthreatening. Indira moves closer to the door, the peephole. She looks out, sees features elongated and distorted as if in some funhouse mirror. It is the face of a little old woman. She steps back, perhaps sensing she is being watched. The Granny wears a neat blue sweat suit and carries a small paper shopping bag. Her makeup is smeared and the blue-gray hair mussed.

"Please, open the door, honey. Talk to me."

Indira drops her right hand to the .22 in the pocket of the robe. She palms it, swallows. "I think you have the wrong house." Her left hand strokes the little cell phone as if it were a lover.

"Gretchen, I do not. Now open up."

Gretchen? "Ma'am, you have the wrong house. There is no one by that name here." She backs away from the door.

A long silence, fraught with tension. And then a muffled, whooping sound. Indira cringes and steps back to the door, peers out. The old woman, seemingly dazed and confused, has begun to sob. "Please don't send me away. I have nowhere else to go."

Indira, still looking through the little peephole, opts to test her. "Would you like me to call the police?"

The old woman nods furiously. "Maybe that would be best. I'm very lost, you see. My memory is not what it once was."

"I'll call 911, then."

"Yes, please. Would you call them for me, dear? Perhaps they might help me to find my Gretchen." She leans forward and one blue eye enlarges at the peephole. A conspiratorial whisper follows. "You see, my husband is trying to take me back to the home."

"The home?"

The woman twirls around like Cinderella at the ball, a chubby little octogenarian in powder blue sweats. "There's nothing at all wrong with me, mentally or physically. I can still dance up a storm and my mind is sharp as a tack." She pauses to thump the fingers of her right hand against her temple. "Sharp as a tack," she repeats. "Sharper, even." She taps those fingers on the door and whispers. "And I know perfectly well it's you, Gretchen. So stop playing around and let me in."

She's not afraid of me calling the cops, I've got a gun, and she's eighty if she's a day. Indira doesn't know if it is the wine, a whim, or her loneliness, but she figures the thick screen door will protect her. She cinches up the robe and opens the front door. Indira looks out into the night at the foolish old woman and smiles a bit sadly. "As you can see, my name is not Gretchen."

The old woman looks her up and down. Her lower lip begins to tremble and her eyes fill. She seems hopelessly depressed and baffled. "Oh, dear. My, my. Perhaps there is something wrong with me after all, then."

"You just have the wrong house."

"Oh, I'm sorry to have disturbed you, then."

"It's all right. I wish I could help you."

"Perhaps you should call the police to report that I am here with you. I do seem to be lost."

"Certainly," Indira says gently. "What is your name?"

That lower lip, those eyes. "Oh, dear. This is awful. I can't seem to remember my name, either."

"Perhaps you have some identification on you."

The woman searches her bag, and her heartbreak is achingly visible. "There's nothing in here but candy and some tampons.

Imagine that! I haven't had a period in many, many years. Why do you suppose I bought tampons?" She looks up. "I think I may be ill, dear. May I use your phone?"

Indira opens the screen door slightly. "You can use my cell." She is about to offer up the phone when the old woman grabs the screen door and opens it. Indira steps back, startled. The old woman breezes by her, chattering up a storm, calling out: "Gretchen? Gretchen? Come out and talk to me!"

Indira keeps her hand on the gun. "Ma'am, you need to leave."

The old woman moves from room to room, ignoring her, calling out for the invisible Gretchen. Finally she ends up back in the living room, that hollow look in her eyes again. "Who am I, dear? What is my name?"

Indira takes one arm and steers her to the door. "You need to leave." Surprisingly, the woman allows herself to be led, although Indira finds a startling amount of muscle in the arm and elbow she holds. She moves the chattering crone out onto the porch again. Once she has her back to the house and the screen between them again, Indira realizes how terrified she has been for the last several moments. She holds up the cell phone.

"One last chance to use this, or I am going back inside."

"That won't be necessary."

Another voice startles Indira; it is a man's voice this time. A distinguished-looking man of about the woman's age comes striding up the walk. His features are stern. The old woman crumbles against the porch railing. "Don't let him take me back there, dear."

Indira reaches down to close and lock the screen door. To her horror, the man steps up onto the porch, whirls the old woman around and slaps her across the face. Hard.

"I told you to wait in the car, damn you!"

The redness on the woman's cheek is clearly visible. She covers her face and her shoulders quiver beneath the blue jogging suit. The man raises his hand again. His eyes are murderously angry.

"Stop that. Let her go." Indira steps out onto the porch. Confident it will stop him, she raises the Koch .22 waist high. The man's hand freezes in midair and he looks down at the little gun. Before Indira can react the old woman whirls, a lithe dancer again, and her two small hands grab the gun and the wrist that supports it; they twist and turn. Indira cries out and the pistol is no longer hers.

The sobbing old woman is smiling now, a wickedly satisfied expression of disdain. Indira gasps as the gun is wedged under her chin. "Twenty-two shells rattle around in the skull a lot, dear. One has to use them in close for them to be effective. Now get back in the house."

Indira floats on her anxiety, backs into the living room thinking, *Oh, Burke I've screwed up, I'm so sorry,* as the old man opens his coat and removes a hypodermic needle. He squirts a drop of clear fluid from the tip. He is making an annoying, condescending clucking sound with his tongue. "Hold her, Mrs. Farnsworth."

The old woman grinds the gun into her chin and Indira finds it painful to swallow. She manages to speak. "No. Please don't kill me."

"Oh, sit down, you silly little bitch," Mrs. Farnsworth says. "We're not going to kill you."

"You see, we are also Shahr-e-Khamosh," Mr. Farnsworth chortles. "*Mo* is going to kill you."

Indira sits. She is the one crying now. The old woman yanks the robe down and grips her arm tightly. The needle slides home with a bitter sting.

Fifty-Three

Burke came through the open front door already knowing in his heart that she was gone. He swept the rooms anyway, 9mm at the end of one extended arm like an accusing finger. The throw rug was bunched up near the wall, the coffee table slightly out of place. Infuriated, he slammed the screen and locked it. He kicked the front door shut and put the cell phone to his ear.

"Where the fuck is Pal?"

"He's not home, that's for sure," Gina said. "In fact, he's left town."

"What the fuck?" A cold wave of sadness ran through Burke. He sat down on the couch. "Explain."

"The home phone was disconnected, so I did a quick search. He's history. Pal has even cut off his utilities."

"When?"

"First thing this morning. His E-mail addy is no longer in service and the Web site says he has resigned his position at the university for health reasons."

"Shit. Indira is gone."

"Which means?"

"Pal took her, or had somebody else do it." Burke closed his eyes. "Let me think for a minute." The last few days had been frantic. He worked to bring the disparate pieces into a cohesive whole. "Gina, we need to know if he went to Mexico."

Gina's fingers busily clacking on the keyboard, a small intake of breath. "Son of a bitch."

"I'm right? What have you got, Gina?"

"I just hacked the school's system and I found an E-mail between two other instructors. It says that he's gone there, supposedly for some kind of cancer treatment he can't get here in the states. It doesn't say *where* in Mexico, though."

Burke opened his eyes. "I think I know," he said, with a sinking feeling. "Leave that for now. Have you got anything else on what happened to Doc?"

"Not yet. But get this, Jack. I started fucking around with the name Stryker registered under at the Sheraton. Dan Ira Palski. It sounds weird. I got to thinking it was in code, or it meant something, and you said Stryker liked word games. So I started doing some anagrams, shit like that."

"Damn it. It's her name. He knew she would talk."

"That's right. Dan Ira Palski is an anagram for 'ask Indira Pal.' "

Burke rocked sideways. "Peter Stryker was leaving clues behind. He probably checked in to meet somebody from Pal's cult, and was pretty sure he wouldn't be checking out again. What about the letter that came to Nicole, anything from Cary?"

"He wants to talk to you."

"Yeah," Burke said quietly. "And that's a damned good idea. Did he say where he wants me to meet him?"

"Online." Part of Gina's mind was elsewhere, the magic fingers still occupied. "ASAP, the man said. He told me via the emergency route, whatever that means to you two."

"Okay, but stay on the line."

Moments later Burke was at the computer, typing code sequences. He removed the small camera from its plastic case. The piece was designed for a one-time use and had been encoded to a specific frequency. Burke lined it up, rolled the office chair backwards on the hard plastic sheet. The monitor flickered and rolled, then burst into white static. After a few seconds he saw a split screen with his face on one side and Cary's features on the other. The images ran together and then resolved. Cary sat alone, in some nondescript office. He was holding a sheaf of papers. He looked exhausted.

"Well, it works, anyway," Cary said. "I always wondered if it would, or if it was more high-tech bullshit from people with nothing better to do."

"The lady I've been seeing just disappeared," Burke said quickly. "Probably kidnapped by a cult headed by a man named Mohandas Hasari Pal. I think it factors into your troubles in Mexico."

"I wouldn't be surprised. And catch this, the sheet of formulas you faxed me?" Cary raised the paper. "It's got the kids at the Center for Disease Control in Atlanta pretty excited. One of them actually called me on an open line to tell me what it is."

"Tell me, make it quick."

Cary read from the page. "This is a direct quote, Burke. The guy from CDC said 'this is the cure for a disease that doesn't exist.' "

Burke leaned closer. "What the hell does that mean?"

"It means that if a certain super strong influenza virus just happened to be manufactured somewhere, a bug that would have a mortality rate nastier than Ebola and one hell of a long life in the open air, then this sheet of equations Stryker sent his daughter would offer the chance of a cure."

"The note at the bottom, in Stryker's handwriting? It said 'for the government, when the end begins.' " *He was trying to save his daughter's life.* "Jesus Christ, Cary, is that what I think it is?"

"I don't believe in coincidences. We have a lot of bits and pieces coming together. I'm just not sure what they mean yet."

"That's because it's time to factor in Mexico, Cary."

It took Ryan a second to catch up. "Buey?"

"That's right, and now my girlfriend Indira, too. Hang on." Burke raised the cell phone. "Gina, what have you got now?"

"I hope you're sitting down," Gina said. "Doc just sent us an E-mail."

"What?"

"He must have mailed it on time delay from his office computer, Burke. It's a file. I forwarded it to Cary's private E-mail because you both need to see this. I mean right fucking now."

Burke to Cary: "You get something from Gina? Open it."

"Got it."

Burke bristled. "You're the geek, Gina. I can't do it and talk to Cary online. One of you tell me what it is."

"Oh, shit." On the monitor, Cary's jaw fell open at the hinges. "Looks like Doc was doing some extracurricular lab work on a homeless lady brought into the morgue. It's the start of a report on the fact that there was something odd about the virus in her body. He never finished it." Cary looked up. "What do you want to bet?"

Poor Doc. "That's all the confirmation I need," Burke said. "The only missing piece was Mexico. Not anymore."

"The pile of dead bodies underground at Los Gatos. Shit. And now someone took your girlfriend down there?"

"Cary, you need to do all the workup you can on Dr. Mohandas Hasari Pal. Gina has a leg up and she will send you what she's gotten together. Like I said, he runs a cult of some kind, very secretive, a perversion of Tantra. I can tell you that he has a preoccupation with death and he's just found out he's terminally ill, also that he and Stryker knew each other. So the virus must originate in Mexico. And Cary?"

"Yeah?"

"I want that mission you offered."

Fifty-Four

The young woman awakens with a soft moan, and her head rolls sideways on the pillow. She reaches out for her lover, can almost smell the tang of his sweaty chest hair, but her fingers grasp empty air. She lowers her hand to the pillow and discovers it is wrapped in clear plastic.

She opens her eyes. Her heart sinks.

Indira Pal finds herself in some kind of a hospital room, or perhaps a prison cell. Her surroundings are made of mirrored glass, shiny metal, and clean porcelain that reeks of cleanser. Everything is sanitized to a fault and the recessed lights are painfully bright. She tries to sit up, but her head pounds. She notices an unpleasant taste in her mouth.

"She might be waking up."

The voice is muffled and tinny and comes from somewhere in the wall above her. Indira rolls onto her side. One light rustling sound tells her she is wearing a paper gown that is backless; she can feel a slight breath of air flowing over the skin of her buttocks. The air smells of disinfectant and polished metal. Embarrassed, she rolls onto her back to cover her nakedness. She keeps one arm over her eyes and pretends to fall asleep again in order to buy herself time to think.

Indira remembers that terrifying old couple, the Farnsworth woman dancing madly through the house. Now she understands that the woman was making sure no one else was on the premises. She recalls the senility routine, the old man striking the woman, how abhorrent his action seemed at the time. The way the old woman skillfully disarmed her, the old man's eerie calm. The injection that followed. Her arm still feels sore. *It has not been long, probably less than a day.*

But where is she? Have they taken her to a local hospital? Why, what sense would that make?

"Good afternoon. Are you hungry?"

Indira feels her flesh swarm with goose bumps. There is no sense continuing to pretend she is not yet awake. She removes her sore arm and opens her eyes. The bright light hurts. "What the hell have you done to me?" Her attempt to sound brave is feeble and she knows it.

"All in good time, Mrs. Pal," the voice soothes. Indira remembers: *they told me Mo sent them.* "I have permission to offer you some yogurt if you are hungry. Although you have ample water in your cell, there is no food at present. This may be your last opportunity to eat."

"Before what?"

No answer.

Indira uses her hands to brace herself against the mirrored wall. She pulls herself upright. Her temples throb. *Buy some time.* "Yes. I would like to eat something. Thank you."

"Of course."

"And may I have some aspirin, please?"

"I'm sorry, Mrs. Pal. No medicinal items are allowed."

Indira looks around the sterile room. She is sophisticated enough to sense that the mirrored walls are two-way. She is being observed. She becomes even more conscious of her naked behind, and pushes her back against the pillow. She hugs herself against the cool air.

Something rattles and rumbles in the wall behind the tiny sink. After a ludicrous amount of whirring, a panel opens to reveal a lightweight plastic container about the size of a cigar box. The container extends into the room on a shelf made of thick paper, which then drops to the floor. The container, which is clear, contains a small, sealed package of store-bought yogurt and a white picnic spoon.

The surface of the wall is completely flat mere seconds later, and the mechanical noises fade away.

"Hello?"

Indira feels tightness in her chest and her breathing becomes ever more shallow and rapid. The extensive medical precautions and cold, impersonal treatment are working to create a stark, lonely terror. She wonders what has been done to her, and what is to come.

"I know you're watching me," she ventures. "Can't we talk about this?"

Fifty-Five

Biff Gerber is a sour-faced condo of a man who is easily twice as athletic as he seems. Thick arms strain the fabric of his blue uniform. He raises the cigarette to his veal-colored lips, jerks his head, indicating the passenger door of the patrol car. "Get in."

Scott Bowden goes around behind the back of the car. He gives a few seconds of serious thought to pulling his throw down and putting two in the back of Gerber's head, but the man's piggy eyes watch him too carefully in the rearview mirror.

Bowden takes a quick look around the quiet Van Nuys neighborhood. An ancient Oriental man is mowing a yellowing yard four doors down. He doesn't look up. The street seems virtually deserted. Bowden reluctantly opens the door, gets in. The first thing he notices is that Gerber has a cocked Colt MK4 series .45 sitting in his lap. The handle and trigger are taped to obscure fingerprints.

"You wanted to see me."

Gerber takes a deep drag on the cigarette and throws it out into the street. He exhales a plume of smoky bad breath heavy with garlic and onions, then rolls over onto one immense ham and farts.

Bowden waves his hand in the air. "Thanks for sharing."

Gerber slaps a broad hand against Bowden's chest. He runs it up and down, gropes his crotch. Bowden allows the search because of the .45 but his temper is close to flaring. He fantasizes about cutting off one of the fat man's ears just to hear him scream. "I'm taking over for Grace where you're concerned," Gerber says, finally. "You take orders from me from now on."

"How come?"

Gerber shrugs to indicate his lack of enthusiasm for the topic. "Grace did himself."

Bowden, hesitantly: "Anybody know why?"

"Maybe his wife finally found out he was laying pipe in them gay bars or something. I don't know and I don't give a shit."

"You always were a caring individual, Biff."

"Save the smart-ass routine."

Bowden looks down at the gun. "You going to use that on me or yourself, Biff?"

Gerber does not smile. "Depends."

Bowden sees a pack of unfiltered Camels on the dash. He takes one and lights up. The radio squawks for a second, but is turned down so low it sounds like static. Bowden inhales deeply, feels the nicotine rush to his brain. Meanwhile, Biff Gerber sits perfectly still except for the slow lift and fall of his huge chest. His mind seems far away.

Bowden exhales. "What they got on you, if you don't mind me asking?"

Gerber grunts. "I mind you asking." But then, after a pause, he speaks quietly through tightly compressed teeth. "Hey, I have a thing for the horses. I got in over my head. Borrowed from guys I shouldn't have."

"Yeah, the bent nose bunch."

"No, the Russian version."

"Damn."

"Grace came and bailed me out, so long as I worked for him. It was no biggie at first, a little bag detail here and there or some enforcement. I was still a good cop."

There is genuine pain in the man's gruff voice. A new silence hangs heavy as fog. "Yeah," Bowden replies. "So was I."

Gerber warms to it, the words bumping together like a five-car pileup on the freeway, spilling out of his mouth in a pressured whisper. "Somewhere along the way I lost track of what I was doing and why I was doing it." He looked down at the gun. "Now, I've done some things I wouldn't tell a priest about. Here comes another one."

Bowden wonders if he is about to die, eyes the gun nervously, knows he could never reach his own in time. "What are we talking about, here?"

Biff Gerber sighs dramatically. The stench of garlic and onions permeates the car. "I ever tell you about my ex-wife, Bowden?"

"Can't say you have."

"Name is Betty. She's a little redheaded twist with big tits, man. You know the kind, a real spinner. We split up maybe eight years ago, before I put on all this weight. I never got over her."

Completely lost, Bowden takes another drag on his Camel. He lets his other hand slide a little closer to the holster clipped on his belt. "I'm listening."

"So Betty had this kid, a real looker herself, kind of a stepdaughter to me, you know? One day last fall I tell Paul Grace I don't want to do this shit no more. He can stick it up his ass, take my badge, whatever. You want to know what happened the very next day?"

Bowden is shocked to see one solitary tear roll down Gerber's pudgy cheek. He edges his hand closer his own gun, takes another drag on the cigarette, and waits things out.

Gerber finally continues. "Kelly, the stepdaughter, she's walking home from school. Three gangbangers pull over and yank her into the car. They shoot her up with dope and do her six ways from Sunday, but they finally let her go." Gerber looks up, eyes black with rage. "They tell her to say hello to her mom's ex, the cop."

"Jesus," Bowden murmurs. He is picturing his own daughter now, and his stomach churns. "I'm sorry, man."

"That's who we're working for, you see." Gerber forces a chipper quality into his voice, and somehow that makes his statement all the more chilling. "All we have to do is play ball and do what we're told and things are cool. We get little bundles of cash and promotions and things roll our way. Just don't ask too many questions, and never turn them down." He looks away. "Never."

Bowden feels the cool, reassuring metal of the gun beneath his fingers. He flips the cigarette out through the passenger window. He changes position in the car so he will have quicker access to the weapon. "Can I ask you something, Gerber?"

"Sure."

"Who the fuck *are* we working for? Who are 'they'?"

Gerber picks his teeth with a yellowing fingernail. "Bowden, if you try to pull that weapon I will blow your guts to ribbons. Just so we're on the same page."

"Okay." Bowden lets his hand slide back into plain view. "Like I said before, I'm listening."

"The people we work for are rich and well-connected," Gerber says quite calmly. "They all know each other, but none of us know who they are. One time I got curious and tried to find out."

"And?"

"I followed one broad, a woman I saw leaving Grace's house one night. She goes into the ladies' room of a bar with a small suitcase, okay? So I'm standing down the hall pretending to be on the pay phone. A couple of minutes later the door opens and a fucking man walks out, plain as day. I only know it's her because this guy is carrying the same suitcase."

"You followed him."

"Damn straight I did. All the way across town and up into the hills. Something about him looked familiar, but I couldn't place him. So I make a note of the address. Know who it was?"

"This a fucking game show? Tell me."

"It was a big, hot-shot writer name of Peter Stryker. You know that dude who wrote all those horror novels. I tailed him a couple other times, always the same story. He meets somebody in drag and goes home as a man."

"So?"

"Hey, I'd write it off as kinky sex, but I know a couple of the people he's meeting, and they ain't into trannies."

"Then it was just to keep things cool. And now Stryker is dead."

"Very badly dead, man. Anyway, so Peter Stryker and Grace I knew about, of course, and as best I can tell, Grace was the biggest swinging dick in city government, other than a fucking councilman or two."

"Any idea how many there are in the whole group?"

"I don't think it's all that large, but they have balls like watermelons. There are some people in the government involved, but I think they're mostly spooks."

"Spooks? You're kidding."

"Most likely CIA or Homeland Security dudes, you know? The ones who never show up on anybody's payroll but still seem to be involved in all the heavy shit."

"So we're working for the government?"

Gerber chuckles in a dirge. "No government you or I would recognize. Jesus, man, they've had me knock around guys who work for the FBI. Whatever they are, it's not that simple." He turns to his right, looks straight at Bowden, who does not like the expression on his face. "I have your next assignment."

Bowden nods carefully. "Okay."

Gerber raises the gun, aims it at Bowden's belly. "Do I need to spell out what's going to happen to your daughter if you don't follow orders?"

"No." Bowden grimaces. He grinds his teeth.

Gerber shrugs. "They told me I should."

Bowden feels flush with rage but cannot move. His daughter's life is on the line, hanging on the way he responds. He shakes his head. "No need for the rough stuff." He forces himself to sound confident. "I hear you loud and clear."

"I've been told a guy name of Jack Burke is your asshole buddy and that you can get next to him pretty easily."

"I suppose so."

"Well, some out-of-town talent got assigned to take him out but still hasn't gotten the job done. So now it's yours."

"He's my friend," Bowden says weakly.

"We don't have friends."

"Christ, Biff, he was a cop in Vegas. He's one of us."

Biff Gerber nods quietly. "Well, then this really sucks." He almost seems sympathetic. Almost. "But from now on, think of it this way. It's him or your kid."

Fifty-Six

Saturday

"I-I-I don't fucking believe this," Cary Ryan sputtered. His chiseled features were engorged and frustration rendered him nearly inarticulate. He already knew he would lose the argument, but could not let it rest. "Rising international tension? Threats of terrorism?"

"That's what the man said."

Cary slapped his hand on the computer keyboard and spilled hot coffee on a case file. "What the hell are we talking about?"

"What are we talking about?" The balding case officer, Garth Burwell, outranked Cary. He was annoyingly calm, even a bit smug. The fact that he was on a video conference and not in the room was almost as irritating as his message. "I don't know about you, Major Ryan, but I'm talking about the government of a sovereign nation having asked us to stay out of the way for the next few days."

"Sovereign nation? Who's kidding who? This is *Mexico* for Chrissakes!"

Burwell fought down a smile. "You have a point there."

"Back me on this, Garth. Please."

"Sorry, Major. No can do."

Ryan rubbed his face. "What about an overland op, maybe with a tour bus or something? I might have time to get it together that way."

A shrug, a tilt of the head. " 'Stay out of the way' indicates that there are to be no ops at all until they get things straightened out down there."

"This is a setup. Whatever or whoever we're after must have some people in Mexico in their pocket. This is the property of a drug lord, for Chrissakes, you know that!"

"Cary, I have been instructed to ask you to shut things down for the duration of the crisis."

"Damn it, that's my point," Ryan bellowed. "There is no crisis! Someone has drummed this up to keep us out of the way."

"Aren't we being just a bit paranoid?"

Ryan decided to put it all on the line. He tapped the screen with a finger. The case officer flinched as if touched. "I want to speak directly to the Secretary."

"He's fishing in Montana," Burwell replied. "You can try him on the secure line tomorrow, maybe you'll get lucky."

"That's too fucking late and you know it."

"No, I don't know it. That's the point. We have nothing to go on but your suspicions."

"I have to talk to him."

Burwell opened his palms as if to say "what can you do?" "Well, none of the powers that be are willing to send a plane into the canyon and piss him off over evidence as flimsy as what you've provided us with so far."

"One or more of the powers that be are in this bastard's pocket. Believe me, I'm going to find out who it is when this is all over. Even if it turns out to be you."

"Major," Burwell snapped. "That had better not be a threat."

"If you're a mole for Buey or this fucking cult, then you're damned right it is."

"That's it." Burwell appeared genuinely insulted. "I have to go."

Ryan was flabbergasted. "You're tying my hands."

"I'm not doing anything of the kind." Burwell was losing patience. "I am relaying what I have been told to say. You will shut down, Major. Cease any and all operations with respect to Mexico until further notice. And this is an order. Is that understood?"

Before Ryan could respond, Burwell turned off the camera and vanished into a wall of static. Cary Ryan sat facing a dead monitor.

And a dead mission.

Fifty-Seven

The compact, four-person helicopter veered north. It skimmed along a ridge of pinkish stone that surrounded the city of Chatsworth, in the northernmost reaches of the San Fernando Valley. The machine was remarkably quiet for a rental. Peering down from the pilot seat, Father Benny watched the rippling shadow of his chopper swim along the streets of the housing tract like a sleek black fish. His stomach felt reasonably calm today. Benny was grateful to God for the respite.

After a low pass, Father Benny checked the time. He adjusted the foot petals and turned for home.

The Van Nuys airport was jammed, but the vast majority of pilots were flying small planes. Benny circled low and to the south. He eased over the helipad low enough to stir up leaves and trash in the lot behind the diner. Today, he had the magic touch and set her down like a rose pedal. Benny grabbed his clipboard and noted the required information from gauges on the instrument panel. When the engine finally died and the blades whirred to a stop, he was grinning wide and high. He unzipped his Miami Dolphin windbreaker, opened the cockpit, and stepped down onto solid ground.

"Going to barf this time?"

"Jack! What are you doing here?" Burke was hunched over the wheel of a Ford van with panel doors. His features were grim. Father Benny's chubby face sagged. "Oh, my, do I owe money again already?"

Burke smiled, despite the circumstances. "No, it's something else. Get in here, Father. I need to talk to you."

Puzzled, Benny waddled around the front of the vehicle, trailing one hand along the hood to keep his balance. Puffing, he climbed onto the passenger seat and slammed the door. "Is this about that girl again?"

"In a way, yes."

Father Benny clucked. "Oh, son. You need to let go once and for all."

"Maybe I'll do that," Burke replied. "But not yet." He started the engine and drove the van out onto a slender dirt road that paralleled the dusty tarmac. A green Cessna sank down out of the sun and wobbled in for a landing. As Burke accelerated, it paced him down the runway. "You told me once that you believe in facing your fears."

Benny, confused, "Where are we going?"

Burke gunned the engine and headed south, for Sherman Way and the 405. "Benny, did you mean that? About facing fear?"

"Yes." They cut into traffic and earned the long blare of a horn. Benny looked up nervously. He didn't care for Burke's driving. "But that doesn't mean I have a damned death wish, excuse me, Lord."

"I need your help with something, Benny. It's important. And it is going to be dangerous."

Benny stared, his anxiety momentarily forgotten. "Is this something for the government?" He seemed excited by that prospect.

"Yes." Burke wove in and out of traffic. "It's top secret."

Benny nodded eagerly. "You can count on me."

"Wait. Hear me out, first. Then decide." Burke honked at an elderly woman in a Dodge, cut around her and roared up the ramp. He checked the rearview mirror out of habit. *Was that white Ford truck behind us at the airport?*

"Red, where are you taking me?"

Benny awaited an explanation. Burke kept his hands clenched tightly on the steering wheel. His knuckles were white. "We're going to stop by a restaurant to see a friend of mine, run an errand or two, and then we're driving to a small ranch in Arizona, near the border. I am assembling a crew to help me with a very dangerous, very off-the-books mission. This one is a black op we're hiding from the folks who pay for the black ops."

Benny started to ask a question, hesitated. Burke continued, "Here it is. I need you to fly me over the border to a specific place in Mexico."

"Okay." That sounded easy enough. Benny relaxed a little.

"This will be an illegal run, in the dark and low to the ground."

"Okay." A bit less sanguine now.

"Benny, we may get shot at."

"What?"

"This is the deal. I need you to drop me at an LZ for a rescue mission. I'm going to free a prisoner, blow some charges, go back to the fixed point and wait. You drop me, fly the bird where the mission commander instructs you to go, and get back to the LZ to bring us home."

"In the dark. Low. While getting shot at."

"Maybe nothing will go wrong."

"Burke, did I hear you correctly? Did you say something about how you were going to 'blow' the place?"

"Sky high."

"Shit. Excuse me, Lord."

Burke noticed the off-ramp he wanted. He forced his way into the right-hand lane. More honking. He checked the rear-view mirror, spotted a flash of white paint but was not certain it was from the same truck. His pulse was racing. Benny had to agree to do this. Burke had no time and no other option. He exited the freeway and took surface streets the rest of the way.

Benny coughed, shell-shocked. "Let me back up a bit. This whole deal will be highly illegal, right? Even the people who plan such things won't know about it?"

Burke shrugged. "Some will. My friends. Nobody else, though."

"And people will get killed."

"Only the bad guys. We hope."

Benny shook his head, began searching for viable excuses. "I can't leave the church for very long, Red. You know that."

"Benny, you can call in and tell your assistant you're away on a personal matter. You'll be home in less than forty-eight hours." Burke ripped his eyes from the street. He faced Benny, pleading. "I need your help. I don't have time to find somebody else." He glanced in the mirror again. The white vehicle, whatever it was, seemed to have vanished into traffic.

Benny's right hand slipped into his pocket, seeking rosary beads. "I'll help you, Red. You know that. But I guess that's why you came to me in the first place, isn't it." It was not a question.

A warm rush of gratitude. "Yeah. That's why I came to you."

"Okay, okay."

"Thank you, Benny."

"One good thing about being a priest," Benny whispered. "You don't really need to make a last will and testament."

They pulled into the parking lot behind Fredo's. Father Benny's eyes darted. He looked even more confused than before. "We're going to lunch?"

"Not this time," Burke said, unbuckling. "We need to move faster than that."

The tall, broad-shouldered bodyguard eyed Benny's white

collar with suspicion. He allowed the two men to enter the restaurant.

Tony Monteleone was seated in his usual booth, long fingers scratching noisily on the red-and-white-checkered tablecloth. He had a bottle of Chianti open and three glasses filled. Monteleone half rose, winked and motioned expansively for Father Benny and Burke to join him. The dazed expression on the priest's face was comical.

"It's good to meet you at long last, Father," Tony Monteleone said with a welcoming smile.

"Should I know you, sir?" Benny sat down heavily, grabbed a glass of wine. He slurped like a camel gone dry.

Burke sat at the edge of the table, in a wooden chair. He hated having his back to the room, but Benny had accidentally left him no option. "Benny, this is Tony. He represents the people you still owe a lot of money to."

Benny blanched whalebone white. "You're him?"

"Your friendly neighborhood bookie."

Burke patted Benny's trembling hand. "Relax, Father, he's not half as dangerous as he looks."

Monteleone had a small notepad in his shirt pocket. He opened it. "I see you still owe me four large and change, Father."

Father Benny's head wobbled. He wondered if he'd been set up. "And I will pay it back, every penny. Haven't I been keeping up with the vig?" He glanced at Burke. "With some help, of course."

"You've done fine," Monteleone said. He made a show of taking a pencil from the same pocket and crossing out the amount. "And if you go through with helping out my friend here, despite some hits I've been taking lately, I will agree to erase your entire debt. You and I, we'll just call it even."

Benny gaped. "It's not necessary, sir, although I would certainly be grateful if that turned out to be the case."

"Consider it done," Monteleone said. He winked. "Call it tithing."

"Of course, now I really have to go through with this, don't I?" Benny was trying for a joke, something to lessen his own growing tension. Burke and Monteleone chuckled politely and then Burke pressed on.

"Everything else we talked about ready to go?"

Monteleone referred to his notes again. "Father, you rent your helicopter from a parishioner named Timothy O'Reilly, is that correct?"

Benny nodded, sipped more wine. Despite the alcohol, he seemed startlingly close to one of his patented vomiting episodes. "Usually for a couple of hundred dollars an hour, yes sir." He raised a guilty eyebrow. "It is my only indulgence, you see. Other than a penchant for profanity, that is."

"And unwarranted confession," Monteleone said. He produced a flat sheet of paper. "Well, some of my people had a conversation with Mr. O'Reilly a few moments ago, and he faxed over this document."

Father Benny read it and guffawed. "He donated the helicopter to the parish? But why?"

Monteleone rolled his shoulders and scowled. "I made him an offer he couldn't refuse. I told him his brains or his signature would be on that document in sixty seconds." When Benny gasped, Monteleone grinned. "I've always wanted to use that line. Even if the fucker is dumb enough to talk about it, nobody is going to believe him."

"But I can't possibly . . ."

Burke adjusted his chair and it screeched. Having his back to the room made him edgy. "After this is over with we don't care what you do with it, Benny. Give it back, sell it, whatever. Believe me, the guy got a good price for it."

Monteleone nodded. "In cash."

"This is unbelievable." Benny was shaking his head, pouring more red wine, doing his best to adjust.

"It's about to get worse."

Burke's shoulders went tense. He started to slide his hand down from the table but the familiar voice came again. "Don't."

Tony snarled. "Who the fuck are you?"

"Turn around, man. Keep your hands in the open."

Burke turned. A man wearing a ski mask had the taller bodyguard by the throat and was pointing what appeared to be a silenced mini-Uzi machine pistol. The Israeli weapon holds between 25 and 40 9mm Parabellum rounds. Burke's eyes zeroed in on the combination safety catch and fire selector on the top of the pistol grip, just above the man's hand. The weapon was set for automatic fire.

Burke recognized the voice. "Scotty, talk to me. Brothers, right?"

Scotty Bowden ripped off the mask, spun the bodyguard, kicked the back of his legs and drove him to his knees. The big man was shaking, although it was difficult to know whether from anger or terror. Bowden palmed a weighted sap in his left hand and expertly crashed it down on the back of the man's skull with a rich *thwack*. The bodyguard collapsed into a heap. "You used my name, Red," Bowden said. "That was stupid. Nobody had seen my face."

"Now I guess now you'll have to kill us all."

Bowden sighed. There was true grief in his reddened eyes. "I don't want to do this, man."

"Then don't."

Scotty closed the distance. Burke knew him well, could see him sizing up the three men by location, height, body weight. He was preparing to spray them down rapidly.

Father Benny folded his hands and started to mutter the rosary.

"A priest, Scotty? You're going to kill an old friend and a priest?"

Tony Monteleone, for his part, seemed less concerned. "Get one thing straight, dickhead," he barked. "You do me and there will be nowhere on earth you can hide. You may as well blow your own brains out right now."

Bowden's hair was mussed and his clothes looked like he'd slept in them. Then, eyes fixed on the three men before him; he moved a chair away from a nearby table. He flipped it, sat down backwards. The small Uzi was rock steady, and so close Burke could read the Hebrew script on the side of the blue-gray metal above the stock.

"Can it, greaseball. Because of you two the truth is I just may *have* to shoot myself next, so shut the fuck up."

Burke forced himself to reach for a wineglass.

"Don't."

But Burke did, sipped to buy some time, turned to face Bowden fully. "Talk to me, Scotty. Who's got you by the balls?"

Bowden shrugged. "What difference does that make?"

"Maybe we can help."

"A priest, a Guinea, and the mark I'm supposed to hit? What a joke." He raised the weapon. Even Monteleone gasped for air.

But Burke noticed a slight tremor in the hands that translated to reluctance. "I'm working on something right now, Scotty," he said quietly. "It's big. In fact, it's big enough that it might interest you."

"Save it." Bowden was steeling himself to pull the trigger.

"Two minutes, then go ahead. Hear me out. I've been getting messed with a lot lately, okay? I think a cult is behind it all, a cult with members placed carefully in industry and government. They have a lot of money behind them. Any of this sound familiar?"

Bowden tilted his head. "Go on."

"I believe a man named Mohandas Pal leads them. They had Stryker murdered. They also had Doc killed, and are also responsible for the death of at least one homeless woman he e-mailed me about. A drug dealer named Buey is tangled up with them. He hates my guts. There seems to be a virus of some kind, something really lethal. They'd do anything to cover up the fact that it exists and that they're manufacturing it. Anything."

Bowden was feeling pieces come together like clicking tumblers, the parts he didn't know. He lowered the gun. "Okay, I'm listening."

"I think these same people took Pal's wife, a lady I care a lot about, down to Mexico, where Buey is helping them culture the virus. They intend to kill her, Scotty. We are going to stop them."

"We?"

Burke winked. "You and me, bro. With a little help from the padre here and some friends of mine that still collect paychecks from Uncle Sam."

Bowden lowered the gun to his side. He closed his eyes like a man inviting a firing squad. His face crumbled into exhaustion. "Red, they are going to hurt my little girl."

Monteleone grabbed his cell phone. "Give me her name. Then be quiet and wait a few minutes before you go and blow up our shit."

Burke poured a glass of wine. He was pleased that his own hands were still rock steady. He extended a glass to Bowden. "Here. You look like you could use a drink."

Eleven long minutes later the cell phone rang. Monteleone listened intently, grunted approval, and closed the phone with a flourish. "Your kid and her mother will soon be on their way to Vegas for an extended vacation. All they'll be told is that they won a prize package and chips from the casino."

Bowden's face showed hope for the first time. "But what if . . ."

"Some of my folks will stay with them night and day. They are pretending to be a film crew. They won't tell the truth unless they absolutely have to."

"We should be back long before that becomes necessary." Burke glanced at Father Benny, who had finished praying and seemed calm. He nodded approval.

"Back from where?"

"We're doing one last op, pal. We're going to fuck with the guys who did Doc. Just you and me, okay?" He offered a clenched fist. "Brothers."

They slammed knuckles. "Brothers."

"But the truth is that we may not make it out this time. Does that sit okay with you?"

"That's fine. Does it pay?"

"Not half what it ought to considering the risk."

"I want two hundred and fifty large life insurance on me, with my daughter as the beneficiary."

Tony made a note. "Okay."

"Then I'm in." Bowden finished the wine, but to Burke's pleasure did not ask for more. "What about the rest of the members of this . . . cult, or whatever it is. Won't they still be in place afterwards, despite whatever we do?"

Burke offered a low-key smile. "You know the game I'm in. I have friends who are very good. These people might try to run, but they will be found, and they will be dealt with."

"Your way," Monteleone said quietly, "or mine."

"It's a done deal."

The bodyguard began to stir and moan. Monteleone called over to him, "DeMartini, get up and get the fuck out of here. And by the way, you're fired."

Bowden rose, the Uzi dangling on his left. He approached

the table and extended his right hand to Monteleone. "I'm in your debt."

Monteleone shook vigorously. With a straight face, he said, "I guess maybe we greaseball, Guinea motherfuckers are good for something after all, huh?"

Fifty-Eight

With Bowden in the van, Burke and Benny hurried northwest into the R4 industrial area situated close to the far end of the Los Angeles basin. The streets were lined with a pastiche of old houses and nondescript storage facilities; small business owners liked the cheap rent and relatively good security provided by the tall, barbed-wire fences and armed guards, and the residents couldn't afford to move. Burke drove to the prearranged location and honked his initials in Morse code. Bowden looked at him askance.

"Don't look at me. That was Cary's idea."

A bearded man with white hair emerged from the parking garage carrying an open *Playboy* magazine that barely disguised a silenced automatic; behind him in the doorway, with half of her upper body hidden in shadow, stood a thin woman in a smart business suit.

"Oh, shit. It's Dave and Cora."

Bowden sighed. "Great. Someone you've pissed off."

"I'm afraid so."

The agent Burke humiliated in the coffee shop reluctantly lowered his weapon. He tucked it into his belt, dropped the magazine. He opened the heavy metal gate and shoved it out of the way while his partner kept watch. Burke steered the van into the enclosed area and remained in the vehicle, hands on the wheel, until the area was secure again.

Dave, his broadcaster's voice heavy with irony, spoke first.

"Oh, so one of my favorite people needs a favor, eh?"

"Look, I'm sorry about grabbing your nuts and all that," Burke offered weakly. "I was having a really bad day."

The man known as Dave glared. "Yeah, well thanks to you, so did I. If it wasn't for the Major's orders, I'd . . ."

Burke hopped out of the van. "You'd likely kick my ass. I wouldn't blame you. But right now we've got work to do."

Cora, from the doorway, "He's right."

Burke, over his shoulder, "Wait in the truck, Father."

"No, I want to help."

Father Benny slid out and trailed the three men and one woman into the darkened storage unit. Cora slammed the door behind them, flipped on the lights. The cement-floored facility was packed, floor to ceiling, with wooden crates and cardboard boxes. Most were marked with the names of fruits and vegetables.

Dave sighed and calmed himself, then found a plastic clipboard. He started scribbling. "Tell me what you need."

Burke touched his arm. "First thing I need is that we don't write anything down."

Dave gnawed at his moustache and sucked air through his lower teeth. He slowly set the clipboard down on a metal desk. "Major Ryan said anything you wanted. How hot is this going to get?"

"Scalding."

Dave looked at Cora; Cora looked at Dave. Finally, they both shrugged. "The Major has covered our asses more times than we can count. What the hell. We're in."

"Scotty? You know what to do. Start unpacking some gear. Dave, I'll explain while you help me load the van. Fair enough?"

"Fair enough."

Bowden located a hammer, knelt on the filthy floor and made some nails squeal, then yanked the lid away from a slatted wooden box marked RADISHES. He reached inside and removed two brand-new thermobaric "bunker buster" charges and some small, portable rocket launchers still packed in a light coating of grease. Father Benny went a bit pale. Burke unpacked two Assault Rucksacks, already filled with emergency food, water and medical supplies. Bowden moved to a crate marked CARROTS and eased out a pair of vintage black M4 carbine rifles with PEQ2A laser sights, two 30-round magazines and two CA-15s with pump shotguns attached to the bayonet fixtures. One crate contained nothing but grenades modified to be powerful to the nth degree. Meanwhile, Cora and Dave were unpacking rope ladders, black flak jackets, and other safety equipment.

"How many on your team?" Cora asked.

"Actually, I was going in alone at first," Burke replied. He looked up. "But now there'll be two of us on the ground."

Bowden belched loudly, injecting some easy laughter. "I can hardly wait."

Burke opened a Dragon Eye system, small enough to fit into his backpack. It was a five-pound reconnaissance craft that could beam video directly to a camera on a soldier's wrist. But after mentally running the mission—and the speed that would be required of them—he replaced it in the carrying case.

"Let's take one anyway," Bowden called. "Just in case."

"Forget it." Burke turned his attention to collecting ammunition. He also packed several modified grenades and a large amount of plastic explosive. The grenades, medical supplies, new-age devices and eerie-looking NVG night-vision goggles rapidly covered the cement. Father Benny went from white to green. Moments later he was outside, vomiting in the dirt. Dave and Cora looked puzzled.

"Don't worry," Burke said. "He's just the designated driver."

Fifty-Nine

"Can't someone please just talk to me?"

Indira Pal is cold and hungry but afraid to eat the yogurt. She has handled the clear plastic container but the top could easily have been penetrated by a needle. Her surroundings are already horrifyingly medicinal, and the idea of eating something that has been tampered with makes her stomach curdle.

"Hello?"

She would love to pace the room just to get some blood flowing but the paper gown is backless. Indira is emotionally shaken, and she can feel she is being watched through the ubiquitous two-way mirrored tiles. The drug they have given her is wearing off and has left behind a pounding headache and a deep thirst.

Shahr-e-Khamosh. Kali-Ma, help me.

She is thirsty but also afraid to drink the water.

Her conversation with Burke sticks in her mind. She knows that there were drugs in the food and drink at the last spiritual retreat, that most of what she has wanted to believe for years is almost certainly false, that she will soon be drugged again . . . and then burned alive, along with the body of her husband. The City of Silence cannot let her go. She knows too much. But how much has she told Burke? Ah, and that is what they will be hoping to find out.

"Are you comfortable?" The voice comes from nearby and startles her.

Indira clutches her legs and squirms back up onto the cot.

She works herself deeply into the corner. Her eyes roam the room and finally land on the tiny metal speaker set deep into the sealed surface of the ceiling. "What?"

"I asked if you were comfortable."

Indira begins to cry. "Mo, I know that it is you. What are you going to do to me?"

"Hush, now," his voice soothes. "Don't work yourself up. There are many things to come that will truly horrify you, my dear, but nothing that is going to happen just yet. You must save your energy."

"Why?"

"You will need it for screaming."

Indira feels her innards quake. She knows the darkness in her husband. She has seen him beat servants and abuse followers not obsequious enough to suit him. He has beaten her many times as well, carefully and systematically, and always in ways that left no mark.

"Why are you doing this?"

Pal laughs, the speaker rattles like phlegm. "You dare to ask that question after laying with another man, grunting like a pig with him? After violating your vows just before we are to share the sacred rite of Sati?"

"Sacred to you," Indira replies. She can feel herself gathering strength. "Personally, I don't want to die yet, Mohandas."

He mocks her. "Why, neither do I, my dear. Who does?"

"This is just to satisfy the bottomless pit of your ego."

"Oh, it is for so much more than that," the disembodied voice intones. "It is to prepare the earth for the return of Kali-Ma, to create the sacred City of Silence on the face of the earth."

"Nonsense." Indira hurls her darkest feeling. "Your religion is a lie. You drugged us and tricked us, Mo. You're a fakir, a charlatan."

After a long moment, Pal chuckles. "Oh, I suppose you do

have a point. I played a trick or two on the group. And I may have fudged a little here and there to impress the heathen . . . but I can assure you, I mean everything I say in the larger sense."

Indira hugs her knees again. "I don't understand you."

"No mortal could." Another laugh, a bit shriller. "But then I suppose that sounds like I'm quite mad, doesn't it? And I'm not, I assure you."

"Let me go."

"Quite impossible. But to be sporting, I will give you a choice in how you die. You may die of a horrible sickness and have your body burned, or you may be burned alive along with my body instead. It's rather a Hobson's choice, eh? If I were you, though, I would take the burning. If you inhale the flames you will die more quickly and with considerably more dignity."

"Go to hell, Mo."

"I will give you a few hours to come to a decision. If you refuse to make one, I will toss a coin. Does that seem fair enough?"

Indira shudders. "Burke will stop you."

"Not a chance that he even knows where you are. It took much effort to manipulate the two of you into bed again, but with the help of my followers and Peter Stryker, I have succeeded."

"You *wanted* us together?"

"I want his wounds to be fresh, for Mr. Burke to suffer as I have suffered. And now he will."

"Jack will find me."

"Hold on to your hope. How much have you told your lover, hmm? How much does he know of my organization, my plans?"

"Everything."

A laugh, followed by a deep, wracking cough; it takes Pal some time to recover. "Why, that is simply impossible, sweetheart. Why, even you don't know everything."

Indira thinks, takes a shot in the dark. "He knows about the formula."

She can hear the hissing intake of breath and takes satisfaction in having startled him. She makes herself grin wickedly, as if filled with feelings of triumph. The speaker clicks off. Indira sits, waiting for the torturer to arrive, waiting to be beaten or drugged. But no one comes. She remains still, completely isolated in the empty room.

Sixty

They sat quietly in a deserted, dilapidated hangar near a private airstrip a few miles north of the Mexican border, listening to a swirling breeze claw some dried sage across the tarmac. Burke opened his cell phone, punched some numbers to retrieve messages. He waved to Bowden and sighed. "Gina and Stryker's daughter are okay. She just left a message that they're at the hotel in Vegas."

"The one your friend's family owns?"

"Yeah, same place as your ex and the kid. One less thing to worry about."

Scotty Bowden stopped screwing around with the Dragon Eye monitor long enough to flash Burke a wan smile. "Too bad we can't hump this sucker. I have one more question. Just out of curiosity, how exactly do you plan on not getting us killed?"

"What do you mean?"

"Didn't you tell me that Cary Ryan already lost two teams over this dude? How are we going to keep from getting toasted?"

Burke walked to the makeshift chalkboard, combat boots crunching through small twigs and pebbles. "First of all, there will only be the two of us going in, and from a different direction. Look." He made an elaborate sketch with blue chalk as Bowden watched. "You've already seen the sketch of the layout. The property is about eight miles outside the town of Los Gatos, which is pretty much under the control of Juan Garcia Lopez, also known as Buey, The Ox."

"Okay, so it is kind of a hacienda in the middle of a military compound."

"That's about right, Scotty. It is a pretty fancy hacienda with fountains and horses and all the accoutrements you'd expect, but it's fenced off in a seriously organized way. Buey is one of the only guys I've seen who plays house a couple hundred yards from his drug lab."

"Maybe he gets high on his own supply?"

"Could be." Burke sketched some more. "Now, let's take a look at the land around the hacienda."

Bowden lowered the weapon, rose and moved a few steps closer. "Okay, shoot."

"This rock ridge is about twenty feet higher than the compound. It's on the east side, maybe one hundred yards out. Then you have one wall with a guard tower, a gate, and the side of the barracks. To the north, a long electrified fence, another guard tower joins the west wall and sits above a second gate. That long building, kind of a reverse 'L,' is what we believe to be Buey's private residence. At the ass-end of the 'L' is another gate and an extension of the electric fence."

Bowden pointed. "And that's where the satellite photos show a shit load of dead bodies."

"Unusual pockets of gas and other materials that indicate decomposition, yeah. So knowing what we know now, it's a mass grave under the ground."

Bowden nodded. "But why are they letting them rot underground, Red? Why not burn them up, especially if they are fucking around with some kind of new biohazard as a WMD?"

"We don't know."

The door slid open with a clang. Bowden looked up and past Burke's shoulder, then smiled broadly. "Well, fuck me."

Cary Ryan entered the room briskly, carrying a large stack of computer discs and file folders filled with photographs. "We're going to have to rush this up, gentlemen. I'm getting waved off big time."

"It's been a long time, Major." Bowden shook his hand. They locked eyes a moment longer than necessary, an acknowledgement of shared history and mutual respect.

Cary dropped his cargo, moved to the blackboard. He tapped the drawing to indicate a drab, square two-story building that squatted near the middle of the drug lord's compound. "We think that's the lab where he makes his drugs and probably this spooky designer virus."

Burke studied Ryan's face. "Cary, who's fucking with you?"

"Everybody."

"You look pissed. Where is the pressure coming from?"

"I don't know," Ryan replied. "Someone doesn't want this mission to happen, and ordering me not to stage it was only the beginning. Now some of my own people are trying to hack me, follow me, and track my whereabouts. I had to call in every favor in the book just to get here safely."

"The agency has been penetrated."

"At least to some degree."

Father Benny had been sitting quietly in the corner of the room, ashen-faced and almost forgotten. "So let me get this straight," he said. "We are going into a situation that is so dangerous that two other groups of men have already died. The naughty boys probably know we are coming. If they do not manage to kill us on the spot, they will have a deadly new virus on the premises that may poison us later. Have I left anything out?"

"Well," Bowden offered, deadpan, "we'll be outnumbered."

His timing was perfect and the laugh provided a much-needed release of tension. Cary Ryan gathered them around the metal desk and a flat computer screen. He tapped keys. "Here is some footage directly from the Predator drone." Actual photographs of the target area rolled by, now artificially colorized and digitally enhanced. "You can run this as many times as you want, but trash the disc when you're done, okay? And now watch this, carefully."

Cary adjusted the angle. The computer slanted down and to the side of the buildings, penetrated and explored hallways and individual rooms. "This is our best guess at what's waiting for you inside. We don't know for sure because the other teams were stopped too early."

"When?" Burke and Scotty asked in unison.

"The first team got torn up right outside the north gate. The second inserted safely but ran into a meat grinder near the porch of Buey's home, before they managed to get inside the laboratory."

Bowden and Burke exchanged glances. "And now you think somebody who works with you might be affiliated with Buey's gang?"

"More likely this new cult being run by Mohandas Pal." Ryan sighed. "And if I had an inkling of that I would never have sent the first team in, much less the second."

"So Buey knew they were coming, how and when. Most likely down to the minute," Bowden said. "That's just terrific."

"Yeah, but he won't know this time."

Burke lifted his eyes from the computer screen. "No offense, Major, but how can you be sure?"

"I'm sure."

"You mind explaining?"

Cary Ryan perched on the edge of the desk. He slapped two folders together. "Let me put it this way, I got an urgent phone call about forty minutes ago reminding me that my orders were to stand down. I told them I had done so. They accused me of lying and demanded I call off this highly illegal mission."

"Shit," Burke growled. "Then they already know."

"I argued with the fellow for a long time, even threatened to resign. Then I struck a compromise." Ryan grinned broadly. "The materials we're borrowing ostensibly belong to the Department of Homeland Security. The Director is in Athens for an international conference on terrorism and won't be back in the States for another six days."

"So?"

"I demanded some face time with him to discuss my concerns about the compound in Mexico, and why I thought another attempt at incursion was warranted. Finally, he agreed to that meeting."

"So what?" Bowden was glowering.

"So I also agreed that we will postpone any mission until after that meeting has taken place and the Director has approved the appropriation of these weapons for this specific purpose. This op has now been rescheduled. It will take place Friday night of next week."

"Fuck that," Burke said. "We don't have six days. Indira will be dead by then, and whatever Pal has in mind will already have begun."

"I know," Cary Ryan replied. "That's why we're going ahead tonight anyway, but completely off the record. No one else is going to know about it, as long as you don't get caught."

"All right!" Even Bowden was pleased. "I always liked that 'don't get caught' part. It keeps things interesting. Just like the old days."

Ryan went to the chalkboard. He looked it over carefully. "Looks good. The only thing I would add to what Red has sketched here is that the guards in the two towers to the east are probably going to be wearing night-vision goggles."

"Just them?"

"Yeah. The reason is that the only roads in the area are located on the west side of the compound. Buey probably figures that if the cops or another gang comes after him, it will be from that side because they'd need access for heavy vehicles. The guards there have lighting that spreads out into the gulley and down the roadway. The acoustics are probably terrific, so those guys would see or hear someone coming from a long way off."

Ryan tapped his pen against the sketch of the rock face that lay on the east side of the compound. "This ridge is a natural barrier to any sizeable force. Nobody smart would try to move a unit down this rock face, for starters. It can't be done without making noise, and the poor bastards that try it would be spotted crossing the flat because of those guards wearing NVG."

Burke nailed the underlying issue. "So how did you try to come in the last two times?"

"The first time we came from the north, where any decent military planner would logically have attempted it. We dropped the squad in the dunes about a mile out. Boom. The second time we came from the south, intending to cross the basin near the edge of the gaseous area. That seemed to work out better."

"And this time?"

Ryan began to pace. "I wish I knew. Like I said, the south worked the best. The boys made it into the compound."

"How did you handle the insertion by air?"

"People got paid off like they do when it's a small plane carrying drugs. Radar gets shut down for a few minutes then turned back on again. A particular flight pattern gets ignored, that sort of thing."

"That's how you got the guys over the border." Bowden grinned. "You pretended it was a drug run. Pretty damned clever."

"And it should work again this time."

"Here's what I want to shoot for." Burke ran two fingers through the chalk on the blackboard, illustrating his point. "Let's say Scotty and I get dropped by chopper maybe two miles to the east, jog across the flats to the top of this rock ridge. We climb by hand, then rappel and drop down the other side. We cross the open area."

Bowden pondered. "Not bad. And the two guards?"

"We take them out before we cross the open ground. It's a tough assignment from there, but not impossible. Maybe a hundred fifty yards from higher ground. All we need is one head-shot each." Burke thumbed through his notes. "Cary, you picked up radio transmissions that indicate the guards check in to the central command every fifteen minutes, right?"

"Right."

Bowden got it immediately. "We fire seconds after they check in, leave the sniper rifles there. We drop down the face, cross the open ground, get into the compound and do our thing. That will give us, what—maybe eight to ten minutes inside before they start to realize something is wrong."

"I hate to be a wet blanket," Father Benny sputtered from the corner, "but what about the noise? I mean, from the shots?"

"There won't be any to speak of, Benny. Silencers." Burke looked at Bowden. "We could also create a distraction. Some barely noticeable noise from the west that sounds like something might be coming down the road."

"That would help," Scotty agreed. "But we'd need at least one more man to pull that off. I say we keep it simple."

Ryan pondered the idea of a third member of the team and the security issues involved. He shook his head. "No, you're probably right. Less to go wrong." He touched the sketch of the square, two-story medical building that was located at the center of the compound. "Seven hours ago a van came down the road from the highway. It entered Buey's compound and parked next to this building. An older couple went into the residence. Moments later another gentleman and a man with a shaved head, who is presumed to be Mohandas Pal, got out and went inside the laboratory. Then someone on a stretcher was also taken inside the lab and the van left."

"Indira," Burke said.

"That seems likely. But we don't know who the other people are. We estimate there are already maybe thirty to thirty-five other people currently occupying the compound, most of them armed."

"Only thirty or so against the two of us," Bowden observed, wryly. "Aw, don't seem fair to them poor fuckers, does it?"

Cary Ryan laughed. "Strange world, isn't it? We have equipment that can peer down a man's throat and tell you what he ate for lunch, but just over the border one drug lord and a religious fanatic with connections can keep us paralyzed for months."

"Okay," Bowden continued, "let's say everything goes smooth as a papaya shit and Red and I get inside without drawing fire. I know we're out to bring the girlfriend back, and if she's unconscious that's problem enough. What else do you want us to do?"

Cary blinked. "I would have thought it was obvious."

"Let's just say I'd rather have it on the record."

"There won't be any record. You know that."

A strange moment of tension flickered between Ryan and Bowden. Then Ryan looked away and shrugged, as if to say *what the hell.* "Those fuckers erased a bunch of my guys. One of them deals drugs and the other may be planning on blackmailing the world . . . or something even worse."

"Yeah," Bowden cracked, "I get that they're the bad guys."

Ryan continued as if he hadn't heard. "So we are going to take them out, Scotty."

"Take them out. How, one by one?"

"I don't give a damn, as long as it happens. And afterwards, I want you guys to plant enough C4 in that lab to incinerate everything within two miles of the area. We're about to show you how to get that part of it done."

"I'm no scientist," Bowden said, "but how do we make sure this virus doesn't get spread around in the process?"

Ryan pointed to the blackboard. "Our guys believe the only two places we need to worry about are in the basement of that laboratory and perhaps underground where we believe all the bodies are buried. The first two rounds of explosives will bring the two upper levels down, first the top and then the bottom. That will bury the concrete area, seal it off."

"Okay."

"The last explosion will be from a thermobaric device I want you to plant in the lab before you leave. The blast will be trapped in concrete, under tons of rubble. It will generate enough heat to fry every bug in there to cinders."

Burke frowned. "What about the burial mound? There might be some live virus there that could get disturbed at some point."

"It's forty feet down, Red. My scientists say that's good enough for the time being. Besides, do you have a better idea?"

"Maybe." Burke touched the area indicated as the body dump. "We plant one charge here on the way out, right on top of the dump. Raw stuff, ready to ignite. We set a timer." He traced the route back to the rock ridge. "If it doesn't go off, then from up here, on the way home, we fire one thermobaric rocket directly at that mass. The explosion should be hot enough to kill anything likely to leak, and if the dump has any open areas, the explosion should collapse and seal them, too."

"It could work." Bowden was running the plan through his mind. "We might even get out again, guys." He tapped his teeth with a finger. "Problem is we need another couple of men to carry all this gear and a few more days to pull it off."

"We don't have either."

"How about we come in really low, maybe fifty yards behind

the ridge, and shove the extra rifles and explosives out? We could maybe drop them wrapped in a reserve chute. That way it would be there after we jog across the flats."

Cary Ryan clapped his hands together. The sound startled Father Benny. "Yeah, we drop it on the first pass to the LZ, but how about wrapped up in a life raft for a little extra protection."

"You got stuff that isn't traceable back to Uncle Sam?"

"Most assuredly."

"It'll have to do." Burke felt satisfied they could complete the mission and had a reasonable chance of survival.

Bowden leaned closer to Ryan. He was not smiling. "You got the life insurance policy I asked for? Two hundred fifty thousand?"

"You're all set."

"Oh, what the hell, then," Bowden said. "I wasn't doing anything else this weekend anyway. Let's go for it."

Sixty-One

Saturday

At first there is only silence, except for the vaguely erotic sigh of the evening wind. Then there comes a man-made explosion as an engine roars to life, the darkened helicopter rattling, whining, and thumping as it lifts off and away, flying blind. The uncertain pilot flies dangerously close to the sandy, rock-freckled ground, hoping to avoid detection. Inside a greenish, shadowy cabin rests the human cargo: two tense, former "D" boys.

"I am most definitely too old for this shit." Bowden chewed gum furiously. He checked and re-checked his pack. "How the fuck you talk me into this?"

"It was that or let you pop a cap in my ass."

"Damn, Burke, I'm really scared," Bowden said, as if amazed. "This shit was sure easier when we were kids."

"Yeah. It was, wasn't it? We were too stupid to be afraid of dying back then. Now we know enough to pucker up."

"You feel it, too?"

"More and more the last few years, bro," Burke said. "Lately it's been keeping me up at night, the not knowing how or when, or what happens after."

"Not knowing sucks."

"Hell, yes."

Scotty Bowden leaned back against the vibrating seat, pack between his knees. "How you doing up there, Father?"

Father Benny did not turn around. "Don't bother me, my

son. I'm praying my Italian ass off, excuse me, Lord."

Bowden laughed. He had a fine line of perspiration forming above his eyebrows and the skin beneath his left eye was twitching. "Burke, can I ask you something personal? You really love this girl, don't you?"

Burke, eyes closed. "Yeah, I think I always have."

"For some reason that's hard for me to imagine," Bowden said. "I don't get women, except for my kid, of course. I'll bet it feels nice."

"I have loved two women in my life. *Really* loved, I mean." Burke's mind went far away. "I guess that makes me a very lucky guy."

Bowden giggled. "You'd better be, or we're coming home in body bags."

"Scotty, we may not be coming home at all this time."

"You really know how to cheer a guy up, don't you?"

"It's a talent I have."

Bowden's jaws working on the wad of gum. "Do you ever have dreams?"

"Mostly of the times something went wrong, you know?"

"Yeah, I have a bad one that I still get pretty often, actually. It's about the night Doc got blown up. I'm watching it happen from a few yards away, and I keep trying to get my rifle aimed to do something about it but I'm moving too slowly, like I'm stuck in clear mud. So I just have to stand there and watch him take a burst. That really sucks."

"Scotty, did they kill him? Did they do Doc?"

Bowden spits the gum out, head bobbing up and down. "It was them, man. And that's all the more reason to get some tonight, right?"

"Damned straight." After a time, Burke shifted in his seat. "I get this weird dream about that same night when I'm all stressed out. It's about the guy Yousef Dahoumed, the one we went after in Djibouti, or at least I think that's what it's about. It's him, but it's not him."

"You lost me."

"Well, when I stitched the bastard he was sitting there in a bunch of gore, you know? Blood and guts and human shit. And he was laughing and laughing. Really spooky. So this dream is a little like that, except it's not him, it's somebody else. And it's not there, it's somewhere else. Somewhere I've never been."

"Funky."

"Anyway, I'm there, and here is this guy, rolling around in the blood and giggling like mad. And I want to shoot him, I try to shoot him, but he keeps moving, almost like he knows what I'm going to do. I can't seem to kill him, no matter what."

"Then what happens?"

"Nothing. I wake up."

"At least you don't die. Those are the fucking worst, man. Sometimes I dream I'm back in the old days collecting ears on a string again, and get myself plugged. I can feel the bullet go in and rip things up, feel my heart slowing down, and then I can't get my breath. You know what I mean?"

"Gentlemen?" Father Benny gripped the controls like a man with dengue fever. "Would you mind changing the subject? I have to fly this thing."

Burke and Bowden laughed. They punched each other on the shoulder. Father Benny clearly did not appreciate gallows humor.

"Here comes the border. Jack, are you sure the Mexican army isn't going to shoot us down?"

"They look the other way now and then, Benny. It's all been arranged."

"I certainly hope so, because here we go."

Benny dropped as low as he dared and urged the bird forward. Bowden stared out the window at the rocky desert, then into Burke's eyes. It was on. They both sensed it. There would be no turning back, they were in-country. The dark, empty land beneath them looked the same, but now the vibe in the chopper felt as wild and crisp as heat lightning.

Sixty-Two

Juan Garcia Lopez has an impressive collection of modern art. The sparely furnished room is appointed with sleek contemporary furniture, which makes the large, ornate wooden dining table with antique candelabras seem truly anachronistic. Still, Mohandas Hasari Pal feels comfortable in this room. After all, dreams have come true here. He listens to the musical selections, some classic recordings of Ella Fitzgerald in her prime, and enjoys the champagne, a fine 1982.

"You need to relax."

The alcohol has dulled Pal's pain, and he is feeling sweetly victorious. He can afford to jest. But his companions, the tattooed man known as Gorman and the somewhat effete Mr. Nandi, do not smile. Gorman has barely touched his wine, although he did partake of the meal. Mr. Nandi, ever the good servant, stands unobtrusively in the corner, ready should his services be required.

"What are they doing?" Gorman whispers from the side of his mouth. "Why have they been gone so long?"

"Be at ease, my friend," Pal replies in a low voice. He pats Gorman's hand. "We are very nearly finished with our work. Nothing can stop us now." He finishes his drink and motions. Mr. Nandi glides forward and refills his glass. "If I know our friend Buey, he is dawdling over his collection of tapes and DVDs, trying to select the perfect film to complete the evening. He will return shortly."

"Then why has Esteban gone with him?"

The door opens and Buey enters, a very sleepy Esteban trailing behind. Indeed, the Ox has brought a DVD and a second bottle of champagne. He grins, raises the liquor. "A movie for after we finish with the night's business."

"We have little more to say, my friend. Please, feel free to open it now should you wish."

Buey, a thick and bearded man worthy of his name, plops heavily into his chair. "Perhaps I will, if only to drink to your genius, Mohandas." As he busies himself with the bottle his lieutenant, a compact younger man who has struggled and failed to grow a decent moustache, sits groggily beside him, clutching a DVD of *The Exorcist.* The bottle opens with a *POP* very reminiscent of a gunshot. Esteban jumps a bit, then giggles and sags into a stupor.

Buey pours champagne for everyone. "A toast." He raises his glass. "To the man who offered me revenge, and who is about to make me one billion dollars with a telephone call." He downs the drink, pours another. He is very drunk. "You know how I hate gringo bastards like this hombre Burke. They have hunted me for years, paid off my own people to pursue me, and forced me to live like a prisoner in my own house. Twice in the last month more of those fuckers have tried to come into my home to assassinate me."

"I can sympathize," Pal soothes. "The United States government can be so utterly ruthless."

"But now he will suffer, this man who shot at me and fucked your wife?"

"I assure you, he will soon know the taste of hell."

"This is a good thing." Buey grins widely. "And it will give me more pleasure than you can imagine blackmailing America for such a sum, Mohandas." He turns to Esteban, kisses the boy on the cheek and fondles his crotch. "And with a billion perhaps we will go down to New Zealand and buy land to raise cattle. We will tell everyone we made money in the stock market and we will be known as generous benefactors of the arts. We will be loved, eh?" Another kiss. To Mr. Nandi and Gorman, he offers, "And you, gentlemen, what will you do with your money?"

Buey has forgotten that Gorman seldom speaks. After a long moment, he tries to cover his misstep by cracking a joke. "Perhaps our silent friend here could visit a spa for a decent bath and a facial!"

But no one laughs. Mr. Nandi makes a small clucking sound of disapproval. Suddenly afraid, Buey gulps and rips his gaze away. Gorman does reply, this time. "I will do whatever my guru wishes."

"Mr. Nandi?"

"The same."

"And you, Mohandas?"

A genial Pal sips champagne. "As for me, I will insure my legacy. Fortunately, I am still here to see that it happens."

"With books and films and temples, my friend?"

"That is how it shall begin."

"So esoteric an addiction," Buey chuckles, "is quite foreign to me."

"Unlike you, Buey, I am not a devotee of the flesh. I wish only that my name live long after I am gone—and that it is celebrated along with those of the other great teachers." Pal catches himself. "Oh, my ego. I must apologize. The wine has loosened my tongue and made me immodest."

Buey laughs heartily. "Not at all my friend, we are none of us without fault." He wraps his arm around Esteban, who has fallen asleep. "Whatever makes you happy. This is all that matters in the end." Buey turns to his young lover. "I do not understand. Esteban never drinks so much as to pass out like this." Looks back at Pal. "In truth, I feel very tired myself. It has been a stressful day. Perhaps you would forgive me if we do not watch a film this evening, after all?"

"But of course." Pal speaks soothingly. "You are always a most gracious host, Juan. If you need your rest, we can certainly see to ourselves and see you at breakfast."

Buey's large head is sagging forward. He startles himself by snoring. His voice begins to slur. "Mr. Nandi, unless you can help us, I must ring for assistance. It is time to get Esteban to bed." He mumbles something else. His hand crawls like a drunken crab toward the ornate dinner bell.

Pal speaks crisply, "Do it now."

In a flash, Gorman is on his feet. He crosses the carpet soundlessly and clasps Buey by the wrist. "Don't bother to ring," he whispers. "We have already taken the liberty of eliminating most of your people."

"You *what?*"

Pal chuckles warmly. "Mr. Nandi and others of my people have already eliminated the majority of your guests and staff. Even your beautiful concubines. The medical personnel making the drugs have also been accounted for. Only the guards in the towers remain. We will see to them, too, in good time."

"I don't understand. We are partners." Buey humiliates himself by wetting his pants. This makes Gorman laugh out loud. Mr. Nandi clucks again.

Pal mocks him with a sad, sighing sound. "You think so small, my friend. I was never interested in blackmailing anyone with the threat of a plague. I am only interested in unleashing one. What we have here is a disease which will change the world."

Buey is shaking his head, mumbling something incoherent in Spanish that sounds like "but you can't do that."

"Oh, I can and I will. And the only people inoculated against the plague will be my disciples. Jesus? Buddha? They will be as dust. I will have become Shiva himself, the destroyer—and savior—of worlds. I'm sorry to sadden you, Juan, but your usefulness and that of Los Gatos is done."

Gorman pats his cheek. "And you see that ugly man who you think needs a bath? He will be dealing with you in just a moment."

Buey's eyes are glassy. He is now struggling to stay awake. Mohandas Pal leans forward on the table and addresses him with some urgency. "Juan, my friend, have I ever spoken to you of the Thuggee?"

Juan Garcia Lopez shakes his head. He tries to speak, but can only grunt.

Pal lectures, "Their history is fascinating. I shall be brief, considering the circumstances. The real origin of the religion is lost in antiquity, but the cult may have been initiated by Mahomedan vagrants who plundered India after the invasion of the Monghuls and Tartars. The Hindu belief is that the divine spark came from the goddess Bhowanee. The first written accounts were uncovered by the British occupiers around 1810, if my somewhat inebriated memory serves."

Buey tries to speak again. What emerged was the babbling of an infant as Gorman, who stands behind Esteban and near Buey, begins to unwrap something from under his dinner jacket. Something he has kept hidden around his waist. Meanwhile, Mr. Nandi has removed the sash he used for a belt. He glides closer. His eyes are feral.

"The Thuggee worshipped the Mother Goddess Kali, as do I," Pal continues. "A gentleman named Philip Meadows Taylor collected the accounts of one Ameer Ali into a classic tome called *Confessions of a Thug.* I have read it many times, as has my friend Gorman, who seldom reads."

Buey finds words. "Wha-wha-what have you . . ."

"Shhh, my friend. There is no point in becoming aroused or upset, certainly not at this juncture. To continue, the Thuggee believed in wining and dining their victims before offering them to Kali and, of course, relieving them of all their money and possessions. It seems that at a suitable point, well after dinner and a drugged drink, their leader would issue a command, and the slaughter would begin."

Buey's dull eyes widen. His large heart is racing fast, but he cannot regain control of his limbs.

Pal leans closer, smiles warmly. "Would you like to hear an example of that command, my friend?"

"N-n-no."

Pal chuckles. He looks deep into Buey's eyes, savoring the moment, and then raises his gaze to his two assistants. Gorman grunts in impatience, Mr. Nandi is more discreet.

Finally Pal gives it voice: *"Jey Kalee!"*

"No!"

The cord drops around Buey's thick, muscular neck. He struggles to grab it with his hands. The ring finger of his left slides just under the cord as it tightens around him. He desperately fights to save his own life. His fat legs kick at the table. His eyes redden and bulge out; the tip of the captured finger turns purple with blood and becomes obscenely engorged. Gorman tilts away from him, at an angle, using all of his substantial upper body strength. Buey twists and bucks like an unbroken horse but he cannot break the hold. He grunts and moans; finally he wheezes into a red-faced stillness. Mohandas Pal leans in even closer, his eyes fixed on Buey's dying eyes.

"Farewell, Juan. Prepare Hell for my arrival."

Buey wheezes, voice high and squeaky, like air seeping out of a balloon. Watching him, Pal has a vapid, slightly bored expression on his face, like a man studying an event of minimal interest. Suddenly Buey's bowels open and a stench floods the room. Next, the delicate Mr. Nandi gracefully drops his scarf and strangles the sleeping Esteban, who dies as quietly as a helpless child.

Sixty-Three

"Go!"

Father Benny praying soundlessly, rapidly, as the chopper bobbed and weaved in response to their hurried exit. Canvas, metal, and sweaty flesh; twin grunts as Bowden and Burke hit the ground bent over double. They rapidly beat feet away from the already departing craft. The equipment drop at the edge of the ridge had gone smoothly and from this point on they would communicate via hand signals or through the sparce use of high-tech headsets. They reached a gully, rolled sideways, dropped to their knees as the helicopter circled away.

The warm night was silent, the desert floor crunched rock and pebble and sand.

They ran forward in short bursts. Their gear had already been taped down to limit noise. What struck Burke immediately was the incredible, overwhelming *loneliness* of the experience; this sliver of Mexico offered only the exhausted yawn of a graveyard, everything dead except for blood rushing through his ears and the soft, ragged caw of their breathing.

It was a world of gray slate, like the pocked surface of the moon, nothing moving but the black silhouettes of two men, running breakneck through the hard-packed sand, carrying automatic weapons and a grudge.

Having dropped the sniper gear on the first pass allowed them to make better time, but also upped the possibility of being discovered. Hopefully the guards would buy that the chopper was on a drug run for a rival cartel. If the bad guys got to the weapons stash before they did, Burke and Bowden were dead men walking. They moved, dodging the occasional succulent that tried to stab at their heavy boots. Jack Burke felt a nasty stitch in his side, knew it was happening sooner than it would have in his wayward twenties. *I'm getting old.*

Nearby, Scotty dug deeper and caught a second wind. His big arms and knees pumped slowly and steadily, like parts of an oil rig. He started to leave Burke behind. His face seemed ecstatic; he was grinning like a pumpkin. Burke could remember the last time Scotty had seemed this alive. An odd feeling of buoyancy overtook him and, like a young boy, Burke challenged Scotty with a fresh burst of speed. When the two men arrived at the rubber craft containing their gear, they were both in pain and out of breath but laughing silently, running on adrenaline and endorphins. Bowden stabbed the raft with his knife and rapidly unpacked the canvas cases containing their sniper gear. He tossed a scope to Burke, who scurried up the slope on elbows and knees to have a look at the drug lord's compound.

Peering through the greenish filter, Burke scanned the entire area. He quickly located the first guard tower. The dimensions they had been given were slightly off and the compound was bigger than they had estimated, but that wasn't surprising. Burke panned down the top of the wall and found the second guard. The man, face a white oval in the green smog, was smoking a cigarette between cupped palms, confident he had nothing to fear. *Good, good.*

Burke slid noiselessly back down the sandy slope. He held up two fingers. Bowden had already assembled one of the rifles. He tossed it to Burke, who climbed back up and sighted on guard number two. Moments later, Bowden was a few yards to the left and locating number one. Burke checked his watch. Three minutes to go. He slowed his breathing, took a reading on the mild wind and marked the exact distance to the target. Bowden did the same. Burke held up one hand, five fingers. He kept his eye on the mark.

As the man finished speaking into his handheld microphone and returned to smoking, Burke counted down five-four-three-two . . . and fired on one. Two soft thumps, like fists against a pillow broke the eerie silence; the sounds quickly faded away without creating an echo.

Burke scored a perfect head shot. The guard dropped like a felled steer without making a sound. He swung his scope down to Scotty's tower and ascertained that the second guard lay slumped over the edge of the station, arms dangling.

Burke looked up. Scotty pointed to his own temple and grinned with obvious pride. They nodded at one another and simultaneously let the rifles slide back down the slope behind them. Up and over. They started down the rock face, climbing by hand rather than rappelling. And this was the most terrifying part, climbing with your cheek plastered against the sharp edges of the rock face, splayed out like a starfish with your back to an armed enemy. Say one stray guard wandered outside to take a piss, well then *boom,* they were both ground hamburger. Hell, a kid with a pellet gun could have knocked them off when they were this vulnerable. Fingers growing numb, nose full of dust and dirt, feet slipping and sliding . . . then, at last, the ground.

Bowden landed first, took a knee and raised his laser-modified, silenced Heckler & Koch 9mm MP-5. He swept the area and waited for his partner to hit the dirt. Burke was only a few seconds behind. He carried a black CAR-15 with a pump shotgun attached to the bayonet fixture. The two men paused long enough to feel confident they had not been discovered.

Burke adjusted his flak jacket and raised the small microphone around his neck to mouth level. "Read me?"

"Yeah, you okay old man? You look wasted."

Burke flipped him off. The two old friends rose, ran bent over and then split into a widening V as they crossed the open ground, heading for the gates to the compound. Bowden slipped on some rocks and tumbled for a long and worrying moment but then he was back on his feet and in stride. Burke reached the wall first and flattened against it. Bowden, now twenty yards north, did the same a few seconds later.

One thing the spook Predator drone had not been able to tell them was the precise location of the doors. Bowden worked his way south, feeling for clues, while Burke held his position at the southern-most gate. Scotty was almost upon him when he raised one hand and pointed up. It was some kind of doorway that rose up from inside. Bowden gauged the height of the obstacle. He signaled for Burke to climb up onto his shoulders.

Burke flipped the rifle behind his back, loosened a thin but remarkably strong nylon cord and a supple plastic hook designed for silent entry. He ran up onto Bowden's body, stepped in his clasped hands and climbed up onto the broad shoulders. He tossed the hook over the wall. On the third attempt he hooked something that held his weight.

Burke shimmied up to the top of the wall, swiveled his head, checked left and right. To his relief, the entire courtyard seemed empty. He could see lights burning in the long hacienda building, and someone moved behind closed drapes. Burke dropped over the ledge, let the rope down and helped Bowden come over the wall. So far, so good.

The two men trotted down the unguarded stairs, footsteps echoing now, and then split up again. Bowden took the left side of the next entry point and Burke eased down to right. Another pause to catch a little breath, a check of the time, a wan smile exchanged because they were ninety seconds ahead of schedule. Then Burke reached for the doorknob, locked down cold when he heard voices, one man and one woman with American accents. The couple was arguing in fairly loud bursts, moving down the barracks hallway, coming closer to the exit. Burke made a hand sign to signal they would each take the target nearest when the door opened. They moved back out of the way.

The door opened. A gray-haired old woman in pearls stalked through it and turned toward Scotty Bowden, lipstick-coated mouth running a mile a minute, saying, "I'll be damned if I do the shit work again, Mr. Farnsworth, I just won't have it, I'm telling you!" She registered the presence of death, face blackened and eyes wide, poised there in the darkness. She searched for a way to scream . . .

. . . And meanwhile, the elderly man she'd called Mr. Farnsworth was only two steps behind her, clutching at her clothing, swearing in a gravelly voice that she was "a shrew and a bitch." Burke took the male's left hand and wrist, twisted hard and leveraged the man to his knees. Burke clapped a hand over the mouth to buy a few seconds, hesitated because they both seemed so old that somehow killing them didn't seem right, but when he glanced over at Bowden, the woman's throat had already been cut and blood was arcing out into the dirt like a small, dark fountain. Burke released the old man's arm, grabbed his skull in both hands and *SNAP* broke his neck. In less than five seconds, two bodies lay sprawled in the dirt under indifferent stars. Bowden shot Burke a puzzled look and a shrug, as if to say: *that was a shame, but what the hell are these two little old people doing in a place like this, working for an asshole like Buey?*

Burke and Bowden trotted through the door and further into the compound, knowing they had to keep moving, stay on the clock or be left behind.

Sixty-Four

Mohandas Hasari Pal is very, very pleased with the cognac, a VSOP rarity that the ever resourceful Buey somehow procured. He sips. "I will miss you, Juan, you fat pervert, particularly for your bottomless greed and prurient interest in all things intoxicating." The corpse does not respond. Its eyes are red-streaked golf balls and milky drool runs from the mouth. After a moment a small amount of gas escapes, creating a ripping sound which causes Pal to giggle.

"Well said, my friend. Your sad demise is indeed lacking in dignity. But since I knew you were planning to betray me as well, and keep both shares of what you believed to be blackmail money, I simply moved more efficiently than you to bring things to a close."

A discreet knock. Mr. Nandi opens the door and glides into the room. "We have accounted for all of his men. I went to attend to the guards in the tower but found that one of the others must have already dispatched them."

"People need to learn to follow orders."

"Yes, sir."

"Well and truly done, Mr. Nandi. We are quite pleased with you. Now, as Gorman has gone to fetch my unfaithful bitch of a wife, would you take the young one away with you?"

"Yes, sir." Mr. Nandi grabs the body of Esteban by the shoulders, drags it out. The chair falls to the carpet. Mr. Nandi pauses to right it before resuming his task. He leaves as soundlessly as he arrived.

As Pal stands and walks the length of the table, glass of VSOP in one hand and the other down, his delicate, manicured fingernails trail along the surface of the wood. "You thought my purpose was mere blackmail. How shortsighted of you, my friend. If you had any imagination, you too could have been inoculated with the sacred cure, but that was not to be. You were too much of a hedonistic dullard to become a believer and follow me. Once my biochemical demon has been unleashed, the whole world will be ripe for the taking. The prize I seek is civilization itself, not just a measly billion U.S. dollars."

Pal begins to cough, and for a few seconds the severity of his illness is apparent. Then the weakness fades. "Those who we have already inoculated, the loyal few who will survive, revere me as a living embodiment of the sacred. This is what you could not understand, Juan. My body may die, but my legend will survive. It will outlive not only me, but most of the human race. Thus I shall be worshipped for all time."

Mohandas Hasari Pal leans down over the body of Juan Garcia Lopez, which now reeks of excrement, vomit and urine. Pal inhales deeply. "Sweetness. The left-hand path teaches us to savor all things." Another taste of brandy, another deep inhalation. "So I savor even the stench of your death." Another sip. "Forgive me my theatricality, old friend. But this is the most significant moment of my life and I am determined to enjoy it."

Pal sits next to the slovenly corpse. He puts one arm around the shoulders and kisses Buey on the cheek. "Thank you for being such a simpleton, Buey. I shall be eternally grateful for your single-minded stupidity."

Another knock, more forceful than the first. Pal, who is now slightly inebriated, looks up. He forces himself to focus. "Come."

The door opens and Indira, still wearing the backless paper gown, enters the room. She falls inward, pushed from behind.

Indira struggles to keep her body covered. She is furious, sobbing from anger and humiliation.

Gorman appears and looks down upon her with a horrid blankness. He awaits instructions.

"Darling, won't you join me for a drink?"

Indira recognizes the voice of her husband. Her gaze follows the rug, the chairs, the table, and finally comes to Pal. She sees Buey's corpse, the arm casually flung around his neck, the sneer on her husband's face. But rather than scream she is determined to at least appear unfazed.

Indira must keep him talking. She knows it is her only hope.

"Slumming again, my husband?"

Pal bellows laughter. "I have always enjoyed your feistiness, Indira. You are seldom boring, even when being a slut." He sweeps one hand across the table, sending glasses and dishes to the floor. "Come, sit down and join us."

Indira stays huddled on the floor for one moment too long. Gorman moves, rapidly as a cobra. He seizes her ear and her hair and yanks her to her feet, then propels her forward. She slams into the table with an expulsion of air, her bare buttocks exposed. Humiliated, she covers herself and sits down across from Pal, who sips from his glass and winks.

"That's better. Tonight would not be complete without you here to share in my triumph."

She does not respond at first, but cannot keep from trembling. Finally: "So now you are a murderer as well as a hypocrite."

Pal throws back his head and laughs again. "Such venom from my little princess." He kisses the cheek of the corpse. "You call that hypocrisy? I am doing exactly what I said I would do, my dear. I am embracing death and shit and becoming one with the Mother. And very soon I shall join her."

"It could not be soon enough for me."

Her continued defiance irritates him. He leers, somewhat

comically. "I hope you enjoyed your hot little tryst with the soldier, Indira. It won't be the last fucking you get, but it will surely be the more pleasurable of the two. Would you like to know what I have in store for us this evening? Are you the least bit curious?"

No reply.

"Listen carefully, darling. First, know that I have perfected a virus so extremely lethal as to have a mortality rate of nearly one hundred percent. Yes, you heard me right. I said nearly one hundred percent. Second, my scientists carefully crafted it to be airborne."

Indira raises her head, shocked by both his statement and his obvious insanity. "Why would you do such a thing?"

"As the ultimate offering, of course," Pal replies. "The entire world, destroyed as a sacrifice to Kali-Ma, made in my name." He grins and winks. "Oh, and by the way, there is an antidote. But only a chosen few are to receive it. Those, like my friend Gorman here, who are among the most loyal of my students. This will insure that my name is immortalized, the man who has become as one with Kali-Ma, both the destroyer and creator of worlds."

His wife is soon sobbing quietly, tears rolling down her cheeks. "Mo, I can't believe you would do this."

Pal leans forward. "Oh, but I already have done it." He glances at the obscenity that is Buey, shoves with his left hand. The bloated body falls heavily to the carpet. Pal snaps at Gorman. "Remove this piece of shit."

Gorman obeys. Pal does not speak again until he has left the room. "And tonight's festivities will be capped by my ritual suicide, Indira. My pain has become so intense the drugs no longer contain it. You, my wife, shall die with me in the sacred rite of Sati. Two bodies, burned as one . . . however, you will still be alive to feel every moment as your flesh bakes, your blood boils, and your skin fries like bacon in a pan."

"Go to hell."

"Oh, I have already been there, Indira. It is home to me now. And soon you will join me."

Her eyes shine with contempt. "Why do you hate the world so?"

Pal finishes his cognac. "I do not hate the world, my dear. I merely embrace its true, dark nature. When Mr. Burke is unable to get here in time and sees film of how painfully you died, he will no doubt embrace it as well. You see, when I sought someone to create my virus, Kali brought me to Buey, another of Mr. Burke's enemies. I knew at once that this was our destiny. Such synchronicity cannot be denied."

A soft knock. Mr. Nandi floats into the room. Pal tilts his head, motions to Indira with his right hand. "She is to be taken downstairs, Mr. Nandi, and bound." Pal looks at his watch. He seems to have difficulty focusing his eyes. "At precisely eleven fifty-five, bring her to the burial mound. Mr. Nandi?"

"Sir?"

"When I am dead, burn her alive."

Indira, hearing the expected sentence pronounced, jumps to her feet and flees the room. Mr. Nandi starts to pursue her.

"Wait!"

Pal has ordered him to stop, so Nandi does, with one hand on the doorknob. Pal smiles. "Give her a moment or two head start and then go chase her down. I rather like that she will enjoy a tiny bit of hope first. It is certain to intensify and prolong her suffering."

Mr. Nandi nods with understanding, yet trembles like a horse at the starting gate. Once Pal raises a finger in acquiescence, he is gone.

Dr. Mohandas Hasari Pal finishes his brandy. At first the diffuse warmth of the alcohol helps to dull the persistent pain in his bowels. But after a few moments his system begins to react badly. With a cry, Pal collapses. He is doubled over, writhing; his shaved head raps against the wooden table and he stuns himself. The medications no longer help. Death anxiety floods his already overloaded system with adrenaline. Pal shakes like a man in the throes of a jungle fever. This paralyzing terror has long been his deepest and most persistent enemy. To fight against it, Mohandas Hasari Pal has marshaled and nurtured an overriding hatred for the indifferent world that will live on without him, virtually undisturbed by his passing.

Oh, but now they shall remember me, he thinks, rocking himself like a small child awakening from a nightmare, *oh, now I shall never be forgotten!*

Sixty-Five

Harsh in the headphones: "Go!"

And Bowden leapfrogged ahead of Burke. He raced along the porch and further down the outside wall of the hacienda. He kept low, crawled under the plateglass window, careful despite the drawn curtains. He raised a fist, motioned to stop. Burke, several yards behind, immediately melted into the shadows. Bowden heard breathing in the headset, then Burke whispering, "Your play."

Bowden, who had locked down purely from instinct, waited quietly for the bad guy to reveal himself. After a few seconds he sees the orange tip of a cigarette. Bowden shifts in the darkness, slips his goggles on. Now the thin guard's greenish figure was clearly outlined. He stood leaning against the wall, smoking. His rifle was looped around his shoulder, over the front of his arm with the barrel down. Given warning, he would still be able to fire and at minimum alert the others.

Bowden slipped free of his weapon. He set it down carefully, put his large knife between bared teeth, and approached. He moved silently, staying low and behind the man. He was patient, even though the minutes were ticking away, willing to trade precious time to preserve the element of surprise. One board in the porch gave slightly, made a faint squeak like a trapped rodent. Bowden locked his muscles into place, despite being trapped in an awkward duck-walk position, ready to charge.

The guard took another drag on his smoke.

Bowden crossed the last few steps in a quick rush. The cigarette went flying and the guard, whose reflexes were excellent, groped for his weapon and managed to turn partway around. Scotty reacted quickly to the change in position and successfully clamped his hand over the man's mouth. He stabbed the knife deeply into the thorax, yanked it free but held on tight. A soft, muffled grunt of pain followed. Bowden drew the knife across the man's throat, blood splattered dirt. He yanked the rifle away and stepped back, but held on to the man's greasy hair.

Hissing blood and gasping for air, the guard dropped to his knees, clutching at the wound. As the life left the body, Bowden lowered it forward onto the wooden planks. He dropped the rifle in the dirt, kicked it under the porch with one foot. Bowden motioned Burke forward, whispered in the headset, "Let's move."

As Burke, wearing night-vision goggles again, trotted up the stairs leading to the hacienda, the porch light flicked on, probably triggered by a motion detector. His eyes were flooded and the sudden change momentarily blinded him. Flashback: *everyone blind and Doc and Top and Bowden trapped in the open and the cult members all start firing* . . . Bowden had already removed his goggles. He knelt in the dirt and raised the silenced Heckler and Koch MP-5. The door opened and three men emerged backwards, all bunched together, chatting amongst themselves. Meanwhile, Burke backed away into the dark, blinking frantically and rubbing his eyes.

Bowden's jaw drops a bit. Each of the men was dragging a body by the legs. Two of the corpses were older females; their fancy dresses rode up on pudgy thighs. The third wore the uniform of one of Buey's own guards. Bowden saw the first guy focus on him, drop the woman's legs to go for a sidearm. Bowden takes out all three men with a measured burst of 9mm ammunition. The silencer makes a sound like popcorn in a lidded pan. The men were flung against the wall and all six bodies landed in a cluster fuck.

Burke trotted over to Bowden's side. The headset made his low voice seem oddly out of synch. "The fuck is going on around here?"

"Looks to me like the bad guys are taking each other out."

"Fine by me."

"You okay now, Hawkeye?"

"Very funny." Burke moved up the steps carrying the CAR-15. He had yet to fire a shot, but when he did it would be loud. He stepped into the hall, goggles around his neck. The corridor was carpeted, the walls covered with flocked, obnoxiously ornate, gold wallpaper. Burke moved further into the hacienda, eyes roaming. He hesitated at the first doorway, moved to the side. Scotty Bowden backed into the hall with his silenced 9mm raised. Burke opened the door.

"Empty."

Burke moved to the next door, opened it. Bowden looked, shook his head and whispered, with some relief, "Clear."

They came to the end of the corridor and turned in tandem. The hallway was empty. Burke eased another door open. They saw a long, mirrored wall, some gold-plated toilets but no urinals. It was a bathroom for the whores.

"Time?"

"Four minutes."

Both men were perspiring heavily from an intoxicating mixture of excitement, fear, and dread. "Okay," Burke whispered into the mouthpiece. "Let's keep moving."

Bowden was up next. There were two blue doors, side by side, with odd metal handles that looked like leaping dolphins. Scotty entered the room, Burke followed. One naked woman lay on a bed as if sleeping, vomit near her face. Bowden crossed to her side, sought a pulse. He shook his head. "Probably an overdose."

They examined the bedroom, which was enormous. There were large round beds, mirrors on the ceiling, video cameras on tripods, and large-screen television monitors. "Either Buey is into making porn now, or he's been taping his escapades for posterity."

"I've seen his picture," Bowden said quietly. "That is one nauseating thought."

They slipped out of the room, closed the door behind them. Burke motioned for Bowden, who had the silenced weapons, to go ahead. The two men trotted down a long stretch of corridor, past more doorways and more empty rooms. Soon they arrived at wooden double doors, clearly the entrance to some kind of master suite, probably Buey's boudoir. Bowden took the right door, Burke the left. They turned the golden handles at the same time and rushed inside.

"Shit."

The room stank of spoiling meat.

It was indeed a master suite, with a huge waterbed, a long bar, and a large flat television on one wall, but the entire bedroom was filled with bodies, human beings stacked waist high. Some of the dead men were dressed as women. Burke and Bowden exchanged looks. Burke knelt next to four of Buey's men in blood-spattered guard uniforms. He examined the bodies. "Scotty, it looks like they've all been strangled. This one here got his throat cut, maybe because he started moving again."

"Like I said, I guess the bad guys are killing off the bad guys. This is a good thing."

"Maybe it is," Burke replied, "but it also means the ones that are left are some really ruthless motherfuckers."

"You think Pal did this?"

Burke jumped to his feet, even more frightened for Indira

than before. "It has to be him, man. Most of the dead guys are in uniforms and the girls look like hookers or transvestites."

"Except for our cross-dressers, here."

"Peter Stryker wore dresses sometimes. It was a cult thing. I'd say Mohandas Pal and his followers wiped out Buey's gang and a few of their own weak links tonight, all in one shot."

Bowden whistled. "You can't strangle a drug lord and a shit load of gang members without drugging them first."

"Or exposing them to something lethal." *Christ, are we all already infected?*

But Bowden's mind was elsewhere. "Let's get a move on, we're running out of time."

Burke hesitated. "Scotty, if he's already released the virus, we can't go back. You know that, don't you?"

Scotty Bowden looked at the pile of bodies. Flies were already feeding. He shrugged and nodded. "Aw, shit. I know that. Hey, but then my kid gets a quarter of a million bucks. So let's go do what we came here to do."

"Can you set the charges alone?"

Bowden was puzzled. "Why deviate from the plan?"

"I guess because the plan was built around us getting in and out alive," Burke answered. "If I'm going to die here, I want to do it with Indira around. If she is going to die here, I need to be the one who . . . sees to it."

There was nothing Bowden could say in response to that. He moved for the doorway. "I'll set the charges." And that is when Burke heard her screaming.

Sixty-Six

Mohandas Hasari Pal has battled his way back into control of his own, tormented body. The excruciating pain has sobered him up; he is soaked with sweat. Pal knows he cannot take more medication and remain in control of his faculties, but he has done nearly everything he set out to do. The virus is ready, the sacrifice prepared, the wife in position.

And he will be remembered.

It's time to finish this. Mohandas Pal hears another knock at the door. He struggles to his feet. "Come."

Gorman enters the room. His busily tattooed arms are damp with sweat. "Your orders have been carried out." He waits silently for further instructions.

"Help me get down below." Pal quotes with wry humor, "It is time to cry havoc and let loose the dogs of war."

Gorman takes his arm with a firm but sympathetic grip. He guides Pal out into the hallway.

"You will be the Prince of Man," Pal whispers seductively. "It is the dawn of *your* era, my loyal student."

Gorman responds in a voice thick with emotion. "And you shall be remembered as the incarnation of Shiva himself, the creator and destroyer of worlds. This is a promise, my guru."

"It is a shame that fool Stryker got cold feet," Pal wheezes. "With his writing talent he could have created works that would have survived us all by thousands of years. Would that he had only remained true to the cause."

Gorman grins wickedly. "His bowel tasted like fine pork sausage."

The two men laugh, which causes Pal to stumble and lean against the wall. Gorman holds him, looks down upon him lovingly like a grown child doting over a senile parent.

"I have prepared the virus for you, Gorman. As discussed, it will be contained in your suitcase, in a coffee thermos. There is one thermos for each of the cities on your route. Your airfare has been prepaid, the tickets and your passport are in the locker at the Mexico City airport. Do not fail me."

"I will not fail you."

"Your hypodermic with the antidote will be in the suitcase, along with the containers. Remember, the antidote will not be effective *unless you have already been exposed,* so do not use it until you have opened the first thermos. Perhaps when you are about to leave Los Angeles airport would be best."

"Yes, sir."

"Then you are scheduled to visit airports in New York, London, Zurich, Tokyo and Moscow. Then India."

"Then Beijing, Ho Chi Minh City, then to Africa, Australia. I know the whole route, sir. I have it memorized. I will be living on airplanes for a fortnight."

"And the world will be changed forever."

They come to the end of the hallway, turn right, and arrive at the stairwell. Down below, they hear a woman shriek in terror or pain. Gorman raises an eyebrow inquisitively. Pal chuckles. "That was my unfaithful wife, no doubt. This nonsense is taking far too long to suit me. Perhaps it would be best if you fetched her, Gorman. Just send Mr. Nandi to join me in the laboratory at once."

"Are you well enough?"

"I will be fine, Gorman. Bring Indira to me where the subject's bodies are kept, and be sure to carefully bind her hands and feet."

Gorman bows respectfully, a slight leaning forward from the waist. He turns on a dime and jogs down the hall. Pal straightens against the wall. He feels a wave of dizziness and a razor-edged cramp grips his bowels. To his humiliation, a small squirt of diarrhea escapes into his trousers. *But soon I shall leave this useless body behind, and be as a god!*

Pal steps carefully down the carpeted stairs, clutching his abdomen. He does not want to take more heroin until he has finished one final task. He steps out through a side door into the courtyard. A guard lies dead near his feet. Pal assumes this is the work of his own people. He is pleased. He stumbles across the lawn by moonlight, through the dirt and up the steps to the laboratory. He uses his key and steps inside. Another guard is lying in a pool of blood near the desk.

A fresh, electrical shock of pain causes his flesh to quiver. Pal closes his eyes and leans against the wall. After a long moment he forces himself forward. The discomfort passes as he finds himself moving more rapidly through the sterile, white complex. Pal takes an elevator down to the basement. When the door opens, he sees the white-coated scientists who worked for Buey piled in a corner of the room. Their throats have been cut. The sight makes him giggle.

"Thank you, ladies and gentlemen, for your dedication."

Pal goes behind the stainless steel table and opens the door marked DANGER in English, Spanish, and Russian. He moves into the room past the white cell where several test subjects were imprisoned, injected, and observed. A red-and-black checkered suitcase lies open on the floor. It is filled with silver cylinders that contain the deadliest poison ever created by man.

Pal sits on the floor, cross-legged, and tries to go deep into meditation. Nonetheless, he feels a flutter of fear grip his heart. Pal's dark secret is that his faith in the surreal is less certain than his driving ambition to be immortal. Still, he slows his breathing and tries to relax. He soothes himself that he has enough heroin to insure that his own demise will be painless. No one need know that he fears and rejects the pain required of self-immolation. That bitch Indira shall be denied anesthetic, however. Pal wants to see her tormented flesh burning before he administers his own, merciful overdose.

"Sir?"

Pal opens one eye, looks over his shoulder. It is Miyori, one of his Japanese followers, who is on a paid sabbatical from the Los Angeles Coroner's Office. Dr. Miyori is a chubby man with an annoying alcohol problem. Pal has arranged for Gorman to dispose of Miyori later, so as not to leave any potential embarrassment behind. Pal forces a thin smile. "Our work here is nearly done."

Miyori bows rapidly. "I am joyous, guru. Is there more that I can do?"

You have probably done nothing since the executions but drink and pass out in the back room, Pal thinks, his mind sour with cynicism. But aloud: "Go and find Mr. Nandi, perhaps he will have some more work for you."

Miyori bows again and backs away. Pal returns to his meditation. He summons up the image of the Goddess Mother, Kali-Ma, with her necklace of human skulls and her sleek, black skin. He is vaguely aware of a *ping* as the elevator arrives to take Miyori upstairs. Some time passes.

PopPopPopPop!

The distant sound invades his consciousness, a metallic noise he cannot quite place. One second later Pal's eyes open wide as he registers the sound as silenced gunfire. Perhaps one of Buey's men has survived and removed Mr. Miyori for him? But that also means the man must be descending into the laboratory. Pal curses himself for being without a weapon. He pushes the suitcase out of sight, behind the lab table, and looks around rapidly. He settles on a closet, steps inside with the lab coats and jackets. He shrinks into the clothing and closes the door behind him, leaving just a narrow slat open for viewing the laboratory.

The man who enters is dressed in black and his face has been painted garishly. He has a pair of night-vision goggles dangling around his neck and holds a silenced weapon at the ready. Pal barely contains a gasp of astonishment. Someone has invaded the sanctuary. Although he wears no formal uniform or identifying insignia, the man is Caucasian, perhaps American or English. Pal curses silently and his fists curl in frustration.

Pal observes as Bowden slips his pack off and starts removing small containers filled with enormously powerful explosives. He works rapidly, smoothly, like someone quite familiar with the task. He has nearly emptied the pack. The entire laboratory has already been wired to blow. In the closet, Pal twists and turns, wondering what to do.

Another sound, a *ping* from down the hall as the elevator arrives.

Startled, the man in black raises his weapon and steps back out of the way. Pal knows the visitor is likely to be either Mr. Nandi bringing Indira, or perhaps—far worse—his heir apparent, Gorman. The man seems unfazed and more than ready to use his silenced rifle.

Without thinking Pal starts to open the door.

The intruder whirls at the sound, his eyes searching the room, but only sees the wall and a closet. Before he can turn around again a knife penetrates his right arm. It seems to go numb, fall straight, and the man reaches for the rifle with his left arm, but by then Mr. Nandi is upon him. A second knife slices into his neck, right at the shoulder. Mr. Nandi holds it there; the threat presented by the blade near the artery speaks for itself.

The man lowers his hand and allows Mr. Nandi to disarm him. Mr. Nandi kicks the side of his knee, full force. The man grunts and falls to the ground in pain. Pal opens the closet and steps into the room.

"Tell me who you are," he orders. "Who sent you?"

The man's eyes roll up, exposing white. Mr. Nandi kneels by him, yanks his hair back and places the tip of the knife in his right nostril. "You will answer the guru, or be mutilated," he says in his soft, respectful voice.

The man says, "My name is Scott."

Mohandas Hasari Pal stumbles to the table and pulls the suitcase into plain sight. "You have not even slowed us down, Mr. Scott. The virus will span the globe within a matter of days. Your life will have been sacrificed for nothing."

"I doubt that," Scott says in a whispery voice. He is in pain and barely able to remain conscious.

"Oh, believe it," Pal replies. He removes one vial from the suitcase. It is different from the others. It is tied to a tightly bound package of plastic and a second, smaller bottle.

Pal cannot resist gloating. He holds up the package. "And this one is my gift to the corrupt populace of Mexico." Pal mockingly pronounces it properly, *Me-he-co.* "When I activate this brilliantly designed little balloon, it will float up to a height of several hundred feet. The internal guidance system will take it fourteen miles to the nearest highway rest stop, where it will explode into a mist. Every traveler who passes through that area tonight and tomorrow will be infected. Within ten hours their first symptoms will appear, but by then they will be lost in crowds all over the southwestern United States and down into South America."

Bowden is losing it, but he wants to know and still manages to ask: "Why?"

Pal chuckles, mockingly. "Because I am the physical incarnation of Shiva, consort to Kali-Ma, and the destroyer of worlds. You should feel honored to be in my presence. You do, don't you?"

Bowden snorts in disgust. In a flash, Mr. Nandi has sliced open his nostril. A thin tendril of bloods spurts. It hurts. Bowden squeals, but the pain helps him recover his senses.

Pal clucks with his tongue. "Such needless suffering. Please, refrain from being macho, Mr. Scott. Now, I will ask you a question. You will answer immediately and honestly, or Mr. Nandi will do you harm. Do you understand?"

"I understand."

"Who came here with you?"

"I am alone."

Mr. Nandi clasps the wounded hand. He raises the knife and severs his two smallest fingers. Bowden shrieks and then grunts in agony. "God damn you! You bastard, that's the truth. I came alone!"

"And why did you come, Mr. Scott? Remember, you have many more fingers. Mr. Nandi and I are very patient men."

"To rescue your wife, asshole."

Nandi removes his thumb. Bowden passes out. Annoyed, Pal looks around, locates a pitcher of water. Moving gingerly, he picks it up and hands it to Mr. Nandi, who tosses it in Bowden's face. Bowden does not seem to regain consciousness. Pal sighs. "We must assume we have been compromised, Mr. Nandi. Regrettably, I must dispatch you with the suitcase to locate Mr. Gorman. Send him on his way immediately. I will proceed to the burial ground alone. Once Mr. Gorman is en route, bring Indira to me. You shall assist in the rite of *Sati.*"

Mr. Nandi bows, takes the suitcase. He stops by Bowden and leans down to cut his throat. The goggles are in the way. Irritated, Mr. Nandi begins to saw at the strap holding them in place. Pal waves him off. "I will shoot him. Go." Mr. Nandi leaves and the heavy case seems as light as a shoebox in his grasp.

But when Pal tries to operate the rifle, he is puzzled by the safety lock. He fumbles with it for a moment, but another icy sheet of agony overwhelms his bowels. He drops the rifle and bends over the table, losing precious seconds, but the captive is bleeding to death regardless. Pal kicks the rifle away, out into the hallway, and stumbles toward the elevator.

Sixty-Seven

Indira backed rapidly out of the master bedroom, one hand to her mouth. The sight of so many bodies in a pile tore a ragged scream from her throat. The fact that so many are men in ritual women's clothing had also stunned her. *Mo is killing his own people.* She realized immediately that she had given her location away. She raced down the hall, head swiveling, looking for a place to hide. She ran barefoot, her passage virtually silent.

She could hear the steady footsteps of the man who was now pursuing her, even over the thudding cadence of her terrified heart. This man was large and unbelievably fast, especially now that the scream revealed her position. Her only advantage is that she has been here before, in the drug dealer's hacienda.

Move. Keep moving . . .

A locked door, another door, a room that contained video equipment; Indira barely noticed the nude body on the bed. There was a second door at the back of the room and she pushed herself that way, even though it was probably just a bathroom and she might be trapped, but that door was locked. Indira thought and stripped away the paper gown. She flung herself facedown on the round bed, beneath the mirrored ceiling.

Her bare skin broke out in bumps at the uneasy proximity of the woman's cold, dead flesh. Her nostrils caught the vague stink of urine. Her gorge rose and soured. She forced herself to breathe, stay loose, and allowed one arm and one leg to dangle over the edge of the bed. The man's footsteps pounded down the hall and paused at the bedroom doorway. The door opened, whispered across the shag carpet like the hissing of a large snake. Indira, face pressed against the stained bedspread, held her breath.

The man entered the room. He was moving swiftly, someone familiar with his surroundings. He passed the round bed and went straight for the locked door. Indira, eyes closed, knew when he tried the handle. She heard an eerie, throaty chuckle and the jangling of some keys. The door being yanked open. The man searching the other room and emerging back into the bedroom. Her chest was beginning to tighten now and she desperately needed to breathe, but somehow held herself motionless, praying, hoping to remain undiscovered.

The man moved away. Her mind sang of freedom.

Then Indira smelled an awful odor, a body that reeked of excrement and charcoal, and felt humid breath stroking her neck. *Gorman?*

"Don't move, pretty," he whispered and fingered her back. "You are so lovely this way." It was Gorman. His odor was terrible, as usual. He spread his body on top of hers and his hardness pressed against her bare buttocks. Indira struggled but froze when something thin and sharp entered her right ear.

"Oh, yes," he sighed, almost erotically. "If I push in here, even just a little, you will go deaf. A bit further and you die . . ."

Make him do it, make him kill you, it will be merciful and quick this way. Indira knew that to be true. He was accidentally offering her a way out. She gathered herself to shove against the needle, but he withdrew it before she could act. A rustle of clothing and the sound of a zipper. Indira shuddered and tried to buck him off, but he was holding her down and her left side was pressed against the dead weight of the corpse.

"I will fuck you both, as a tribute to Kali," the man whispered in her trembling ear, "first the one who is still alive and then the one who is dead, then back and forth again."

"Get off me!"

"In due time, my pretty."

His freed penis presses against her clenched buttocks. Indira decides she would rather die than have this happen, but she cannot move. He pushes hard, looking to penetrate her; Indira screams in rage and frustration. The man strikes her once, expertly on the right temple, and her limbs collapse into mush. But before he could enter her there came another, somewhat distant sound, footsteps moving rapidly down the hall, almost as rapidly as the killer's had just moments before.

The rapist pauses for a split second, zips himself and backs away from the subdued captive. Indira still cannot move, but she watches her attacker via the mirrored walls and ceiling, that stocky body, those strong, tattooed arms. Gorman moves to the side of the open door, clearly preparing an ambush. Indira, lying helpless beside a corpse, can see the doorway. She wants to warn whoever is coming. Anyone Gorman was afraid of offered hope. Her voice began to come back to her. She blinked rapidly and gathered breath. But when the other man stepped into the room she hesitated, convinced she was dreaming, for it was Jack Burke.

Gorman landed on Burke's shoulders, his strong right hand already trying to strip away the heavy CAR-15 rifle. The men struggled. One powerful, deafening shotgun blast demolished the side of the bed and removed the left arm of the dead girl. Mattress stuffing, gore and smoke soared through the moist, red air. The rifle slipped to the carpet. Burke kicked it away before Gorman could grab it. Indira screamed and rolled onto the floor, then to the other side of the bed. She watched Burke and Gorman struggle. For a long moment the two men, evenly matched and rigid, strained against one another. Then Gorman stomped down on Burke's instep. Burke managed to avoid the worst of the blow, but lost his balance.

The two men crashed into a clothing rack and disappeared into a pile of ritual dresses and nightgowns.

The gun!

The rifle was within reach, so Indira, eyes riveted to the spectacle of the two men, crawled toward it, one foot at a time.

Burke and Gorman alternated between rapid bursts of feverish physical activity—myriad attempted blows and effective blocks—and brief periods of intense, silent struggle. Gorman managed to produce a knife and sliced at the front of Burke's shirt. The blade was stopped by the ultra-thin Kevlar vest. Burke's hands moved in a blur to trap Gorman's forearm and wrist, turned and twisted and disarmed him. Burke caught the knife in midair and opened a long gash in Gorman's shoulder. Gorman kicked with blinding speed and sent the knife flying. The hand-to-hand battle smashed the two men into the mirrored wall, spider-webbing the tiles and raining down fragments of broken glass. Some of the fine dust got in their eyes. Burke, blinking and shaking his head, lost a fraction of a second. Gorman brought his palm up, aiming to drive Burke's nose into the brain and kill him with one strike. The blow slid off but managed to crack Burke's cheekbone. He grunted from the pain and grabbed at Gorman's testicles. Burke twisted. Gorman screamed.

Burke lowered him to the carpet, still tightening and twisting. Gorman rained blows on his head and shoulders but the pain had weakened him. Burke turned Gorman's back toward Indira. His face was grim with concentration.

Indira had the gun, raised it. She could see herself in the mirror, wild-eyed and naked, cradling a huge shotgun in thin, shaking arms. She tried to aim it, but before she could, Gorman managed to flip Burke in a tangle of arms and legs, removing what had been an easy target. Uncertain, Indira lowered the weapon and watched helplessly as they fought to the death. Burke lay pinned on his side, but did something with his legs and quickly rolled free. He slammed Gorman into the mirrored tile once, twice, and yet again. Blood from a scalp wound splattered upwards like a fine, Zen painting of the rising sun. Burke clapped his palms over Gorman's ears with precision, breaking the eardrums, and Gorman howled with pain.

Burke rolled away, tried to retrieve his weapon, but somehow the nightmarishly indefatigable opponent grabbed his ankle to keep him from reaching the gun. Burke rolled over onto his back and kicked with both feet. Gorman slammed backward into the mirrored wall. His bloody head smashed into the glass with a dull *thwaaack.*

Stunned, the deafened Gorman slid down the wall and sat still. His nose and forehead were bleeding, eyes red-veined and dazed. Burke again turned for the gun, but unbelievably Gorman was already moving again. Burke turned to face him with a snarl and the two men collided right over the naked girl. Their hands and arms moved rapidly again. Gorman seized Burke's right arm and tried to break it.

"Let him go!" Indira bravely brought the gun up and around, forcing Gorman to release Burke and react. Gorman turned sideways and kicked Indira in the stomach. She dropped the shotgun and rolled over onto her side.

Burke saw the world turn red and black, welcomed the rage. He slammed into Gorman from behind and grabbed the killer by the skull. He stomped into the back of Gorman's legs and dropped him to his knees. Burke clutched Gorman's head in his powerful arms and hands and began to twist it around, as slowly as possible; wanting the deaf man to know what was coming, to suffer right to the end.

Gorman struggled and the inhuman, screeching sounds he

made were horrific. Burke kept turning. Gorman kicked and wet himself as he fought back, but Burke had the correct angle and would not be denied. Indira shocked herself, for at the first small *craaaacking* sound, she felt only an overwhelming sense of joy. Gorman's bloodshot eyes went wide with surprise and pain. His expression was now one of unimaginable terror.

"No," Gorman croaked. His gravelly voice was loud now, like a man wearing headphones. "Don't! Not me!" In his agonized deafness, he was already hearing the onrushing sound of eternity. His expression announced he'd seen the truth—that God would show him no mercy.

"Yeah, you." Burke yanked hard and snapped Gorman's neck at the spinal cord. He released the body and fell backward, chest heaving.

Indira rushed to be near him, and for a moment all they could do is hold on tight. Burke broke away, grabbed a plain evening dress and some flat shoes from the pile of women's clothing. "Hurry. Put these on."

"Jack, what are you doing here?"

"Later. Let's move."

Indira, nakedness covered, felt stronger immediately. Burke found the shotgun and took her hand. They hurried into the corridor. "Stay behind me," Burke whispered urgently. "I have to go check on my partner." He spoke into the mouthpiece. "Scotty?" But Burke couldn't be sure it was working any longer, after all the chaos. He moved down the corridor, the rifle up. Indira held on to his belt and followed close behind. She kept her eyes fixed on his back, and deliberately avoided looking at the carnage in other rooms. The hacienda had become a tomb, a monument to her husband's insanity.

"Who else is here?" Burke asked, without turning his head. "Who else would Pal have brought with him?"

"He never goes anywhere without Mr. Nandi."

They came out into the night and Burke paused, chest heaving, to allow his eyes to adjust. "That's the laboratory over there. I'm afraid Scotty's been hurt."

He moved rapidly away from her. Indira lost her grip. Unnerved by being separated, even for a moment, she hurried to catch up. Burke paused at the door to the lab. He motioned for her to stand behind him. He pried the door open with the barrel of his gun and went inside. The two moved smoothly across the room to the waiting elevator. Burke made sure it was clear. He took her downstairs, into the bowels of the building. When the doors opened he swept the room with his eyes and dragged her into the hall. "Scotty?"

No answer.

Burke flattened against the wall. He kept his gun up and motioned for Indira to wait a few steps behind. He moved to the doorway and spun around the corner in a crouch, weapon raised.

Blood *everywhere*. "Where the fuck you been, cowboy?"

Scotty sat propped against the wall, with Mr. Nandi laying half across him. Burke took a knee just in time to watch a last bit of pinkish air bubble from the smaller man's open mouth. Bowden was white with shock, but managed a macabre grin. His trembling hand held one severed ear. "Hey, look. I took this for old time's sake."

"Scotty, hang in there, man. Indira is with me."

"That's good."

"We're going to boogie to the chopper in a few, okay? We're going home."

"*You're* going home." Bowden moaned and flinched. When the pain passed he could barely speak and there was an odd, hoarse rattle deep in his chest. "I'm not."

Burke blinked away tears. He pawed at his medical kit. "That's bullshit."

"Save it, no time," Bowden whispered. "I'll patch myself. You've got orders."

Burke looked down and away. "You're right."

"Do something for me."

"Name it."

"Brother, you take this motherfucker Pal all the way out, okay? Me, I think I'll just rest here for a while. And when the pain gets real bad, I'll make sure to get my sinful ass blown all the way to heaven. Only way I'll ever get to see the place."

Sixty-Eight

Dr. Mohandas Hasari Pal sat calmly among the stacked, putrefying bodies of plague victims, stoned out of his mind, preparing to inject a fatal dose of heroin. He had covered the basement area with gasoline, adding to the already stultifying stench of offal and decay. When Indira walked into the basement he roused himself long enough to speak.

"I asked them to leave you naked."

She challenged fate. "If I am to die, I wish to be clothed."

Pal shrugged. "This does not matter. I am far from being able to respond to your sexuality at this point, although it surprises me that Gorman has not seen fit to partake of it along the way."

"Gorman is a pig. He raped me."

Her expression was so bland, so defeated that Pal coughed and barked a dry laugh. "Oh, that's good. And I hope he was quite perverse."

"He was."

"Where is he now?"

"I told Gorman and Nandi to wait outside."

"Ah."

She crossed the floor, nose wrinkling, barely able to contain her revulsion. She studied him and the expression on her face was a complex mixture of shock and bravado.

For Mohandas Pal sat naked and cross-legged among the stacked dead. He was indifferent to the stench of rotting flesh, vomit, blood and emptied bowels. He looked around, dreamily. "The left-hand path carried to its logical conclusion," he offered. "There is nothing in life or death that should shock us, nothing we cannot incorporate. It can all be absorbed."

"And this is how you assure yourself of immortality?"

He patted something resting by his thin, hairy buttock. It was a canister wrapped in plastic. "No, *this* is how I become immortal." Pal raised something that looked like a garage-door opener. He pushed the button.

Indira heard a *whirring* coming from the ceiling. She looked up and saw that the braced roof of cement, wood, and dirt had a long chimney of sorts and that a glass panel was sliding away. It hid a chimney that rose all the way to the starry night sky. Pal twisted something near the canister and a balloon began to inflate. "This is my present to the world. It will be followed shortly by several other gifts, presented to the nations by my designated successor Mr. Gorman. Oh, I assure you my dear. My name shall be long remembered."

The balloon filled up and the doomsday device began to levitate. Indira moved to the right, away from the doorway. Pal followed her with his eyes. Meanwhile, Jack Burke eased into the room. He stayed low to the ground and approached Pal from the opposite side.

"Shall I trust you?" Pal kept his eyes fixed on Indira. "You wouldn't lie to me, would you, dear?" He called out. "Mr. Nandi! Come in here!"

Burke could not believe his eyes. The area reeked of gasoline, filth and rotting meat, and the scene was eerily reminiscent of his nightmarish experience in Djibouti. Pal, covered with gore, even began rocking and giggling, a man in the throes of sensual ecstasy. Burke shook off déjÀ vu, closed the gap, but somehow Pal sensed something. He released the lethal balloon device and groped for a nearby cigarette lighter, intending to immolate the room.

Burke was torn for a second, stared as the virus carrier floated upward toward the skylight. He moved toward it just as Pal's hand grabbed for the lighter. Changing gears in midair, Burke kicked the lighter away, vaguely aware that the remaining drugs Pal was intending to inject were also on the same small metal tray. Pal, seeing him, dropped into a kind of comical shock, jaws open and his eyes sprung wide.

"You?" Then Burke jumped as high as he could. He grabbed for the canister of virus beneath the balloon; got it with one hand but came down awkwardly and lost his balance among the bodies. To his horror, the virus escaped his grasp and floated upwards. Burke, mind working feverishly, backed away. Pal was shouting in triumph. The balloon carried the device relentlessly higher. It bumped into the ceiling, appeared to be stuck for moment, but then drifted into the open chimney. It moved up toward the bleak night sky.

Burke raised his pistol.

Pal screamed, "No!"

Burke aimed and fired. The canister exploded. A fine mist of the intensified, deadly virus drifted back down and covered the room.

Burke and Indira were now infected.

Pal shrugged. He laughed softly. "No matter. Gorman will see to the rest."

Burke spat on the ground. "I already killed Gorman, Mo. And my partner killed Nandi. Your fucking dream dies with you."

"So you got here anyway, Mr. Burke, how resourceful of you." Mo Pal shook and rocked and laughed, hugged his own naked, hairy knees. He had gone completely mad. "But now you will both die here with me tonight, too, no? You and our beautiful slut."

Indira was sobbing. "You bastard, you fucking bastard!"

"Indira, leave." Burke motioned her out of the room. She did not want to go, but saw something primeval in his dark eyes. She backed away rapidly, shaking her head, both terrified of death and disgusted by her arrogant husband and what he had become.

Meanwhile, Burke reached down to the floor and picked up the butane lighter. "I need to burn as much of the bug as I can, Mo." He stomped on the vials of painkiller scattered across the cement floor, crushing the glass. "You're going to get part of your wish, I suppose. But you'll still be alive, and without an anesthetic. Think of yourself as an honored wife."

Pal's eyes registered his fate, then terror. He sank into complete despair. He senselessly slapped his own face, like a man struggling to wake up from a nightmare. "No, no, *no!*"

Burke stepped away, flicked the lighter and tossed it onto the pile of corpses. The various dried body fluids smeared on the concrete retarded the spread of the fire, so there was no real explosion. Pal moaned in fear. He tried to rise, but his legs had either gone to sleep or deserted him. The white flames spread into a smoking curtain several feet high and equally thick. They approached to lick hungrily at his rapidly blistering flesh. His shrieks of agony echoed through the concrete tomb.

Burke slammed and locked the door behind him.

He and Indira rode back up the elevator. Pal was still screaming. Indira covered her ears. Meanwhile, Burke contacted Bowden on the headset. "We're coming to get you, buddy."

"No, you're not. The door is locked."

"Scotty, don't give up."

"Clock is ticking, dude. And what these timers don't blow, I intend to take care of personally. Get your ass back to the LZ."

"Scotty, we got exposed."

"What?"

"The virus. Both of us have been exposed."

"Shit."

"Yeah." They reached the lobby and trotted to the entrance. "That's just how it went down. So we may as well come and check out with you, buddy." Both Burke and Indira were weeping.

"No," Bowden replied. He moaned once, clearly in great pain. "Go up, my man. Go out there under the stars and be together. Just wave the chopper off and tell Father Benny to go home. Have him tell Cary to napalm five square miles and worry about the consequences later."

"Scotty . . ."

"Go, man. Just be sure my kid gets that money."

"I will." Burke checked his watch. There was no more time. He looked up and pulled Indira to him. "I guess this is it. Sleep well, brother."

The voice was faint, couched in static. "Yeah, Red. The same to you. There are three minutes left as of right . . . *now.*"

Precious seconds were ticking by. Burke and Indira crossed the open area. They reached the wall. Burke helped her up onto his shoulders. She caught the rope and clawed over to the other side. Burke followed, still hearing Scotty's ragged breathing in the headset. He was losing ground.

Burke scrambled rapidly up the rope, ignoring the pain of his cuts and bumps and bruises. Even a few extra moments of life with Indira suddenly seemed terribly important, and he could not bear the thought of losing them. To his own amazement, he was no longer afraid of dying, just of being without her when it happened.

"One minute."

Burke dropped to the other side. He took Indira by the hand

and they raced across the mesa toward the LZ. She stumbled and fell once but he picked her up and encouraged her to keep going, while in the headset, he heard Bowden's now whispery countdown get to "twenty."

"Run, run!"

Burke urged Indira forward. When Bowden finally reached ten, he pulled her to him and they both lay facedown in the dirt.

"Brothers, Burke." Then Scotty chuckled morbidly. "What the fuck. Blast off."

The world erupted like a volcano behind them; the sandy ground trembled and shook and heaved them several inches into the air. The sky turned white and stayed bright for a few endless seconds before it darkened again for good. Burke's ears were numb and ringing. He turned her face and kissed her. They held on tight and cried wordlessly for lost opportunities. "I'm so sorry, I'm so sorry," both were apologizing so rapidly it was hard to tell one voice from the other. Burke rolled three grenades between them, and willed himself to pull the pins when the first symptoms appeared. Their night vision slowly returned. They wait for death.

The chattering of the approaching helicopter finally penetrated the hissing in Burke's ears. He changed frequency, searching for Benny, and decided to pull the pins the second this last conversation was over. Fuck waiting, it was a good night to die.

"This is ground team. Abort. Abort."

No response. The chopper circled and a small spot lit up the area, which constituted an odd breech of security, although after the size of the explosion it seemed unlikely to make any difference one way or the other.

"Benny, abort. Do not pick us up. This entire area might be infected, and we have been exposed. Abort at once."

"Negative."

Burke shook his head. The voice was not Father Benny's. Something seemed terribly out of context. The light grew brighter. The chopper was going to touch down for a landing! Burke was horrified. He screamed into the mouthpiece. "Damn it, Benny, don't land! We are infected!"

"Settle down," the voice said calmly. "We have the antidote ready. Just get your ass on board."

Burke and Indira struggled to their feet, hair flying, blinking into the blinding white glare. The door of the chopper opened and someone dropped down to the ground, someone lithe and slimmer than Father Benny.

"Move it," Cary Ryan shouted. "We made just enough to handle this. We'll shoot up, too, once we're on the way back. Where's Bowden?"

Burke pushed Indira into the chopper. He turned to Cary, weary face devoid of expression. "He's not coming." His voice broke on the last word. Burke dragged himself onto the right rear seat.

Ryan grunted as he clambered into the front. "I kind of figured maybe that was the way he wanted things to go down."

"Me, too."

"We changed that life insurance policy. I moved it up to half a million. I asked Nicole Stryker to kick in a little cash, too, and she's game. Scotty's kid will do okay."

Burke hugged Indira, closed his weary eyes. "Good. That's good."

"Oh, and Burke?"

"Yeah."

"Gina says we should both pack it in now. It's time to retire."

Burke sighed. "I'm thinking maybe she's right."

Sixty-Nine

One Week Later

The woman is nearing the end. Her breathing has slowed and taken on a coarse, husky quality. The two men who stand on opposite sides of the hospital bed observe her without speaking. The older man is smiling, although tears course down his reddened cheeks. He reaches down and strokes her frowning, once-pretty face.

"Shhh, baby. Don't fight."

Although the mind is surely gone, the body continues to struggle for air. Beside her, the younger man's face contorts. His emotions are raw, more conflicted. His eyes reveal his agony. With a Herculean effort of will he remains still and does not allow himself to intervene. And neither does Father Benny, who stands patiently in the open doorway, although it clearly wounds him, too. He mutters the rosary over and over again.

"Just let go, baby girl."

Harry Kelso reaches over to the end table and turns the music up. It is a CD of songs Mary loved when she and Jack were courting. "Listen to the music."

Mary Kelso Burke hiccups a dry breath. Her torso writhes a bit. Suddenly her eyes open wide and impossibly, miraculously, appear to focus on what is actually happening in this barren, white room. The men are stunned by the vague possibility that she is actually conscious.

Jack Burke leans closer. "I loved you, Mary." Has she smiled?

Her expression softens; perhaps because some previously numb part of her recognizes either his voice or the soft, familiar strains of music, perhaps both. But Burke will never be certain. Behind them, in the doorway, Father Benny quietly begins to recite the last rites. His voice caresses her face with a melancholy whisper.

Mary locks in place for a long moment. She seems to look deeply into her husband's damp, reddened eyes. He jumps, as if touched by an angel. Mary rolls her head on the pillow as if to acknowledge her sobbing father. She grunts and shakes a bit.

"Sleep, honey."

For a horrified second Burke fears she will continue to fight for life, further shattering his already tormented heart, but Mary does not. Her eyes close peacefully and a small smile curls her beautiful upper lip. Her head falls back on the pillow and her features relax. She looks just like the woman he married a few short years before.

Father Benny raises his voice slightly. He finishes the last rites and begins the rosary. Mary Kelso Burke sinks into the bed. One last, feathery breath rattles free . . .

The monitor flatlines. She is gone.

"Good-bye, baby girl," Harry Kelso whispers. He kneels by her bedside and prays. Burke feels like an intruder now. He turns to go.

"Jack?"

Burke looks back. He is pinned by the gratitude in his father-in-law's eyes.

"Thank you, Jack."

"I loved her, too."

"I know you did."

"Good-bye."

"Good-bye, Jack."

Jack Burke will never remember the hug Father Benny gives him, or his long, sobbing walk down the hospital corridor, nor the silent ride in the crowded elevator, where the other passengers fall silent in shame and confusion before the intensity of his unbridled grief. The moments he spends in the lobby, turning mindlessly in circles, will also be lost to him. He will not remember stumbling into the gift shop and hiding in the corner until he is able to calm himself. That anguish will be forever erased.

Mercifully, he will only recall that precise moment when he emerges into the bright sunlight again and sees Indira standing by the car, waiting for him, her eyes deep with sympathy and understanding, wide-open arms full of love. That is what he will remember.

. . . and the rest of his life, from now on.

ACKNOWLEDGMENTS

Anyone who has ever endeavored to write a novel will cheerfully tell you that it is impossible to accomplish such a daunting task without the support of a great many friends and advisors—too many, in fact, to list here. I asked several different folks from various professions for input along the way, and they were all abundantly helpful. However, in the end, I just flat-out made up a bunch of stuff to suit my nefarious purposes, so please know that any errors contained herein are my own. All of the people and events are products of my overheated imagination.

I feel compelled to publicly appreciate the following folks: author and ex-cop Gina Gallo for sharing some particularly nasty crime-scene memories, Dr. Bruce Ballon for some psychiatric perspective on oral sadism and anthropophagy, editor/authors Kealan Patrick Burke and Patricia Wallace, LAPD Officer J. D. Kasper, author Ray Garton, fellow author (and retired Army soldier) Weston Osches, my good friend Lynwood Spinks, Ms. Alexa Carpena who during a conversation reminded me of the existence of the obscure sect in India called the Aghora, Mr. John Boylan for his proofing and invaluable suggestions, also author/producer Marc Brener, Ms. Leya Booth for the editing help, and (as usual) my brilliant wife, Wendy.

As for the fictional disease Pal created, this tale was obviously written as entertainment, but I hope it also serves as something of a warning. Bird flu is yet another wake-up call. The world needs to get its act together. Any day now, a new virus, manufactured or otherwise, will appear like a blip on the radar screen but become a global public health disaster within a matter of weeks.

ABOUT THE AUTHOR

Harry Shannon has been an actor, a singer, an Emmy-nominated songwriter, a recording artist in Europe, a music publisher, a film studio executive, an acclaimed author of horror fiction, and a freelance Music Supervisor on films such as *Basic Instinct* and *Universal Soldier.* He is currently a counselor in private practice. Shannon's short fiction has appeared in a number of genre magazines, including *Cemetery Dance, Horror Garage, City Slab,* and *Crime Spree.* Shannon's horror script *Dead and Gone* was recently filmed by director Yossi Sasson. You can learn more about the movie at www.deadandgonethemovie.com. Harry's Mick Callahan novels, *Memorial Day* and *Eye of the Burning Man* are also available from **Five Star Publishing.** He can be contacted via his Web site, located at www.harryshannon.com.